Jewel in the Evening Sky

MaryAnn Minatra

HARVEST HOUSE PUBLISHERS
Eugene, Oregon 97402

Cover by Left Coast Design, Portland, Oregon.

JEWEL IN THE EVENING SKY
Copyright © 1997 by MaryAnn Minatra
Published by Harvest House Publishers
Eugene, Oregon 97402

Library of Congress Cataloging-in-Publication Data

Minatra, MaryAnn, 1959–
    Jewel in the evening sky / MaryAnn Minatra
        p.   cm.
    ISBN 1-56507-668-0
        1. Germany—History—1933–1945—Fiction.   I. Title
PS3563.I4634J49 1997
813'.54—dc21   97-9437
                                                                                   CIP

Printed in the United States of America.

97 98 99 00 01 02 03 / BC / 10 9 8 7 6 5 4 3 2 1

For Christa,
a special little girl who is teaching me about faith—
and who will always be
a jewel from Him.

Prologue

The sun, wreathed in mists of yellow, scarlet, and pearl, was slipping into the horizon over a city scarred and ravaged. The guns of war had fallen silent three years earlier. Warsaw had been a glittering European jewel of cosmopolitan society; now it was a city, like so many across the continent, struggling from the ruins. The heaps of stone, brick, glass, and charred embers had been carted off, yet nearly every building and street bore the marks of invasion, occupation, and battle.

The intersection of Nalewki and Gensia streets was quiet now, except for one lone city worker who was sweeping the pavement, even though it really didn't need to be swept. He paused occasionally, resting on his broom, to gaze at a recently unveiled monument. Sometimes he looked down the empty street as if he could see and hear things. The streets were empty; everyone had gone home. But earlier that day there had been a ceremony at the intersection. Over five hundred citizens and dignitaries had gathered.

A thousand acres in the center of the Polish capital had felt the heat of the Nazi torch. The pavement, the gutters, the few trees, the skeletal remnants of buildings all spoke an eloquent testimony—bullet holes, pitted sidewalks, scorch marks that looked like the claw marks of a great beast that had fallen in its death agonies. The Jews of Warsaw had taken their stand against the Third Reich here. Most of the thousands had perished in the struggle—but not before they stalled the German machine for nearly three weeks. No other civilian resistance in all of Nazi-occupied Europe could make such a boast. But it was a costly boast. Now the monument to their struggle had been raised.

The platform, the chairs, the guests were gone. Only the thirty-foot column of granite and bronze remained amid a city wasteland. The city worker lingered, reluctant to go home. He didn't know why. He wasn't a Jew. He hadn't known anyone who had perished here. Yet. . .yet he didn't want to forget this place just because the ceremony was over. He wanted to pass it each day on his way to work and give a silent tribute to the brave Jewish Poles.

He heard steps behind him and turned. A man and woman were coming slowly up the street toward him. The woman looked at him, but the man's gaze was fixed on the monument. Yuri swept and watched as they drew closer. The man was tall and slender, graying at his temples. Yuri couldn't estimate his age. Late 30s, early 40s perhaps. His face was thoughtful and undeniably sad. The childlike woman was younger than the man and holding onto his arm. They stood very still and quiet before the monument for a full five minutes. Yuri, unashamed, watched them. The woman reached out and patted the stone and smiled up at the man.

"Here it is. It's pretty."

Finally the man turned as if he had suddenly sensed another's presence. He swung his piercing blue eyes toward the city worker. Yuri cleared his throat awkwardly.

"They had a ceremony for the unveiling earlier," Yuri said with a nod.

"Yes, we . . . just arrived in the city."

"Oh? I'm sorry you missed it."

"We . . . mostly we wanted to see the monument."

Yuri was surprised at the tone of sadness. "Well, I was here for the whole thing, and I can tell you it was a pretty fine ceremony. The premier gave a short speech. He said that what had happened in Poland would never ever happen again. There was quite a crowd. I heard that Jews came from all over Poland to be here."

"I would imagine there are very few Jews in Poland left to come to such a ceremony."

"Well . . . yes," Yuri shrugged, "but they were here. I saw them. Some did survive the camps and others by hiding with the partisans. There were several who were survivors of this ghetto uprising. A small number, but . . . it was a miracle."

The man looked at Yuri curiously. "You . . . believe in miracles then?"

"Yes, I do," Yuri replied firmly. "Adolf Hitler and his kind tried to kill every single Jew. He tried to smash courage and decency but he couldn't. This monument proves it. I bet Hitler was pretty pleased the day they told him the Warsaw ghetto was burning. But look, he's dead and the Jews live on to raise a tribute to their courage."

The man was silent, looking down at his shoes. He sighed deeply and Yuri knew this man had suffered much. *I want to . . . help this stranger—somehow,* he thought.

"There were all kinds of miracles when the Nazis were here. Have you heard about the Jews that escaped through the sewers? Or the Jews in Lvov who lived in the sewer for eighteen months?"

The man said nothing.

"Yes, they were helped by two Gentiles—two city workers—who provided food and water. There are many stories."

"Yes, many stories. Those who lived through them remember them well," the man with the piercing eyes said. He looked back at the monument. "Even when they try to forget."

Yuri didn't know what to say. Twilight deepened.

Finally the man turned away from the monument, "Are you a pastor?" he asked.

Yuri laughed and held up his broom.

The tall man searched his face, his voice very tired. "You have a . . . great faith in God."

Yuri smiled again. "Who else could there be to put your faith in?"

The man stepped up to the monument. The granite was smooth and cool under his fingertips. Yuri stepped closer also.

"They did a fine job. Have to give the Frenchies credit, they do good work."

"This didn't come from France originally," the man said slowly.

"Oh? Well I read in the paper last night this granite came from France, a gift from the French Jews to the Polish Jews."

The man shook his head. "It came from Sweden."

"Sweden?" Yuri echoed.

"It was quarried in Sweden. It was ordered and paid for. The designs were made. It was ordered from . . . Berlin."

"Berlin! How do you know that?"

Again the tired sigh. "I was there . . . just . . . just as I was here." He looked down the deserted street.

Yuri studied the street a moment.

"You were here during the uprising?"

The man shook his head. "I left the day before it . . . began. I tried to come back . . ."

Yuri was uncertain what to say. "I'm sorry."

Now the man appeared to be speaking to himself, or to the shadows, or to the memories.

"All of us who lived then, who survived ... we carry a deadness in us that never quite heals. I lost my faith in miracles. I stumbled in this darkness. Then ... light finally came."

Yuri spoke up. "God has not forsaken you! He could not! You standing here tonight is no small miracle!"

The tall man was crying now; silent tears slid down his slender cheeks. The woman put her arms around him, leaned into his shoulder, and murmured something Yuri couldn't understand. He felt like he was an intruder here. *This man is on some sort of pilgrimage. I should leave.* He patted the man's arm awkwardly, then turned to make his way home. He walked to the end of the street, away from this quiet place, to the city where life still flowed. But he stopped at the corner.

The man walked past the monument a few yards, leaving the woman. He stood in the center of the street, remembering the last time he had traced these steps. Then the sun had been shining. It had been a calm, cloudless spring day. He could remember the weather quite distinctly. He breathed deeply. He had come here to find some peace that the three previous years had not relinquished to him. He must live with what remained.

He remembered then an old friend, an old man who had spoken to him from his deathbed. It came back now, as if the old man were speaking just over his shoulder.

Someday you will find yourself where I am, Thomas, unable to do anything but either turn to Him or turn away. There will be no other distractions. Trust Him, trust Him.

He spoke to the memories, to the shadows, the pain and loss in his soul.

"Lord, please forgive my unbelief ..."

Then, for the first time in three years, he felt like singing. The rich tenor of his voice filled the clear air of twilight.

What wondrous love is this, O my soul, O my soul!
What wondrous love is this, O my soul ...
To God and to the Lamb, I will sing, I will sing!
To God and to the Lamb, I will sing, I will sing!
To God and to the Lamb, who is the great I am,
While millions join the theme, I ... I will ... sing!

Standing at the corner, Yuri was spellbound. He felt an unexpected nervousness—an expectancy—as if the night air was charged. He shivered. Silence had settled over the street again. The young woman stood watching the man.

Suddenly another voice sounded from the end of the street behind Yuri. He turned swiftly. Another woman was coming up the street. She was smiling and she was singing.

And when from death I'm free, I'll sing on, I'll sing on,
And when from death I'm free, I'll sing on,
And when from death I'm free, I'll sing and joyful be,
And through eternity, I'll sing on,
And through eternity, I'll sing on ...

Yuri's mouth fell open. The tall man near the monument had swung around. The woman with him stood with clasped hands. The singer drew closer. She walked past Yuri, her smiling face illuminated, tears trickling down her cheeks. The woman at the monument ran to her. Yuri's heart hammered in his ears. What was happening on this spring night in Warsaw, on this battlefield of courage and sorrow ... and miracles? Dawn had swept away the darkness.

PART 1

Thomas and Maria
1932–1942

Deliver those who are being taken away to death, and those who are staggering to slaughter, oh hold them back. If you say, "See we did not know this," does He not consider it who weighs the hearts? And does He not know it who keeps your soul? And will He not render to man according to his work?

—Proverbs 24:11 NASB

We were willing to overlook his [Hitler and company's] excesses [his brutality toward the Jews] for what he was doing for the economy. His character did not matter to us. We were trading the freedom from starvation for the slavery of our souls.

—German citizen, 1950

Nothing is more difficult and nothing requires more character than to find oneself in open opposition to one's times and to say loudly, "No!"

—Kurt Tucholsky, 1935

1
A Mighty Fortress

September, 1932—Wittenburg, Germany

Sixty young men rose silently, as one body, as a tall man dressed in black church vestments strode purposefully to the altar. Sunlight poured in through the high windows, shafts of radiance fell across the platform in significant testament. The young men stood expectant, as they had each Friday morning for the last year to hear this man speak.

Castle Church, Wittenburg, Germany. Every German Protestant was proud of this place. The great reformer Martin Luther had nailed his Ninety-Five Theses to the door 415 years earlier. The young men gathered in this place of glorious German history; they gathered as part of Germany's glorious future. The speaker waited until every eye was upon him. Then he smiled and nodded, and the group sat down. He gripped the edge of the altar and began to pray.

He prayed for Germany, her leaders, and the church. He prayed for the young men assembled before him. As pastor candidates nearing the end of their term, they too could shape the new Germany. They were the spiritual leaders of the Fatherland.

"For my message this morning, I will begin with the Scriptures, Romans 13:1,2."

The sound of Bible pages turning could be heard in the great room. The speaker cleared his throat.

" 'Let every person be in subjection to the governing authorities. For there is no authority except from God, and those which exist and are established by God. Therefore he who resists authority has opposed the ordinance of God; and they who have opposed will receive condemnation upon themselves.' "

He leaned toward his listeners, his eyes scanning the crowd, to make sure every man was listening, captivated.

Then he straightened and brought his fist down upon the altar.

"I tell you there are many voices raised in our troubled country these days. Many voices that would deceive and would divide. But we are a proud people; we will reject these deceptions! Yes, you will know the truth, and the truth will set you free."

He wiped his brow.

"In the pitch-black night of church history, Adolf Hitler is a wonderful transparency for our time—the window of our age through which light falls on the history of Christianity—as the light falls upon all of us from these windows in this great church. Through Adolf Hitler we see the deliverer of the German people. God speaks through our authorities, our leaders. God has ordained this time for Adolf Hitler just as He has ordained this time for each of you. You are obeying God when you obey your elected leaders. One state, one people, one church!"

He pulled out a handkerchief and wiped his brow again. "I rest in the confidence that I send you out well equipped."

He stretched out his hands toward them.

"I send you out with the blessing of God upon you." He paused, then continued, "And of one I am especially fond—Thomas Picard, will you come up and lead us? I have a strong desire for us to raise our voices in this cathedral with the great song, 'A Mighty Fortress Is Our God.' Thomas?"

A tall young man rose from the congregation. He had been momentarily oblivious to the dean's calling. He had felt a warmth that rested on his head when the man had blessed them. *Such a moment! I will treasure it forever.* He climbed the platform and was warmly embraced by the dean. Then he faced his fellow pastors and raised his clear, strong voice in the ageless anthem.

• • •

"Will you join me for lunch, Thomas?" the dean asked when the service was over.

Thomas Picard hesitated. He respected this man so much, and they had grown close over the past few years.

"Other plans?" Dean Wagner pressed.

"Well, sir, I . . . I have another appointment. I sort of . . . promised."

Dr. Wagner smiled. "I would prefer a young fraulein's company for lunch over an old seminary man. I understand, Thomas."

"Well, sir, I . . . it isn't a fraulein. Dr. Begg asked me to come over, and this is the only time I've had all week."

Wagner was gathering up his papers and Bible from the altar. His face and voice conveyed clear annoyance. "Dr. Begg summons you from his bedside, eh?" He shook his head. "I've always failed to see what you students find so charming in that eccentric old man."

Thomas didn't know what to say.

Wagner's voice was chilly. "I trust you can . . . discern things Dr. Begg may tell you in error, Thomas. I don't think my esteemed colleague has the same perception of the current tide in Germany like men such as you and I."

"Yes, sir."

"I suppose we can have lunch another time." The voice had the edge of poutiness. They were moving down the wide central corridor of the vast sanctuary. Thomas opened the door for the dean to pass through into the winter sunshine. The dean ran his hand across the old door as if he could draw some power from it. "I tell you, Thomas. As important as that day Luther nailed his theses here, so are the days you and I stand in."

"Yes, sir."

The dean slapped his back. "Well, you'd better hurry off to your companion."

"Actually, I am in a bit of a hurry. I need to vote before I go to see Dr. Begg."

"You haven't voted yet?" The dean sounded alarmed.

"It's been a busy week."

"Then hurry along, Thomas. Auf Wiedersehen, and God go with you."

• • •

The room was nearly empty in Wittenburg's city hall. Only a handful of men stood in front of Thomas.

"I was expecting a long line," Thomas said to the magistrate who handed him the voting forms.

The man shrugged in eloquent apathy. "Folks are tired of this voting business. This is the third election this year. They have better things to do. The Nazis keep demanding elections, but I ask, who is paying for all of this?"

Thomas shifted. "Yes . . . but still it is important to vote."

The man grunted and waved Thomas forward.

Thomas contemplated the ballot in his hand. *Better things to do than vote? This election is critical to our nation; indeed, the future of Germany will take shape with this final election. Men of vision can see that.*

Thomas looked up as the words of the men in front of him penetrated his thoughts.

"He's a Catholic. I won't vote for a Catholic."

"He says he can give us jobs and build up the military. Hindenburg had his chance. I say let this new party have its chance."

"He's not to be trusted. Have you forgotten about that affair with his niece? They were overheard arguing and then she turns up dead the next day!"

"He can restore Germany. That's all that matters."

"He hates Jews. That's enough for me."

"The church supports him. That is enough for me."

"I went to my astrologer only an hour ago. He showed me it is in the stars to vote for the Nazis."

• • •

A formidable, middle-aged woman opened the door to the doctor's apartment and led him to the bedroom. Her voice was a little sharp.

"The doctor shouldn't be having visitors yet. He is better, but he still is not strong. Keep your visit short."

He entered the bedroom reluctantly. Ever since the call had come the day before, he had been a little nervous and hesitant. This old man was his favorite professor in his years at the university. . . . And yet Thomas couldn't deny that the old professor had a reputation for being odd. Although he was not accepted among most of the other university staff, like the dean, this man seemed to try to live his faith. He was almost always smiling and cheerful ... even in his threadbare suits. Yet the students loved him. He was a master storyteller.

Thomas stood at the threshold, hesitating. He cleared his throat.

"Sir? Dr. Begg?"

The lids fluttered open. The rheumy eyes took a moment to focus.

"Ah, Thomas! What a pleasure. Pull up a chair, son."

Thomas sat and quickly surveyed the plain room. The old man seemed to read his thoughts. "Not much for a lifetime, eh, Thomas?" he croaked.

Thomas smiled. "How are you feeling today, sir?"

"Better, yes, much better. And you?"

"Fine, just fine."

"Well, Thomas, your internship is soon over. You are very eager to leave, yes?"

"Yes, sir. I feel like I'm ready to go out and ..."

"Take on the world?"

Thomas nodded and smiled.

"Yes, I felt like that forty years ago," chuckled Dr. Begg. "I've had a wonderful, rich life, Thomas. And one of the riches has been having a student and a friend like you."

Thomas stirred uncomfortably. "Well, it's been a privilege for me too, sir. I treasure the talks we've had together."

"I too have treasured them. That is why I summoned you, Thomas. Of all my students, I can trust you. And I know you'll be leaving soon— ready to take on the world and forget an old man in Wittenburg."

"I couldn't forget you, sir."

"Then I must presume on our friendship and ask you a favor. Please humor an old man."

"What can I do for you, Dr. Begg?"

The old man looked so intently at him that Thomas wondered if the man had heard him.

"I want you to listen to me, son. I want you to come here each day until you leave and let me talk to you as long as I can. I'm too weak to put these things on paper, and I want you to hear them from me."

"What kind of things, sir?" Thomas asked slowly.

Dr. Begg looked toward the window. He closed his eyes, and Thomas knew this elderly cleric was praying. *Curious,* he thought. *What had* stirred this man to seek him, to impart something he had seen or heard? For a time, Thomas forgot completely the disapproval of Dean Wagner.

Dr. Begg turned back to him. "I've had much time to lay here and think and pray, Thomas. Sickness either focuses ourselves wholly on ourselves or on the presence of God. Someday you will find yourself where I am, Thomas, unable to do anything else but either turn to Him or turn away. There will be no other distractions. Trust Him, Thomas. He is more real than even your hurt. I lay here and I hear Him speaking to me ... words I cannot ignore. Thomas what is under your feet?"

Thomas smiled. Even in the man's infirmity he continued the methods he had used in the classroom for years. *Begin with a question.*

"Under my feet. Well, I suspect you're not talking about carpet or wood. Below that, dirt, earth."

"Keep going."

"Under the soil? Rock."

"Under the foundation of this apartment, a few feet of earth as you say. Then?"

"I'm sorry, sir, I have no idea."

"The sewer runs under the buildings of a city. There is a sewer under our feet, Thomas."

A sewer. Is the old man lucid or has the illness affected him? Dean Wagner's words rose suddenly in his mind. *A man with odd ideas, a different man.* His face reflected none of his thoughts. He was surprised to hear the deep sadness in Begg's voice.

"He has shown me there is a sewer flowing in our country, Thomas, hidden, as the one under our feet, but just as real and just as full of filth. He has shown me, and I must tell you."

Munich

He had been away from home only four months but to him it seemed more like a year. *It is always that way,* he reflected. *The excitement of travel, the adventure of a new place, and the anticipation of coming home. Coming home to Blumenstrasse.* He had been to all the countries that surrounded Germany; he had been to London. He still wanted to go to China and Africa. But his favorite journey so far, in his twenty-five years, had been his trip to the American West two summers previous. But now, this winter night as he turned the corner, he was at the place that he wanted to be. Home—with all its blemishes, with all its glory. He was a happy young man.

He had enjoyed the walk from the train station in the clear night air. He had left the business district of Munich, walking through the largely quiet residential streets. Squares of lights from the windows were muted, yet threw out shafts of warmth and welcome onto the darkened streets. Menorahs were burning in several windows—this was the final night of Hanukkah. Though he was not Jewish, he knew the holidays. He knew his neighbors, the Goldsteins, would be having a party in their big front room. Thinking of Sophie Goldstein's rich Hanukkah culinary creations made him hurry his steps.

He turned the corner on Blumenstrasse. It was nearly eight o'clock, but in the darkness half a dozen boys were playing soccer in the street. *Every scar on my knees and elbows came from my own boyhood days of street soccer,* he reflected with a smile. They saw and recognized him immediately.

"Hey! It's Thomas!" They accompanied him along the street like a welcoming band.

"How's your grandfather, Peter?" Thomas asked.

"Still the same. Gonna come pray for him as soon as you become a preacher?"

Thomas laughed. "I can pray for him without being a preacher, Peter. You know that. Tell him I'll come by in the morning."

"Rudi's courtin' a new girl, Thomas. Did ya know? She's from across town."

Thomas shook his head. He hadn't heard of his younger brother's latest conquest. They changed so often. That his mother hadn't written to him about her loudly revealed her displeasure.

"She's a looker."

"Not much of one beside Maria," one young boy said in awe. "When I grow up, I'm going to marry her!"

Thomas joined their laughter.

Thomas' laugh deepened. *These irreverent boys with their street wisdom. Yes, the lives on Blumenstrasse are an open book.*

They went back to their game. Thomas could see his house. It was dark. He took the steps two at a time up to the Goldstein's door. He slipped into the foyer. Immediately he was assaulted by voices and laughter, warmth and light, and delicious sights and smells. Someone was tuning a violin. He grinned. His father was getting ready to play. He pulled off his long coat. A sudden movement tipped his hat over his eyes. He heard a giggle and swung around. Maria Goldstein was behind him, a shy-looking boy beside her. They had been in the shadowy alcove.

"Celebrating Hanukkah out here, Maria?" he with a serious face.

He lips pouted. "No sermons if you please, Herr Picard."

"I'll leave that to your mother, fraulein."

He entered the brightly lit front room.

"Thomas!"

"Look who's here!"

"Shalom, Thomas!"

"Mazel tov!"

Across the room a young girl of thirteen shrieked and propelled herself into his arms. He hugged her as the Goldsteins and his father came up to him. He drew back.

"You are getting so tall, Gret," he commented.

The girl buried herself in his chest as they laughed.

His father was patting him on the shoulders. "We weren't expecting you till tomorrow. Mother will be disappointed she wasn't here."

"Where is she?" he asked.

No one spoke. Thomas looked to Frau Goldstein. It was strange she wasn't speaking up for his reticent father. Frau Goldstein was rarely silent.

Herr Picard finally spoke up. "Ah, your mother went to ... a seance this evening. With the Shroeder's. She'll be home soon."

"And Rudi?"

The eldest Goldstein son spoke up with a chuckle. "In the daytime your brother is on the soccer field, and in the evening..."

Thomas laughed. "I already heard a rumor of some sort before I even reached the front door. So do we like her?"

"She's a nice girl," Herr Picard said.

"Yes, a nice girl," Frau Goldstein nodded. "Her father is a banker, but she does use too much rouge."

Everyone laughed.

"Maria doesn't like her," nudged Jacob Goldstein. "A cat is the nicest name she's called her."

Now sitting across the room, Maria spoke up in teasing revenge. "Papa, did you hear about the scuffle Jacob got into the other day?"

"Children, children," Frau Goldstein reproved. "To act this way when Thomas is home."

"It isn't as if he hasn't been hearing it all his life," Aaron Goldstein inserted with laconic ease.

The two families laughed again.

"I miss the music of Blumenstrasse, Herr Goldstein. And Maria's the most of all!" Thomas added.

"Doesn't Gretchen look nice this evening, Thomas?" Frau Goldstein spoke up.

"Yes, very much." He looked to his father. "How has she been?"

Frau Goldstein spoke happily, stroking the girl's back and smoothing the thick blonde braids. "She hasn't had a seizure in ten days. We are all so thankful."

"Welcome to our home and our Hanukkah celebration, Thomas," said Herr Goldstein, shaking Thomas' hand.

"Thank you, sir. It's good to be home."

They ate and laughed and enjoyed each other's company. The night deepened as the menorah burned in its final light. Aaron Goldstein stood with outstretched arms and blessed his sons, his daughter, and his best friends: "May the Lord bless and keep you. May you rise up to serve him. When you lay upon your bed, remember His faithfulness."

2
Side-by-Side
on Blumenstrasse

A residential street, Blumenstrasse was ordinary and typical in its architecture but remarkable for the temper the years had given it. Years of change and conflict in the nation had been like small ripples on Blumenstrasse. It had become a small community, a block of sixteen German families who lived alongside each other in comfortable, congenial, loyal friendship. Disputes were rare, minor, and easily mended. Though Eastern Europe was a stronghold of anti-Semitism, religious differences on this Munich street were largely tolerated and accepted. Most families had lived there for decades. It was a middle-class neighborhood with fathers working in white collar jobs and raising their families in neat, narrow, two-story brick homes. The front lawns were abbreviations, the backyards, walled gardens. The side windows gave an eye to the adjacent house. The stamp of individuality was in the color of the front porches, the front-room curtains, the inside decor.

The children trooped off to school in the mornings in noisy parade and returned in the afternoon to their street games and continuing dramas. On a clear summer night, with the windows open, one could stand at an end of the street and hear various musical instruments, laughter, babies crying, and marital conflicts. If a man's castle was his home, Blumenstrasse was his kingdom.

The Picards and the Goldsteins were a testament to the harmony of Blumenstrasse. They had a strong friendship, a true weaving together of two families. It had begun a generation earlier with Aaron Goldstein's father and Michael Picard's father. For ten years they both had worked two jobs, saved their money, nurtured their close friendship and mutual love of music, and nourished their dream of owning a music store together. They married good German women within months of each other. When the store became reality and quickly prospered, they bought homes beside each other. They raised their children and passed on to their sons and daughters their love and affection. The oldest Goldstein son, Aaron, and the oldest Picard son, Michael, inherited their respective houses and the business. It had succeed because both men were as close as their fathers had been. Their business had prospered and their families had grown, intertwined with each other's shared sorrows and joys. Nothing could break the friendship spanning decades. Nothing.

● ● ●

Sophie Goldstein privately held that her kitchen window was really the most important place in the Goldstein home. Most affairs of the household, both trivial and significant, were conducted from this place. Sitting at the table underneath the window, peeling potatoes or thumping bread dough, she could see up and down Blumenstrasse. She cooked and mixed, read and sewed from this position. She couldn't have had a better view if she had positioned herself on the roof with binoculars. Life on this Munich street flowed like a current past her observing eye. From her chair she could read the hearts, emotions, temptations, joys, and sorrows of her neighbors. Everyone knew they couldn't surprise Sophie Goldstein. This surveillance didn't really offend since it had a practical side, Sophie "always knew the need." She always had the first gift for the new baby, the first meal for the grieving. Her involvement, if at times a little too intimate, could be forgiven for her heart sometimes exceeded her prudence. Romance was her particular forte—no one courted without the scrutiny of the woman at the window.

She was a thrifty, energetic German housewife despite her vigil at the window. Her house was spotless, her meals always large and punctual. Her children and husband couldn't understand this balancing act she performed. It was a mystery. They teased her about it—an old standard family joke. Sophie smiled at them in a cheerful, patronizing way. They didn't understand how very useful and fulfilled it made her feel.

Blumenstrasse was her own little world; this Jewish mama knew very little beyond the corner. Let her husband or sons talk of the great affairs of the nation, this election or that, the bickering, the quarrels. The sun rose, the sun set on Blumenstrasse. It was all she wanted to know. She supposed, in some indefinable way, that the predictability of her world would never change. A few new faces, the loss of friends, but the same. A different president, a different philosophy, it did not affect her. This myopia frustrated her growing, worldly wise sons. Over the table their discussions would grow heated as they tried to draw her in. She would listen calmly then tell them that Alfred Rosenburg had failed his entrance exam, and they should go cheer him up after dinner. And wasn't it outrageous, the price of beef in the market? Her sons looked at each other and groaned. *Why wasn't their mama more like Frau Picard next door? She knew everything.*

Sophie Goldstein loved each of her four offspring with fierce maternal love. But Maria, her youngest, her only daughter; Maria, accomplished, popular, witty; Maria, the undisputed beauty of Blumenstrasse was favored above her brothers. Sophie shamelessly pampered her and that made her a very pretty and rather spoiled young girl. The indulgence was enough to stimulate the creative wit of Thomas Picard when they were both young. He had declared during a joint family meal that Maria would be better named "O Petted One." He was privately pleased with himself—it had such a Jewish sound to it. The table had erupted in laughter. Sophie unruffled at the jest merely shook a thick finger in Thomas' direction. Maria had stuck out her tongue in classic response. The Goldstein brothers had declared Thomas terribly clever and seized and adopted the moniker with a passion. The tease had held, and over the years Maria had grown accustomed to it.

But the young girl was not without her own balance of humor. She could tease with her brothers and the Picard boys. She had a name for each of them, emphasizing some defect.

Mealtimes at the Goldstein home were always lively, a chorus of laughter and eating and discussion. The Goldstein children, Abraham, Isaac, Jacob, and Maria carried the weight of the energetic conversations. Their mother participated only long enough to admonish elbows off the table or to laugh at their teases. Her brows could contract and her thick fingers would thump the linen-covered table when one of them became too rowdy. Sophie Goldstein refereed mealtimes. She was a short, broad woman with snapping brown eyes. Aaron Goldstein was a slender, scholarly looking man of fifty who sat at the head of the table as an indulgent, amused patriarch. Though his hair had turned silver, his beard was still predominantly brown. He was still a good-looking man, something Sophie was inordinately proud of. She knew childbearing had rearranged her figure and added lines on her face. Walking beside Aaron, so tall and straight, she secretly wondered at her good fortune to have such a fine-looking mate. He offered opinions when requested and quiet insertions when he felt they were needed. Everyone grew quiet when Aaron Goldstein spoke. Then the banter would resume with enthusiasm. The quiet, soft-spoken Aaron and the voluble, vivacious Sophie was a combination everyone on Blumenstrasse regarded with a little wonder.

At twenty-four, Abraham was the undisputed intellectual of the family, after his father. He was a lanky young man who worked in the family music store as bookkeeper. He was a younger version of his father, reserved and methodical, opening up only in front of his family. Twenty-year-old Isaac was the vibrant son—personable, energetic, helpful. He was the peacemaker of the family and was studying to become a doctor at the university. Jacob, short and stocky, was the family athlete. Like his best friend and next-door neighbor, Rudi Picard, Jacob could be temperamental and moody. He was seventeen years old and wanted only to play soccer. His parents had given up trying to persuade him in another career direction. While Sophie loved them all dearly, she would have occasional bouts of weeping on Aaron's shoulder—to have three sons and none of them a rabbi! Aaron's secret sorrow was that none of them, beyond singing, had any musical inclination. Four offspring, with distinct personalities, strongly held opinions, and fiercely held loyalty for each other.

The Goldstein's were sitting at dinner in their fire-lit dining room. They had stood, with restrained patience, as Aaron intoned the blessing. The Goldsteins were German Gentile in culture and dress and, in worship, some customs, and food, Jewish.

"Don't hog all the bratwurst, Jacob."

"Please place your napkin in your lap, Isaac."

"I wish it would snow."

"Wife, did your oldest son tell you what happened in the store today?"

"Abraham tells me nothing without me having to pry it from him, a tomb our son!"

"Well, a very pretty girl came in. I was busy and he was coming out of the office. He had to wait on her."

"Poor Abraham. Such a fate, to have to speak to a girl!" Maria inserted.

"She asked for piano sheet music and he stammered that we didn't have any. He was standing right in front of the rack!"

Laughter.

Abraham shrugged sheepishly.

"My son, you will never marry if your tongue doesn't become unloosened."

"You just find me a girl, Mama. I will trust your expert judgment," Abraham returned.

Sophie smiled. "There you see, Aaron, he may not have a loose tongue but he has a mind full of wisdom. We should have named our son Solomon!"

More laughter.

Jacob shook his head vigorously, his mouth full. "I think he's misnamed anyway. Didn't Father Abraham have lots of descendants? Obviously he knew how to talk to a girl."

Abraham blushed and bent back over his food.

"I will certainly choose my own husband," Maria said with a defiant toss of her shoulders, knowing this would cause a barrage of teasing.

"There are so many for you to choose from."

"And she is already so busy trying out the candidates. What mark did you get on your history exam the other day, Maria?"

"Steven Weiss nearly faints every time she walks by."

"Such devotion, ah, do you feel like a queen 'O Petted One'?"

"Pass the salt."

"'Please' would be nice, Jacob."

"I think Maria is trying to accumulate as many boyfriends as Rudi Picard has girlfriends!"

"Maybe they should just eliminate everyone else and concentrate on each other," Jacob inserted slyly. He knew well his sister's secret devotion.

Maria tossed a roll at her brother's head.

"Children, children. Your children are wild tonight, Aaron. Rudi Picard needs more ambition than just to play soccer. I cannot imagine that would be a good way to provide for a family," Sophie said practically.

Isaac leaned back. "Ah, well, if he ever gives up soccer, I'm sure Frau Picard will have a profession for him to choose from."

The boys laughed; Sophie tried to look severe.

"Isaac."

"Mama, you know it's true. Isn't Thomas always doing what his mother tells him to do?" A tone of disgust threaded his voice. "Whenever he does start preaching, I'm sure she'll give him his sermon text."

"Now, Isaac, that is enough. They are our dearest friends. How can you talk that way?"

"And in all those girls Rudi chases, we all know Frau Picard will pick the one," Jacob joined in.

"She probably chooses all his clothes," Maria laughed, "and tells him what he is hungry for!"

Aaron Goldstein cleared his throat and the table fell quiet.

"I will pose this question to Isaac, Jacob, and Maria. Would you feel comfortable making the comments you just made in front of Frau Picard?"

The three offenders were silent. Aaron's voice was gentle. "As your mother said, the Picards are our dearest friends. We think of Thomas and Rudi and Gretchen as our own. Frau Picard is likewise devoted to you. She would do anything for you, indeed give her life for you. Remember that, young ones, when you are tempted to tease."

Maria felt properly chastened, and was to recall her father's strange words several years later. Words of a prophet . . .

• • •

Maria Goldstein felt she had been walking to the tobacconist with her father forever. He had begun the journey sixteen years earlier when he pushed her in a pram. It was the only time of the day she had alone with her reticent father; one time of the day when she was more subdued.

"Papa, I was thinking, if we took all the times we have walked to the shop, I wonder how far it would stretch. To Berlin?"

He smiled. "At least to Berlin. But Berlin is a big, harsh city. Let's go the other direction. Where would that take us, daughter?"

She slipped her arm through his. "You are testing my geography, I know."

Her father chuckled.

"Let's see ... if we went east, we would go all the way to ... Vienna!"

"And south?"

"South. Italy. To Rome."

"A little too far, perhaps. Through the Brenner Pass to Milan. We've walked to Milan or Vienna."

"I'd go to Milan then because it sounds romantic!"

"Ah, romance." He stroked his short beard.

"Which would you visit, Papa? Vienna or Milan?"

"Well, you know I went to Vienna years ago for the shop. And in Italy you need to know Italian, which I don't. With a pretty girl, language doesn't matter as much, with an old man it would."

"You aren't old."

He sighed. "I'd go to America if I could go anywhere. Like Thomas did. Ever since he told us about the West, about the plains, I'd like to see it. That's where I'd go."

"Mama wouldn't go with you, you know. She's afraid of the ocean."

"I know." He laughed. "She would think we were silly for dreaming of these trips, Maria. Life for her is Blumenstrasse."

"I know. But Papa, is wanting adventure or romance wrong? Surely Mama has had her romantic moments."

Herr Goldstein smothered a smile. *Yes, my practical wife can be romantic. ...*

"You are unhappy, daughter?"

The young girl shrugged. "No, not exactly. But everything is Blumenstrasse. I feel so ... so confined sometimes!"

"Youth. It is natural, Maria. But with the proper perspective you could find romance and adventure on Blumenstrasse. Perhaps, even someday wish only for Blumenstrasse." Again the prophet.

"That's hard to imagine. Romance and adventure can't be found when you have three nosy older brothers who give me not a moment of respect. And Thomas is no better. I have absolutely no privacy here. Everyone treats me like I'm a child and not a woman of nearly twenty!" she exaggerated.

"They think they know all my thoughts. They think I have to marry someone they know!"

"You know, daughter, not so long ago—and in many places still— marriages are arranged by the parents."

She laughed. "I would trust your judgment to find me a good man, Papa, but I don't know that I could trust you with his looks!"

Her father smiled. "Ah, Maria, you're right. I would look to his heart—not his face—to see how deeply he would love my precious daughter."

They walked in silence a few more moments. "Well, maybe I will just go to Milan someday and have an affair with an Italian!"

She darted a look at her father to see if he was shocked. His step was still steady, his face impassive.

"I'd like you to finish school first, Maria."

She laughed out loud. *Papa. He knows how to poke fun at me without making me mad.*

His tone was still mild. "And, of course, your Italian would need to speak German so Mama could inspect and see if he was kosher through and through."

For the first time Maria frowned. He was teasing, but there was a truth there. Did she dare voice it, even with her unflappable father?

"He does have to be Jewish, doesn't he, Papa?" her voice was low.

"Maria, you are only sixteen. Do you have to be ready for love already? If you take another man, who will walk with me in the evenings?"

Yes, he has to be Jewish. The world is no bigger than Blumenstrasse. With a Jewish man someday. Love could not be with an Italian or Austrian ... or Gentile. She gripped his arm tighter. They both knew he would never see the American West. He would never leave Sophie that long. So she would stay with him, so they could walk together in the evenings, so they could share their dreams.

Maria sat on the front steps. The house behind her was dark. She had crept down the stairs after the thin strip of light under her parent's door had been extinguished. Maria Goldstein was not a young girl who typically indulged in solitary musing. Usually she was the center of a group of girls or her youngest brother's soccer crowd. But tonight, as the half moon was sliding through a deep-blue sky, she felt like being alone. The walk with her father earlier had cast her in a pensive mood.

At sixteen, Maria was a beautiful young girl. She was olive-complexioned with deep brown eyes and dark brows. But it was her hair that people noticed first. Straight, thick, deep brown, glossy, shoulder length. Her own good nature saved Maria Goldstein from complete self-infatuation. She was not above laughing at herself. But tonight, she didn't feel like laughing.

What was really beyond Blumenstrasse? she wondered. *Can I face new challenges with confidence and boldness?* She was usually in a group of girls or with her brothers. *What if I was alone in a city like Milan or Vienna? Could I really be the same laughing, independent me?*

There were things in Munich that could challenge her. She knew that. Just the day before, on the way home from school, her best friend Sara had whispered that her older brother had been called a Christ-killer by a group of Nazi stormtroopers. Then they had roughed him up and humiliated him on the public street. Maria had listened then immediately changed the subject. She didn't want to hear about such things. Over the years, she had read in school or heard in synagogue that Jews were a persecuted people. So she was part of them, part of that history, part of those who could be persecuted. *But why should anyone persecute me? They don't know me and I've done nothing to them. It makes no sense,* she thought. *No, I won't think about those kinds of things. They won't affect me.*

She glanced over at the Picards' house. Like her home, it too was dark. Frau Picard had been sweeping off her porch this afternoon. *She frowned when I inquired of Rudi's whereabouts.* Maria knew the soccer season was over. *Was he doing a delivery for the store?* Frau Picard replied stiffly that she didn't know. The tone spoke volumes—Maria didn't need to be wondering about her youngest son. There were many times, like this afternoon, when Maria didn't quite understand how her mother and Frau Picard could be best friends. Frau Picard could be so formal and brusque sometimes. Then Maria remembered the story of her birth and christening.

The two families were vacationing together in the Alps. The husbands had taken the older children skiing, leaving Maria Picard and Sophie alone in a rented chalet. Suddenly, six weeks early, Sophie went into hard labor. She became hysterical, convinced she was going to die without her husband or doctor near. But Maria Picard took over the situation with cool, composed efficiency. Baby Goldstein was delivered three agonizing hours later, perfectly healthy, to a sobbingly grateful Sophie.

Now, sitting on the porch, Maria knew her mother would broach little criticism of the Picard family. *But sometimes I wish Mother hadn't named me after Frau Picard. Then I wouldn't feel so guilty about not liking the older woman.*

Maria leaned forward, her arms encircling her legs, her chin on her knees. *It's not unheard of to mix Jewish and Gentile in marriage, but I know many people frown on it. Even though my parents love the Picard children as if they were their own, none of them would be acceptable in marriage.*

But that didn't change the inclinations of her heart. She knew she had the reputation for being boy crazy, and most any boy her age and acquaintance fell under the spell of her dusky beauty. She truly enjoyed these flirtations. But her thoughts always returned to the boys next door. She had known them all her life. Thomas had taught her to read. Rudi had taught her to ride a bike and ice skate. They were Blumenstrasse, yes, but they were the best of Blumenstrasse. Rudi Picard was absolutely the most handsome, most winning boy she had ever known. Her girlfriends were reduced to giggles when they saw him. Average height, thick cap of dark curly hair, blue eyes. Well formed. Two years older than Maria, full of energy and brashness, confidence and helpfulness, he was, to her, perfect. *With him around, there need never be a trip to Milan or an affair with an Italian,* she thought. She glanced up at the moon. . . . *Is he as far from my grasp, as unattainable as the moon?* Then she heard someone coming down the street. *Rudi is coming.*

She straightened her posture and brushed back her hair with her hands. With his head lowered, preoccupied with his thoughts, and in a hurry, she knew he would jog up the stairs to his home and never see her sitting there. He was on the first step when she cleared her throat loudly. He stopped and looked around, stretching forward in the darkness.

"Maria?"

"Guten Abend, Rudi. Been with Helen?"

"What are you doing out here? Aren't you cold?"

"No, and I'm just sitting here."

He sauntered up to her steps. "Do your folks know you're out here?"

"Would you stop questioning me like you're my nursemaid?"

He shrugged. "All right, all right. So what's up?"

"Perhaps I'm just enjoying a nice night under the stars. . . . A romantic night."

He looked up and yawned. "Yeah . . . all right."

"Maybe I'm just sitting here thinking."

He smiled. "What's the occasion?"

Normally she would have laughed; normally they would have traded teases. She stood up and marched to the step in front of him.

"You are calling me brainless just like Thomas does."

"We don't think you're brainless, Maria," he laughed.

She remembered the technique Marlene Dietrich had used in her latest film. *Sultry voice, direct approach.* She knew the Picards thought she was pretty. *Still* . . . She tried to lower her voice as she stepped closer. She would bring a new angle to the old Picard-Goldstein alliance. *The bond didn't need to break!*

"Do you think I'm pretty, Rudi?"

"Of course I do. Everyone does. Why—"

"You never tell me. The other day Thomas said, 'The height of your beauty, Maria Goldstein, is in direct proportion to your vanity.' He insults me and thinks I don't know it!"

"I don't think he meant to insult you," Rudi laughed. "You know how Thomas is, how he talks."

"I think you're the most handsome man I've ever seen."

"Well, ah, thanks, Maria. What's with you tonight?"

"The moon and the stars . . . have stirred me."

"Oh. Well, ah, I better go in. You sound like you're coming down with a cold. Maybe you shouldn't stay out here any longer."

Her hands went to his shoulders. "Did you kiss Helen Kruger tonight, Herr Picard?"

He nodded dumbly. *She had never stood so close . . . and she smelled so nice.*

She leaned forward, her eyes closed in clear invitation.

Rudi Picard thought fleetingly of Sophie standing at the parlor window—or worse, his own mother. *Never mind.* He would indulge the moon-stirred Maria. *She is prettier than Helen by miles. And a pretty girl, even a neighbor, is hard to resist.*

They kissed briefly. Then he stepped back and smiled.

"Auf Wiedersehen, Maria."

She was alone again. With the moon and the stars. She felt like laughing. She knew it would be hours before she could fall asleep. *Blumenstrasse! Wonderful, dear Blumenstrasse! Dreams can come true.*

3
The Soul of a Country

Thomas Picard was stretched out on the floor, his feet toward the fireplace, his head pillowed in the lap of a young girl. She was brushing his hair. He was reading to her slowly, stopping frequently to ask her questions. Most often, in stuttered tones, she merely repeated his question.

Gretchen Picard was a slender woman with a pale, oval face and deep-green eyes. While her body testified of her age, her mind was no more mature than that of a four year old. Since she had been a year old, Gretchen Picard had suffered epileptic seizures. She was a gentle, loving girl who adored her older brother.

Thomas watched the softness come over her face as she stroked the cat. He thought of the conversation he had had just an hour earlier with his parents.

Maria Picard sat on the velvet sofa; her husband Michael was teasing the cat with an old tie. Thomas had been reading. The room had been comfortably warm and quiet with only Michael's occasional chuckle. Frau Picard's voice was tired.

"I feel so disturbed about what happened in town with Gretchen."

Thomas looked up. "Mother, that was yesterday."

"Yesterday and I still feel the shock of it, Thomas. It was very upsetting to me and the people around me. I could see the fear and disgust on their faces."

"If they knew about Gretchen I'm sure they would have understood," Herr Picard offered.

"If they had known about Gretchen they probably would have wondered why I brought her. It was so quiet in the room—even with that many people. It was like we were holding our breath. We had such good seats near the front. We could see Göring and Goebbels and Bishop Frank so clearly. Herr Hitler was as close as that chair. Then Gretchen starts screaming. I tell you, Thomas, I felt my blood run cold. I felt every eye in that huge room on me. It was terrible, just terrible."

"Mother, you said yourself it wasn't a full seizure so that should greatly encourage you."

"Screaming loud enough to wake the dead was bad enough, Thomas. It was so strange. Once outside in the hallway she calmed down instantly. But of course I didn't dare take her back in. So I missed all of Herr Hitler's remarks, which I expressly wanted to hear."

The room was quiet. Thomas looked at his father who was leading the cat around the room with the tie while humming some melody. Thomas went back to his book.

Maria Picard sighed loudly. "If you had gone with me, Michael, I could have stayed and listened. Or if you had stayed at home with her."

Michael Picard looked over at his son.

Thomas spoke up quickly. "Frau Sophie could have watched her. Or Rudi."

"Sophie was preparing for their Hanukkah feast; I didn't want to burden her. And Rudi doesn't watch her closely enough. His head is in the clouds more than ever since that new girl came into his life. Your father should have gone with me. The most important political figure in Germany comes to campaign in Munich and your father refuses to go."

The unmistakable bitterness. All three in the room could hear it. Herr Picard had no political interest to the frustration of his intensely politically interested wife.

Michael flopped down in an overstuffed chair, all animation and pleasure erased from his face. Thomas studied him a moment and realized that in the months he had been in Wittenburg, his father seemed to have aged or grown tired. *There are lines around his eyes and mouth that I haven't really noticed before. Is he working at the store too much?*

Michael Picard was a slender man of fifty-seven. His iron-gray hair was wavy, his blue eyes usually sparkling behind silver-rimmed glasses.

His lean face and slender hands belied his real demeanor. When he smiled, he was a pleasant, very cheerful man interested in life and full of jokes and warmth. He was constantly humming a tune. Merely drop the hint and Michael Picard would break into song. The love of music flowed through his veins—a gift, a passion from his father. Nothing delighted Picard more than to be asked by some group in the city to come and play the piano for them. He was a self-taught, highly gifted pianist.

His mother's voice pulled Thomas from his concerned thoughts for his father.

"Yesterday's episode only convinced me that tomorrow, when Bishop Frank and Pastor Shraeder come, I will send Gretchen over to the Goldsteins."

"Mother, I really wish you wouldn't do that," Thomas requested softly.

Frau Picard straightened in her chair.

"Thomas, these men are coming because of you; they are your future employers. Think what it would be like if Gretchen started screaming or, worse, had a seizure." She hesitated. "And Otto is coming."

"Paul Shraeder is my best friend, Mother, and he's been around Gret before. I'm sure that is the case with the bishop as well. He would understand."

"Well, it would be very upsetting to me. Besides, Pastor Shraeder is your friend, our friend, and our pastor, but he comes in a different capacity tomorrow."

Thomas stood and walked to the fireplace. He could feel his mother's eyes upon his back. "If you do that, Gretchen will be hurt. She'll know she's being sent away."

"Thomas, in your love for your sister you give her too much understanding. She will only know she is going to visit the Goldsteins. You know how she dotes on Maria."

Thomas looked at his father. The man had closed his eyes. Thomas shrugged. It was useless to argue.

Even a man of twenty-three isn't above an occasional bout of pettiness. Thomas was annoyed like a small boy at the prospect of a visit from his less-than-favorite relative. There would be tension at the Picard dining table.

Mealtimes were usually subdued anyway. Maria discouraged bantering between the boys and their father and Gretchen's chattering. Michael or Rudi would attempt a few jokes only to receive a disapproving frown. A discussion of the days events, told briefly, was tolerated.

Now Uncle Otto was coming unexpectedly, visiting from Frankfurt. Normally Maria Picard looked forward to her younger brother's visits because he always knew the details of those stories in the paper. He was a well-traveled man and knew what was going on in Germany. But Maria was nervous at her brother appearing at the table with two religious leaders. Otto Beck had absolutely no use for religion. It was the one issue that divided brother and sister.

Thomas was in the kitchen helping his mother with the meal preparation when Rudi stuck his head in at the doorway.

"Did you take Gretchen over?" Maria asked.

"All tucked away, Mother."

She turned from the steaming stove, frowning. "I do not like your implication, Rudi. I am not trying to hide your sister. I merely want a peaceful dinner. Is that too much to ask?"

Herr Picard peered around Rudi. "Smells wonderful—I'm starved."

"Michael, we can't eat until our guests arrive so don't attempt to bribe me."

"I would not attempt such an offense, my dear. Besides our guests are here: Otto and Paul."

"Michael, why didn't you tell me!" Maria Picard was hurriedly untying her apron.

"I was trying to tell you, my dear."

"And Bishop Frank? He will be late?"

"No, he's not coming. Something came up at the last moment."

Maria Picard sighed and leaned heavily against the counter.

"It's all right, Mother," Thomas soothed.

"I was so looking forward to meeting him. He is such an important man, Thomas. Can't you see that? He can do things for your career."

Rudi sauntered in and snatched a piece of fresh bread. "I guess Thomas would rather God did things for his career than Bishop Frank."

Maria was very annoyed. "Rudi Picard, go change your shirt."

Rudi shrugged and left the room.

"Dinner will be fine with Paul, whether he's here as our friend or a church officer," Thomas said as he put his arm around his mother.

Maria nodded reluctantly, disappointment clearly etched on her face.

Maria knew as she greeted her guest with smiles and calmness, she could expect little from her family in making this meal a success though the food was perfect and the table looked lovely. Only Thomas could help her, that is, if he wasn't pouting about sending Gretchen next door. They were seated and Maria looked to her eldest son. She smiled and relaxed. Thomas had a steadying, calming affect on people, and she was no different. She depended on him, always had. There were times they had made decisions and met crises that Michael had no part of.

Yes, I can depend on Thomas, Maria thought. *Such a fine, tall, handsome son to be proud of. He never disappoints me. He never will. And now, in a matter of weeks, he will be an ordained minister. Such an honor! Rudi? Rudi with his wit and charm and athletic abilities, more like his father. Thomas is truly of my flesh and mind. And Gretchen. Sweet Gretchen with her timid smile . . .*

Maria's heart had broken long ago for her fragile-minded daughter. So many times she had held her gasping and vomiting little girl as she experienced a seizure. So many nights she had sat beside her daughter's bed, holding her hand while she slept to make sure she kept breathing. So many times she had prayed for the defect to leave her daughter's body and take residence in her own. But Gretchen hadn't changed. She had only grown taller, her body moving toward maturity. Maria Picard felt the heavens had been deaf to her prayers.

Thomas couldn't remember when he had started disliking his mother's brother. Uncle Otto, a bachelor, always brought them wonderful, expensive toys. Yet the big, florid-faced man always put Thomas off with his loud, brash, manner. He was forever boasting about who he met and where he went in his business travels. Each visit meant a litany of his financial success and what he had paid for his fine Italian leather shoes. Otto was a dogmatic man, confident and forceful in his views, and scornful of anyone who didn't share them.

Though Paul Shraeder was five years older than Thomas, they had been good friends since primary school. Paul had gone to the university and into the ministry, forging ahead on the same path that Thomas would take. The Picard family had been delighted when Shraeder had been called to their small, Protestant neighborhood church.

Over dinner everyone laughed and talked together before Paul struck up a conversation about church music with the eldest Picard. Rudi, Thomas could see, was watching his uncle. Otto was eating with typical relish as he chatted with his sister. Rudi looked up and winked at Thomas.

"So, how is the teeth trade these days, Uncle Otto? Is that what brings you to Munich?" Rudi asked.

Maria Picard shook her head slightly. Rudi and Thomas persisted in calling her brother's occupation as a dental supply salesman a "teeth trade."

But Otto appeared unruffled. He blotted his lips with the fine-linen napkin.

"Flourishing, Rudi, thank you. Southern Germany belongs to Finkel-stein!"

"Put a Finkelstein in your mouth and smile," Michael Picard hummed lightly.

Everyone laughed, but Thomas didn't miss the look Otto gave his sister—a mocking smile on his lips, something else entirely in his eyes.

"And you, Rudi? Helping your father in the store or still out on the field?" Otto asked with false pleasantness.

"Season's over," Rudi replied, his mouth full of food.

"So what does a man of eighteen do when the season is over? What career are you pursing?" Otto pressed.

The young man jabbed a fork at his uncle. "I seem to remember you asking me that the last time you were here," he said good-naturedly.

Otto's head bobbed. "Yes, I did. A young man's vocation interests me, especially my nephew. Our days are full of . . . opportunity for a man. Not like a few years ago. Germany is emerging, coming out of the dark-ness the Treaty of Versailles cast her in. Great times are coming, Rudi, very soon. I want to see a Picard in the forefront."

"Well, I can tell you it won't be in teeth or music. Something in between," Rudi laughed.

"Chasing a white ball? Can you make a living from that?" Otto asked, leaning forward.

Rudi's voice was still pleasant as he shrugged and said, "I could. But who knows, perhaps I'll find a girl with a rich father. That's the ticket!"

Maria gave a nervous laugh. "Rudi Picard! Michael, did you hear your son?"

Pastor Shraeder spoke up, winking. "You could enter the seminary, Rudi, if you can't find a young girl with a rich father. Follow in your brother's footsteps."

Everyone chuckled. Maria smiled. Perhaps dinner could be salvaged.

"Thomas's footsteps are too big for me to fill, Paul, thanks."

"Germany doesn't really need more pastors or priests. Certainly no more rabbis!" Otto offered loudly. He ignored his sister's furious look. *Her foppish husband has dulled her wits. It's time she saw the realities of life in Germany,* he thought. *Even if her husband and sons ignored them. Poor Maria . . .*

"You sound like a Nazi, Uncle Otto," Rudi said.

Thomas watched his brother. He didn't like this uncle any better than he, but Rudi could be volatile at times, his composure suddenly ignited.

Otto drained his wine glass with a flourish and reached for the crystal decanter.

"Thank you, Rudi, that is good. I am a member of the Nazi party. In fact, it is not just Finkelstein that brings me to Munich. It is party business as well."

The table was deathly silent. Everyone resumed eating. Except Otto. He seemed amused.

"You all understand that the Nazi Party will be the power in our government very soon? The decadent Weimar republic is falling. Do you know that, Thomas?"

"Well," Thomas said slowly, " I . . . I did vote last month for the party. They have many good ideas."

Otto was beaming. "There! At last, Maria! You see—Thomas understands!"

Pastor Shraeder spoke up. "Even pastors are important to this new Germany you speak of, Herr Beck. The church is to safeguard the soul of a nation. Thomas will be a part of that. We are all very proud of him."

Otto sat back, still smiling, but Thomas could see the look the man was giving the pastor. Measuring, calculating. Thomas had seen it before.

"Safeguard the soul of Germany. Well, you see it is very simple. Let the pastors and priests take care of the church; our leaders will take care of the rest. I have heard our leader say these things."

Shraeder nodded slowly. "Yes, there are many, even in the church, who believe there are two spheres or realms in life. One sphere belongs to Christ, the other to the government or state. However, I believe there is only one realm, and Christ must be Lord over all."

Maria Picard closed her eyes. *Why didn't I insist that Otto come for dinner another night?* Otto would not be silent; and this pastor could influence Thomas' future.

"And you agree of course, Thomas?" Otto prodded.

"Well, that has been a debate long-held at the university. I . . . I have not come to a definitive conclusion on that. I do think a strong government means a strong church. A strong church means a strong government."

"Otto, we don't normally discuss politics at the table," Maria said smiling.

"But what if one, the church or the government, becomes stronger than the other, what then?"

Everyone paused. Michael Picard had spoken.

"The government cannot be too strong, Michael," Otto said scornfully. He glanced at his sister and rolled his eyes.

Then Thomas knew. *I've never liked Uncle Otto because he is always condescending to Father.* He wanted to think more about this, but his father interrupted his thoughts.

"It seems to me that if the church is strong and the government is strong, they are bound to collide."

Thomas was stunned. His father rarely talked this way. He was looking so serious.

"Why should they collide, Father?" Thomas asked.

Picard was examining the beef on the end of his fork, a crease between his eyebrows.

"Because two powers will not want to share power; they will feel threatened by each other."

"If the Nazi party comes into power, they will respect the church," Thomas returned. Many of our leaders have spoken to the party officials. We all want to work together for a better Germany."

"Exactly! Well said, nephew!" Otto was nearly clapping.

"I think it's time for dessert, Mother. Want us to move into the parlor?" Thomas asked.

"Yes, that's a fine idea Thomas, thank you."

But before anyone could stand, Herr Picard's voice stopped them. Those at the table froze. Maria was horrified. *Why, why of all nights did he have to speak this way?*

Picard leaned back in his chair, his voice gentle and thoughtful.

"The Nazi party speaks very harshly about Jews. How do you explain that, Thomas?"

"Michael, I've never heard you talk this way!" Maria sputtered.

He smiled. "I listen to my customers. We do more than talk about Mozart and Beethoven!"

"Then you have been listening to the wrong customers, Michael Picard," Otto snapped.

"Otto, please."

"I confess I too have felt a little concern for the Nazi party's position on Jews," Pastor Shraeder added. "They are God's chosen people."

Thomas could see that his mother was terribly upset. Every eye was upon him.

"Every political party has rough edges. They usually pick some real or, in most cases, some perceived enemy." Thomas smiled. "That's why I don't want to get into politics. I don't want any enemies. But think of it. The social democrats blame the communists, the communists blame the social democrats. The Nazi party has chosen the Jews. I don't agree with it, but it's hardly what they are all about. Once in power, they'll turn their energy to the reforms they promised."

Picard nodded thoughtfully. "Let us hope you are right, son."

Otto's smile had vanished and his face was redder than usual. He stood abruptly.

"Delicious meal, Maria. Thank you. I can't stay for dessert because I have a business appointment. Auf Wiedersehen."

Maria hastened after her brother, out into the foyer where he was pulling on his overcoat and hat with swift, jerking motions.

"Otto, Otto," her voice was barely above a whisper. "You know how they are, why did you start all that?"

He leaned down, his voice hissing. "Maria, you must see how things are. Your sons should have been in the Hitler youth groups long ago. You have a successful business that you own with a Jew!"

She laid a hand on his arm. "Otto, I will not have you talk about the Goldsteins that way. You know how I feel about that."

"Maria, you are wanting it both ways like Thomas, but it can't be that way. Don't you see?"

"Otto, please—"

His hand was on the doorknob. "I will come back tomorrow, when they are gone, and we will talk some more. You must see that Thomas has potential. But not if he listens to weak types such as your beloved Shraeder. If you really want your son to succeed you must understand and accept the way the new government will dictate."

"You aren't a Christian man, Otto. Are you saying Thomas shouldn't go into the church?"

"Let him go. But let him understand," he emphasized with significance, *"two spheres!"* He was shaking his head as he closed the door.

Michael and the pastor had adjourned to the parlor for coffee. Rudi and Thomas were left at the table. Rudi sat back, leaning and stretching. Thomas was staring at the table, his fingers laced together in front of him. He was frowning.

"Interesting meal, eh?" Rudi chuckled.

Thomas sighed. "Suddenly I'm glad Gretchen wasn't here after all."

Rudi stood. "You know, the funny thing about tonight—you were on the same side as Finkelstein."

January 30, 1933
Berlin

He understood that to aspire to a throne of power, you must first sweat in the corridors of power. It never surprised him that this understanding of the mechanics of greatness was something inborn and instinctive for him. It had been a day of high tension in the capital. His aides around him were almost feverish with anticipation. He too had been visibly nervous as he paced the carpet of his room at the Kaiserhof Hotel. Nervous for the process, not the outcome. He was supremely confident his hour had finally come. His aides could wonder, speculate, worry, strategize. He knew.

He had practiced the ancient arts, telepathy, hypnosis, and pagan rituals since those bleak days in Vienna when he had been a vagrant. He had consulted the stars; he had invoked the powers of darkness. He had stood before the spear that supposedly had pierced the side of Christ and possessed supernatural powers. He had called upon those powers to indwell him. He had bullied, bribed, and flattered men to support him. He had lied. He had been charming. He had made promises; he had inspired. He had worked hard and suffered privation, scorn, and ridicule. His minions had likewise given much to him and the cause. But in this hour, this triumphant hour, Adolf Hitler stood alone. The Third Reich was born this day. He had done it.

4
Ignorance and Innocence

Rich, warm light filtered through the lace curtains of the Goldstein front room and onto the slushy sidewalk outside, casting liquid pools of amber and gold at the feet of any who ventured out on such a sharp, cold night. The curtains revealed the scene of uncomplicated friendship as the Goldsteins and Picards sat down for an evening of cards. It had been a Friday evening ritual for years: a little food, a little music, and some games. Begun when the children had been in diapers and underfoot, always interrupting, fighting, breaking, and spilling things, the tradition continued. Now grown, the children often left the parents to continue the tradition.

It was obvious what knit Aaron Goldstein and Michael Picard together in friendship, what made their business a success. They were so much alike—in temperament and interests. To the casual eye and a few people on Blumenstrasse however, the friendship between the two wives was not so easily dissected. They looked, and in most respects were, opposites—right down to Sophie's short, unruly brown hair and the customary crooked inch of white slip hem showing to Maria's tightly coiled, smooth, gray bun and her gray silk perfection with white starched collars. Maria was punctual, correct, modest; Sophie was late, emotional, earthy. Maria was undemonstrative; Sophie bordered on theatrical. Maria was meticulous and a perfectionist; Sophie was energetic. Maria was opinionated on politics; Sophie studied a candidate's looks in the newspaper to confirm her logic.

Side by side for more than twenty years, they had laughed and wept together, held each other's sick children, done hundreds of errands for each other, traded meals, shared frustrations.

Sophie, ignoring the fact that most of the children gathered in the hallway were old enough to have children themselves, was bustling among them with eager hands and tart tongue.

"You can't possibly go out in a thin jacket like that, Maria Goldstein. Go up and get your coat."

"Mama, really!"

"She wants everyone to see her new sweater," Jacob pointed out with wicked honesty.

Sophie swung around on Thomas, who was leaning against the balustrade.

"Thomas, you look at my rebellious daughter! Look at her sweater so she'll be satisfied," Sophie pleaded.

Maria turned red. "Mama!"

Thomas pushed away from the stairs, cocked his head, and squinted his eyes.

"Thomas Picard, stop it!" Maria laughed. *If only it were Rudi. Rudi as he had looked the night we had kissed. Rudi seeing me as a pretty girl. But Rudi was already at the cinema ... with Helen.*

He bowed deeply. "Beautiful sweater, O Petted One."

Sophie clapped and shooed her frowning daughter up the stairs. Thomas stepped into the room with his parents and the Goldsteins. Gretchen was sitting with her father.

"Go, Tom?" she asked eagerly.

He nodded. "As soon as Maria passes inspection."

The parents laughed.

"You go back to Wittenburg tomorrow?" Aaron asked.

"Yes, sir, on the noon train."

"Any prospects where you will get a church?"

"Well, nothing definite. I've talked with a few church leaders—"

"The church in Dachau wants him very much," Frau Picard interrupted pleasantly. "He did such a fine job for them last summer. The elders have already spoken with him."

"Mother, they talk with lots of candidates. Nothing is for certain."

"Nonsense. They want you. It will be perfect. You'll be close enough to come home on weekends."

"Well ..."

"Of course, it will be really perfect when you get a church in Munich. Then you can live at home. I would be delighted to host your congregation."

An embarrassed silence fell over the room. Thomas was grateful when young Maria entered the room.

"Well, I suppose I'm ready," she said mournfully. She spread her arms. "Dressed as I am in sackcloth."

Maria bent over to kiss her father goodbye.

"The inside, my Maria, the inside. There is the beauty," he whispered softly in her ear.

She nodded and smiled, then helped Gretchen with her coat. Maria Picard was watching her.

"You look very lovely tonight, Maria."

"Thank you, Frau Picard," Maria returned with unconcealed surprise.

"Now hurry along, hurry along, children," Sophie waved.

Gretchen thrilled to be with her big brother and Maria, swiftly kissed her parents. Her mother held her face in her hands a moment, and everyone in the room knew Maria Picard was loving her little daughter. Then her eyes sought her son's.

He smiled. "I will be careful. She will be fine, and if she gets too tired we'll come straight home."

"To the movie!" Gretchen Picard squealed.

• • •

While it was a pleasant evening for the Goldsteins and Picards, an event had transpired earlier that Sophie—the diary, the dictionary, the authority of Blumenstrasse—knew nothing of. Old Frau Zimmerman, who owned the pretty brick house exactly in the center of the street, was ill in a Berlin hospital. Her grown, Berliner son had moved her there a week before. Now, quite suddenly, she had died. Alfred Zimmerman had many things weighing on his mind as he orbited the bleak world of grief.

What do I do with the house on Blumenstrasse? It's mine now, but my home is in Berlin. He pulled a paper from his pocket that held the name of a man who was interested in the house in Munich. *He can pay cash for the house. With this uncertain economy, that's impressive,* he thought. *Yes, I'll sell the old place. I'll go there to collect my mother's things and say goodbye to Blumenstrasse. The new owner will be a credit to the street. A hard worker, which Blumenstrasse would admire, a family man, and a strong Nazi party member.*

• • •

Maria's scarf was wound tightly around her throat, and a soft wool cap was pulled over her head. Only an island of face showed. She didn't care about her looks now; she was too cold. Her gloved hand gripped the gloved hand of Gretchen who walked between her and Thomas.

"You all right, Gret?" Maria asked somewhat absently.

Gretchen nodded and squeezed her hand. Her head jerked toward the sky. "Stars!"

Thomas chuckled. "Our Gret loves the stars. Maybe she will be an astronomer when she grows up."

But Maria didn't answer. She was thinking of the film, *Morocco,* they had just seen. She loved films. They transported her into another, far more glamorous world. *Movies ... now there would be a profession. An actress! Just like the German-American star, Marlene Dietrich. So sultry ... yes, I could play that part. Isn't Mother always calling me dramatic?* She chewed her lip. Here it was. The same old nagging battle. *What am I going to do with my life? What am I skilled at? What do I like to do?* She sighed with the weight of youth.

"What?" Thomas asked.

"You know what you are going to do with your life. In a few weeks, you'll be a pastor. Rudi wants to be a professional soccer player. Jacob wants to be a mechanic. Isaac wants to be a doctor. I'll be seventeen in three weeks and all I can see is being a permanent fixture of Blumenstrasse like, like Frau Reinhardt's hideous hydrangeas!"

He laughed. "You told me that all you ever wanted to do was have fun. I distinctly remember you saying, and I quote, 'I want to have prolific amorous adventures before I become the captive of a solitary man.' So what happened to that vaulting ambition?"

It was hard for a tease such as Maria Goldstein to be indignant, no matter how hard she tried. She could hardly keep from laughing.

"I never said that!" she said as she punched his arm.

"You did. Maria, you forget I was your tutor for nearly four years. I was like a diary to you!"

"You have a cruel streak, Thomas Picard! Gretchen, your brother is so mean."

Thomas was laughing loudly as Gretchen vigorously shook her head.

Maria was silent a moment as she watched her brothers up ahead on the sidewalk.

"You and Rudi, along with my own brothers, think of me as a child interested only in boys. You think I have about as much value as a pretty potted plant!"

He held up his hands. "All right, all right! You are trying to tell me that you want to figure out what you want to do with your life beyond boyfriends."

"Exactly. Your mother told you what to be, but I really don't want mine—" She could feel the heat flooding her face. *Such thoughtless, impulsive words! If Mama had heard them she'd be wagging her head like a dog just bathed.*

Thomas Picard could be a terrible tease, but he had always listened to her. And after the teasing he had been kind and encouraging. Besides her own father, Thomas was who she always talked to about important things. He had defended her when her brothers had wanted to exclude her. She had always been closer to him than any of her brothers ... even the dashing Rudi. She cast an eye at him. He was looking forward.

"Thomas, I'm sorry. I didn't meant that. I ..."

"It's all right."

They had now come to Blumenstrasse. Gretchen was skipping before them.

"That is what you really think, that my mother made me become a pastor?" he asked slowly.

He stopped walking and faced her. Her eyes looking up at him were dark and alert.

"I am going into the ministry because I want to, Maria, because I feel God has called me."

"And I want to be taken seriously for a change."

For a moment there was no longer six years separating them. They were equals, both capable of hurts and hopes. They had reached their homes.

"Then I suppose we are a little alike, fraulein. Both misunderstood."

The two combatants had fled the battlefield and were now sitting, bruised and bleeding, at the Goldstein kitchen table. Sophie, also sitting, was fanning herself. The sight of blood had such a weakening effect on her. Isaac was patting her shoulder. Maria was brewing tea and looking very angry. Frau Picard was applying a compress to Rudi's forehead. She had bandaged Jacob Goldstein's cheek and torn knuckles. Her lips were drawn into a hard line. Her movements were brisk and efficient, and both boys winced several times under her handling.

"Should we call Dr. Jensen, do you think, Frau Maria?" Isaac asked. "Those lacerations look deep."

Maria Picard straightened, a hand pressing against the small of her back, her face pale. She did not turn. Her voice was clipped.

"Rudi needs stitches. Jacob needs his shoulder looked at. Yes, Isaac, call him."

Sophie lowered her face in her hands, moaning. "Oh, our boys."

Frau Picard tossed down the rag with obvious impatience.

"I think we should call Papa and Herr Michael," Maria Goldstein ventured as she handed the boys tea.

Frau Picard's voice was firm. "No. They are busy at the store." She glanced at her watch. "Thomas is leaving in an hour." Her voice cracked a fraction. "Where is he?"

"I passed him on Bannerstrasse. He said he had an errand to do before he left," Rudi offered.

Frau Picard swung around on her youngest son. "How could you, Rudi Picard? How could you be brawling on this day when your brother is leaving? Don't I have enough distress? I was up with Gretchen until midnight."

Rudi met eyes with Maria. She wanted to put her arms around him. He looked away, and she swung around to the stove, chewing her lip and furious at Frau Picard.

"I'm sorry, Mother," Rudi said softly.

"It was all my fault," Jacob volunteered as he winced.

Rudi shook his head and looked back at his mother. "I'm sorry that this has upset you and Frau Sophie, Mother, but I would do it again. I had to."

Maria turned from the stove. The strength of his voice didn't surprise her. She held her breath to hear his mother's reaction.

"What's going on?" Thomas stood in the doorway. No one had heard him enter.

Sophie went back to sobbing. No one said a word.

Thomas stepped into the kitchen, looking at his mother then the two boys.

Rudi smiled weakly. "We had a little trouble at the soccer field. We got a game together and some fellows joined us. They..."

"They said no Jews were allowed on any field in Munich again," Jacob said.

"They said no Jew will play soccer in Germany very soon. They started shoving Jacob around," Maria interjected.

"I should have left," Jacob said sadly.

"No!" Maria flared, and every eye turned to her. "No you shouldn't have, Jacob Goldstein! If you had, you'd have been a coward and not worthy of Rudi's friendship."

"Maria," Sophie wailed.

"The doctor has been called," Frau Picard said calmly as she touched Thomas' arm.

"No one makes you get off the tram or a soccer field just because they say so. So you're bruised, so what?" Maria continued on the verge of tears. Today it had reached out and touched her family. Hoping had not kept it away.

"Your brother may have a dislocated shoulder, and my son needs stitches. That's more than a few bruises," Frau Picard said stiffly to Maria.

Maria turned scarlet and the room was deathly still. Rudi winked at her. She turned back to the stove.

"Mother, why don't you go over to the house and get Gretchen ready. We'll go on to the station. I can't be late and you don't need to be here while Dr. Jensen patches them up," Thomas said steadily.

Maria Picard stalked purposefully from the room.

Thomas looked around, smiling slightly. He bent over Sophie.

"Are you all right, Frau Sophie?"

She nodded and patted his arm. "Mazel tov, Thomas."

His smiled deepened. "Thank you. The boys will be all right . . . don't worry."

He turned to his brother. "How'd the other fellow fare?"

Rudi's smile was roguish. "I got in a few good ones."

"Well, maybe next time you could use your head a little more than your fists and not upset mother and Frau Sophie."

He shook hands with Isaac. Then he leaned over Maria's shoulder and whispered, "I decided to get your birthday gift early. It's out in the hall. Wait till I'm gone." He gave her a wink that was almost as good as Rudi's.

She waited until she saw him hurry down the front steps. Sophie followed her into the hallway.

"He got you a gift early? That was so thoughtful of Thomas," Sophie sniffed.

Maria stopped. A big, beautiful pot of African violets sat on the hall table. Purple, her favorite color. She pulled out the card, and Sophie peered around her shoulder.

"Now what does that mean?" she asked.

"Now *this* is a potted plant, fraulein. Happy birthday, Thomas." Maria understood and smiled.

Wittenburg

"You must keep your notes in here," Dr. Begg said as he leaned stiffly forward and tapped Thomas on the skull. Thomas winced at the sour breath. "Keep my words there."

"All right, sir. I'm ready for what you have to say," Thomas replied. *Since the church at Dachau has called me, this will be my last visit with the old professor,* he thought.

"Tell me what I told you last time, please."

"Well, you said that our country is rebuilding, growing stronger. You said it looks very impressive, but the foundation is built on a sewer."

"I love my country, Thomas. I have lived my entire life here. I love the land; I love the people God called me to share the truth with. Yet such love gives me sorrow."

"Why?"

"Because the country I love, the people I love, are about to be tested, to be shaken. You will be tested, Thomas Picard."

Thomas paused and looked at the worn carpet a moment. *No, not tested—I'm about to assume my career,* he corrected silently.

"I want to serve God as you have Dr. Begg," Thomas replied with a trace of desperation.

The old man nodded. "And so you will." He looked into the fire.

"Why is the foundation of our country built upon a sewer?" Thomas asked. "The economy is improving, there are more jobs. People feel secure. When you ride the train or are on the street, you hear the optimism in their voices."

"A sewer. Their faith, their optimism is resting on a sewer."

"Why do you keep saying that?"

"It has been coming for many years, Thomas. Crumbling. And now, now at the end of my life, I am seeing it fall...."

Sewers, being tested, crumbling, falling. The old man is rambling. He is no longer the brilliant, logical thinker he was in the classroom. I'm seeing the decline of a great man... Thomas wiped the sudden perspiration from his brow. *Dean Wagner is right! This was ... is heresy! I'll just have to listen politely,* he decided.

The old minister leaned forward, his eyes feverish-looking.

"Thomas, the church is being tempted, seduced by this wave of national pride. The people are feasting on the boasts and promises that Germany can be even greater. Why must we be greater in such a way? Why aren't we trying to be greater in our love for our fellow man? In our devotion to God?"

He was breathing hard and Thomas was worried.

"Sir, sir, please—"

"Now I hear that Germans are not only strong, but they must be kept racially pure. What is this talk? The church should have called the people to repentance long ago." He fell back into his chair. "Perhaps it is not too late."

"Dr. Begg?" Thomas hurried to get the man something to drink. He held the glass to the old professor's lips, then helped the man to his bed.

"I'm not finished, Thomas," he rasped weakly.

"I know, but you should rest now. I'll come back tomorrow."

The old man clutched at the young hand.

Thomas smiled. "I promise I will come back tomorrow. Now, lean back, there. Now rest. I'll sit here until you fall asleep."

The white, woolly hair fanned out against the pillow, and Thomas found himself wondering if this is the way the Old Testament prophets must have looked.

"Thomas, you ..."

Thomas leaned forward. "Dr. Begg? Are you all right? Shall I get you your medicine?"

The man shook his head; his voice was weak.

"Tell them, tell your people they must not trade their souls for their bodies. They cannot gain the world and keep their soul."

"Yes, all right. Now—"

"And you, Thomas, you must . . . see that it doesn't always come with horns and a trident and cleft feet. It comes disguised."

"It?"

"Thomas, the sewer is hatred."

"Yes, sir, all right."

"Thomas, they are our brothers and sisters. Thomas . . ."

Because he had been busy in and out of his apartment all morning, Thomas didn't receive the call. He didn't know until he climbed the stairs and looked at the pale, angry face of the housekeeper. She looked at him accusingly. Thomas looked past her at the closed door. He looked back to the formidable woman. Her eyes were rimmed in red.

Thomas stepped back as if slapped. He swallowed hard as he studied the ground.

"I'm sorry," he rasped.

He was shocked at her soft tone. "I was with him. He went peacefully."

"Yes . . ." He felt too addled to speak. *Of course I shouldn't be surprised. He was old and has been ill. And he was so excited the day before. This annoyance, this heresy is over . . . is finished.* He turned slowly toward the stairs. Her voice, still gentle, stopped him.

"He was very clear, very lucid in his last moments. He said, 'Thomas doesn't believe anything I told him, that is why I told *him*.' "

• • •

Maria felt like a queen as she descended the stairs. She wore a dress of royal blue velveteen trimmed in satin. At the last moment, she had piled her hair up, leaving a few dark tendrils hanging down. She was wearing new pearl earrings. Aaron Goldstein, waiting at the bottom of the stairs, caught his breath. *She has never looked so beautiful. To be seventeen with your whole future before you, exciting and mysterious.* He felt his throat tighten as he thought suddenly of the things he had read that morning in the newspaper.

He blinked rapidly against the tears. Maria kissed him on the cheek. "Papa," she said tenderly.

Then there was clapping and cheering as she entered the front room. It seemed as if all of Blumenstrasse had crowded into the Goldstein's front room. And with a few exceptions, they had. Sophie had invited everyone. Her daughter's seventeenth birthday was a grand event. Her mother's sister and cousins from Stuttgart were here, her father's parents from Bonn. Maria's three best friends ran up to her, laughing and hugging and thrusting beribboned packages at her. Then Thomas started up the birthday song and the whole room began singing. She blushed with pleasure.

There was laughing and singing and feasting in the crowded room. Aaron and Michael played duet after duet. The young people pushed back the carpet in the dining room and danced. Maria was not without a dance partner all evening since Sophie had invited many Jewish boys. Maria loved it. There were nearly a hundred people in the house, but she noticed one boy whom she didn't know. He had to be her age, perhaps a little older. She liked his looks: tall and blond. He stood alone, watching.

She saw the young man turning toward the front hallway, and she followed him.

"Hello," Maria said.

He turned, hands thrust in his pockets.

"You've come to my birthday celebration, but ... I don't know you," she laughed nervously.

He shrugged. "Your mother came to my house and invited ... us. I was in the other room; I heard her."

Maria was puzzled. "My mother? Where do you live?"

He jerked his thumb over his shoulder. "We moved into the Zimmerman place yesterday."

"Oh! You are the new owners on Blumenstrasse! Welcome," she extended her hand.

He shook it awkwardly.

"I'm Maria Goldstein."

"My name is Eric Hager."

He dropped her hand and stepped back. She liked his shyness.

"You know ... you are very pretty," he said.

"Thank you," she said, giving him a little curtsy. "Come in and join us. We were dancing. I'll introduce you to everyone. Mama has made these great . . ."

He was shaking his head and stepping toward the front door.

"I can't stay. I have to leave."

"Why?"

"My parents don't know I came."

"Well, they are welcome too. Mama invited them. It's my birthday! Come on!"

She stepped toward him, but stopped. His face was no longer shy or pleasant.

"I have to go now."

He opened the door, looking over his shoulder. "I'm sorry . . . but you are a Jew."

Maria stood perfectly still. Her mind was thinking slowly and her body felt cold, such a strangeness sweeping over her. *Any moment someone will come looking for me,* she thought. *I can't face anyone right now.* She opened the front door and fled down the steps.

The street was dark—most everyone being in her house, where light poured from every window. The wind was cutting, moaning, acting like it would chase her if she started to run. She wanted to run into the darkness away from everything. As suddenly as it had left, feeling came back to her. She was very cold. She glanced up. A light was burning in the window of the Picards. Earlier, across the room, she had seen Thomas taking Gretchen home.

She entered without knocking, and went into the front room, trembling. Thomas was seated on the sofa, reading. He looked up startled.

"Maria! What's the matter?"

She shook her head, clutching her hands. "I . . . nothing."

"Why aren't you at the house? I can hear the party still going on."

She shook her head again. "I . . . I came, to, I forgot, I didn't have a chance to tell you earlier, I mean, to thank you for the flowers. Thank you, Thomas."

He had set the book aside. "You're welcome. Maria, what's wrong?"

"Nothing, I told you, nothing." She looked around wildly. "Rudi . . ."

"He's in the kitchen fixing himself something to eat. But—"

She turned and hurried toward the kitchen.

Rudi was just recovering from a terrible cold, so his mother had told him he couldn't go to the party. He was fixing himself some hot chocolate when Maria entered breathless and disheveled.

"Maria! Say, that's some dress. You look great. I mean . . . hey, what's wrong?"

"Rudi, tell me something. Tell me the truth."

"Sure."

Tears slipped down her cheeks. "That night . . . did you want to kiss me?"

She could see he was embarrassed.

"Sure, " he admitted slowly.

"Really want to?"

He nodded. "Maria, what's this about? Why aren't you at your party?"

"Is there a chance . . . could you . . . could you be my boyfriend?"

"Well . . ." He was scratching his head. "You know Maria, I have a girl—Helen Dietl."

"But you could like me if you didn't like her. If . . . if you didn't care what . . . your mother thought. If you wanted me, nothing would matter, right?"

He nodded slowly. *Girls!*

She drew a deep breath.

"Maria, you look kind of pale. Why don't you sit down and tell me what this is all about?"

She backed up, shaking her head. "I have to get back to my party. Good night, Rudi."

He stood up, feeling very confused. "Good night. . . . Hey, happy birthday, Maria."

5
Melodies from Blumenstrasse

1934

Sophie Goldstein was sweeping with an energy and purpose that defied any particle of dirt to land on her front stoop. Typically good-natured and easy to laugh, she had not even smiled when Rudi Picard had jogged past her, waving and tossing over his shoulder, "I bet your broom is an inch shorter than when you started, Frau Sophie!"

No, she had not even smiled. And she could tell you why she didn't feel like smiling this bright blue March day in two succinct words: The Hagers. She couldn't look out any of her front windows without seeing their house. Perfectly clipped lawn, perfect starched curtains. The doors never slammed, the trash never overflowed, the voices never raised. Perfect. But they didn't belong to Blumenstrasse—according to Sophie. She was a friendly, generous-hearted woman. Over the years she had dealt with nearly every kind of trouble or sorrow or emotion that people fall prey to. But this? Hostility was foreign to her. So every time she looked and saw the house or one of the family, she felt herself growing annoyed. She also felt herself burn with embarrassment as she remembered their second meeting a year ago.

She had waited until they had time to settle in. Then she had tidied her hair, straightened her dress, and grabbed her basket filled with soup and bread. The children were away and Aaron was at work, so she had gone alone. She knew that a few of the closer neighbor women had already been to say hello. But she was the first with food. Of course.

The door had opened instantly at the first ring, as if, she later reflected with bitter tears, they had been waiting for her. A woman her own age, heavy-set, dull-eyed, had greeted her timidly. Sophie had bustled in with boisterous welcomes. The husband, Herr Hager was there, but Sophie didn't notice his stiff manner or look. She did note that the teenage son seemed nervous. All three stood staring like statues while she stood smiling and shifting the heavy basket from one hip to the other.

"Where are you from?" she asked.

"Berlin."

Ah, Sophie thought to herself, *Berlin, of course they were unfriendly. It would take awhile for Blumenstrasse to thaw them.*

"I have brought you some supper. Good, hot, mushroom-and-barley soup. I know the hard work of moving, though it has been years, so of course you are tired and . . ." her voice trailed off.

They were still staring. Silent.

"My Aaron, he has a music store downtown, a fine store. . . . He could help you tonight with any of the heavy pieces you have to move." Her tongue slid over her lips. "I have three sons and one daughter. My Jacob looks your age. How old are you?" She would try to engage the tall son. He gave a quick wary glance at his parents.

"I am seventeen."

She nodded. "Well, fine, fine. . . . And what do you do for a living, Herr Hager?"

"I am a magistrate."

She turned to smile at the pale Frau Hager. "I'll just put this in the kitchen for your dinner since you must be tired."

Again that frightened look at her husband. He picked up a box and motioned to his son. "Thank you, Frau Goldstein, but we have dinner already."

Sophie had never encountered this before. *Won't I have a tale for the table tonight? Oh how the boys will hoot.*

"But you see," she lifted the cloth cover, "it is good and hot. But you don't have to eat it today. I'll leave it for your meal tomorrow. I am in no hurry for the dish. I made stollen too."

Herr Hager exhaled loudly as if someone had shoved him in the back.

"No, *thank you*, Frau Goldstein, we don't want your food. Now, if you will excuse us we have more unpacking to do."

The woman hurried past her to another room. The son picked up a box. She could feel he was watching her under his dark brows.

"But ... but ... I ... I always ..."

He turned his hostile eyes away and went back to his work. Sophie felt she was going to faint. She almost hurried out the door and down the steps. She nearly ran into ten-year-old Herman coming home on his bike. She looked at him wildly. He paused. He had never seen Frau Sophie looking like this. She scanned his face, as if looking for something familiar.

"They wouldn't take my food," she gasped.

Herman looked up at the house behind her. He squinted a moment, pushing a thick lock of blond hair from his forehead. He reached out and patted her arm consolingly.

"You were taking food to them?"

She could only nod mutely.

He leaned forward over the handlebars, his voice confiding. "They are Nazis, Frau Sophie. They don't like Jews. I'm sorry."

Sophie squeezed his young hand as if she could squeeze back the tears.

"My mother is feeling bad today," he said cheerfully. "See, I have been to the store for bread for her. You could take the food to her, you know. You are such a good cook, the best on Blumenstrasse. What do they know?" he said jerking his head disdainfully toward the house.

Yes, Sophie would never forget that day.

Sweeping with a vigor that she hoped would remove a few equilateral pounds, Sophie thought about the changes in the last year. *Isaac! Finally a child had married! The only sorrow is that he moved to help his grandparents in Bonn and continue his medical studies in night school. Shy Abraham is still working in the store and quaking before girls. I'll get no grandchildren from that one. Jacob.* Here the sadness came to her heart. *Jacob gave up his soccer and his dreams. He is sullen and unhappy. At least he's doing menial odd jobs as he can find them. I'm afraid for him,* she thought. *He is so angry at what the Nazis have robbed him of. I can't soothe or console or bandage or chide away his troubles,* she murmured sadly to herself. *They are bigger than both of us.*

Maria, at eighteen. Sophie was growing a little worried. *Haven't I paraded a seemingly endless line of proper Jewish youth before her? She's rejected all of them! Who is she waiting for? She can't continue this courting and flirting forever.*

Then there was this . . . this change in Maria Picard. Yes, Aaron told me I am imaging things, but . . . no. No, there's a new stiffness to Maria these days. As if she is always thinking of things she can't or won't share with me. We spend less time together these days too. I miss the days of morning coffee we had before Maria began helping out in the store.

Sophie set aside her broom, her hands going to her broad hips. She sighed deeply. With the antagonistic Hagers, her brooding Jacob, her unmarried daughter, and her cold friend, Sophie Goldstein had more than enough troubles in her little world.

Maria Goldstein believed on such a spring day as this that human flight was indeed possible. When she had raced Jacob from the corner to the front steps, she felt that, given the proper altitude, mixed with the proper attitude, she could launch into the piercing blueness. She thought about the prospect and laughed to herself. *Imagine gliding over the heads of my family and neighbors, soaring above Munich, and then . . .*

She galloped up the Picard steps two at a time, panting as she went through the front door. Frau Picard was pulling on her gloves as Maria entered.

"I'm sorry I'm late, Frau Maria. They were having a parade, and I got stuck. Then I saw this gorgeous dress in the window at—"

Maria Picard was not smiling. "It is all right, this time Maria. Rudi is not quite ready. Gretchen has eaten; your dinner is on the table."

"Thank you."

Maria hurried into the front room so the older woman wouldn't look too closely at her. *How can I look chastened on a day like this?*

"Gret," she said, and the girl hopped up from the floor and into her arms. Maria laughed.

Watching from the doorway, Maria Picard couldn't smother the tenderness that touched her at the sight of this beautiful young woman embracing her daughter. *Their love for each other is so obvious.* Maria looked over Gretchen's head and their eyes met. *Frau Picard always looking so distant yet . . .*

"You are very good with Gretchen, Maria. Michael and I are very grateful that you have taken this position."

"Gretchen is good for me."

"And I'm good for nothing," Rudi Picard laughed as he came up behind his mother.

"We are going to be late. Auf Wiedersehen, Maria. Be a good girl, Gretchen."

Rudi paused only a moment to wink at Maria. She laughed and, as had become their custom, winked back at him. A year ago her heart would have done leaps at the sight of the darkly handsome Rudi Picard. But a year had passed, and though outwardly to her family she still looked like the same pretty, pampered girl, Maria knew there was a difference inside herself. Since the night of her seventeenth birthday, she had come to some conclusions about Rudi. He would always hold the spot in her heart reserved for deepest dreams. But Rudi would never see beyond the girl who was like a little sister to him, that lived beside him on Blumenstrasse. Maria had hated to untie the tether to her heart he unknowingly held, Romance was something Maria Goldstein was not sure could exist in 1934 Germany.

Then the house was still and quiet.

Suddenly the front doorbell rang and, before she could stop her, Gretchen had dashed over and jerked it open. In the front room, Maria was startled to see the girl backing up as if in a trance. Maria hurried forward.

The man was already in the house taking off his hat. His eyes narrowing on Gretchen. He was heavy, balding, and dressed ostentatiously Maria decided swiftly. He was also vaguely familiar. Then he saw her. His small, pale eyes widened.

Maria didn't like some stranger taking such liberty and entering the Picard foyer uninvited. If he was a salesman he was certainly bold, and she would give him a tongue-lashing that would make Frau Maria and her own mother proud.

"Excuse me, but if you would please step back on the front stoop," she said, going toward him. The smell of his cologne came like a wave toward her. His eyebrows raised.

"Who are you?" he asked with unvarnished arrogance.

"At the moment, I am the mistress of the house," she replied evenly. "Now." Her hand was on the knob.

Gretchen had backed up to the stairs and was making an odd, guttural noise. Maria recognized it—the girl was afraid.

The man had laughed when she had spoken, and now his eyes roved over her with a boldness that made her grit her teeth.

"What is your name, Mistress of the Moment?"

His smile reminded her of a gargoyle.

"None of your business," she said curtly.

He laughed again. "You're a tart one. Does my sister know you're so high and mighty to strangers?"

Frau Maria's brother, the tooth salesman that Thomas and Rudi didn't like. Well . . .

"I didn't recognize you," she said, a concession to apology. "But really, you shouldn't have come in the house like you did. It frightened Gretchen."

"Where is my sister?" he returned evenly.

"Frau Picard works at our store now. I keep house and take care of Gretchen."

"What is your name?"

Thomas and Rudi's dislike of this relative is thoroughly justified, Maria decided.

He spoke before she could answer. "Our store. You are the Goldstein girl?"

"My name is Maria Goldstein."

He nodded. "Now I remember . . . but you've grown up." Again that appraising look.

"You probably know I am a member of the Nazi party," he continued. "But what you don't know is that I am privy to inside party information. Tomorrow you and all of Germany will know what I know. So—"

"I'm sure, Herr Beck, that there is nothing that you know that I would care to know."

She was a little startled with her own audacity. *Would this man malign her to Frau Picard and threaten her care with Gretchen?* It was too late to retract her words or conceal her feelings.

"If you are as smart as your pretty tongue, then you would do well to listen. I will tell you anyway. It will give you time to . . . understand. As a Jew your time is over."

"What do you mean by that?"

Gretchen began pulling on her sleeve.

"Just a minute, Gret."

"Michael Picard cannot be in business with a Jew. I have been telling my sister that. Soon you will no longer be housekeeper here. Jews cannot be employed by good Germans. It is coming." He turned to the door. "Perhaps you have seduced one of my nephews already." He shrugged. "You will understand."

• • •

Aaron Goldstein was proud of his store. Every morning as he rounded the corner and caught the first glimpse of the rising sun striking the tall panes he felt an inner gladness. Not all men were as fortunate as he—to love their work, to look forward to each day, and to be their own boss. And the store was so impressive-looking on this busy Munich corner: two stories of cream-colored brick and highly polished windows with "Goldstein's and Picard's Fine Instruments" in gold gothic letters. In smaller letters, near the sill was written, "Since 1830."

He unlocked the wine-colored front doors and the bell announced his arrival. It was quiet. He locked the door behind him. The wooden floor was almost as highly polished as the windows. A mosaic of colors, muted and in harmony, filled the vast room: the wine-colored wood of the counters, the shiny black of the huge grand pianos, the burnished russet of the smaller pianos, the gold brilliance of the horns, the soft hues of the violins, and the velvet blues and greens from the cases.

An hour later, the three clerks came. Abraham was busy at his books upstairs and Michael was doing scales for a young couple when Jacob burst through the front door. Aaron was checking over a new order of violin music when he looked up. Jacob saw him and rushed to him. He was clutching a newspaper.

"Have you seen this?" he demanded, thrusting the first edition of the paper at his father.

"Calm down, Jacob, calm down." He pulled his youngest son toward the back of the store. "Why aren't you at work? Don't you help Herr Olsen with his deliveries today?"

"Papa, I couldn't go to work when I read this!"

Michael Picard had joined them now, sensing trouble from Jacob's appearance and tone.

"What's the matter, Jacob? Is everything all right?"

Jacob gave the man a measured look, a strange, almost suspicious look.

"No, sir, everything is not all right."

Aaron cleared his throat. His words slow and deliberate. "Son, I would post a sentinel at the entrance to your mouth." He read the lead article swiftly then handed it slowly to his friend. Michael reluctantly lowered his eyes to the paper. They watched him. Almost arthritically he pulled off his glasses. Only then did Jacob notice that Michael looked very tired and very thin.

Abraham had seen the commotion through the little window from the second floor. He descended the steps behind them.

"What has happened?" he asked.

Wordlessly Picard handed the young man the paper. He read the article, and his eyes widened. Tomorrow, April 1, the government was demanding a boycott of all Jewish-owned businesses throughout Germany.

"Well . . ." was all Aaron could manage.

"What are we going to do?" Jacob demanded. "We are a Jewish-Gentile business. On the way, I saw them. They are putting posters on windows: 'Don't buy from Jewish swine.' "

"We are a Jewish-Gentile-owned business and we will stay that way," Picard said smoothly. He turned to Abraham. "What do you think, book-keeper? Don't you think tomorrow would be a fine day for Goldstein's and Picard's to have a spring sale?"

"Sir?" the young Jew asked blankly.

"A sale, a sale! Our biggest yet! Run up and put together an ad, Abraham. Jacob will run it to the printer. Yes, a sale. We'll have the whole staff. We'll bring your Maria and my Maria so that Aaron and I can hold a concert all day. We'll open the front doors and fill the streets with Mozart!" He reached out to put a thin arm around Aaron's shoulders.

"What do you think of my plan, my friend?"

But Aaron Goldstein could only nod.

• • •

Maria was not especially glad to see her brother. When he had rung the bell just after dinner, she had hurried him into the kitchen. Michael and Aaron were practicing in the front room.

"Well," he scowled, "they are in there together."

"Of course they are. They are nearly every night." She turned back to her sink of dishes. "Really, Otto, I'm very tired. I've had a long day at the store, and it looks like it will be a long day tomorrow. So please, don't start with any words against our friends."

He sat down heavily in the chair. "Where is Rudi?"

"He is with his girlfriend."

Otto laughed shortly. "He is at a Zionist meeting in the old Mann heim warehouse with your *friend's* son."

She swung around. "No!"

"Yes, my blind little sister. I have seen the reports. Your son is involved with Jewish scum. The Gestapo are getting interested."

"Otto."

"Otto what? I've tried to warn you over the years." He shook his head. "You know about tomorrow?"

She nodded mutely.

"Well, what is he going to do?"

Maria braced herself for the retort. "Otto, you know our families have been joined in friendship and business since the last century. You can't expect Michael to change that in one day."

"He's had time to change it, if you gave him my advice. If he had . . ." He shook his head. "Maria, your husband's foolishness could cost you this precious business." He leaned forward. "The cost could run very high. You know Jews have no place in the new Germany, and if you ignore that or wish it away, you'll get caught in the whirlwind and be swept away!"

Her voice was a hoarse whisper. "They are our friends."

"They are enemies of Germany."

"There is nothing I can do. He is my husband."

Otto stood up. "I thought you were stronger. I thought you were smarter. There will be much more after this boycott. If you don't choose now, you will choose later. Or," he jerked his head toward the music, "he will choose."

Then he was gone and the only sound was the rumble of the teakettle about to boil.

"I cannot choose," Maria whispered. "They are our friends."

In this bedroom they had shared for thirty-six years, Michael stood pulling off his vest and tie. Neither had bothered to turn on a light because moonlight flooded in through the window. He wished they could simply stretch out on the bed and hold each other, enjoy the spring night, and forget politics. But that was not Maria's way.

"I know you're angry. I'm sorry," he said suddenly in the stillness.

She studied him a moment. "I'm not angry with you, Michael. I'm frustrated. I'm concerned with what you did today."

"It won't change anything that today was one of the best days our store has ever had? It was also one of the best days Aaron and I have ever had together."

"This isn't about money."

"It's about friendship."

"It's about the law, Michael. It's about obeying our government. And it's about what might happen if we don't."

He exhaled loudly, rubbing his eyes. "Maria . . ."

Her voice was steady. "Michael, there is no use ignoring this any longer. We have a big problem. Today was a one-day boycott. You know the authorities are aware of what you did. They will have seen the crowds. They—"

He was pulling off his socks. "They will see that a good German businessman made a good business decision," he chuckled. "We took in over—"

Her severe look silenced him.

"Michael."

"Maria, they didn't put one of their disgusting little signs on our store."

"But everyone knows. And it is only a matter of time. Otto says that this boycott is only the beginning. We have to be prepared for what is coming."

"Be prepared? How?"

"I don't know!" She could imagine Otto shaking his head at her. *Little sister, little sister, tell this man, make him grow up. . . .*

She stood up suddenly, exasperated, and went to the window. *Blumenstrasse.*

His voice was gentle. "Perhaps you shouldn't listen to your brother so much, Maria. He brings you this upsetting business."

"No, Michael. You are upsetting me. You won't face facts."

Michael Picard was terribly calm. "What facts?"

"That our business, our children's futures, our very home could be threatened if we ignore what the government is dictating."

His head was cocked; his nearsighted eyes peered at her across the room. Suddenly she felt like crying.

"I don't follow things as closely as you, Maria. I never have. But if you are saying that our friendship with the Goldstein's must be sacrificed because of some ignorant, small-minded dictates of the government you know what my answer will be."

She sat statue-still. There were too many conflicting voices in her head. Too many.

"Let's go to bed, Maria. I'll rub your back and we can listen to the crickets. Hmm?"

She shook her head. "I will not see Thomas' career jeopardized because of our ... I won't see the business your grandparents sacrificed for and worked so long for ... Without our income, what will become of Gretchen? Will you put your family at risk, Michael?"

"Maria, it will not come to that. Otto has frightened you with such talk." He stood up and firmly pulled her toward him. For a moment he waited for her to defy him. But instead she leaned against him quietly weeping.

6
Seduction

Berlin

He received the church leaders in the inner sanctuary of the chancellery after they had been led through a maze of corridors hung with swastika flags and eagles. All of the twelve church leaders felt awe and nervousness as they passed through the tall double doors to the fuehrer's office. They were in the room with the most powerful man in Germany. The man received each one warmly. He was smiling.

They took chairs arranged in a semicircle and settled in for one of Hitler's famous hour-long monologues. His words were not new to them, but he had summoned them to deliver the plans personally.

"It was important that you understand how much I respect the church. Christianity is an essential element in safeguarding the soul of the German people. You can feel secure in knowing I will respect the rights of the church. I desire to have a peaceful accord between the church and state. I will seek an improved relationship between Berlin and the Vatican."

The twelve heads facing him nodded in amazement.

Hitler rose from his chair, still smiling, and started pacing in front of them, his hands loosely clasped behind his back. He began to outline his proposals for a Reich church. "This would be the best way of uniting the German people and building a strong church that would benefit everyone," he said.

The seated men had been receiving literature on the Reich church and, in many cases, had talked to ambassadors from the chancellery for months concerning this plan. All of them had disseminated the outlines to hundreds of pastors.

Again they nodded and Hitler smiled broadly. He stopped and introduced a man sitting a little off to the side of the circle, whom none of them had really noticed until then. He smiled faintly as Hitler introduced him.

"This is Ludwig Wagner, pastor and head of the seminary in Wittenburg. I propose Herr Wagner as bishop of our new Reich church."

Hitler stopped and stood before them; his smile was gone.

"I am a very busy man with the many affairs of this great land. There is work to do in our economy and our military. I am faced with constant threats and opposition from enemies of Germany." Now his dark eyes focused on each of them with that hypnotic-like quality that many were to feel over the years of his rule. "I am too busy to be bothered with opposition from the church. Let the world see that the church and state of Germany are in peace and agreement."

They all rose and applauded.

Dachau

Walking hatless and in short sleeves, through the little German village, with a market basket on his arm, he looked more like a civil servant or rural schoolmaster than a popular young minister. People called out to him, and he smiled and waved. He went through the village and traveled half a mile down a dirt road, barley fields maturing on either side of him. The sky was an intense blue; the breeze mild. For the first time in years, Thomas Picard felt his soul was his own. He was very happy serving among these simple German people. They were so receptive and encouraging. They accepted him with all his youthful arrogance. Settled in Dachau, Thomas largely ignored the events of Germany in his first year of ministry, the first year of the Nazi regime.

For most of the walk, he had been critiquing yesterday's sermon. But as he passed from the village and into the countryside, the warmth and smells drew him away from pulpit analysis, and he thought of Gretchen. *She would love this place. Next time I go home I'll ask Mother if Gret can return with me.* He frowned. The only problem was that it would mean taking her from the care of Maria Goldstein. *Well then, I'll not separate them. I'll bring them both here.* He stopped on the path to the church and laughed aloud. *Bring Maria out of the big city to this little provincial place! Bring a pretty girl into his home? Well now, the church matriarchs might find something to admonish him about!*

"Have you unknotted the problems of the universe, Pastor Picard?" a voice boomed at him.

He looked up, startled. A big, black, sleek car had pulled up in front of the stone cottage beside the church. Dean Wagner was smiling broadly as he came forward to shake Thomas' hand.

"Sir! Dean! I . . . I didn't see you," Thomas stammered.

He laughed. "I know, I know. Which of your flock were you praying for?"

Thomas smiled. "Actually, I was thinking about my little sister in Munich. I'd like to bring her here for awhile. I know she'd like it, and the people would take her into their hearts."

"As they have you."

"Well, I like to think so. They're good folk."

"Back in Wittenburg we hear only good reports from this district. You are making a name for yourself, Thomas."

"Thank you, sir. Please come in for tea."

They sat down together.

"What brings you to Dachau, sir?"

"I've been on the circuit visiting preachers for weeks. You . . . have heard of my appointment?"

"No sir, I'm afraid I haven't."

"Then I'll have to trumpet my own horn. Our fuehrer has appointed me as the first Reich bishop, Thomas. I'll be moving to Berlin."

"Congratulations, sir." Thomas hoped the dean wouldn't ask him if he knew what being Reich bishop meant.

"Thank you, thank you. I am thrilled that the Lord has seen fit to give me this new responsibility. Now, have you received your papers from Berlin on the formation of the Reich church?"

Thomas looked a little sheepish. "Forgive me, sir, but I confess I haven't read them yet." Thomas pointed to his desk. "They are there, under some work. I've been busy and haven't had a chance to read them."

Wagner leaned over and patted the young man's knee. "I understand, Thomas. We knew at Wittenburg we had a hard worker in you. But you must get to them soon. They are important to your church and to you personally. Now, on to the other reason I'm here to see you. What are your intentions here, Thomas?"

"Well, just to serve the people as well as I can."

"You like it here, obviously."

"Oh yes, sir, very much. I could stay here perfectly content for years."

"But the Lord could have a greater sphere of influence for you, Thomas. A different future than the one you have planned."

Thomas wasn't sure what to say.

"To speak frankly, Thomas, we allowed you this church as a training place, so to speak, to learn the ins-and-outs of a small church and its flock. Among the hundreds that pass through the seminary, only a select few come to our attention. You are one of them. Like Jesus' example in Matthew 25, you were given a small talent and you have been faithful. Now you shall be rewarded and given more."

"Given more?" Thomas asked blankly.

Wagner laughed. "I can't say more right now. I'll contact you in a few weeks. Suffice say there may soon be an opening that would suit us and you far better than your little hamlet here."

Thomas entered the foyer quietly. He stood concealed and watched Maria and Gretchen dance to the music of Strauss. They were giggling, and Thomas felt slightly guilty for spying. When they finished, they curtsied and bowed to each other. He entered clapping. Both girls turned red.

Gretchen's hands went to her hips, "Thomas, no!"

"He is very ungallant, Gretchen," Maria whispered loudly. "I thought I had locked this," she said, brushing past him to check the front door.

He dangled a key in front of her. She shook her head.

"Why did you have the door locked, fraulein?"

"Well," Maria laughed, "I didn't want your mother coming in. She wouldn't approve."

"Ah . . ."

Looking up at Thomas, she suddenly looked about ten. "You won't tell, will you?"

"I didn't ever tell when you snuck out your window to meet what's his name or when you went to the dance at the river and you told them you were at the library."

She shook her head. "Nothing is hidden from you, Thomas Picard."

He tapped his temples. "I have the eyes of a minister. I can see into your very soul, Maria Goldstein."

Her head tipped, her face flushed, she now looked fully eighteen.

"You can, can you?"

"To the depths."

She turned and reached for her sweater. "Then there is no point in me telling you anything. I'll see you tomorrow, Gretchen. Enjoy your time with your omnipotent brother."

Thomas laughed. "Now wait, wait. You don't need to go."

Maria was at the door. "Your mother will be home in less than an hour, and I need to get ready for an important date."

"Maria has a boy!" Gretchen said swinging her friend's hand.

"A new boyfriend! Who's the victim this week?" Thomas asked.

She arched her brows. "You should know, all-knowing one." She paused on the front steps. "Auf Wiedersehen, dear Thomas!"

Maria Picard cried at the unexpected sight of her eldest son. Now, with him drying dishes beside her, she felt a calmness settle over her. Thomas would smooth the churning Picard household.

"I could sense there was something upsetting at dinner, Mother. Father was so quiet. What's wrong with Rudi?"

"Rudi is involved in a ... group, Thomas. I have asked him to quit going because it is dangerous,—but he said he won't stop. He said he will keep going even if it means moving out. I haven't told your father."

"What kind of group?"

"A group that opposes the government. They are mostly composed of Zionists."

"Zionists? Rudi isn't Jewish!"

She faced him. "No, but Jacob Goldstein is."

Thomas looked away and sighed.

"Thomas, I'm afraid for Rudi. He can be so head-strong and impulsive. This involvement can only bring trouble."

Thomas nodded slowly. "You're probably right."

"I wish you would talk to him."

"Like you said, Rudi is head-strong. I'll try, but don't put much hope in it. How did you find this out? From Frau Sophie?"

She turned back to her sink, her voice lowered. "Your uncle."

"Good ol' Uncle Otto."

"Thomas, he means well."

"Hmm . . . What's wrong between you and Father?"

"Since the boycott last month, we . . . your father wants to ignore the things that are changing. Oh, Thomas." She sat down suddenly. Thomas had never seen his composed mother so flustered.

"We are in a unique position."

Thomas nodded. "Our business partner is Jewish."

"Exactly. We'll be punished."

"What do you expect Father to do?"

She drew a fortifying breath. "I have thought this out very carefully. I think it's the best course for us and the Goldsteins. We should buy out their share."

"Father will never agree to that."

"To save both families, he may have to. Why not do it now before he is forced to? Buy Aaron's share, but retain him as a working partner."

"You mean . . . take off the Goldstein name?"

She nodded slowly. "I don't see any other way."

Thomas felt his homecoming mood suddenly deflate. "Maybe you're right," he murmured.

• • •

"What I'm trying to say is that my parents and my grandparents had this meeting last night, and we've decided to leave Germany. We are emigrating to Palestine. We have the passports and papers. We leave in three weeks."

Maria was still sitting on the stone bench of the park. She looked at the fountains, the trees, the flowers—anywhere but at the young man who was peering anxiously at her. *I won't cry, I won't!* she decided. *I don't really love him anyway.*

"Maria?"

"They are making you go?"

The Jewish youth shook his head. "The Nazis are destroying our homeland. They are taking the best from it. I don't want to stay. I'm sorry."

I guess this handsome, enjoyable man isn't my future after all, she thought sadly, remembering the passion she felt when he held her and kissed her in the shadows.

She pushed away from the bench, her tone brusque. "So the Nazis have won again."

"Maria—"

"I wish you and your family well in Palestine, Eli. Auf Wiedersehen."

She walked home alone. Angry, terribly angry. She felt foolish in this new dress she had paid for with a month's salary. Foolish in her tiny, private hopes. *Fine. Let him go,* she declared to herself.

As she turned the corner of Blumenstrasse she nearly ran into Eric Hager. They both stopped abruptly and stared. Her eyes were flaming, defying him to say any of his little Nazi slanders. He stood there so tall and polished in his tan uniform with the black armband. He felt the scorch of her stare. He looked away.

"Does your uniform and those big black boots make you feel so very very strong and mighty, Eric Hager? Does it give you the courage to go push around some rabbi on the street or run some little Jew boys off the playground?" She punched his chest. "Does it?"

He paled and stepped back.

"It . . . pleases my father," he said in a low voice.

Maria felt the tears come to her eyes. She hurried past him, across the street, and up her steps. In the foyer she stopped. She had planned to rush up to her bedroom, away from her mother's inquisition, but she heard singing. Clearly Thomas was in their kitchen. She entered. He was sitting on a stool with a towel around his shoulders, some sheet music on his knees. He looked up.

"Home so early?"

"Uh huh. Where's Mama?"

He nodded to the left. "Frau Bowen called and wanted Frau Sophie to see her new grandbaby."

"And Mama can't resist a new baby." She stood in front of him. "I can't believe she walked out on you with half your hair cut—no, actually I can."

"She's almost done. See, only the back."

She reached out and fingered his hair. "Very nice . . . you are quite handsome."

He laughed. "It's Thomas, Maria. Not brother Rudi."

"I am quite aware of that, Thomas." She was caressing his neck.

"You ah, shouldn't . . . do that."

"Why?"

"Because your mother could walk in ... and she'd be horrified."

"Oh, I don't know ... I thought it was because you didn't like it."

"No, I do, I mean, I don't. Maria, you—"

But Maria had placed her arms around his neck. His eyes widened. Then she leaned forward and kissed him. After what seemed like an eternity to her, she finally felt him relax and respond. His arms encircled her waist. She was unprepared for his passion. Then abruptly his arms dropped away. He stood up and the stool fell over—like an alarm going off in the still kitchen.

"Maria, what's the matter with you? Why did you do that?"

She laughed. "Well, Thomas, why did you do that back?"

He was wiping his forehead. "Oh for goodness' sake, Maria ..."

She said nothing.

"Don't ever do that again!"

"Why? Because I'm a Jew? I'm not a perfect Aryan? I'm impure and a race defiler? That is what your Uncle Otto says. He says I have ..." She covered her face with her hands and began to cry.

"Maria." He placed his hands on her shoulders. "I'm sorry about whatever my uncle said to you. He is not a gentleman." He tilted her chin up to face him. "Maria, you can't kiss me, because I don't want to be teased like your other conquests."

"I wasn't thinking of you like a conquest. Besides, I'm finished with conquesting." She laughed nervously.

"I ... didn't mean to ... respond like I did."

She stepped back. "I'm sorry for acting so silly." She turned toward the doorway. "But you know, I have wondered before if you were really flesh and blood, Thomas Picard."

After she left he stared at the door for a long time. "Yes, I am flesh and blood, Maria Goldstein."

The man was surprised to see Thomas, but he greeted him warmly. Yet Thomas could see the man's face was shadowed and anxious, his usual banter missing. They talked for nearly an hour about Thomas' parish. Then Paul Shraeder looked down at his hands spread on the desk before him. The silence lengthened. Finally, he looked up and Thomas was shocked to see the pain etched in the man's eyes.

"What is it, Paul?" he asked softly.

"The little rumors haven't reached you out in Dachau?" His voice was bitter.

"I don't know what you're talking about."

He exhaled loudly, looking down at his hands again.

"Thomas, someone has brought charges of ... sexual misconduct against me. Someone in my congregation has accused me. I have no idea who."

Thomas was speechless.

"I know, you don't know what to say." Shraeder stood up. "I didn't know what to say at first. I just sat there, staring. I honestly couldn't think of anything to say. I mean, to even have to deny it. I felt insulted and sickened when they told me ... the details."

"Who is they?" Thomas asked finally.

"Our district superintendent. The charges came to his office. So he came here with three other church leaders. Finally, I managed to say that it was all lies—terrible, filthy lies."

"What happened then?" Thomas asked slowly.

"They've suspended me until they can look into it further."

"I'm sorry, Paul. If there's anything I can do ..."

Paul swung away from the window, giving Thomas a curious look that made him uncomfortable.

"I've been going over in my mind every detail of the last few weeks—everywhere I've gone or visited—and I can't come up with anything that even remotely could be compromising. I've prayed and prayed for the Lord to show me.... All I can think of is something I said at a meal I had with some of the men in my church a few weeks ago."

"What was that?"

"I said I wasn't very impressed with the Nazi plans for a Reich church." Paul sat down again across from Thomas.

"Thomas, the government is moving so swiftly in reform, touching every area of life. Everything has a Nazi stamp on it. I'm concerned with them becoming involved in the church. I think that it's dangerous to the purity and purpose of the church."

"I think the government wants the best for the church. They are affecting every area of life true, but they want the best for the people. So they want to be involved in the church. A strong church makes for a strong nation. We all want that."

"You sound like Ludwig Wagner, Thomas."

"I will take that as a compliment then." Thomas didn't conceal the irritation from his voice.

He left Shraeder shortly after that, walking toward home deep in thought. Nearly to Blumenstrasse he stopped, suddenly thinking of his father. He glanced at his watch. Michael Picard would soon be closing his store. Thomas changed his path.

His father was locking the front doors when Thomas came up behind him.

"Can you spare an oboe?" he said in a deep voice.

His father turned smiling. "Only for a solo." It was an old joke Rudi had made years ago.

"Been a good day?" Thomas asked as they headed home.

Picard nodded. "Sold a Steinway. It's such a beautiful evening, isn't it?"

Thomas looked around. "I hadn't really noticed, but yes it is."

"You should take the time to notice it, Thomas. Do you think God makes it for us to ignore?"

"Well, no."

They stopped at a corner.

"Ah ..."

"What?"

"I had a catalog I needed to bring home tonight. I'll have to go back for it. You can go on so your mother won't be waiting."

"No, I'll go back with you."

They walked in silence until they came to the entrance of the store. Michael Picard had never been one to openly display affection to his sons. Looking at Thomas, so tall and straight in the twilight, he suddenly wished he had. He cleared his throat.

"I want you to know that your mother and I are very proud of you. I'll be right back."

Thomas stood waiting on the sidewalk.

Finally he entered the darkened store. "Father?"

There was no answer, only a small light burning in the back office. "Father?"

Thomas found his father sprawled on the floor, sheet music scattered around him. Michael Picard had played his final solo.

● ● ●

Adolf Hitler was in a gloating, expansive mood. He sat with his feet propped up, an opera playing on the phonograph behind him. He held a plate of strudel and a cup of tea in his lap. His secretary was tidying papers at the desk behind him. Hitler's friend and party comrade Herman Rauschning sat across from him sipping scotch.

"It's been a good day. Lovely spring weather we're having," he remarked.

"Hardly have the time to notice the weather anymore," Hitler chuckled.

"It was perfect for the confirmation in Wittenburg. You would have been pleased. It was quite a spectacle. There must have been a hundred swastika flags in the church. Wagner gave quite a stirring speech. The applause was thunderous."

"I would have liked to have been there," Hitler commented.

"Well, I think we can feel confident there is peace with the church. They are in line. We can expect no further trouble from that quarter."

Hitler sat his plate aside roughly. He had swung into a mood, so typical of his nature.

"Peace today, yes. But you understand there is no future for either the Catholic or Protestant churches." His eyes were snapping. "Protestant pastors are insignificant little people—submissive as dogs and they sweat with embarrassment when you talk to them. All they care about is their miserable little incomes." He stood up and stalked the room, his voice rising. "Making peace with the church will not stop me from stamping out Christianity in Germany—root and branch! One is either a Christian or a German. You cannot be both!"

7
A Servant Who Pleases God

Their steps sounded cold and hollow on the wooden floor. They walked silently up the center aisle, looking at the benches and stained-glass windows and pulpit as if they had never seen them before. Yet they had been coming to this church for years. And only six weeks earlier they had come to this place for the final tribute to Michael Picard. But though it was familiar, it was new because now this was Thomas' church. He would stand behind the pulpit on Sunday.

Maria Picard held his arm as they walked, still wounded with grief yet exalted with this triumph for her son. How many times she had sat in the pew and imagined him tall and proud in the pulpit. *Her son. Finally, a dream come true.* She looked up at him.

"You're not still missing Dachau, are you?"

"I liked it there very much. They were good, uncomplicated people. I will miss it. But this can be a good place for me too." His voice was unconvinced.

"It will take time, Thomas. Time."

He nodded. When they reached the front of the sanctuary they finally noticed the man hunched forward on the bench. They started to turn away, but he lifted his head. It was Paul Shraeder, the former pastor. He stood up. Thomas could hardly keep himself from gasping. The man looked shrunken.

Paul looked at them both. Finally he smiled and reached out his hand. "Welcome, Pastor Picard."

"Guten Tag, Paul," Thomas returned awkwardly.

"I've finished packing the office, but I wanted a few moments ..." Paul looked to the pulpit.

Thomas glanced uneasily at his mother. She was standing very rigid and unsmiling.

"We didn't know you would be here, Paul. I meant to come by earlier, but things have been very busy, getting things in order since my father's passing."

Paul's hands were in his pockets, his eyes fixed on the cross. Maria tightened her grip on her son's sleeve. Slowly, Paul turned back to them. He seemed to see Maria for the first time.

"You have my heartfelt condolences, Frau Picard. Your husband was a very good, kind man."

"Thank you, Paul," she replied stiffly.

"Michael came to me just a few days before he died," he continued easily. "He was a great comfort to me as he expressed his conviction in my innocence." Then Paul smiled, his arm sweeping the empty benches. "You will have a lot of good men and women in your congregation, Thomas. They will be a blessing to you."

"Thank you. I'm sure they will," Thomas replied softly.

"Thomas, we should be leaving. We can come back later."

"There is no need, Frau Picard," Paul said, smiling. "Continue your tour. I'm all cleared out."

"Paul, I . . . I'm sorry. Truly sorry. Like my father, I have no doubt of your innocence. I never did. I'm here . . . but there were other authorities making these choices for you and me. I hope that it will turn out well for both of us."

Shraeder had stooped to pick up a book satchel. He stood slowly, almost arthritically, Thomas noted. Their eyes locked, and Thomas was instantly reminded of their other visit. *How do I interpret this look my old friend is giving me? Is it accusing? Pitying?* It was like the unpleasant repeat of a dream. When he should have been feeling an inner pleasure because a step of success had been reached, he felt instead an odd mixture of uneasiness and sorrow.

"Other authorities are making our choices," Shraeder said deliberately. "There you have said it, Thomas. It's those other authorities that have caused me my greatest frustration in all of this. I know God has allowed this to happen to me, but there is no way He or His influence designed it."

Thomas said nothing.

"You'll be very busy with this church in the coming weeks. And of course, as you said, there are your responsibilities to your family. Perhaps in some spare moment you'll think about all of this in a different way."

"What way?"

"Thomas—" Maria Picard began but both men ignored her.

"You receive the church record in Dachau. You know there has been an alarming incident in 'pastoral difficulties' in the last six months. I've become one of those statistics. 'Pastoral difficulties' used to mean a pastor taking too many vacations or his congregation stagnating or chronic illness or, the most serious, taking too freely of the communion wine. Do you know what it means now, Thomas? Sexual misconduct, treason, theft of church funds. I did a little study in our denomination and the Catholic Church in all my free time the last few weeks. There have been at least twenty separate removals of pastors or priests. Just last week I was told about a nun in Frankfurt who was charged with things I won't speak of."

"Why are you telling my son this?" Maria demanded with open hostility.

"I am telling your son this because he is in the church and he should be terribly concerned."

"He has no intention of engaging in any of the offenses you list, Paul," Maria said archly.

"Mother, please."

"I had no intention—and I didn't. And neither did these other accused."

"Then you are saying our church leaders made up all these terrible things!" Maria said shrilly. "Surely you can't be implying that."

"I took the time to talk with a few of the men who were accused. All of them have strong views against the persecution of the Jews our government is engaging in. This racial purity stuff is straight out of the pit of hell. The Jews are our brothers! . . . The accused believe Berlin shouldn't tell the church how to conduct itself like it is through the Reich church. "Do you see the pattern?"

Neither Picard responded.

"I read an item in the paper today. Maybe you saw it too. The state is now offering infant dedications and marriage ceremonies. There are plans to have alternate holidays to the 'Christian' ones. Christmas this year is to be called Yuletide. Nativity scenes are forbidden in public. Prayer and Bible-reading is forbidden in school. So, Thomas, tell me. What's the point of the church? I'll tell you. There is no point. Make the church unnecessary, and it becomes extinct. Hitler and his gang are phasing the church out slowly, and the pastors are nodding it along!"

"No!" Thomas declared firmly.

Shraeder's voice was sad. "We've been friends a long time, Thomas. I wish you well here. I will continue to pray for you. And I will pray that your eyes will be opened."

Rudi stormed into the kitchen where Maria and Gretchen were making bread. Maria looked up, flour to her elbows.

"Careful, Gretchen, your brother has a stormy countenance," Maria teased.

Rudi slumped into a kitchen chair. "A stormy what?"

"You're frowning."

"Hmm . . ." he muttered.

"Good. Now let's add a little more flour . . . careful."

"Makin' bread, Rud," Gretchen piped.

"Great."

Maria observed him with a hand on her hip.

"So what's your trouble?"

"I've been dumped. Well, I kind of dumped myself."

"The fair Charlotte?"

He nodded.

"Why?"

Rudi leaned forward, tapping the table with impatient fingers.

"Her family is very pro-Nazi. Didn't want their daughter with a soccer player who didn't 'heil Hitler' every time he kicks the ball. Her father wanted me to go into the military."

"Ah . . ."

"I detect very little sympathy from you, Maria Goldstein," he said, wagging a finger at her.

Her chin was in her hands. "You detect correct, Herr Picard. I was dumped by a Jew because I'm a Jew and he has to leave Germany. I was flirted with on the streetcar by a nice young man until I told him I was Jewish. Chilled his passion in record time."

He shook his head, hardly hearing her words. "The thing is, she would have been so good for me. You know, a rich wife. I could play ball and not have to worry about anything else. It could have been a perfect arrangement."

Sitting there with his dark curly hair, his strong chin, he was still so handsome. But suddenly, in the light of the kitchen, he looked different. *Perhaps ... perhaps he had never been the one for her for more than the old reasons,* she thought.

She stood up and went back to the counter. She knew he was watching her.

"You can either be a Nazi or a Jew, Rudi. There is no in-between anymore."

"You've changed, Maria," he said slowly.

She was fingering Gretchen's long braid. "I had to. Even ... even if I didn't want to."

He sat up, animated. "Let's forget all this! Let's you and I go out tonight. We'll go to Demel's for dinner, then to the club on Benderstrasse for dancing—"

She was shaking her head. Jews weren't permitted in those places. Besides, she could vividly imagine Frau Maria's disapproval.

"No thank you Rudi," she said, smiling sadly.

Maria entered the dining room breathless and smoothing her hair. Everyone was at the table, waiting for the blessing, waiting for her. She sat down quickly, noting that everyone was looking very ... strange. She glanced at her mother. She looked like she had been crying. Her father drew a long, ragged breath. Maria peeked at him with her head bowed. He looked very pale. She glanced at Jacob. He was watching her, frowning and slightly shaking his head.

Her father's voice was steady. "The earth is the Lord's and all it contains. Praised are you, O Lord, our King of the universe, who brings forth bread from the earth."

Sophie began filling the plates.

"What's the matter with everybody?" Maria asked with false brightness.

Sophie spoke up eagerly. "Nothing, nothing. Hand me your plate. Such a day today! Little Gregor fell down the front steps and split his lip. You could have heard him in Berlin! And the boys' soccer ball went into the Hager's front flower bed, and there was Herr Hager raging at them as if they had brought down his roof. Such an intemperate man! But what do you expect! Gretchen was coughing so bad over here at dinner I thought she might go into a seizure, poor thing. Oh, the soup needs salt. Abraham, please remove your elbows from the table. Herr Fritz told me his knees indicate we'll have rain tomorrow. What a funny man! Did you have a good day shopping, Maria?"

"Yes."

Only Sophie was animated. Everyone saw through her strategy.

"What is wrong with everybody?" Maria repeated.

"You were on the streets all day and you didn't hear?" Jacob's voice was patronizing.

"If I had I wouldn't be asking," she countered.

"Children," Sophie warned.

Her oldest brother was pulling at his black beard; he ignored his food. His voice was patient. "Berlin has announced a law that will take effect tomorrow."

"What kind of law?" Maria asked with growing dread. Their faces told her volumes.

"It says that Jews are no longer citizens of Germany. We are denied all rights. We cannot vote or buy property. We are barred from public office, civil service, journalism, radio, farming, teaching, theater, films, medicine, and the legal profession." His voice slowed. "We are barred from the universities. We cannot own businesses. We . . . are . . . subjects."

Maria scanned the table. Only her mother continued eating. The boys were looking out the window or down at their laps. She laid her fork down slowly.

"Papa, what does this mean?"

But Herr Goldstein did not seem to hear his young daughter. He had withdrawn into his own private pain.

Abraham spoke up again. "Slaves, Maria. Like the Jews in pharaoh's Egypt. Slaves."

"Slaves?" she echoed. "Slaves? How can that be? We are Germans. We . . . how can they make laws. . . How can we no longer be citizens overnight?"

"This is what happens when you don't pay attention to the things that are going on around you because you are so busy playing and swooning over some boy," Jacob said in a tight voice.

"Leave her alone," Abraham added with equal firmness.

"Boys, the last thing we need is quarreling among ourselves. You need to calm down, Maria. There is no need to spoil or waste a perfectly good dinner," Sophie said practically.

But Maria had stood up, tossing aside her napkin. She was flushed and staring at her mother.

"Are you serious? Our country has just said that we're slaves! And you tell me to calm down and eat?" She turned and fled up the stairs.

Her voice reached out to him in the darkness. "Papa, I'm afraid."

Aaron had waited until the end of the meal to slowly climb the stairs to his daughter's bedroom. His throat constricted to hold back the screaming of every fiber of his body. *Why should my beautiful girl have to be afraid?* He had never lied to her. But what she needed now was not his sympathy but his strength.

"I understand, Maria. But you must overcome your fear. It is more of an enemy than they are."

She was clutching his hand. "Papa, they don't know me. How ... how can they hate me?"

He reached out to stroke her hair. "If they did know you, they wouldn't hate you."

"No, Papa. Just across the street, that Eric Hager, he hates me."

"He doesn't know you."

"He knows I am just a girl, that standing beside a Gentile no one would know I am a Jew."

"I know, I know."

"Papa, what shall we do?" her voice cracked.

What shall we do? Aaron Goldstein knew all the Jews of Germany were asking themselves that question. He could do only the thing he knew best.

His head was bowed and Maria in her youthful terror fell asleep with his rhythmic voice, like one of the sweetest melodies he had ever played, comforting her.

"O Lord, our God, hear our prayer! Have compassion upon us and pity us. Accept our prayer with loving favor. Let Your tender mercies, O

Lord God, be stirred for the righteous. We thank You our God and the God of our fathers. He who never slumbers nor sleeps. Defender of our lives, shield of our safety. Hide us in the shadow of Thy wings." His voice trembled. "This is my beloved daughter. May she have the kindness of Ruth and ... and may she have the courage of Esther. Hear, O Lord, I cry unto You."

"Sophie, please don't cry," Maria Picard said with a tenderness that had been absent from her voice for a long time.

Sophie, so expressive and voluble, had no words to return. She wept into her handkerchief.

Aaron reached out and patted Maria's hand. "She'll be all right in a few days. She just has to get used to the idea ..." His voice faded, revealing that he was clearly having trouble with the idea himself. But he was a man who concealed his complaints, his frustrations, his fear. Perhaps, in the end, a steadfast calmness was all he could bequeath to his family.

Jacob stood at the window of the Picard dining room with a sullen face, his hands jammed into his pockets. He snorted out loud at his father's words.

Abraham drew the pen and papers out of the case and gave them to Frau Picard to look over. She read swiftly then nodded to him.

"Everything looks in order, Abraham. Thank you."

She signed her name then carefully passed the papers across the table to Aaron. He adjusted his glasses as he read. No one met each other's eyes. After a five-minute interval, the elder Goldstein picked up the pen and carefully signed his name.

Jacob came from the window and looked over his father's shoulder. Huge tears formed in eyes that had not cried in many years. He reached out and put his hand on his father's shoulder.

Maria Picard studied her fine sideboard and china across the room.

After fifty-six years, "Goldstein's and Picard's Fine Instruments" was gone.

Berlin

Dietrich Bonhoeffer was already speaking to a half-full sanctuary when Thomas slipped in. Thomas was surprised. He had visualized a tall, scholarly looking man. This slightly chubby, balding man looked barely thirty. He seemed to squint through his gold-wire glasses. His voice carried with a strength Thomas had rarely heard.

"The church must remain the church! We must confess! Confess! Confess! As long as Christianity remains Christianity, and as long as National Socialism remains National Socialism, conflict is inevitable," Bonhoeffer stated. "The totalitarian National Socialists is a pagan faith that cannot but regard Christianity as alien and antagonistic. There is only one altar before which we must kneel, one cross before which we must bow."

There was nothing hidden or veiled in this man's words. Every person in the sanctuary understood. Thomas stirred uneasily. Suddenly the closed front doors rocked with a loud thud. Thomas was sweating. *It was a mistake to come here, to have given in to curiosity,* he thought. Everyone was silent and motionless. Then muted murmering broke out, which soon became shrill screaming. This raging made Thomas feel there was something supernatural outside the walls of this church—an angry legion of demons. A man approached the pulpit and spoke into Bonhoeffer's ear.

The pastor spoke with a slight smile. "It appears the Nazis have joined our meeting."

• • •

Aaron Goldstein had been staring into his coffee cup for several minutes. Against the kitchen glass a bare branch of the almond tree was scratching, demanding their attention.

"You know, I planted that tree the year you were born, Maria," Aaron said softly.

Maria and Abraham exchanged a look over their father's head.

"Papa, we have to talk about this. We have to come to a decision, make a plan," Abraham said.

Aaron focused on him. *This tall son with a full beard, speaking with such maturity, a man. When had he grown up?*

"Yes ... yes," he nodded. "a plan, you are right."

Maria refilled their cups than sat down across from them. *This little conspiracy would be exciting,* she reflected, *if it was about something less ... painful. The three of us in our kitchen, trying to make a way in the world that was somehow out of balance.*

"I went to the emigration office during the noon hour, and I was able to talk with a clerk," Abraham began. Then he sighed. "So we emigrate. We leave our ... home. We leave all we know," Aaron murmured. "We leave our home, our business, our—"

"We have already lost our business," Maria interrupted with audible bitterness.

Aaron took her hand in his. "Maria, you know there was no other way. Frau Maria was trying to make it easier for us. We are not without an income. We must be grateful for that. There are many who are having a very difficult time."

"Yes, Papa." But Maria knew she would never forget her father's face that first morning when the front glass had been different. "Picard's Fine Instruments." She had walked to work with him, holding his hand the entire way. He had stopped before the entrance, studying the window. The brick, the instruments—everything the same, yet so very different.

He turned to his daughter. He was pale, his eyes watering.

"You know, Maria, change is good. If you never change you can become narrow-minded. Well, have a splendid day, Maria!" He kissed her cheek and paused at the front door. "Thank you for walking with me."

"Emigrate," Aaron repeated, shaking his head. "Sophie will never agree to this. It would break her."

"Papa, we will help her understand," Abraham soothed. "And if it comes to her not agreeing in spite of that, well, she will just have to come under protest. There is no other way."

Aaron stood up, suddenly angry. "Why must I think about this? They have taken away our citizenship, what else can they do?"

"It isn't going to get better Papa," Abraham said. "Deep down you must know that. Hitler is taking little steps at a time with no opposition. Not even the Christian church is speaking up for us."

Aaron hung his head. "Yes ..."

The kitchen door swung open with a bang. Sophie was framed in the light, her hair wild, her eyes wild, her hands on her hips.

"I have been listening," she said dramatically.

"Now, Sophie—" Aaron began with an outstretched hand.

"She'll just have to come under protest, eh? What does that mean?" She slapped the side of her son's head. "Have your father drag me by the hair of my head? Or maybe you? Ha!"

Abraham lowered his head. It was useless to try to stem this tide.

"Now!" She jabbed a thick finger at the defendant. "He says there is no other way. Ha! We are the Goldsteins of Blumenstrasse in Munich. We do not run when a little trouble comes. We hold our heads with dignity, and we wait out this storm of weak-minded fools! This is our home! And I will not hear another word of this treachery in this house. Tell them . . . tell them, Aaron. This is our home." She collapsed, weeping, into the shelter of his arms.

He held her. "It's all right, Sophie, it is all right. This is our home. We will stay."

8
A Gulf Called Blumenstrasse

1935

The sky was flat and gray like a smooth slab of rock. The day before her nineteenth birthday, Maria was sitting in the window seat of her bedroom. She was passing through a quiet evolution in her response to the Nazi control of her homeland. Shock, disbelief, boiling fury, and indignation were changing to acceptance.

I can tolerate the situation in the new Germany, she thought. *This is a drama I haven't chosen, but one I must take part in. And I'll perform my role with dignity. I might have to live by the rules and die by the rules, but they will never numb my mind or steal my spirit! And I will resist in whatever ways I can find,* she decided fervently. *I won't be like my friends and passively accept what is happening—I could never do that!*

Besides, I have my faith, Maria reflected. *I'm proud to be identified by my heritage. I'm part of a persecuted race—a people who are called God's chosen ones. We're the apple of His eye—like Papa has been telling me since I was a little girl.*

Maria Goldstein had discovered quite suddenly that God was bigger than Adolf Hitler. And if sides were chosen, she was on the side of the Creator of the universe. She could survive the taunts, the meanness, the ostracism.

A figure coming down Blumenstrasse caught her eye. It was Thomas Picard coming home. She pulled back behind the curtain so that he wouldn't see her and wave. He bounded up his steps. She pursed her lips. *Thomas has no troubles. Thomas has the future unfolding just the way he wants. What happened to his heart?*

What do I feel for Thomas Picard? She had thought it through. Anger. Smoldering anger. *Thomas, for all his kindness to me over the years, has stepped on the side of the Reich church, which hates ... me. I doubt whether I can ever forgive him,* Maria decided. *In all the changes and pain of the past few years, this is the hardest.*

• • •

Maria Picard dreaded these unannounced visits from her older brother. There had been a time, now receding, when his advent was like a breath of intellectual and cultural stimulation. He brought the wide world of Germany to the narrow world of Blumenstrasse. He talked confidentially about people Maria read about in the papers. It was he who had secured her a place in the gallery when the Nazi leaders had come to campaign in Munich, their old gathering ground. But now his coming meant only conflict.

Maria sat nervously on the edge of her chair, grateful her sons had proposed a quiet evening for their mother and an outing for Gretchen.

Otto leaned back in the chair. "How are you these days, Maria?"

His question, while not so gently put, took her by surprise. The badgering tone was absent.

"I know you will find this difficult to understand, Otto, but despite our differences I ... I loved Michael. I miss him."

Otto nodded. "I am not so hard-hearted that I can't understand that, Maria. Give me a little credit for feeling. It is feeling for you that made me leave my meeting early. I'd like you to know that."

Her hands twisted even as her stomach knotted. "What is it you've come about, Otto?"

"I have seen files tonight, and I was not surprised by them. Fortunately, the men with me didn't look closely enough to see that Frau Picard was once Fraulein Beck, sister of Otto Beck." He let his words sink in.

She drew a deep breath. "All right, tell me plainly, Otto."

He smiled and nodded. "I knew you were a smart girl. We can understand each other. The Gestapo is compiling a file on your family. I have
seen worse files—but it is far better to have no file."

"What is in this file?" she asked with synthetic calm.

"Rudi Picard is not a registered member of any Nazi group. But
worse, he's running with Jews. The Gestapo is only bidding its time until
the net is fuller, so to speak, before it draws the net in." He paused. Maria
had turned pale.

"Thomas Picard is not registered with any Nazi group."

"He is a pastor!" Maria flared.

Otto shrugged his flabby shoulders. "There are many pastors registered on the Nazi roles. Even that might be overlooked . . . but we cannot
overlook that you have two Jews still working in your music store." His
voice had risen.

Maria leaned back and closed her eyes. She was very tired.

"They are clerks, Otto. Abraham and Aaron are clerks. They know
the store and the music business of course. They are the best—"

He stood up, his face red. "They are the best? Maria, they are Jews!
Only Jews can figure out how to blow in a piece of metal or pluck a string
to make a tune? Is that what you're saying?"

She shook her head.

"You have them out by the end of the week or you will have signs in
your store windows that won't be advertising a sale," he menaced.

She made a motion with her hand. "Otto ..."

"Don't start your whining at me. 'Otto, please Otto,' he mimicked. I
can't stop what will happen to you and your precious store or your precious worthless sons, I can only warn you!"

She stood up, shaking. "How dare you say these things!"

He was unmoved by her defiance. "One last thing—"

"Yes, it will be the last thing, Otto. You are never to come to this
house without my express invitation," she said in a voice of steel.

"You employ a Jewess in this house—a clear violation of the law.
If I know this, the SS and Gestapo know it. Think about that. You are
risking everything you want for this Jewish trash to care for your
halfwit—"

Frau Picard's scream kept her from fainting. She had seen a swift,
blurred movement in the room. Suddenly, as if he were one of Gretchen's

dolls, her brother was jerked backward. He stumbled but not before a fist connected with his chin. He fell back, knocking over a table.

Otto shook his head like a staggering bull and looked up. Someone was a shadow over him, his breath panting as was his own. Finally, his eyes cleared. *Thomas Picard.*

"You won't ever step foot in this house again without *my* invitation," Thomas stated forcefully.

"Don't worry, I won't come back. Save your own skin, little sister. I won't try to help you again." The big man stood up shakily. His eyes narrowed on Thomas.

"So you can do more than lift your skinny hands to some God, eh? Well, at least I can see the evening isn't a total loss. Finally the Picard boy shows he has some backbone."

"Get out," Thomas said through clenched teeth.

Otto paused at the door, wiping the blood from the corner of his mouth. He managed a thin laugh. "What is it your disgusting friends say? Mazel tov? Yes, you'll need it."

• • •

"Alex not home, not home. He'll be cold, Maria. Find him, come on, please. He's lonely without Gretchen," the young girl said, her face a mask of anxiety.

Maria stood up. "Gret, there's no telling where the cat might be. He's probably in our garden or out courting." She put her arm around the girl. "He'll be crying for you in the morning on the backstep. Thomas or Rudi will hear him and let him in."

She wagged her head vehemently. "No, Maria. Gotta find him."

Maria went to the window. The rain had stopped and the fresh night air did seem appealing. She studied Gretchen. *Frau Picard and Thomas are at an evening church service. Rudi was unpredictable,* she reflected.

"Mother Soph," Gretchen said, rocking back and forth.

Maria laughed. This girl had known her thoughts again. She went for her sweater.

"Curl up in the chair. I will look for Master Alex Cat."

She dashed up the steps to her own house to ask her mother to care for Gretchen until she returned. Maria walked briskly down Blumenstrasse calling the cat. At the end of the street she stopped. There was no way to know if he had gone further. She would go a few more streets, far enough to pacify Gretchen. But after a block or so, the crisp, rain-washed night felt good to her. To walk alone under the canopy of darkness gave her a heady feeling of freedom. She would perhaps walk as far as the little pastry shop on Brennerstrasse. The pastry there was delicious and, more importantly, there were no signs in the window. Yet. She would buy a pastry for herself, Gretchen, and her mother.

She passed a few darkened shops, a tavern that emitted the tones of an off-key piano, then the lights from Jensen's Bakery beckoned. She hurried across the street. The door jangled when she entered, but it was so crowded that few looked up. There was laughing and eating. She went to the broad counter. The owner, Hilda Jensen, was behind the counter, presiding with a jovial and generous air.

"Guten nacht," she said to Maria.

Maria met her eye-to-eye and smiled. It was wonderful to be greeted in such a commonplace way. Maria took her time to select the three treats. It was difficult since Fraulein Jensen bragged on everything. Laughing, Maria finally made her selection. The woman wrapped up her pastries. As Maria paid the woman's whispered words went straight to her heart: "God bless you, child."

A stranger gave me a blessing! Looking across the expanse of counter, Maria had the odd feeling this gray-haired woman knew she was a Jew. She smiled back.

"Thank you."

Out on the street Maria pulled in a long breath of moist night air. She felt like skipping the three streets over to Blumenstrasse. No cat for Gretchen but a delicious pastry for the three of them. They would be worrying after her if she didn't hurry back.

Suddenly Maria felt like she was being followed. She stopped and realized her heart was pounding. She swung around, but no one was there—only the darkened shops and the beacon light of pastry shop. She continued walking. *I'll pass through the vacant lot where the old drugstore had stood. It's a quicker way home,* she decided. Yet the charred shell of the building rose up in the night like a hand clutching for the heavens. She had seen this relic a thousand times, but on this moonless night it was different. The wind picked up, thin and moaning. She pulled her sweater collar closer around her neck.

She was halfway past the building when she heard the appeal of a cat. She slowed and stopped. He was somewhere in the building.

"Alex?" she called. A cat answered back but didn't show itself. "Alex, come on!" She stepped into the gaping, darkened entrance. "Kitty, kitty!" But nothing, no sound, no shadow. She turned.

A man was standing in front of her. Only two feet away. She jumped back a little, stifling a scream. Instantly she smelled the pungent odor of alcohol.

"Little Jew . . . mistress out in the night to find her cat," his laugh was throaty. "Very foolish. Haven't you heard what the Nazis do when they find a Jew on the street? I will show you personally what they do to a Jewess." He stepped forward.

Maria gasped. *It's Otto Beck!* her mind cried.

"Please," she whispered, putting her hand out instinctively.

"Ah, now not so high and mighty . . . Plead for my mercy."

The arrogance of his voice wrenched her from her fear. Her hand went out in a stinging slap. He lunged and grabbed her wrists. In that moment, Maria knew she should have turned and ran. Her swiftness would have been no contest for his strength. He had wrestled her back into the ruins, cursing and foul, encircling her with his thick arms. He pulled her to the wall and pinioned her there. His hands were on her.

Once again, Otto was jerked in the darkness and staggered over some broken beams. Maria was huddled against the wall watching the stranger wide-eyed. He was tall and slender. He grabbed the drunken man and pulled him back through the open door, out into the lot as if he were no weight at all. "Go on you big coward. Go on, get out of here!" His voice was shaking but stern. Maria didn't recognize it.

Otto staggered up, cursing, and backed toward the lighted street. They stood motionless until he was out of sight. Then the figure turned back to Maria, who was leaning in the doorway. Though she couldn't see his face, she knew he was watching her. Then he stooped down and picked up the bag.

"I think they're all right, a little smashed maybe." She could hear the youth in his voice.

"I feel sick . . . I think I'm going to faint," Maria murmured.

He took her arm. "Sit here. Now breathe deep. That's it . . . just sit and you'll be all right."

Maria closed her eyes, breathing deeply, willing her heart to a steadiness. She knew he still crouched in front of her.

"A little better?" he asked softly.

She nodded. Reluctantly she opened her eyes. The sky had peeled back from the storm and a half-moon was shining. It fell on the man before her—on his polished boots, on the outstretched arm with the black band. Maria recoiled, trying to find a reserve of strength to fight again.

"Don't. I'm not going to hurt you." He stood up. "If you want, I'll go get your father or one of your brothers to help you home." He sounded a little angry. The light fell across his face.

Eric Hager.

"Make up your mind," he said curtly. "Your family will be worrying after you."

"How did you see me here?" she whispered.

"I saw you come out of Jensen's. Under the streetlight I knew it was you." His voice was hurried, as if he was embarrassed. "I saw that pig Beck come out too. I could tell he was following you . . . so I followed him."

He waited then reached out his hand. "Let me see you home safely, Maria Goldstein."

She hesitated. She still felt weak. Everything had happened so fast.

His voice was soft. "You have no reason to trust me, but you can. Come on."

With a shy smile and a swift good bye, he left her at the corner of Blumenstrasse.

Maria sensed the strain as soon as she walked through the front door.

"Let's go into the parlor and talk Maria," Frau Picard said as she led the way.

Maria followed, her nervousness increasing. *What did I do to offend this woman? Perhaps it was something I didn't do.* Maria searched her mind quickly. *Or . . . or Otto. Certainly he wouldn't have said anything to his sister about the night before. Why would he do that? I didn't even say anything about it to my family*—it would only have multiplied their fears and worries. Frau Picard couldn't know of her brother's attack.

Frau Picard's hands were fluttering in her lap, picking at the fabric. Maria suddenly realized this woman was very nervous.

How could I make her nervous? Maria wondered.

"Maria, you are a very intelligent, very capable young woman. You have been very … very good for Gretchen, and when Herr Picard was alive, he was very grateful for your … your loving service to our daughter … as I have been."

Maria felt she should say something. "I feel like Gretchen is my sister."

"I have … been faced with difficulties over the years … trials. This is difficult for me now."

Maria Goldstein suddenly understood. It was as if the lace curtains had let in a powerful, penetrating light. She stood up, her voice calm and steady though her heart was pounding as it had in the vacant lot with Otto Beck. Here was another fear she must face.

"You're trying to tell me you don't want me to care for Gretchen anymore," she stated calmly.

"Yes, Maria, that is what I'm trying to say."

They stared at each other.

"Of course you … can continue your friendship with her. I simply can't employ you any longer."

Maria was silent. I won't give this woman any more help. Let her say it.

"You are smart, Maria, and you understand my position. I don't want any of us in trouble or attention brought on any of us. I have Rudi and Thomas to think of."

And Gretchen, Maria added in her mind. She bit back the words. Papa wouldn't want her to be small in spirit.

"It is the law, Maria. I have no choice."

It took all of her young will to speak evenly. "Yes, I understand, Frau Picard."

Berlin

Thomas hadn't expected to journey back into the inner chambers of the vital Nazi heart, then into the personal study of Adolf Hitler. He had been summoned for an eleven o'clock appointment. He appeared outwardly composed as he and ten other church leaders were led past the SS guards and through the corridors of the chancellery. They waited outside the study doors. The heavy, paneled doors swung open. Bishop Wagner stood beside the fuehrer.

The bishop was smiling as he gave each man a personal introduction to the German leader. Hitler pressed Thomas' hand stiffly. Unlike the bishop, he was not smiling. Yet Wagner's words were warm and conversational.

"This is Thomas Picard, mein Fuehrer, the young pastor I was telling you about. He has recently taken a church in Munich. Besides being a dynamic preacher, I can also boast that Thomas has an exceptionally fine voice. One day he will treat us to a little concert." He winked at Thomas and said, "Perhaps when you are working in Berlin."

The last man in line brought an immediate tension to the room. Noticing this, Thomas realized for all of the bishop's smiles and gracious words, tension had permeated the room.

The churchmen were seated in Hitler's favorite semicircular arrangement. He stood like a general on the battlefield. Hitler was no longer in a conciliatory mood. He began swiftly by reproaching them. They misunderstood him and, as a result, there was this church conflict.

"Peace is all I want between church and state. You, in your leadership positions, have sabotaged my efforts to achieve this peace. Men like Bonhoeffer! I will no longer stand this treachery against the Third Reich!" He glared at one man in particular.

No one moved or shared a look. Thomas felt as if the entire room had stopped breathing.

Hitler slapped his fist into his palm. "Tell me this is not true! Tell me I am wrong!"

Thomas took a closer look at the tall, gray-haired man who had received the withering stare from the fuehrer.

Niemöller cleared his throat.

"I cannot and will not attempt to speak for my fellow servants of our Lord. I speak to you, mein Fuehrer, only for myself. If these with me share my sentiments, they will have to say this. My object is not to cause dissension or disharmony in our church. That is the last thing I want. My object is the welfare of the church, the state, and the German people."

Hitler stood in stony silence for a moment, then in a suddenly high-pitched voice he said, "As a former patriot in the last war we both fought in, your words confuse me, Martin Niemöller. You do cause dissension and disharmony! So I say to you, you confine yourself to the church, I'll take care of the German people!"

Hitler then directed the monologue to other church themes. Forty minutes later the churchmen were preparing to leave, saying stilted, nervous, abashed goodbyes. Thomas had his eye on Niemöller. This was an intimate of Bonhoeffer's. Thomas immediately noted this man didn't seem anxious or disconcerted. He appeared quite calm. It was Niemöller's time to speak. He looked at Hitler with the same penetrating stare he had been given.

"You say that 'I will take care of the German people,' but we too, as Christians and churchmen, have a responsibility to the people. This responsibility was entrusted to us by God, and neither you nor anyone in this world has the power to take it from us."

A surge of purple rose up Hitler's neck to his face. Sharply he turned his back on the speaker.

Thomas looked over and found the bishop's eyes fixed on him.

● ● ●

"Gret had a seizure a little while ago. She's resting now, but she's asking for you," Thomas said from where he stood in the Goldstein hallway. "Could you come, Maria?"

Maria sat on the edge of Gretchen's bed and heard the door close behind her.

"I went 'way," Gretchen slurred.

Maria nodded. Gretchen always referred to her seizures as going away.

Maria squeezed her hand. "But you came back. We're glad you came back."

Gretchen picked listlessly at the covers. "With him. I . . . come back, it's all sad. Mother sad. Maria gone. Gret doesn't want to come back times."

"I understand. Sometimes I want to go away too . . . and never come back."

"Why? Maria is pretty smart."

Maria smiled. "I'd go someplace where it didn't matter about who people are. I'd go where I'd be liked." She fell silent. Five minutes passed.

"Thomas, tell Maria where she can go be liked."

Maria swung around in her chair. Thomas Picard was leaning against the door.

"I didn't know you were there," Maria said stiffly.

"I thought you did. I wasn't trying to eavesdrop—but this may be my only chance to talk to you."

Maria reached out and stroked the girl's forehead until she drifted off to sleep.

Finally she stood up, knowing she'd have to face him. She didn't look up until his voice pulled at her.

"I can never tell you how much your love for my little sister means to me," he said. There were tears in his eyes. The hardness in her heart melted for a moment. *Thomas of old, who was her friend, who tenderly loved his sister.*

"Maria, I . . . don't know how to begin, what to say."

"There is nothing to say."

"No, there is so much to say. Mother dismissed you while I was in Berlin—"

"She had to. I've accepted it. You don't need to suffer any guilt over it. The Picard family can rest easy knowing they are not law-breakers."

He gripped her arms. "You have to know I don't like this. You have to know that there is nothing I can do about it."

"You can speak from your lofty pulpit on Sunday and preach that the Jews are not Christ-killers and race-defilers. You can speak the way this Bonhoeffer and Niemöller speak."

His mouth had gone dry. "I can't do that ..." He gazed down at her, feeling as if he had been stabbed.

"It cannot be the way it was, Thomas. You know that in your heart. I'm truly sorry for both of us."

His arms reached out as tears spilled down his cheeks. She allowed herself to be held, to feel his beating heart against her cheek. But it would be the last time.

9
Requiem on Blumenstrasse

1937

Swiftly passing, 1936 and '37 were memorable years for the Goldsteins and Picards.

The Goldsteins were generally homebound now. Aaron took in a small handful of children to tutor on the violin. Abraham continued to do the bookkeeping for "Picard's," but at home now. Frau Picard was the legal and figurative bookkeeper. Maria worked parttime at the bakery shop nearby. She washed dishes and helped with cooking. She was never seen by the customers up front. From her place behind the green curtain, she heard of the world: new fashions, current movies, popular music, and Germany's success in the Olympic games. It was a difficult exile for a vivacious girl.

Sorrow had visited the Picard home as well. Rudi had died in a bloody fight with a Nazi street gang. At eighteen, Gretchen Picard had grown into a tall, slender girl. She could identify letters but couldn't read, she could dress herself and do small chores, and she could draw beautifully. The grief of her family caused her to further withdraw into her private, tranquil world. The only happy note was that Thomas was now the pastor of the largest Protestant church in Munich. His zealous preaching and fine voice were gaining him a reputation throughout Germany.

• • •

"Maria, wake up!"

She rolled over, momentarily straining in the darkness, afraid.

"Jacob? What are you doing? Get out of my bedroom!"

"Hush, you loud-mouthed goon," he said, hunched beside her bed.

She pushed herself up into a sitting position. Her breathing became steadier. She pushed back her hair.

"What's the matter?"

"Maria, I'm leaving and ... well, I wanted to say goodbye to you. Only God knows when we'll see each other again."

"Jacob, what are you talking about? Where are you going?"

"I'm leaving Germany. Some of us ... we're going tonight while we can still take the train."

"Jacob, this ... Mama will be destroyed!"

He held her arm. "I know it will hurt her at first. But it's the best way for all of us. After Isaac and Rudi ... I am not going to stay here and let them take me!" his voice was fierce.

She sighed. "Oh Jacob ... Do you have money?"

He nodded. "I've been saving for this." He stood up. "You'll tell them in the morning? Tell them I'll be careful and that somehow, someday, we'll all be together again."

Maria began to cry.

Awkwardly, Jacob leaned down and kissed her on the forehead.

"You've been a good sister most of the time, O Petted One."

Then he was gone.

• • •

Thomas was sitting hunched over in front of the fire, staring moodily into the flames.

"Trying to get inspiration for a sermon about the devil?" Maria Goldstein asked from the doorway.

He raised his head slowly. Maria was shocked at his ragged appearance. He didn't smile at her joke.

"Are you sick?" she asked gently.

"Maybe ..." he replied cryptically.

She held up a deck of cards. "Papa sent me over to see if you wanted to play. Obviously not."

"Obviously. Did you come in through the kitchen?" he snapped.

She nodded.

He stood up. "I don't like that and I don't want you to ever do that again. No one in this house has ever told you to stop coming in through the front door."

Maria had never seen Thomas like this.

"You're as grumpy as Jacob. You're right, no one told me to come in the back door. But Mama and Papa said it would be best so that . . ." her chin went up, "so that no Jew would be seen entering your home."

He was unaware that his fists were clenched at his sides. But Maria noticed.

"How's Gretchen tonight?" she asked by way of changing the subject.

"She's asleep; she's fine. She was here alone when I got home."

"Alone? What happened?"

Thomas was clearly boiling, and Maria knew she had struck another nerve.

"I don't know where Mother is. Gretchen couldn't tell me. Nor do I know why Mother didn't send for you if it was something urgent."

"You really don't understand why she didn't send for me?" Maria asked impulsively, instantly regretting her words.

They gazed at each other across the unspoken gulf. Finally Thomas turned away from her to the fire; Maria returned home.

An hour later, Maria Picard entered the front room to find Thomas still in front of the fire, his face in his hands.

"Thomas, Thomas, what is the matter? Are you ill?"

"Why did you leave Gretchen alone? Especially when there is a fire in the fireplace!"

She drew off her hat and coat slowly. "I don't like your tone, son."

He sighed. "I'm sorry, Mother, but I don't like finding Gret here alone. Maria could have stayed with her until I came. . . . Were you at one of those meetings again? Is that why you left before I came home?"

Her spine straightened. "They are called seances, and I didn't want to be late."

He groaned into his hands again.

"Thomas, I know you don't approve—but you don't understand."

"I understand enough to know that seances are part of the occult, which is expressly against our Christian faith."

Her voice cracked. "They have told me I can ... speak ... to your father—"

Thomas stood up impatiently.

Her voice was pleading. "I can speak to him and Rudi. You don't know how much that would mean to me, what a comfort it would be. I'm desperate, Thomas, try to understand. I miss them!"

He leaned on the chair. "Mother, you cannot be so desperate you forget what is right and what is wrong. Trying to contact the dead is wrong."

She searched his face, this face she loved.

"Thomas what is wrong with you tonight? Why are you so angry? What has happened at the church?" she asked.

He slumped back into the chair. "Nothing happened at the church. Everything is very ... smooth at the church."

Maria Picard paled in alarm just as Maria Goldstein had done earlier.

His voice was low, almost a whisper. "Did you hear what I said? You cannot be so desperate that you forget what is right and what is wrong. I said that."

Frau Picard swallowed with difficulty. "Thomas, you are clearly overworked. You must tell your elders you need a vacation. I'll tell them, if you can't. We can all go to the sea like you've been promising Gretchen."

He shook his head morosely. "I can't go on a vacation. I leave for Berlin tomorrow. Bishop Wagner has summoned me again."

• • •

The pastor had plenty of time to think as he stared out the window of the train traveling from Munich to Berlin. He kept his hat pulled down and his scowl pulled on to prevent any passenger chitchat. Hours to think ... and, strangely, he gave this latest summons hardly any thought.

He knew when this inner sickness had begun—or at least when it had finally made itself felt. He would never forget that day, that bright warm day that had thrown a chill over him. A chill that in all the accolades and ceremony he had not been able to shake. It had begun when he stepped off the platform to thunderous applause. He had just taken the oath of loyalty to the Nazi government. His mother, tightly clutching Gretchen's hand, had been beaming through her tears in the front row. Even Bishop

Wagner appeared teary-eyed. A man's life is made of forward steps, and he had just taken a tremendous leap.

Afterward, he would plan sermons in his well-appointed study, and in the silence he could hear a trio of voices: Dr. Begg's, Paul Shraeder's, and his own father's. It had taken him months to come to the gripping realization that they all had been saying the same thing—like a symphony in his mind that he could not ignore.

If you go into the church, and the Nazis take power, I fear you will find yourself with a new enemy. The Jews.

You will be tested, Thomas.

The church is being tempted, seduced by this national pride. The church should have called the people to repentance long ago. They are our brothers and sisters.

When the old professor had said "they are our brothers and sisters," Thomas had been uncertain who "they" were. He had been too busy and too uncaring to find out. But now the man's words were plain: "They" were the Jews, the very ones the church—his church—was helping to destroy. There had been the day all Reich churches had been ordered to remove the cross and all Bibles.

In the last two years Thomas had been carried away in the vortex of his ascending career and the Nazi gains, but something was missing. Never had his preaching been more inspiring, never had his singing of the old church anthems been better—and never had he enjoyed it less. He saw the haunted eyes of the Jews on the streets, hurrying like rats caught in the light of day. He saw the random street beatings. And he saw his extended family, the Goldsteins, turned prisoner in their own home. There were times he felt the blood was on his own hands. And he had kept silent about the cancer that was threatening to kill him.

Then, there was the day the government ordered all the Reich churches to remove the cross and all Bibles from the church, Thomas reflected bitterly.

The outskirts of Berlin were coming into view. He shifted in his seat. *Begg told me I was responsible for telling the people they must not sell their souls to gain the world. I've done that.*

What were the dying man's words to his housekeeper?

Thomas does not believe, that is why I told him.

"Make him work for his faith, make him work for the truth, as he had once worked for a grade," Thomas mused.

The same long, tiled corridors, the same unsmiling SS guards, the same gilded eagles and swastika banners, the same study, the same dark-eyed man, only he was now wearing a drab army uniform. The same bishop grinning broadly as if he held a tantalizing secret. But unlike the first time, Thomas felt more wary than impressed and excited. He had a strong urge to tell these two men that, though he looked outwardly the same, he was not.

But I won't tell them that, he decided.

Wagner greeted him with the customary cordiality, pulling him aside and speaking in a lowered voice.

"Welcome, Thomas. Welcome back to Berlin."

"Thank you, Bishop Wagner."

"The fuehrer had some unexpected business come up. We will just wait quietly."

Hitler and a man Thomas didn't recognize were leaning over a large table near the long windows. Their voices were not hushed.

"The Swedish company has agreed to our terms, mein Fuehrer. I have just spoken to them on the phone. They will ship us their finest granite as soon as we request it."

Wagner bent close to Thomas' ear, "Albert Speer, the fuehrer's architect."

Hitler was nodding vigorously. "Excellent, Albert, excellent."

The leader turned abruptly to the churchmen, and for a moment it seemed to Thomas that the man's eyes were unfocused and that he didn't recognize them.

"What do you think of that, Wagner?"

"Sir?"

Hitler strolled toward them, hands in his pockets, smiling.

"Oh, don't pretend you didn't hear. Of course you were listening," he said.

"Well, I …" the bishop sputtered.

Thomas was surprised at the tremor of nervousness he detected in the normally confident voice.

"Wagner, churchmen must be unfailingly honest," Hitler teased.

"Yes, yes, of course."

Hitler's eyes narrowed on Thomas. "Who is this?"

"Pastor Thomas Picard of Munich, sir. He was part of the church leaders meeting two years ago. I brought him here today—"

"Of course, of course." He gave Thomas' hand a swift, limp hand-shake. "I suppose being younger than the bishop your hearing is better," he chuckled. "Now, to both of you—privy to the highest plans—I will give you a look at the future of the Third Reich. Few men have such a privilege."

Thomas said nothing; Wagner was sputtering again.

"Yes, of course, yes ..."

Hitler gave him a patronizing look. Once he had used this worm of the church, he didn't bother to conceal his true and deep disgust. He nodded to the table. "Come, I will show you."

A huge, colorful map of Europe lay across the table like the geog-raphy of a banquet feast. Hitler was rocking back and forth on his heels.

"The finest granite in Europe will be fashioned into monuments—victory monuments to the great Germany army!"

"Victory monuments?" Wagner spilled out in surprise.

Thomas knew they were thinking alike. *Victory monuments to the army. That meant military conquest. But the fuehrer recently said that the annexation of Austria was all he intended for expanding the Third Reich,* Thomas remembered. *He's said the Germans of Austria had wanted—in fact, begged—to be absorbed into the Third Reich. I'm confused.*

"Yes, Bishop Wagner. Victory monuments! Tributes to our splendid army!" He stabbed at the map. "I shall place a monument in each capital where the Nazi boot steps. Here, here, here, and here."

Thomas and Wagner were leaning forward. *Warsaw. Prague. Paris. Moscow.*

The casual voice of the architect pulled the two men from their shock.

"The Swedes were not entirely certain they wanted to do business with the Third Reich. They did some mumbling about Austria."

"A bloodless conquest," Hitler said in an abrupt, snarling voice.

Speer nodded. "Yes, yes, but you see, the Swedish nation greatly cherishes its history of neutrality, like Belgium does."

Hitler snorted in derision. "Perhaps we will need more stone than originally ordered. Perhaps we need a monument here to shake some neu-trality." He placed a thick fingertip on the map, obscuring Stockholm and almost the entire country. "A swastika will fly from the Eiffel Tower and in Trafalgar Square! I have seen it!"

Thomas swallowed and glanced at the bishop. He was obviously shaken.

Thomas looked back at the map. *Warsaw. Prague. Paris. London. Could this little man's ambitions come true?* He stepped back from the desk, suddenly wanting to be out of this room that seemed heavy and airless—just like that eerie evening when the Nazis had harrased Bonhoeffer. The movement caught the fuehrer's eye.

"What are you here for?" he barked at Wagner.

"The appointment, sir, to the church."

"Ah, the beloved church. She safeguards Germany's soul." He laughed and sank into a deep leather chair, as if the devouring of countries had exhausted him. He reached for a crystal dish and began popping sugar cubes into his mouth. He peered up at Thomas through the lock of dark hair that hung over one eye.

"You have your own little victory monument, Herr Picard."

"Sir?"

"Mein Fuehrer, I haven't had a chance to tell him," Wagner broke in hurriedly.

Hitler waved an impatient hand. "After two years of this church conflict, we are at peace. Men like you Picard, and the good, pure bishop here are entrusted with the church. I have given you the power. I am the way, the truth, the life!" He broke into another spasm of laughing.

The stuffy room felt chilled to Thomas. Instinctively he stepped backward. Wagner was horrified at the fuehrer's imprudence. He knew what his words would do to a sensitive young pastor like Thomas.

He forced his voice to steady. "Thomas, the fuehrer and I have called you here to tell you we have appointed you to succeed Pastor Holtz at the Kaiser-Wilhelm Church. I have already spoken with your mother, and she is very excited and proud." His own excitement reasserted itself as he grabbed Thomas' arm. "The biggest church in Germany, Thomas!"

The biggest church in Germany. Thomas could feel the eyes of both men fastened on him. He was amazed at how soft and calm his own voice sounded.

"Sir . . . I . . . am of course, very, very surprised. But I do need to go home and think and pray about it."

"Of course, Thomas, of course," Wagner continued enthusiastically.

Thomas cast a hurried look at the leader still slumped in the chair. He was smiling as he reached for another handful of sugar.

A cold, driving rain kept Thomas in the corner of the Berlin train station, staring moodily through a grimy window. A sharp pain stabbed him between the shoulder blades signifying tension and fatigue. An inner voice whispered, *you should be exceedingly grateful for this illustrious advancement in your career. You should be as proud as your mother is. You've attained a place that few men—and certainly not of your youth— would ever attain. You're riding the wake of the Reich's rising star.*

But Thomas only felt cold, tired, lonely, and afraid.

Someone to the left of him began coughing. He glanced at his fellow traveler—a slight, gray-haired man. Thomas looked around.

"Pastor Niemöller, are you all right?"

The man regarded him with question and caution. He wiped his brow.

"I'm always a little hoarse after speaking. My wife tells me I get too excited." His thin smile evaporated. "Have we met?"

"No sir, not directly. We were at a pastors meeting at the chancellery two years ago."

Niemöller leaned forward slightly until recognition lit his face. "Picard."

"Yes, sir."

"You are the young man with the fine voice."

"Well ..."

"I remember now. You were Alex Begg's star pupil, his protégé."

"You knew Doctor Begg?"

"Quite well. He was my professor, and we were good friends. You have a church in Munich?"

Thomas nodded. "But Bishop Wagner summoned me here to offer me ... another church ... the Kaiser-Wilhelm Church.

"Ah ..."

Thomas felt the man's awkwardness. He had been offered the largest Reich-controlled church in Germany, and this slender man beside him was opposed to everything a Reich church represented.

"Professor Begg's star pupil in the Kaiser-Wilhelm." Thomas' voice spoke far more to Niemöller than his words.

"You're not happy and pleased with this appointment?" he asked gently.

Thomas let out a wrenching sigh. "This is everything my mother has ever wanted." He studied the floor tiles a full minute in silence, unaware that the older pastor was praying.

"I should be happy. I want to be thrilled about it." He looked Niemöller in the face. "But I'm not, no sir, I'm not happy. Frankly, I . . . I can't remember the last time I could say I was happy." He thought suddenly of the sunlit barley fields and church of Dachau. *Had it been that long?*

He glanced at the man, suddenly embarrassed. "I'm sorry. I don't know why I'm telling you this . . . except somehow you remind me of my father."

"I will take that as a compliment then."

"Yes, he was a very good man. I wish . . . I wish I had listened to him more."

"We all have this wish, Thomas. I would tell you to look at the past only briefly, only long enough to learn from it, then go forward!"

The young pastor nodded slowly. "Yes. Only now I'm looking back to hear Professor Begg, Paul Shraeder, and my father. I can't get their words, their warnings out of my mind. And I see the Jews, and my stomach churns. I see them at night."

"What do Begg, Shraeder, and your father tell you?"

"They tell me I've been unfaithful to the truth. They tell me I've hardened my heart so I could reach what I wanted, that I had my own conquest. . . ."

"Thomas, God will not be mocked. When evil is aggressive the church—the true church—must not retreat. When a government becomes increasingly ungodly, the church must meet that darkness with light. The darkness must not overtake it."

"Two powers colliding," Thomas said softly.

"Pardon me?"

"Something my father said. The church and the state colliding."

Niemöller nodded. "If only more Germans had such vision. This conflict in your soul is the light God has given you warring with the darkness that has come to surround you."

"I let them . . . I let them take down the cross in my Munich church," Thomas said in a choking voice.

Niemöller touched his arm. "It is not too late for the light, Pastor Picard."

"Yes, I know." Thomas nodded slowly.

"Yet I remind you this light is free but very costly."

"Yes."

"I'm sure you've been praying about this."

"Oh, yes sir, very much." Thomas smiled weakly. "My prayer times have grown to feel like wrestling contests!"

"That is good, very good. Now go home and read one of the gospels. Read it over and over, and it will speak to you about this Reich-church appointment far better than I ever could."

"Though you could," Thomas said, smiling again.

"Though I could," Niemöller nodded. "There's my train. I will pray for you, Thomas Picard," he said as he got up.

"And I will pray for you, sir."

Niemöller paused and turned at the door. "You know, I'm just going as far as Dahlm and I usually just take a streetcar. But tonight, well, I felt impressed to take the train."

He smiled and waved.

Though it was well past midnight, Thomas wanted no other creature comfort than to lower himself into a good hot bath. Blumenstrasse was a darkened corridor with only one chink of light burning in the Picard front window. Thomas was not surprised that his mother had left a light for him. But he was very surprised that his key turned effortlessly in the lock. Frau Picard was meticulous on home security. Immediately he was assaulted by an alloyed smell of cologne and vodka. He hurried into the front room.

"What are you doing here?" he asked sharply.

Otto Beck was comfortably ensconced in a chair.

"Thomas, that is a very unfriendly greeting for a beloved family member," Otto chuckled.

Thomas glanced up the stairs.

"She's not here, neither one of them."

Thomas concealed his alarm. He set his bag down and tossed his hat and coat into a chair. "What do you want?"

"Patience, patience, nephew. I'm willing to forget and forgive the way you treated me at our last meeting."

"I'd prefer you didn't forget, Uncle Otto."

"Sit down, Thomas. We need to talk. I will tell you where your mother and sister are."

Thomas sat across from him, tense. "I'm listening but make it short."

"Long ago I recognized you were the smartest one in this household. Your—"

"One word about my father or brother and I will throw you out."

"You are in a temper tonight, Thomas. Did your meeting with the fuehrer not go well? I have heard he can be a frightening man."

Thomas couldn't conceal his surprise this time. Otto was flexing his power.

Otto pressed his fingertips together, his legs stretched out. He was relaxed, confident, and in control. Thomas came to a sickening realization that this man had likely been waiting for this moment of revenge and power for a very long time.

"I have quit the teeth trade, Thomas. I've been appointed party leader of Munich."

Thomas said nothing.

"I am in control of the Gestapo file on the Picard family."

Still Thomas was silent.

"I know, for example, that a certain Protestant pastor has been offered a position in Berlin. Very impressive, Thomas. I also know that this pastor has been to hear Bonhoeffer. In fact, he has the man's writings in his possession—writings the government has declared illegal. I know that his younger brother was killed fighting against the government. His father was not a party member. His mother still pays their Jew friends a percentage of the family business. Bishop Wagner has not seen this file. He would be very troubled I think—if he were made aware of it."

"What do you want?"

"I want you to give the store to me. I want a secondary income in case the Nazi party finds itself in straits."

"I thought your Nazi party was invincible."

Otto shrugged. "I've spelled it out for you. I talked to Maria about it on the way to the train station. She'll stay on as manager and draw a decent salary. She will do whatever her precious firstborn says....You know, your father and I had a conversation once. He was very snobby, I remember, telling me what a fine thing it was to own your own livelihood. "And of course, all those years of you and Rudi and your little teeth-trade jokes. I'm moving to Munich. I want that fine pleasure of owning my own livelihood. 'Picard's Fine Instruments.' " He laughed.

"Or you make things difficult for my appointment to Berlin."

"Exactly."

"Get out."

Otto's eyebrows raised. He leaned forward.

Thomas stood up. "That's right. Your bribery didn't work. Now get out."

"You don't know where Maria is!"

"I'll find out."

Otto was shouting. "From your Jew friends? No! They don't even know. She has gone to Berlin—and you are too late!"

"What?"

"You've been so busy with your church, Pastor Picard. Have you not noticed your own mother's sorrow?" Otto made a clucking noise.

"What are you talking about?"

"Your mother has been under a terrible strain lately. And Gretchen has been so . . . so unmanageable."

Thomas' mind was racing. *This pompous and repellent man is telling the truth. Mother has been unusually withdrawn and haunted-looking.* He closed his eyes in fear. *What is happening?*

"Tell me."

Otto stood up. "Maria has shown good sense at last. She's taken Gretchen to a home for mental derelicts in Berlin."

"No . . ." Thomas groaned.

"Yes."

"Where?" Thomas stood up, his anger and fear and fatigue boiling over. All he could see was this pig-faced man who represented so much evil. He grabbed him by the collar and shook him.

"Tell me!"

But Otto was silent and smirking.

Thomas punched him in the face with such power that it sent Otto backward.

"That's from Rudi. He wanted to do it all those years."

"You're too late! And I will tell you more. I have seen the orders through the party. Hitler intends to liquidate those homes for crazy people. You're too late, Thomas Picard!" He wiped the blood from his lip.

"You will be sorry, very sorry you have treated me this way," Otto snarled. "You have made a big mistake."

Thomas was grabbing his coat and bag. "You and I agree there, Uncle Otto."

• • •

Aaron Goldstein had just given the blessing over the morning meal when pounding on the front door froze them in their places. Sophie's hands went to her mouth to stifle a silent scream. Maria gripped the table for support. Abraham's fork was suspended in mid-air. Aaron sat calmly with his hands folded. They all exchanged glances. Abraham finally found his voice and Maria her feet. She jumped up and rushed to the window. Abraham spoke deliberately.

"I'll go."

Maria was surprised at her father's tone as he leaned toward his wife. "You will do exactly as our Maria says," he ordered quietly.

Sophie's eyes widened as she nodded.

Abraham returned with heavy steps. Three men in SS uniforms came in behind him—and a man in civilian dress. Otto Beck.

They assessed each other in silence. Beck's eyes darted until he found the young woman still standing at the window. *A beautiful girl.* She eyed him with expected coldness.

Aaron Goldstein rose slowly, folding his napkin deliberately.

"Good morning," he said without tremor.

One of the SS officers spoke up curtly. "You are Herr Aaron Goldstein?"

"Yes, I am Aaron Goldstein."

"This is your son Abraham?"

"My oldest son, Abraham."

"Any Noahs or Moseses?" one of the other officers said, laughing.

Otto spoke. "There are only two other sons. One in Bonn, the other, the youngest, has run away."

Sophie cried out, and Abraham went to stand behind his mother. "It's all right, Mama," he soothed.

"What is this about?" Aaron asked evenly. "As you can see we were just sitting down to our breakfast."

"We have been ordered to escort you and your son to SS headquarters for questioning, Herr Goldstein."

"But why?" Sophie gasped. "They have done nothing, nothing!"

The commanding officer spoke slowly ... reluctantly. "I have orders."

"Abraham, you will fetch our bags," Aaron said.

He nodded and hurried up the stairs.

Aaron took Sophie's hands in his and looked deep into her eyes. "I love you, Sophie Goldstein."

She nodded mutely, her tears spilling over.

"Listen to Maria."

Abraham was at his father's side with two leather satchels. Sophie knew then. *They had known this moment was coming. Her Aaron had been prepared.* They released each other. The men pulled on their coats and hats. The SS were stone-faced and silent.

Aaron hesitated as his eyes found Maria across the room. So lovely in her deep-blue dress. She came to him.

"Papa," she said steadily.

He nodded. They had said all the words they needed to say between them already.

He reached out one slender finger to touch her chin. "You will remember."

Still tearless, she nodded.

Then the SS led the two Jews from their home to one of the waiting cars. Otto stood appraising the room, appraising the two women. Maria stood beside her mother, her arm around her. Though a thousand things filled her mind to say to this evil man, she kept her mouth firmly clamped. Sophie didn't have such discipline.

"You are an evil man, Otto Beck, such a dishonor to your sister!"

"You should be begging me for mercy, Jewish scum!" Otto shouted.

Maria's arm tightened. "You have gotten what you came for, please leave."

"I will not beg mercy from the son of the devil!" Sophie continued. "You strutting around in your importance. You are nothing but rottenness inside!"

"Mama—"

Beck's face turned red. "You will regret your tongue, Frau Goldstein." He turned and hurried down the steps to the car.

The Blumenstrasse telegraph had transmitted the news with lightning speed. The SS had come for Aaron Goldstein. A few stood weeping and watching behind their parted curtains, but most had come outside to stand on their sidewalks. The car pulled away slowly. People were lining each side. Men, women with flour on their arms, children, all unsmiling. Some ventured boldly into the street itself, as if they might keep the big black car from taking the good Aaron Goldstein away. But their gesture was too late.

At the corner, the group of boys playing street soccer didn't seem to understand the honking, the shouts, and the gestures of the men inside the car. The car came to a standstill. Then everyone heard the sound of someone running, and turned.

Maria Goldstein was clearly still the fleetest of foot on Blumenstrasse. And many, when they saw her, began to cry. She was running with her dark hair flying behind her, her dress whipped like a blue blur. She was carrying a violin case. She came to the car and pounded on the window.

"What do you want?" the driver demanded.

The SS officer who had questioned Aaron got out of the car and walked around to her. Maria looked into his eyes for a shred of mercy.

"That is your father's?" he asked.

She nodded, unable to speak.

He reached out and took it gently. He stared at it a moment, then looked up at her.

"He will keep this. I promise you." He turned and reentered the car.

The big black car was forced to back up the length of Blumenstrasse and turn at the corner.

10
When Life Is a Sermon

It was the quiet she had wanted, a peaceful stillness declared from every room of the house. But this terrible, accusing silence wasn't what she had expected. She slumped into a deep leather chair, her typical dignity absent. She was utterly spent. For the first time in many years, Frau Picard began to cry. The gentle tears became body-shaking sobs.

The front door burst open with hurried steps. She stood up weakly, wiping away her tears. It wasn't Thomas; it was Sophie.

"Oh Maria, you're home!"

Sophie collapsed into her friend's arms; Maria didn't stiffen. In a way, it was like old times.

"Sophie, Sophie, there, there, calm down. What is the matter?"

But Sophie couldn't stop sobbing.

"They took my father and brother yesterday," answered Maria Goldstein, who had followed her mother. Frau Picard was shocked at the hollowness in the young girl's voice. *She is so pale and ...* Maria Picard wanted to scream. *What has happened to our world?*

"Who came for Aaron and Abraham?" she asked, although she knew.

"The Nazis, the SS ... they ... oh, Maria ..." Sophie gasped.

"Otto Beck brought them to our house," Maria Goldstein intoned flatly.

Maria Picard felt her insides squeeze. *Where is Thomas?* She felt faint, but she managed to lead the crying woman to a sofa.

"Sit here. Now, Sophie, tell me."

"There is nothing more to tell, Frau Maria," the young Maria responded. "They took my father and brother to the warehouse by the train station. It appears to be a general roundup of Jews. I have spent all day there. They will tell us nothing."

"What can we do, Maria?" Sophie gasped. "Maria, I must ask you—"

"Mama, we should leave now."

Frau Picard stiffened. "You are accusing me, Maria Goldstein, because of my brother. I can see it in your eyes."

Maria Goldstein said nothing.

Maria stood up, facing her namesake. "Well, I had nothing to do with this. This is Otto's work and I'm ... I'm ashamed and appalled. He is a Nazi leader now, he has such power. But there is nothing I can do."

Sophie gripped her daughter's arm. "Please, daughter, don't talk this way. Now we must try to help each other."

"Mama, you have heard Frau Picard. She has told you herself—there is nothing she can do."

Sophie stood up, her eyes begging.

Maria Goldstein took her mother's arm gently and led her from the house.

Again the quiet. "There is nothing ... What can I do?" Maria Picard whispered.

* * *

Maria Picard felt listless and apathetic. She couldn't imagine where Thomas could have disappeared to for two days without sending her word. It was not like him to be so thoughtless. But even that couldn't stir any passion. She was beyond anger. She watched Sophie and Maria from her bedroom window as they walked to the warehouse to inquire for Aaron and Abraham. Maria found herself gripping the curtain. *They have each other. They have lost as I have lost. I don't want them to lose each other,* she thought. *I wonder if they have enough food to eat? My kitchen is so full ...*

She entered through the Goldstein's back door and stood in the kitchen. This room was as familiar as her own. *Thirty years ...* She was smiling suddenly at Sophie's little decorating schemes. She was checking the cupboards when she heard a pounding at the door.

This time there were only two. Two SS in their spotless uniforms and shiny boots.

"Yes?" she asked.

One of them consulted a paper. "We have come for Frau Sophie Goldstein."

Maria stepped back, stumbling slightly. "What?"

The young man didn't mask his irritation. "We have come for Sophie Goldstein, a Jew."

Maria Picard found time suspended in that brief moment. She thought of Michael as he had looked at her on their wedding day. *He was so proud. He called me his jewel. Yes, he had been so proud of me. I saw it in his eyes, heard it in his voice. I'll hear it again.*

Her voice was firm. "I am Frau Sophie Goldstein, Jew. And I will thank you to take your hat off in my home!"

The two pink-faced men pulled their hats off in unison.

"Now what do you want? I have soup to make."

"We ... we ..." They shoved the papers at her. "We have orders to take you to headquarters."

"Because I am a Jew you think you can come and make such a demand? Such nerve!"

"Now—"

"I will get my hat and coat and you will wait while I leave a note."

And this Maria Picard did. Her head held high, the men led her to the big black car.

• • •

He was at home: Blumenstrasse, where there was supposed to be some predictability and stability. A sanctuary. But as he stepped into his own cold, dark house, and then the Goldstein's, his fear mounted.

Maria Goldstein was pale and calm as she regarded him.

"Are you ill?" he asked.

She shook her head.

"Maria, do you know where my mother is? I haven't seen her or been able to speak to her since Monday."

"Where have you been?" she asked in a flat voice.

He ignored her question. "Where is Frau Sophie?" he asked.

"She's upstairs resting."

He licked his dry lips. "And your father?"

"The Nazis took him and Abraham five days ago."

He reached for the wall. He could think of nothing to say.

"Where is Gretchen?" she whispered.

He looked up and they stared at each other, comfortless and unable to reach across the gulf.

"Mother took her to a home in Berlin. For mental patients. It took me days to get permission to bring her home . . ." he broke off visibly shaken.

Maria looked away, biting her lip, hugging herself. *How could things get worse than this? To think of what Gretchen had gone through . . .*

His voice was hoarse. "Maria, what has happened to us?"

She bent her head.

"Please tell me where my mother is? What has happened, please?"

Maria hadn't cried since her father was taken. She had steeled herself against the pain. Crying had been a luxury she couldn't afford. But at the sound of this old friend's voice she broke.

"Thomas . . ." She reached out and touched his face.

"Please tell me," he groaned.

She pulled a paper from her pocket. "The Nazis came for my mother the day before yesterday. We weren't here. We . . . had gone to see if we could take anything to Papa and Abraham. And . . . and Frau Maria must have been here when they came . . . and . . . oh, Thomas, they took her. She . . . she went in Mama's place!"

He read the note written in his mother's neat and correct penmanship.

> *Sophie, I have loved you like a sister, though I have been poor in showing you. Please forgive me. Thomas, you know how much I love you. Keep seeking the truth. All my love to my sweet Gretchen.*

He folded the note slowly. "Mother . . ."

Somehow Maria's voice reached him.

"Eric Hager came over this morning to see if he could help us in any way. He went down to the warehouse for us. Thomas, all the Jews have been deported to Poland."

• • •

The sunlight pouring through the stained-glass windows cast a collage of colors on the stone floor of the vast Munich church. The young pastor came to his pulpit. His freshly shaven face was flushed. Many of the single women in the church thought Thomas Picard had never looked more handsome.

"I have so much to say to you this morning ... and so little time to say it. I wish I could sit down with each of you individually and talk with you because I want you to understand. But that isn't possible. I want to thank so many of you for welcoming me into your hearts and homes. For that I will always be very, very grateful."

Some of the congregation cast nervous looks and stirred uneasily in their seats. This wasn't sounding like the typical, well-prepared sermon. This was sounding like some kind of farewell. Thomas sensed their thoughts.

"This is my last Sunday with you. After this morning I will no longer be your pastor. If I thought I could remain here and preach the truth, I would. But I know, finally, that the truth cannot be preached in freedom from a Reich church. I feel very responsible for what I have allowed and what I have been an accessory to since this became a Reich church. It has not been a church under the Lordship of Jesus Christ. It has been a puppet of Berlin. I have been a puppet of Berlin." His voice trembled. "I pray God will forgive me for leading you astray. But a brave man told me recently that it is never too late to try to set things right. That is what I'm trying to do this morning before I leave.

"I tell you plainly—it is wrong for a government to run a church. And this government is evil. It is bent on the destruction of the German people. We have been intoxicated with all its promises that feed our bodies and deliver our souls to the devil. He gripped the edge of the pulpit. "When you or I persecute our Jewish brothers and sisters, we persecute the Lord Himself. This must not be! Pastor Bonhoeffer and Pastor Niemöller and a handful of others have been saying this for the past few years. And now they are silenced. I have been in the darkness; I have led you in darkness; and now I can only fervently pray that each one of you will come out, come out into the light!"

Then Thomas raised his voice in song in the vast sanctuary, tears streaming down his face. "A mighty fortress is our God, a bulwark never failing ..."

• • •

"Was there something you wanted?" Thomas asked tiredly.

"Yes." Eric Hager stood nervously twisting his hat on the Picard front steps. "I was ... Fraulein Maria asked me to tell you."

"Do you know where they are?" Thomas snapped. "Gretchen keeps asking."

The young boy wet his lips and nodded slowly.

Thomas sighed. "Why do I know I'm not going to like what you're about to tell me."

"Fraulein Maria and her mother left for Poland yesterday—to try to join their family."

"Poland, "Thomas repeated numbly.

"I'm sorry, sir."

The twlight had deepened as Thomas crossed back to his home. Never had this place on Blumenstrasse seemed so lonely and cold.

PART 2

Max and Emilie
1942–1943

If you have run with footmen and they have tired you out, then how can you compete with horses? If you fall down in a land of peace, how will you do in the thicket of the Jordan?

—Jeremiah 12:5 NASB

11
Portraits of Nightfall

Tegel Prison, Berlin, Spring 1942

The rats always came just after midnight. Predictable nocturnal visitors to his cell, he welcomed them as something living and as a distraction. Though he had little way to observe the passage of day and night by outside light, he did have his watch. A fine Swiss watch, quite expensive, that amazingly the guards had not discovered and confiscated. When he realized he'd been stripped of all his possessions but this fine gold timepiece, he had smiled ruefully to himself. *What an odd thing for a man to have in prison, when keeping time was of no value—except as a sharp reminder.*

A thin, rectangular opening, not barred or covered with glass, was cut along the top of the door letting in occasional sounds, almost ineffectual light, and the always-present smell of mildew. He was in a small eight-by-ten room with walls and the floor made out of stone. A narrow, rusting bed frame was attached to the wall. It held a thin cotton mattress. It had taken him weeks to tolerate the smell of the mattress. Now it smelled like him—or he smelled like the mattress. A metal bucket in the corner, emptied by the guards every few days, served his personal needs. Nothing else. This had been his home for nearly five months—actually, by the scratches on the wall, 157 days.

Max Farber was allowed no visitors and only restricted contact with other prisoners. The guards pushed in a metal tray of food twice a day.

He always welcomed this—not the stuff they called food, but the attention. It gave him a small sense of being remembered. They had not dropped him into this dungeon and forgotten him. He closed his eyes. *Had they ... could they ... forget him? Joseph? Eric?* There were days he tried vainly to not think of her because it was too much of a torment. *Emilie ...*

The first week of imprisonment had been the worst. He had stepped calmly into the cell at the guards rude, mocking comments and orders. His calmness had quickly turned to claustrophobia and panic. He ran around the perimeter of the room. He pounded on the door. He felt as if they were pulling the oxygen from the room somehow, suffocating him. His exertion left him drenched and drained and ill in the frigid room for several days. He lay in a stupor, all his grand boasts and courage mocking him from the past. Only with great effort did he control his desire to scream.

The second and third week he retreated into a stupor of sleep and lethargy, hardly eating or drinking, a strange reversal for this vigorous, healthy young man. Continually sleeping and waking into this nightmare. Finally, by the second month of confinement, his true self began to emerge. *I can survive this,* he told himself. *It's just another challenge—my greatest challenge.*

He exercised like an Olympic athlete—hundreds of pushups and sit-ups a day. Jogging and shadow-boxing. He pretended he was on skis—one of his best sports—going down his favorite slopes. He hummed all the music scores he could remember and practiced them on an imaginary piano. He recited the plots of books he'd read, stimulating his mind with thousands of questions—especially the *Scarlet Pimpernel,* with its hero Sir Percy Blackney. He reviewed geography and history. A lover of astronomy, he plotted the night sky that he could not see. He did complex arithmetic problems in his mind. Anything, everything, a constant activity—mental or physical. By nightfall, precisely at eight, he was truly tired, in part because of the insufficient diet. He would sleep until the rats came, then drop back to sleep.

He would survive, for Max Farber, German patriot, was in training for freedom.

Berlin

It was the staccato music every citizen of the Third Reich dreaded—the incessant, impatient pounding on the front door. Even the most devoted Nazi feared it. Had a neighbor interpreted some disloyalty? Sometimes, depending on the perceived offense, the knocking was accomplished with a rifle butt. Either fashion, it meant the Gestapo or SS had come calling. This knocking came from a firm, determined hand. And it pulled her from her dreams.

Half-dreams really. She lay across her sun-washed bed. The man in her dream had been playing the piano and singing, filling the huge house with his talent while she clipped roses in the garden. The knocking penetrated her peace. She sat up. Reality was this lonely bedroom. Reality was this quiet house on Tiergartenstrasse. So who had come on this beautiful spring afternoon? She felt her pulse quicken. She went to the open window and peered through the sheer curtains. A long black car. This spring day, when she had drowsed off into dreams, the Gestapo had come.

There was a soft knock at her bedroom door and she hurried across the room. An older man, pale and trembling, stood there. A dog was whining at his side.

"Emilie? I ..."

"I know. I heard them." She glanced back at her room. Should she take the suitcase she always kept prepared in the closet? Pulling it out would frighten Josef. So she reached for her purse, instead. Even so, his eyebrows went up. She steadied her voice.

"Just in case."

She stood at the full-length mirror, smoothing her dress, checking her hair. *Presentable for ... what?* she thought with amusement. Holding hands, the old man and the young woman started down the stairs. The pounding began again. The dog began a furious barking.

"Percy, hush! Get down. Josef, perhaps you should hold him."

The old man nodded. The woman drew a breath and opened the door.

"Good day, Frau Farber."

Usually friendly, she could only nod.

"You are requested to appear at Gestapo headquarters. We have come to escort you."

There was nothing she could say, no protest she could form. There was no point.

"Why?" the old man asked. The dog kept growling.

"We are not privy to orders, Herr Morgan. We are only obedient to them," one of the officers said with a stiff bow.

"Is my niece under arrest?" the old doctor rasped.

The woman put her arm around him. "It's all right, Uncle Josef. They have no reason to arrest me. I—"

"They have no reason to arrest most of whom they arrest, Emilie," the man said with asperity. "But that doesn't stop them."

Emilie smothered a smile in spite of the ominous looks of the men.

"If you are ready, Frau Farber ... you really don't want to keep the Gestapo waiting." *Nazi menace,* she had grown to recognize it immediately.

She ruffled the dog's ears affectionately. "Be a good boy." She looked into the old man's eyes. "Promise me you'll not worry. You'll just pray."

He nodded wordlessly, tears filling his eyes.

She kissed his cheek. "I will be back. I will."

The quick drive was silent. The men in the front seat stared straight ahead. She gazed at the streets and was flooded with a thousand memories. For all the calm and confidence she had shown Josef, this might be her last view of this city for a long time. The first time she had seen Berlin, back in the summer of 1936, it had been so very different than this. She was relaxed and happy then. *He* had been beside her, smiling, kind, confident. Even if she hadn't been in love with him then, there had been much to like and trust in him. She shook her head against the memory. She should really not think of him now, when she needed all her clear resources. Not when she was preparing to meet men who held the power of life and death.

• • •

The Nazis leaders had gathered in the chancellery for an informal meeting. At the far end of the table, a tall, blond, blue-eyed man in polished boots and an SS uniform clenched his hands under the table to conceal his frustration with this philosophical discussion. It was boring, and it was a waste of his time. He had someone waiting for him in a hotel suite on the Kurfurstendamm. Reich business consumed the daylight, his other passions, the darkness. At thirty-eight, his professional zeal and hedonistic lifestyle had fused perfectly, and his handsome frame bore no mark or attitude of dissipation. Of all the leaders gathered this balmy spring evening in the chancellery conference room, including Goebbels and Göring, Reinhard Heydrich was by whispered rumor and tacit agreement second in power to Adolf Hitler. His decisive brutality had garnered him a nickname in and out of Germany: Hanging Heydrich. As head of the military police, Heydrich's responsibility had broadened. He was responsible for an incredible network of informers who could bring him information on enemies within the Reich. He set up concentration camps in Poland. He created and controlled the "Office of Jewish Emigration" that issued select permits for Jewish emigration. He was the primary strategist for the 1938 "Night of Breaking Glass" retaliation against the Jews. He was in charge of planning Nazi terrorist attacks in Britain. And now he was the chief architect for the Nazi secret directive called "the final solution."

On this seductively warm evening, he was thinking of a woman. Not his wife, not his mistress, not the woman waiting at the hotel. Another woman only four streets over from this very building. He could remember no woman whom he had ever wanted this intensely. It made him feel weak and vulnerable. *A Nordic warrior should have no chink in his armor,* he told himself firmly. It was that thought that controlled the war within himself, that had restrained him from forcibly taking her. Yet in the back of his mind, always there, he thought of her. *It's only a matter of time—time of my own choosing—until she becomes mine body and soul,* he inwardly vowed.

Himmler's brusque voice pulled him from his campaign.

"There are many enemies of the Reich. We all know that. *The Gestapo* is a vigilant in pursuing them." The men at the table understood the taunt.

Heydrich's face was impassive, his voice pleasant. "You are suggesting some lack in my duties, Herr Himmler?"

Himmler leaned forward. "I am suggesting a little negligence in the matter of one of the Reich's enemies that has not been fully investigated, fully punished, Herr Heydrich. Perhaps this should be made a Gestapo matter again."

Heydrich was furious. "The case against German industrialist Max-imillian Farber is under my personal jurisdiction, Herr Himmler, and I will prosecute it fully," he spat. "If you have a complaint with that, I suggest you take it up with our fuehrer who gave me this jurisdiction."

The table was deathly still and quiet. A contest between vipers was always fascinating, always deadly. Hitler loved the sparring. It brought out the best and kept everyone sharp.

• • •

Max Farber was tall, broad-shouldered, blue-eyed, blond, and handsome. He was very well traveled, fluent in English, French, and Italian. One of Germany's richest men, Max was the most sought after bachelor. He was a monument to Aryan excellence, and he moved in all of Berlin's highest social circles.

But now he sat in the dank bowels of a Berlin prison. The healthy tan-and-ruddy cheeks had paled, his hair was limp, and he had lost twenty pounds. The bruises and cuts from the initial beatings had faded leaving no outward scar. After nearly six months of confinement, this monument had changed.

Max Farber woke up with a jerk. He was shocked to find himself sitting on the floor, his back against the damp wall, his legs outstretched. A surge of panic welled up in him; his heart beat so erratically that he felt light-headed. *I can't remember the last few days. Is this the first stages of insanity?* He had tried so hard . . . but to find himself on the floor with no memory. He felt an urge to scream, to hear his own voice.

"Max!"

Hollowly it reverberated off the walls, weak, but his own voice. It gave him a moment of comfort and satisfaction. On his knees he went to the bucket in the corner, moved it aside, then clawed frantically at the dirt underneath. He ignored the pain and his own weakness. After many minutes his fingers folded around a cloth-covered object. He exhaled with relief. His one possession—his watch. In the grimy light he peered at it. *Eight-thirty in the morning.* Breathing a little easier, he carefully refolded it and replaced this now-priceless possession. It was a remnant of his identity; it was a slender connection to the present. It could be used for a bribe.

He crawled to his cot and with the same tender fingers felt the marks he had scratched on the underside of the metal frame. Each group represented a month. It was sometime in April. He pulled himself up onto the cot. His fingers feeling for the day marks he had made in the brick. Three marks. April third. *How long since I made that last mark?* he wondered.

I had a fever. His heart returned to a steady pace. His breathing came easier. *Of course. That explains this amnesia. I've been sick.* He heard the scrape of a door outside his cell, the sound of steps. He sat up. *Reality.* His breakfast was coming. But, instead of the tray shoved in as usual, the door swung open. A rectangle of light. Max strained his eyes in the dimness to see.

"You better?" The voice, while not unkind, was not warm and inviting either.

Max nodded. "I suppose I've been kind of sick."

The voice grunted. "Likely a fever. Everyone gets it. Some don't wake up. You're lucky."

"Lucky," Max repeated.

The guard set the breakfast tray down. "Better eat. Fresh water too."

Max was stunned at this unexpected kindness. "Thank you."

The man turned back to the door.

"Please!" Max said, surprised at the strength of his own voice. "Please, could you tell me the date?"

But the door had swung shut with a groan and slam of blunt finality. Max gripped the edge of the cot to steady himself. Losing track of time only showed he was passing each day of his life in a stinking Nazi prison. He hung his head. *All these months I've exercised my mind and body to stave off madness. Now I'm slipping. . . .*

A low voice came to him from the other side of the door. The guard had remained.

"It's Thursday, April 6, 1942." Then the retreating steps.

After he had eaten the thin soup and stale bread and washed his face, he updated his calendar. He felt better. Someone had spoken to him. Someone had given him something beyond a curse or kick. He sat cross-legged on his bed, and in that half-twilight of his room he felt a little like the old Max. The Max on the library floor at home on Tiergartenstrasse making paper airplanes for Percy to chase. *Percy. If only I could reach out and feel the dog's head resting on my knee.*

Max smiled, feeling better. "I am Maximillian Farber, youngest son of Irwin Eric Farber. My oldest brother is Irwin Farber, head of Farber Company. My next oldest brother is Eric Farber, officer of the German army medical corp. I live on Tiergartenstrasse in Berlin. I am thirty-seven years old. My best friend is Dr. Josef Morgan. I have another friend; he's a three-year-old wire-hair terrier named Sir Percy Blackney."

He breathed deeply of the fetid air. He could not . . . he could not say her name to this room, the one closest to his heart. His eyes closed.

"God . . . help me . . ."

• • •

Emilie was led to an inner office at Gestapo headquarters. A tall, thin man in a gray suit stood regarding her from dark, hooded eyes. She waited nervously. She judged him to be in his early thirties. She was puzzled. *There is something familiar about him.* He stood watching her with obvious speculation.

Emilie Farber was a beautiful woman as she stood there in the bland outer office. Her dark-chestnut hair waved and curled around her shoulders. She wore a tan skirt and white blouse that concealed her six-and-a-halfmonths of pregnancy. *Very simple dress, yet classic.* The man smiled inside. *She looked like a rich man's wife. Cool and composed. Yet she is nervous.* That pleased him.

"Sit down, Frau Farber," he said in a detached voice. "My name is Karl Beck."

She could see he expected her to recognize his name, but she didn't. She said nothing.

"You are here to answer my questions about Pastor Dietrich Bonhoeffer, Frau Farber," he said, while lighting a cigarette.

Emilie was momentarily stunned. "Pastor Bonhoeffer! I assumed this was about my husband."

He exhaled a long trail of smoke. "I have nothing to say about the traitor Maximillian Farber."

"But—"

"You will answer my questions about your friend Pastor Bonhoeffer."

Emilie didn't know whether she should be disappointed or relieved.

"What do you want to know about Pastor Bonhoeffer?" she returned evenly.

His smile was a fractional lengthening of his thin lips. "I want to know where he is."

"I have no idea. I haven't seen him in well over a year."

"When was the last time?"

"I can't remember precisely—sometime last fall."

He consulted his paper, his eyebrows contracting. "He visited your apartment last October. You were alone with him for just over an hour."

Emilie felt herself blush, but she kept her eyes level with his.

"What were you doing?" he asked with a smirk.

"We were talking."

"Talking . . . talking with your bodies perhaps?"

It was difficult for her to control her voice. "Pastor Bonhoeffer is an honorable man, Herr Beck, aside from being a devout Christian. I am a married woman—and also a Christian. I am . . . very insulted by your implication."

He shrugged and focused on the ceiling above her head. "Then tell me what you talked about."

A conversation that had taken place over a year ago, she thought. Yet in truth, Emilie could remember it perfectly. Perfectly enough to know she didn't want to share it with this ugly-minded man.

"I don't remember."

"You are lying."

"We talked of our shared faith. That is all I remember."

"He must have told you who his friends are, where he goes to conduct his illegal seminary."

"He never told me any of that. He wouldn't. He knew he was being followed. He wouldn't have put me at risk by telling me information like that."

"He has friends all over Germany who, like the traitors they are, hide him. He is in hiding now and I want to find him." His voice had become steely.

"I do not know where Pastor Bonhoeffer is," she said with careful deliberation. "Please, can't you tell me something about my husband? It's been almost six months."

He stood up and casually walked to the window. He leaned against the frame. "Max Farber. He fell from his pedestal, didn't he? Now he's rotting in a Nazi pit. Always so confident . . ."

Beck. Her horror made her voice choked. "You . . . you were his secretary at Farber Company."

He turned around slowly. "Yes, Frau Farber, I was his secretary for twelve years before he fired me." He watched the fear in her face that she couldn't hide, then he was distracted for a moment by her beauty. *No wonder the great Heydrich is smitten with her. But I won't be. I don't have that weakness.* He returned to his chair.

"As I emphasized earlier, we are not here to discuss your husband. You are in a very . . . unique position, Frau Farber. I wonder if you realize that. First, you are the wife of a man who is imprisoned for his traitorous activities against the Third Reich."

"Accused of treason," she inserted with false calmness. "He . . . hasn't been formally charged."

"Your husband was seen passing information to Germany's enemies in Geneva. While he has not confessed, he is no less guilty. His actions clearly compromised national security. Surely, you cannot be so naïve that you believe he is innocent! Now to point two. You are holding dual citizenship: German and of a nation that is at war with Germany. Your loyalty to the Riech could be suspect. You could be a spy."

She made no move to protest. He was on his way to a total checkmate.

"Point three. We have the file of an unnamed woman who has been seen taking unauthorized photos in the Reich. This could further constitute espionage activities. Perhaps she is in the employ of the Americans."

He was watching her with predatory calmness.

"Finally, Frau Farber, you have been seen in the company of Dietrich Bonhoeffer enemy of the Reich, as I mentioned earlier."

"Everything you've said is absurd, but I won't waste my time or yours protesting. I want to go home now." She was perspiring and felt light-headed as she stood up.

He stood up quickly, his eyes dilated in anger. "You smart-mouthed—" he cursed as a stinging slap slammed into the side of her face. Emilie staggered.

The door opened abruptly, and Beck was cursing again. "What is this?" he demanded in a high, weak voice.

Reinhard Heydrich entered. He was pulling off his gloves as if he had come late to a dinner party. His voice was as Emilie remembered, cool and smooth. He gave Emilie hardly a glance. But his eyes leveled on the Gestapo man.

"What is ... this interruption, Herr Heydrich?" Beck sputtered.

The SS chief's eyes were riveted on Beck, but his tranquil voice was for Emilie. "There is a car waiting downstairs to take you home, Frau Farber." Heydrich had come to her rescue.

12
A Quiet House on Tiergartenstrasse

Puttering around in the walled garden behind the house on Tiergartenstrasse made the man feel better. The strong sunshine felt good on his back. The blueness of the sky, the fresh air, the early flowers blooming and scenting the air calmed him. He eased himself down on a bench with a sigh. His eyes fell on the apple tree that Max had helped him plant years ago. Seeing the tree suddenly reminded him that tomorrow was his sixty-ninth birthday. His eyes scanned the garden and the back of the brick house and spied the terrier lolling in the warmth. The dog sensed the man's eyes on him and raised his head. Josef Morgan smiled and nodded, and the dog came to sit beside him, his head resting on the man's knees.

"I know you miss him as much as we do," Josef sighed, his voice wistful. "And with all our love and attention we don't quite fill his place, eh boy?" He ruffled the shaggy, multicolored ears. "If any present in the whole world, Percy, could be mine tomorrow I would have him walk through that front door."

He continued stroking the dog, drawing comfort from it. "Why couldn't they take an old man in his place?" he murmured. "Why Max?"

His thoughts dwelled on the two people he loved. *I'll always treasure the day Emilie came from America to photograph the Olympics and surprised me.* Now an orphan, with little connection back to the states, he had persuaded her to make Germany her home. Even that memory paled a little when he recalled the day Max and Emilie had married in the old courthouse in Dresden. *Emilie and Max, the beloved son I had never had. My niece and son in love! What a triumph! Then Emilie with her news. There is a child coming!*

Josef had declared then and there he could die a supremely happy man.

But their happiness had been snatched away so abruptly, he recalled sadly. *That was the Nazi way. Max in prison. Max not even knowing that he was going to be a father.*

The past year, with Gestapo threats, Max's dangerous masquerade to help Jews, his own beating and the clinic's destruction, Emilie's perilous efforts to aid Jews and photograph Nazi brutality, had taken its toll on Josef's aging body. The arthritis was slowly but determinedly crippling him. The heart condition he had controlled through medication over the years, was no longer so easily controlled. There were days when weakness engulfed him.

Yet I can say I've had a good, full life. But now, now . . . to see Max again and hold the baby. I'd give my life to reunite Max and Emilie. He sighed.

Percy stretched and began chewing on a loose button of his sweater. Josef nodded. "We just keep hoping, Percy . . . keep hoping . . ."

Emilie knew she had only a moment in the shadow of the backdoor to watch her uncle unobserved before Percy detected her presence. She was relieved to see Josef was relaxed and at ease. She sensed his physical condition was worse than he wanted her to know. *He's slipping away from me, slowly, a little each day. Then I'll be alone.* With his face relaxed, she noticed that he looked more like his younger brother—her father. *First Mom, then Dad, then . . .* Emilie gulped back her tears. She was not ready to lose another one she loved.

Percy had seen her and came yapping and jumping to the door. Josef jerked awake. She hurried to him. He tottered as he stood and feebly enfolded her in his arms.

"You came back," he whispered hoarsely. He began to cry.

"I told you I would."

They held each other for several minutes before they sat back down. He was clutching her hand as if he couldn't turn loose of it.

"Did they hurt you?"

She smiled. "Unless making me wait is painful. No, they didn't. I only talked to one man."

"About Max? What did he say about Max?"

Her smile evaporated. "I'm sorry, Uncle Josef. He wouldn't talk about Max. He wanted information on Pastor Bonhoeffer."

"Then they released you? That was all?"

She nodded. She dare not tell him Reinhard Heydrich had come to her aid. He would only be more frightened.

Josef shook his head.

"Why Emilie? Why are they hunting and imprisoning all the good men of Germany? Germany has become a, a prison with the criminals in control!"

"I know, I know. But we must keep hoping and praying that finally all the people will regain their senses and see the criminals for what they are. Pastor Bonhoeffer says that the German people must repent and ask forgiveness. God is merciful, but the people must turn from their wicked ways."

He looked at her searchingly. "Do you believe God is merciful and forgiving?"

She nodded. "Yes, Uncle Josef, I do. My faith is all I have left to hang on to."

"Then, my young niece, you have something I don't."

She squeezed his hand. "Oh, Uncle Josef, let me share it with you."

Emilie stood before the full-length mirror in her bedroom in the gloom of evening. She wore a simple white cotton slip. She looked at herself from every angle. Yes, dressed like this there was no question. A nicely rounding stomach. *Would Max find me pretty with this changing figure?* She smiled. *Me and Max's child. The Nazis have their secrets. I have mine.* A strong kick on her left side reminded her this was a situation that wouldn't stay forever hidden. She climbed into bed. Percy, in an attempt at stealth, jumped lightly onto the foot of the bed.

"Percy Blackney, you are a rogue!" she scolded.

She leaned back, studying the ceiling.

"Which do you hope for Percy, a boy or a girl?"

The tail thumped.

"A boy. You would. Keep the male ratio of this household dominating, I understand perfectly. A boy or girl ... our little one," she murmured. She placed her hand on her stomach, feeling the progress of what she assumed must be a little heel. Her other hand stretched out to the empty side of the bed.

If only Max were here. I would take his hand and let him feel the energy of his child. She imagined some tease he would make and his soft laughter. *Then he would take me in his arms.* Emilie didn't restrain the tears this time. There was no Uncle Josef to be strong for, no Gestapo agents to hide from ... only a dog on the end of her bed. He would keep her secret. Finally she grew calmer. She rolled over on her side as a soft breeze fluttered her curtains and brushed her skin like a caress. She closed her eyes, but not to sleep. It was a pain and a pleasure to remember the times she'd had with Max.

Max and Emilie had moved from strangers to friends the summer of 1936. Max was so friendly and generous as he showed Emilie Berlin and the Olympic games. Boyishly sweet and terribly handsome, his charm had been hard to ignore. Emilie had to remind herself that she was here on assignment and that this good-looking friend of her uncle's obviously wanted a brother–sister type relationship. Besides, he had something going with his friend from childhood, Elaina Heydrich. They had been an impeccable couple Emilie had noted a little scornfully. Then she and Max had moved from friends to antagonists when their political views collided. How could easy-going, gentle Max condone the Nazi atrocities toward the Jews? Emilie had been disappointed, then horrified. A cool wall of separation had risen between them. Josef had become an emissary of peace between them.

Even now with their child over six months in the womb—a testament to the change that had come—Emilie was still surprised that she had proposed a marriage of convenience to the polished Farber scion. She was surprised and secretly a little gratified, that he had gallantly agreed. It had been a simple arrangement. She needed his name to remain in Germany. She had become Frau Farber with a kiss that had been a little too intense for a purely platonic relationship.

Emilie smiled in the darkness as she remembered the passionate kiss.

She rolled over on her back, staring at the ceiling which acted like a screen to her memories. *That night* ... She finally drifted asleep wondering if there would ever be another.

● ● ●

A sleek black car was parked at the end of Tiergartenstrasse. It had been there ever since Emilie had hurried up the steps from her Gestapo interrogation. It was not the same car that had deposited her. It didn't belong to the Gestapo. It didn't belong to the SS. Now, wrapped in her dreams, Emilie would have been very surprised to know who was watching her. At dawn, it was replaced by another.

Tegel Prison

Max stripped to his shorts to do his exercises. He was feeling stronger, like his old self. He was feeling optimistic again. He had a plan to survive and, barring these prison fevers, when he was liberated he would not be some shriveled skeleton of a man, an apparition of his former self. He would emerge from this pit as jauntily as he had entered. He would be the Max Farber the world of the living remembered and recognized.

All his mental and physical exercises done for the evening, he stretched out on the cot to let his mind do a little wandering. He checked the time. Eight-thirty. With his hands behind his head, he stared at the gray ceiling. *What is Josef doing? Taking Percy out for an evening walk? Are the trees blooming in Tiergarten? She will see them from our bedroom window. What would she be doing at eighty-thirty? Emilie.* He closed his eyes and replayed the very first time he had seen her.

She had come to Josef's office on Friedrichstrasse. A big surprise from America. Max had heard her voice in the waiting room. He had been flirting in the examining room with Josef's nurse. Then he had stepped through the green curtains to pose as Dr. Josef Morgan for a pretty stranger. *Dark shoulder-length hair. A tan suit and white blouse, standing very straight and calm. Very pretty, great legs.* He remembered every detail. She had played along with his charade, then dramatically revealed her identity. Her laugh had been deep and rich.

"What I wouldn't give for the sound of it now," he whispered.

Another file. The night when she had danced with Reinhard Heydrich and he had driven her home. They were both angry. The color had come to her cheeks. He said something about her dress being too little. Rather, too revealing. Especially for a wolf like the SS chief. Or boating on the Spree River. . . . Or the night at the estate when she had come upon him playing "Moolight Seranade" on the piano. She had stood in the shadows, and when he turned, she was like an ephemeral being. He had fought a titanic battle within himself to keep from sweeping her into his arms.

His voice was hoarse. "I would have frightened her. I could have devoured her."

That night she had been his bride, his wife but only in name. Though they had fought and misunderstood, he knew in this young American he had found a person he could trust. She would not betray his love.

Darkness was throwing a shroud over the cell. Could she be laying in bed tonight thinking of him? "Emilie . . ."

• • •

The fading day filled the third-floor office at SS headquarters. Sipping schnapps, Reinard Heydrich was not thinking of love, or moonlight, or melodies. He was thinking of Karl Beck. His mouth curled into a hard smile. Imagine trying to go around me, to supplant my authority! He leaned forward and switched on his desk light.

He pulled Beck's file toward him and scanned it for the second time. He punched the intercom and immediately an SS adjutant was standing rigidly in front of him.

"Sir?"

"Listen carefully. Karl Beck in the Gestapo office. I want him transferred to army intelligence in . . ." He scanned the map in front him that plotted the day's progress of the army. His finger stabbed the place and he chuckled. "Smolnesk in the Ukraine. He will join the army there." He looked back to the man. "You will notify him first thing in the morning. He will have twenty-four hours to get his gear together. Have his tickets and passes in order. Let him . . . enjoy a Russian summer and winter."

13
Cain and Abel

May *was beautiful even in Berlin,* Emilie conceded. From her window she could see into the huge park grounds of Tiergarten, a lush palette of green with shimmering opal and azure of dozens of small lakes. But standing at her window watching the splendor of advancing spring never failed to remind her of spring in Maryland and Virginia. Living there for twelve years, she had loved the famous annual cherry tree blossoming along the Potomac in Washington, D.C. Spring recalled almost another lifetime when she'd been an American citizen, never giving another thought to the very distant land of her birth.

She had been a tour guide for the Smithsonian. Back then, she'd had boyfriends and D.C. traffic snarls and a predictable, easy-going life in Georgetown. She had her faithful best friend, Bess Bennet, to laugh and plot the future with. But in 1936 she had chosen a different path. The path had brought her here. Nazi land. Where she had found love and sorrow.

Emilie's thoughts were interrupted by a knock on the front door. *Has Reinhard Heydrich come calling to collect my gratitude?*

She glanced at herself in the hallway mirror. The loose yellow blouse concealed her figure.

"Hello, Emilie."

It was not Heydrich.

"Eric!" She grasped his hands and pulled him into the house.

142

He laughed. "It took you a moment. Have I changed that much?"

"No, I, I was just expecting . . . thinking it might be someone else. And you surprised me." She was still clutching his hands, then she impulsively hugged him.

"It's good to see you, Eric."

He nodded. "You look well. Is the doctor here?"

"He's upstairs resting. Can you stay for awhile, for dinner?"

"Well," he demurred.

"Come on." She led him to the kitchen and pulled out a chair for him. "Why can't you stay for dinner?"

"I have only a twenty-four-hour pass. I've been posted to Poland."

"Poland!"

He nodded. "But I have to tell you," he said, his face brightening, "that Bridget and I have married. In Paris. She's still there."

She squeezed his hands. "Oh, Eric, I'm happy for you. I'll have fun scouring Berlin for just the right wedding gift."

He smiled again. "You look wonderful, Emilie."

"How like Max you sounded just then."

They both glanced away. There it was. The happy reunion must face reality.

"Then I would be complimented," he said softly.

She looked back to the table. She wanted to tell him she was going to have a baby, that he was going to be an uncle. It would be nice to have the normal congratulations. But even though she trusted Max's older brother, some instinct warned her to silence.

"Have you had any word?" he asked.

She shook her head. "I was hoping you brought some with you."

He shook his head and looked down at Percy who had positioned himself by the visitor's leg.

Emilie smiled wanly. "I have no doubt Percy is devoted to me, but you can see how he longs for a . . . man in the house."

"Josef?"

"He's not well, Eric. Frankly I'm worried. It's his heart. He hardly eats—always says he's full. I know he's giving up his food for me."

"Shortages are that bad here?"

"I'm sure it could be worse. I had to stand in line two hours yesterday for two pounds of beef."

Eric leaned back in his chair. "This sounds like the depression all over again—except the Nazis said this would never happen."

Emilie was silent. She didn't really know where Eric Farber stood with the Nazis. How did he feel about the persecution of the Jews? He was an army officer, but he was not a party member. He had arranged for that brief final meeting with Max before he had been taken to Tegel.

What about taking Dr. Morgan to a physician?"

"There is a shortage of medical personnel. I've already looked into it. There is a long waiting list, and with his age he's hardly a . . . priority. He takes medication. I don't know what else they could do for him."

"I wish . . . there was something I could do for you, Emilie. Do you need anything?"

She smiled her bravest smile.

"I wish I could get that for you," he responded gently.

She stood up. "Oh, Eric, it's like the Nazis have just swallowed him up. They won't let us get any word to him. There's no word about him. I don't even know whether he is still at Tegel.

Eric leaned forward, his hands steepled together, his face in a concentrated frown.

The Farber boys sure don't look at all alike, Emilie thought.

She sat back down. "Two weeks ago the Gestapo came for me and took me to their headquarters. Karl Beck interrogated me—"

"Max's old secretary?"

She nodded. "He's in the leather-coat league now. He wanted to know about Dietrich Bonhoeffer. He would tell me nothing about Max. Then . . ." She stopped.

"What Emilie? Tell me what happened. Maybe I can help in some way.

"Eric, Reinhard Heydrich suddenly entered the office. He . . . had a car waiting to take me home. I haven't heard from him or the Gestapo since."

"That was who you thought might be at your front door?" *Heydrich. Anyone else but Heydrich,* he thought.

She nodded. His eyes had widened at the mention of Heydrich's name. Now he sat deep in thought; Emilie was silent.

Finally he looked up and glanced at his watch. "I've got all kinds of things to do before my train leaves at eight in the morning."

She walked him to the front door.

"Next leave I'll stay longer," he said. "I'd like to try some of your culinary creativity."

She clung to him and he knew she was stifling her tears. "Your Bridget is a very fortunate woman. I hope she realizes that."

He fumbled with his hat, his voice low. "Max and I ... we know we're the fortunate ones."

The car at the corner duly noted the exit of Eric Farber thirty minutes after his arrival.

They walked together in the fragrant beauty of Tiergarten. Emilie tried not to notice that Josef's steps were more faltering and slower. She held his arm as though he was leading her. Percy was dashing in front of them.

"You are far prettier than that bed of tulips and daffodils, my dear," her uncle noted.

She smiled and squeezed his hand. "I don't know, Uncle Josef. I weighed this morning ... and I've lost my waist completely!"

"I don't know how you're gaining much weight with what we eat." He shook his head.

"Uncle Josef, you are worrying needlessly. I have never felt better, and the baby is active."

"But if any complications came up—"

She stopped in the wooded path. "I don't want to be stern with you, Uncle Josef. But I think if you didn't worry so, about the baby, about me, about Max, you would feel better. God is taking care of us."

"I know you're right, Emilie. I'm sorry. I just ... I just feel so feeble and useless. When Germany is needing doctors I can't ... I can take care of you, but when your time comes will I be strong enough? You need to find another doctor."

"Every doctor I've contacted," she sighed, "doesn't want to treat a Farber. They're afraid."

"As if you were a threat!"

"Yes I am so formidable-looking!" she laughed, patting her stomach. Now, have you noticed what a beautiful day it is, Uncle Josef?"

He looked around, smiling. "Yes, yes, I think I do notice!"

• • •

Because they had adjoining country estates, the Heydrich and Farber families had been friends for years. Irwin and Reinhard had been the closest growing up, with Eric occasionally tagging along. But Eric had always been intimidated and a little afraid of Heydrich. Heydrich had teased him and, when bored, bullied him. Eric had always given into Heydrich's goading—even when it went against his sense of right and wrong. And now as a man of forty, dread and apprehension rose up in him like bile at the thought of approaching him. But this time he must. For his brother.

Lena Heydrich approached the door to her husband's study hesitantly. She knew he was in no temper for her or the children. In a way, she wished he would go to his club or . . . wherever he went so often in the evenings. She didn't want to know.

"Reinhard, I'm sorry to bother you. Eric Farber is here. He insists on seeing you."

Reinhard cocked his head, amused. "Eric Farber insists?"

She knew that tone and a part of her went out to the pale, nervous-looking young man waiting in the hall.

Reinhard waved a languid hand. "By all means then, show him in."

Heydrich didn't change his relaxed posture. Eric entered and closed the door behind him.

"Hello, Reinhard."

Heydrich nodded. "Eric. So, you're back from Paris and off to Poland."

"Yes."

"Congratulations on your marriage."

Eric blinked rapidly in surprise. *Heydrich knew everything.* "Thank you."

"Sit down, sit down. A drink?"

Eric hesitated a moment. He was not a drinking man. "Yes, thanks."

Heydrich poured it, making no effort to conceal his amusement.

"I'm sorry to bother you at home," Eric said hurriedly. "I went by your office. I leave early in the morning . . ."

Heydrich nodded. "Do you know what you'll be doing in Poland?"

Eric shook his head. "They'll tell me when I get there. Working with medical engineering is what the paperwork said."

"I know why you're here, Eric."

Eric cleared his throat again. "Reinhard, he's been held for over six months. No visitors, no trial," Eric said hurriedly.

Reinhard's voice was still pleasant and conversational. "He's guilty of treason against the Third Reich Eric. He was aiding enemies of the Reich—the Allies and the Jews. There is no greater crime—" He paused to study his nails before he refocused his gaze on the young officer facing him. "—except the assassination of a Nazi officer. Other men have been rotting in their graves for less than Herr Farber has done. You know that."

"Max hasn't confessed, and there are no witnesses. He—"

Heydrich's voice perceptively hardened. "Three SS officers have positively identified Max as the one who was masquerading in an SS uniform and freeing Jews. A trusted Gestapo official has identified Max as being seen with a representative of the English government in Geneva."

"Max has many business contacts, men he has met in his travels with Farber Company," Eric inserted.

"It was not company business he was on . . . and we both know it. Irwin has confirmed this. I will tell you this privately, Eric, so you can better understand. Goebbels and Himmler are squarely lined up against your brother. They wanted his head months ago. The Fuehrer respects me, and I have been able to restrain him on this case. I reminded him the Farber family is well known, popular, with a rich heritage. He has *two* loyal Farbers. So I have stood between him and your brother. I have kept him out of the people's court that would have hung him within an hour of his certain conviction." The pride was unmistakable in the SS leader's voice.

Eric looked away. *Two loyal Farbers. Yes the fuehrer was no fool. Irwin Farber was a deep financial well for the Nazi government.*

"I understand his crimes, Reinhard," he said slowly.

"Then you understand my position perfectly," Reinhard smiled.

Eric thought of Emilie's tears, her courage, her unspoken pleading. His voice was heavy with emotion. "As you have said, Reinhard, he's my brother."

Reinhard had poured himself another drink. He peered over the glass rim at Eric, smiling.

"He's a traitor."

Eric sat straighter. "We would like to see him, Reinhard."

"*We* want to see him? You and Irwin?"

Eric shook his head sadly. "No. Frau Farber would like very much to see her husband. Reinhard, please allow me to escort her to Tegel, to give her some time with Max. That is all I came for, all I wanted to ... plead with you for."

Reinhard was disgusted. He didn't like weakness, and Eric Farber was groveling.

"Only your brother can arrange such a meeting, Eric."

"Max? How?"

Reinhard stood signifying it was time for Eric to leave. "Anytime he will answer my questions I will contact you and you can bring Frau Farber. Then Max can look at his beautiful wife through the bars. Perhaps I will be his first visitor. Perhaps I will go tomorrow and tell him."

Eric stood up also, drained. *This little chat has been a total waste of time. Reinhard has no soul.* Eric reached for his hat.

"If your brother does not agree to this little arrangement that we've discussed, you will have to wait until the first anniversary of his incarceration to see him. He will determine that."

Eric's voice was low, but firm. "I don't suppose I can ... appeal to you on the strong friendship between our fathers."

"Our fathers are dead, Eric. We carry on the legacy of Germany now. The strong prevail; the weak are crushed. Friendship is secondary to loyalty to the Reich. Good night, Eric."

• • •

The cell was in total blackness yet Max was awake. For the first time since he had been imprisoned the thin light from the hallway was extinguished. The prison walls seemed to thud and shake. It reverberated through the cell. The Allied bombs were falling very close. He thought of Emilie and Josef and hoped they were safe. Perhaps they were at the country house ...

Another bomb shook the cot. The floor rumbled under his feet as if the earth would suddenly split in a gigantic fissure. *I could be buried alive,* he thought, his heart pounding. *I can't remember any time in my life when I've been physically afraid. But I am now,* he admitted to himself.

He took a calming breath and tried to pray.

• • •

Emilie waited a nervous hour in the corridor of Berlin's largest hospital before she realized she was being ignored by the staff. Finally she saw a man in a white coat scribbling on a clipboard as he talked with a nurse. She knew it was him from the description Josef had given her. She drew a steadying breath.

"Dr. Ley?"

He turned and looked her over without expression.

The nurse's voice was low and confidential in his ear. "This is Frau Farber, doctor. She has been waiting to see you. I told her you were very busy."

"I am very busy, Frau Farber. I have more surgery this morning—thanks to the Americans."

"I've come, Dr. Ley, because of my uncle, your old friend from medical-school days—Josef Morgan. He told me of your skill and that you might help us."

He made an impatient wave at the nurse, and she reluctantly turned away.

"My uncle is very sick," Emilie said hurriedly. "It's his heart and he's worse this morning. I was hoping you could come to the house and see him. Give him . . . something . . ." Her voice trailed off. This medical man was regarding her with such hostility.

"Last night, Frau Farber, you were in Berlin. Who were you rooting for? The German defenses or the Americans?"

She staggered back, her eyes widening. "You . . . you are serious?"

He smiled thinly. "The murder of German civilians, yes, is very serious. You are an American. You—"

She was surprised at the strength of her own voice. "I had nothing to do with last night any more than you or my uncle did!"

"Your husband is a traitor to the Reich."

It was very difficult to stay calm. She could feel the baby tumbling inside her. Suddenly her legs felt weak. "I am here for *Josef Morgan*. I am here because he is in need. Will you not come and help another doctor who is in need?"

"I regret Dr. Morgan's illness, but I will not step into the house of a traitor."

Emilie spoke through gritted teeth. "Then I'll bundle him up and bring him here."

The man was shaking his head and moving away. The nurse came up to him briskly. She thrust another clipboard into his hands. "The transport from Tegel just arrived, sir. They're waiting for you."

Emilie caught up with them. "Did you say Tegel? Tegel prison?"

"Tegel prison was hit last night by the allies. The casualties were brought here," the nurse replied.

Half an hour later Emilie was back in her car, leaning over the steering wheel, feeling as if she was going to be sick. Finally she leaned back and closed her eyes. The stressful night had blended into a horrible day. She hadn't been able to help Josef. She glanced at her watch. She'd been gone a little over an hour. She gripped the steering wheel, fighting back the tears of frustration. *If only there was someone ... If only Eric would suddenly appear again. Surely he could do something.*

She had stood concealed behind a corner as the prison transport was unloaded. She discovered she was holding her breath. If Max ... if Max was among them. Finally one nurse had noticed her.

"This is a restricted area. May I help you?"

Emilie lowered her voice. "I ... I heard about the bombing of Tegel. My brother is a—a guard there. I wanted to know if he was among the injured."

Someone called to the nurse.

"I have to go."

"Please, can't you look on your list there? If only I knew. We've been so worried."

The nurse hesitantly reached for a sheaf of papers.

"Nurse!"

The doctor brushed past them, then stopped as if he had run into a wall. He swung around his eyes glaring.

"What are you doing in this restricted area?"

"She wanted to know about her brother, Doctor Ley. He's a guard at Tegel," the nurse supplied quickly.

Emilie turned away. She didn't need to hear his scathing words. Instead he grabbed the manifest. "Max Farber is not listed."

Driving back home, Emilie suddenly thought of Bonhoeffer. He had given her a verse that last time she had seen him.

"Depend on this, when there is nothing else to depend on," he had said.

She couldn't keep the tears from slowly spilling over as she repeated the words: "Whom have I in heaven but Thee? And besides Thee, I desire nothing on earth. My flesh and my heart may fail, but God is the strength of my heart and my portion forever."

14
On the Path
of Salvation

The soft hues of twilight filled the upstairs library. Josef was alternately rolling a ball for Percy to scramble after and watching his niece sew baby clothes. Though the evening was warm, he sat with a shawl loosely draped around his shoulders. It gave him great pleasure to watch Emilie so absorbed in her sewing—a little frown creasing between her eyes, her hair soft and curling. *She's like a Madonna, so peaceful and serene,* he decided.

Emilie had nearly forgotten her uncle's presence. The music that was playing on the phonograph and her efforts at sewing had transported her out of the Berlin room. She was daydreaming of what it would be like to be back in America with Max. She would take him to a Washington, D.C. restaurant where they could dance to these Glen Miller serenades. She thought of herself with her protruding belly as Max attempted to guide her on the dance floor and laughed aloud at the mental picture.

"It's good to hear you laugh. And your own thought provided it—that is good," Josef said.

She looked up. She tried to determine if he was looking better. Only a tad less gray today. But his mind was sharp.

"I like this Miller fellow, he's very . . . snappy!" he added.

She laughed and stretched. "He's very popular in the States. The Nazis would be very kind to their citizenry if they'd allow some of his music to be played."

He leaned back and closed his eyes. "Someday Germany will welcome composers regardless of their religion!"

Emilie strolled to the window, nodding. She thought of beautiful music and religious freedom again. And when the Jews would no longer be persecuted. She realized she never saw the yellow-starred figures on the streets of the city anymore and her heart constricted. *Have they escaped or are they safely hidden? I wish I could have done more for them, but I can barely provide for Josef and me. I guess my photographs that were smuggled to America hadn't made any difference.*

"You won't be able to conceal the baby much longer," Josef spoke up. "The baby always puts on more weight in the final months."

"I suppose I shouldn't be concerned that anyone knows. I'll be strolling this little Farber out in Tiergarten one of these days."

Josef nodded.

Emilie turned back to the window. Only a matter of weeks and this baby would be even more of a reality. More responsibility. It could overwhelm her. Staring through the glass, she began to pray. *Lord, please provide a way . . .*

The phone rang, making her jump. She went to it.

"Yes . . . but . . . all right."

She put the phone down slowly. She was too surprised to mask her emotions. Josef was watching alertly from his chair. She couldn't keep this from him.

She made her voice casual. "That was a secretary from Reinhard Heydrich's office. Heydrich wants to see me. They're sending a car."

The words fell as devastatingly as an Allied bomb.

"At this time of night? That is peculiar," he said in an unruffled voice. He knew his young niece didn't need the additional burden of his fears.

Emilie smiled. "Heydrich's peculiar. It shouldn't take long. I'm going to go freshen up."

In her room her hands were shaking as she brushed and pinned her hair. She wore the most concealing outfit she had. *This man has been stalking me since I first came to Germany seven years ago. This man of immense power. This man who holds Max's future.* She remembered Max's warning: "Reinhard is predatory and ruthless." She didn't feel the threat so much for herself as for her unborn child. *If he knew he had yet more leverage against Max. . . . With his practiced eye, how could he not see my swelling figure?*

"O Lord, please help me. I'm afraid ..."

Josef stood when she reentered the library.

"No point in telling me to go on to bed. I'm staying up." He gripped her hand and smiled. "And I'm praying."

• • •

Heydrich went into the washroom off his office and shaved. He applied his best cologne. His uniform was spotless and pressed. He stood back and gravely assessed himself in the mirror. *Perhaps I should change into a civilian suit that's less intimidating. Yes, a fine, gray Persian suit would be better.* He changed quickly. He assessed himself again. *Better.*

Back in his office he ordered dinner from a nearby restaurant. Then he leaned back and poured himself a brandy while he waited. He thought back on the first time he had seen her. It was the summer of the Olympics, and he had decided to go to the Farber dinner party because he was bored at home. His wife was heavy with their third child. He had arrived late and paused inside the library before he joined the party to look over the changes Max had made to his country home. He had found more than books and oil paintings in the room. A young woman who had been sitting in the window seat was regarding him with curious, wide eyes. He had swiftly evaluated her figure. *Good. Face and hair, beautiful.* She was a stranger, and she had a charming American accent. She also didn't accede to his own charm immediately. *That was novel. Cool and aloof. I liked that. It suggested a pursuit. Then Max had intervened and claimed her.*

Max can't intervene now. He smiled.

Emilie paused outside the heavy door. She didn't miss the significance of the empty offices and the deserted hallways. Everything was shadowy with twilight. *I'll be alone with the SS chief in this vast building.* In the short drive from Tiergartenstrasse to Wilhelmstrasse she had prayed for wisdom. *I must try to be somewhat civil to this man. Perhaps even ... even charming.* She had inwardly sickened at the thought.

There was a discreet knock and the door opened. He stood as she entered. Any pretense at indifference evaporated at the sight of her. She was more beautiful than he remembered. *She was ... There is something different about her face, her figure, fuller, more womanly.* He clutched his hands behind him and swore at his nervousness. *Even her hair is darker and shinier,* he thought. *There is something almost . . . angelic about her!*

"Please sit down," he said as he indicated two chairs and a table that had been set between them. It was placed before the tall windows that looked out over the busy Wilhelmstrasse. The lights of the cars driving up and down reminded her of a string of jewels. *Very impressive.*

Another knock and two aides entered carrying trays. They set the table silently, swiftly, and with lowered eyes. Sitting across from her, watching her nervously arrange her skirt, helped him regain his balance.

He uncovered the trays and delicious smells wafted up to her. Smells of things she had not smelled in months. Finally she looked up. He was smiling at her.

"Thank you for coming at such short notice," he said.

She stifled the impulse to say they both knew she had no choice. *So he's going to try to disarm me with the gentleman angle,* she thought.

She leaned forward slightly, her hands in her lap. "My uncle is not well and I don't like to leave him too long," she said gently.

He nodded and smiled. "I never discuss business while eating. Let's enjoy this first."

She looked down at the food and sighed imperceptibly.

"It does look . . . good."

"Please enjoy." But he was watching her with unconcealed desire.

She took a bite. "I could enjoy this more if you would talk while you eat."

He laughed. "You have not changed since I saw you last, Emilie Farber. You are direct, and I like that." He took a sip of wine and met her eyes over his glass. "Not changed—except to be lovelier."

"We have a saying in America: Flattery will get you nowhere."

Again he laughed. "Beauty, wit, and intelligence." He pointed his fork at her. "A lethal combination in a woman, I have always thought."

"We are talking about me. That really doesn't interest me. I'd prefer . . ." She looked away. "I'm asking you, Herr Heydrich, can you give me any word on my husband?"

His voice was calm. "I would prefer to finish my dinner in peace. And I'd prefer you call me Reinhard, Emilie."

Emilie picked at her food nervously.

He poured himself another glass of wine and refilled hers. Then he leaned back, his legs crossed. Emilie lay down her napkin carefully. He watched her as she perused his office. Only one desk light was burning, throwing muted light in the room. Emilie tried to ignore the atmosphere.

"What is wrong with Dr. Morgan?" he asked finally.

She knew it was useless to hide anything from this man. "He has a heart condition. He needs to see a doctor but..." Her eyes leveled on his. "The Farber name is not very popular right now. No one wants to treat us."

"Us?"

"The doctor."

"That is understandable. Many good Germans are sacrificing their sons for our war. They would naturally resent anyone who was selling information to the enemy."

They both knew there was nothing she could say.

"The bombing raids at night make the capital a difficult place to be ... with a heart condition, I would think," he added.

She nodded. "Yes. It is very ... painful for me to see him like this, to be unable to help him. I love him very much—he is all the family I have."

"I understand."

There is no sarcasm or cynicism in his voice. Almost caring ... Emilie felt a stirring of hope. It faded as quickly as it had flared.

"I can help you. And I can help Dr. Morgan," he said slowly.

The words hung heavy in the shadowy room. His eyes rested on the base of her neck.

He said he liked directness from her. She took a plunging breath. "Reinhard, I know you can help me in ... every way I want ... but I ... I can't ..."

"Because you don't love me?"

Her nails were biting into her flesh. She knew what the mention of Max would do to him. But what choice was there?

"Because I love my husband."

He stood abruptly and walked closer to the window. He didn't look at her.

"You wanted word of your husband? He is a traitor to the Reich. He's imprisoned at Tegel."

He waited a full minute, and when she didn't respond he swung around.

"Did you hear me?" His voice had taken a hard cast.

"Yes."

He walked around the table and stood behind her. For another full minute he said and did nothing. Then his hand rested on her shoulder. The fingers slid up her neck.

"You don't love me. That doesn't matter to me. That you love him doesn't matter to me. What should matter, Emilie, is that you . . . you have power." He leaned over, whispering into her hair. "Life can be better for you, for the doctor . . . and for the man who sits in a cell only an hour from here. Perhaps you could even see him. It's in your hands."

He straightened back up, but his fingers continued to travel around her neck and shoulders.

Emilie had clamped her eyes closed and was biting her lip. When his fingers rested on the top button of her blouse, her eyes closed.

"I can't, Reinhard. I won't."

The caress tightened around her neck. "You will always remember this opportunity I gave you. You will regret your decision."

He came around in front of her and pulled her to her feet.

She was trembling inside. If he pulled her into an embrace surely he would discover . . .

"Reinhard, please, I've been away from Josef too long. He'll be worried."

The SS leader smiled. "He shouldn't worry. His niece is with the most powerful man in the Reich." He leaned forward. "That is the safest place to be." He reached out and ran his fingers through her hair. His voice was low and husky.

"You are discovering that I am a patient man, Emilie. But I have my limits. I am also considerate. I know that you would be uncomfortable in Berlin with me. So I am placing you under house arrest at your country estate."

She gasped. "What?"

"A little formality that will satisfy Himmler. We will be able to talk about what you know regarding Herr Farber's activities with the Allies and who was helping him in the inside."

"I know nothing about that. I told that to the officers months ago."

"And they believed you because I told them to. Now I will play the interrogator." He fingered a tendril. "You know you are very beautiful to me. You have known that from the very first." He let the hair fall and took a step back. He was rigid and unsmiling now.

"You will have two days to gather whatever belongings together you want. Then I'll send a car for you and the doctor. It will take you to the Farber Estate. It will be safer for you there and healthier for the doctor. There will be a staff in place. You will have the finest foods. And, depending on how our ... interrogation sessions go, I'll have the best heart doctor in Germany at your door. He won't care that you're a Farber."

He took her arm and led her to the door. His hand rested on the knob.

"My family is spending the summer in Bavaria. I'm staying at my estate on the weekends. It's safer and cooler than Berlin. I'm looking forward to that."

An SS officer had come from the shadows to escort her to the car.

Heydrich was still smiling. "We understand each other don't we, Frau Farber?"

Her throat had constricted. She could only nod.

• • •

"She was in there with him for over an hour," the driver of the sleek black car reported bluntly.

The big man behind the desk was frowning as he rubbed his chin. His eyes were piercing, and his subordinate was glad this particular situation didn't in any way involve him. Germany's leading industrialist was known to have a volatile temper. He could be generous; he could be punitive.

"In with Heydrich for an hour ..." he mused. "And yesterday she went looking for a doctor for Morgan."

"Yes, sir."

"Nothing said about her need for a doctor?"

"Nothing. She told the doctor she met with that Dr. Morgan is having trouble with his heart."

He held up a slip of paper. "And she went to Potsdam to do a little shopping. Let's see: diapers, yarn, baby clothes." His voice fell heavily on the word *baby*.

The subordinate nodded. "She was very cautious that day. She parked at the end of the street. She told the salesclerk she had just moved to Pots and her husband was in the army. She wore a head scarf. Obviously she didn't want anyone to know she was shopping for baby things."

The big man nodded slowly.

"It's pretty obvious when you put it together. The doctor placed an order for iron tablets."

"Pretty obvious . . ." the boss murmured thoughtfully. "Can we speculate if Heydrich came to the same conclusion?"

The man in front of the desk smirked. "If things got frisky in the office, he knows."

"Keep watching her. Report to me immediately if Heydrich sends for her again or she leaves the city."

"Yes, sir."

He was alone again. He had a stack of work to do, but he didn't reach for it. He was tapping his pen against the desk in thought. *Emilie Farber is pregnant.*

Irwin Farber was very pleased.

• • •

They left Berlin early—before Heydrich's escort arrived. The beauty of the countryside, the spiraling road from Berlin held many memories. The first time she had been on it Max had been driving this car. *He had been so debonair and suave . . .*

Percy sat between her and Josef. He was clearly thrilled with leaving the city. He dashed from the front to the backseat whining and barking.

"Percy's a little excited," Emilie laughed.

"Tell me again what Heydrich said," Josef asked.

"He wanted to formally question me about Max's activities. He's convinced someone within his own SS helped Max. He thought I might have remembered something that would give him a clue. And, of course, anything I might know about Jews in hiding."

"Are you sure about this move? If you got to feeling bad . . ."

"It's perfect," she returned with false brightness. "I only wish we had done it sooner. Everything will be so beautiful. It will be much better for both of us."

"Yes, you're right."

"Herr Heydrich is very thorough. He has a staff in place because he didn't want us to try to hide Jews or anything. Kind of keep an eye on us."

"Very thoughtful."

"Yes ... very."

For the first four days Emilie waited anxiously. *There is nothing hiding it now. If Heydrich doesn't suspect, he will the moment he lays eyes on me. And this is his staff. Do they report by phone to him after I go upstairs?*

Emilie blossomed. She waddled. At night she wondered what affect this would have on his desire. *Will it impede him? Will it enrage him?*

It was a perfect place for them; it was good to be away from Berlin. Josef was almost ecstatic with the bounty of fresh, nutritious food. But she could hardly enjoy the serenity of this place. Though weak and crippled, he was not blind.

He found her on the patio, staring listlessly out at Percy on the back lawn. At the sound of his shuffled step, she jumped.

"Oh ... I ..."

He lowered himself into a chair. "You were expecting someone else?" he smiled.

"No. I was just thinking."

"About?" he prompted.

She tapped the newspaper on her lap. "Just reading the latest war news. Rommel in Africa."

"And Rommel in Africa makes you nervous these days?" he smiled, taking her hand.

"Well, no. Thinking about the baby perhaps, not worried though."

"This was supposed to be such a perfect place for us, so peaceful out here. Yet you've been anxious-looking and jumpy. You can't hide it from me, Emilie. I've been looking at faces and bodies for over thirty years for clues. Yours tells me you're nervous about something. So let's go through a little checklist."

She smiled. "You are feeling better."

He nodded. "This place has helped me in only a few short days. Have you had any pains?"

"No."

"Anything different in any way?"

"No."

"Baby still active?"

"Yes."

He pulled out a stethoscope from his sweater pocket. He listened to her heartbeat, then he listened to the baby's.

"Nice and strong." He checked her blood pressure. "Just right. After lunch, we'll do your monthly check. Now, what's troubling you, Emilie Farber?"

"Uncle Josef, there is nothing. Heydrich upset me the other day with his accusations about Max. He really is . . . enjoying Max's position. He bested an enemy."

Her ploy had worked. Josef frowned. "Heydrich was always a bully. He could shove Max around, bloody his nose, but he couldn't make Max afraid like he did everyone else. He now has Max in a place to be afraid."

"If only I could . . . just get one word to Max. If only Eric had been able to do something."

"I want you to stop worrying about Heydrich. It's not good for the baby. I want you to enjoy the sunshine, and I will tell you about Max and I fishing here. Small men like Heydrich won't stand forever; men of honor like Max continue."

Emilie smiled and nodded. But Heydrich was standing now, blocking the sun.

• • •

Max had gone to his cot early in the evening with a headache. He had dozed for an hour or so, then awakened suddenly. His heart was pounding. His cell, his world, was as silent as a tomb. The light from the hallway shown thinly into his room. He sat up. What had wakened him so suddenly, filling him with dread? *Emilie. My wife is in trouble.*

• • •

She had known that he would come. Reinhard Heydrich didn't appear to be a man of hollow boasts. It was a matter of when. So the first Saturday night they had been at the estate she expected him. He kept his word. He sent a servant.

The man appeared nervous as he entered the library. She stood up.

"Frau Farber, Herr Heydrich has sent me to invite you to a late dinner. He'd like you to come within the hour. He sends this with the invitation." He held a white box out to her.

She stepped forward slowly. "I ... Will you wait in the hallway please?"

He closed the door behind him. Her heart was thudding in her ears. How grateful she was that Josef was already in bed. She opened the box, pushing back the layer of tissue.

A silver evening dress. Very expensive. She held it up. *Maybe six weeks ago,* she thought. Any other time or under other circumstances this would be outrageously funny. She thought of her old American friend. Her response would have been succinct and dry: "Maybe you could slip your big toe in it ... maybe."

She placed it carefully back in the box. She took a deep breath and stepped into the hallway.

She handed the box back to the startled man. "Please thank Herr Heydrich for his gift and invitation, but I'm feeling ill this evening."

She looked at the box in his hands. *The rejected dress ... no, I'd better keep it, if only to forestall the inevitable.* She smiled shakily as she took the box from him.

"I'll keep the gift. Good night."

She couldn't go up to bed. There was no way she could sleep though she was exhausted with tension. She returned to the library. She paced and prayed and tried to determine what her options were. She could waken Josef, pack, and drive into the night, to put as much distance between them and Heydrich's grasp.

"All of Europe is under the Nazi stamp, how far can we go?" she said aloud, then shook her head. It wouldn't work. Unless we hide. We could register under aliases. But a very pregnant woman and an elderly man would be easily spotted. Heydrich would have no trouble dropping a net over us.

"And he would enjoy it," she added out loud.

She still had her American citizenry—even if she was under suspicion by the government. She could go to the Swedish embassy if needed. *Yes, that was it.* She and Josef could return to Berlin in the morning and seek refuge in the neutral country's diplomatic office. But that was in the morning. *And what could they do for me after a few days, especially if pressed by the second in command of the Reich? It would only be a temporary deliverance.*

She walked along the bookshelves, her fingers running over the rich leather. *Max's books ...* She sat down on the sofa. There was another option.

She could submit. Her mind recoiled automatically. *But ... it would help Josef. It would help Max.*

"Oh, Max ..." she whispered hoarsely.

She heard the sound of a car in the drive before she saw the lights. He had come. Trembling, praying that Josef would not waken, she stood up. He was unlocking the front door. *He had a key to Max's house!* She felt a surge of anger. She went to stand by the light, her hands clutched behind her. The paneled doors slid opened.

He was dressed casually. His eyes found her swiftly. His smile was roguish. "Well, we are back to where we met Emilie, how fitting." He took a step forward, his eyes fastened on her face.

"You rejected the car, now you say you're ill. My man said you looked quite fine. So—"

He came halfway across the room before he finally allowed his eyes to take in her figure. He stopped abruptly and his smile dropped. The silence lengthened in the room. He was angry. He didn't like surprises.

"Well, well, well ..." he said in a tight voice.

"Please leave."

"This is the traitor's child?" he asked through gritted teeth.

"This is my husband's child. Now I'm asking you to leave."

He shook his head and grabbed her wrists. "Not so fast, not so fast." He pulled her painfully close. "I told you I was a man of patience ... when I want to be. I know you are worth the wait." His grip tightened and she winced. "But my patience does not stretch forever. This," he glanced at her stomach, "this does not matter. It hasn't saved you. Now the only question remains is if you will fight me or come willingly."

She had lost. There was no escape. She wanted to cry. *Max ...*

Her voice was low. "I don't come willingly, Herr Heydrich, but I won't fight you. Because of the child."

He leaned toward her. "You are as wise as I knew you were. You will call me Reinhard tonight."

"What is going on here?"

Reinhard swung around so swiftly that Emilie stumbled and almost fell against the desk.

Irwin Farber stood in the library doorway.

"What are you doing here?" Reinhard hissed.

Irwin looked carefully and slowly at Emilie. His eyes traced over her. He was not smiling. He looked back at the SS chief. His voice was even.

"I've come to see my sister-in-law, Herr Heydrich."

15
The Proposition

When he didn't appear at breakfast, Emilie knew something was wrong. She hurried to his room. He looked very gray, but weakly lifted his hand at the sight of her. With shaking hands she administered his heart medication.

"What else can I do, Uncle Josef? Should I call an ambulance?"

He shook his head, but Emilie was afraid. She had never seen him this debilitated. Her mind was racing as she held his hand.

He had come the night before, delivering her from the hands of an evil man. Could she appeal to him now? Heydrich had brushed past them, fury clearly etched on his marble face. Irwin had regarded her a moment in silence before he spoke.

"It's late. I will contact you tomorrow and we will talk."

His words conveyed unspoken meaning—Heydrich would not molest her. He spoke in blunt and clipped tones, his face an emotionless mask. Emilie could understand why he was such a successful businessman.

She summoned a maid while she went down to the library phone. She was surprised at how quickly she reached him after giving her name to the secretary. She swiftly explained the problem. She was afraid Josef could be dying. There hadn't been even a moment's hesitation. He spoke in the same succinct fashion—he would bring a doctor within the hour.

As Emilie sat waiting at Josef's bedside, she tried to think over the scant profile she had of Max's oldest brother, the scion of Farber Company. She had seen him only two brief times. Because she and Max had had such a short time together, and Irwin seemed so irrelevant to them, they had hardly discussed him. But Emilie knew from Josef, and from what Max had not said, that this older brother had been a large part of her husband's unhappy childhood. How she wished that this man who was coming to help her was less of an enigma and more like the pleasant Eric.

They sat across from each other in the library. She poured him coffee, but he didn't touch it. His eyes scanned the room, again without any indication of emotion.

"You are in a most . . . interesting position, Frau Farber."

So he is going to dispense with any pleasantries, and familiarity. This is business. Emilie was very tired, completely drained, but she knew that as much as she had needed her wits the night before, she needed them more now.

"I've been told that before," she replied.

"The Gestapo and the SS both want the wife of Max Farber."

She was surprised by his bluntness.

"They want her, a prize for them both. They both want her desperately. And only one of them can have her. She can't be shared."

"Reinhard Heydrich is obsessed with her, the Gestapo wants her. Even though Karl Beck has been shipped off to Poland, the Gestapo will continue their hunt. They will use her, and then they will kill her . . . if they are inclined to."

Emilie's hand went to her mouth in a wave of sudden nausea.

"You have heard the doctor's words. Morgan needs medication, a proper diet, and rest. For at least a few weeks he needs a trained nurse."

"You are very direct, Irwin," Emilie said slowly.

You also need medical care, Frau Farber."

Their eyes met. Hers, blue and pleading for a little kindness, his gray and stony. She laid her hand on her stomach protectively. She was so tired, and all of her energy must be preserved for the coming of the baby. *No more intrigue and threats. No more Heydrich.*

"Why are you telling me the SS and Gestapo want me? Max—your brother—has been in prison for months. Why do you care now?"

Only then, watching carefully, did she see something flash in his eyes. Then it was gone.

"I can protect you and your child."

"How?"

"You will come to my home. You will live with my wife and me. You will be safe. Everything you need will be provided. You and the doctor, and your baby, will receive the finest care. You can trust me on this."

He sounded so positive, even in the face of the powerful Heydrich, that she was confident he could do this.

"Why? Why are you doing this?"

He was reaching for the door. "For my little brother."

• • •

Reinhard Heydrich had the work load of half a dozen men. And of course the efforts against the Jews continued. He didn't have time to brood about some woman who had slipped through his fingers. He didn't have time to take her from Irwin's hold. *Very clever,* he admitted. *Very clever of Irwin.* Heydrich, a man of scheming designs, knew exactly why Farber had taken such a sudden interest in his sister-in-law. *Well . . . that is fine for now. For now.*

• • •

It was the largest house in the Berlin suburb of Dahlm. Emilie had expected a place of obvious wealth since her brother-in-law was one of the richest men in the expanding Third Reich. She knew he had entered the Nazi regime a very wealthy man and, she suspected, the war had swollen his fortune. But she didn't expect the mansion the Mercedes stopped in front of. Percy was whining beside her.

They had passed through tall, black, iron gates, down a spiraling drive past lawns that reminded her of a small park—something out of a Jane Austen novel. The landscape was perfectly manicured. The red-brick house rose up solid, dignified, cheerless. A hundred vacant eyes. She found herself shuddering. *Would Max . . . would he approve of this sudden decision to stay with his brother?* Josef was too incoherent in the ambulance behind them to know anything of the move. She had made the decision alone and could only hope it was the best one for all of them. *Still . . .* She stepped out on the brick drive and glanced around. The skyline of Berlin was obscured. This had to be a safe place. The car had brought her to another world, a world away from the war, away from shortages, and away from Heydrich.

Once inside the house the feeling of sanctuary continued. The staff greeted her formally and showed her to a suite of rooms. A huge bedroom of luxury, a large sitting room, a bathroom with a huge tub that she eyed with immediate interest. She went to the French doors and stepped out onto a sunny stone balcony. It looked out over a garden in full bloom. She had thought Max's estate lovely if a little neglected. Her breath drew in sharply. *This was . . . amazing!* Back in the room two maids were already unpacking her things.

"Oh, I . . . I can do that . . . thank you. I'd like to . . ."

They left her. She waited then tiptoed to the door and cracked it open. The richly carpeted hall was silent and empty. She felt like a schoolgirl. Finally a door opened at the end of the hall and a male servant appeared. She smiled shyly. He looked at Percy at her side and didn't smile.

"Dr. Morgan is installed."

"Thank you. I was wondering . . . what all these rooms are?"

"These are guest rooms. They are empty."

"I see. Thank you."

He disappeared. So far she had not seen anything of Irwin or his wife. Emilie could hardly remember her.

She went to Josef's room. He was in the large bed and Emilie stood at the end looking at him. *He seems so small, so . . .* She looked to the nurse who was arranging things on the bedside table.

"How is he?" she asked.

The nurse smiled. "He awakened briefly. He asked for you and I told him you were fine. His heart is very weak—any move can be difficult. The doctor will be here again soon."

Irwin had kept his first promise.

For the first four days in Irwin's house Emilie stayed in her room, which was like a small apartment. She was vaguely aware of someone taking and returning Percy and of huge, delicious meals served on silver in the sitting room that was daily brightened with fresh flowers. She took baths and sunk into the huge bed. She couldn't ever remember having such a great need for rest and solitude. Lying on the expanse of bed, the tensions and worries of the past months seemed to melt away. She was surrounded by beauty and comfort and safety. For hours she would lay drowsing and smiling as she felt the baby cartwheel inside her. She had been sleepy and agreeable when a doctor had listened to her heartbeat and the baby's and asked a few questions.

"You are doing fine, Frau Farber, and your baby is strong."

"How much longer do you think?" she asked, yawning and stretching.

"A few weeks, three perhaps."

"And my uncle?"

"I'm not in charge of his case, but I understand he is doing better. You have nothing to worry about, Frau Farber."

By the fifth day she was ready to see more of her new world. She would go to see Josef after she had done a little investigating. She dressed and brushed her hair and tied it back with a yellow ribbon. She surveyed herself in a full length mirror.

"You look huge, Emilie Farber, like a zeppelin!"

A maid informed her that Herr Farber was never home until very late, and the mistress was in the garden.

Frau Katrina Farber had never had much natural beauty. But she had a perfect pedigree. Any beauty was from her gentle kindness. And when she stood up from the rose bush she had been tending, Emilie saw she wore the same sad smile she had remembered.

"I'm sorry I've been so out of things for the last few days," Emilie apologized. "I just wanted to sleep."

"There is no need to apologize. I understand."

"You are very kind to have me here. Everything is so lovely."

The woman looked back to the bush, hesitating. "We hope you will be happy here."

And yet the mistress of the house looked so very unhappy.

Tegel Prison

He had been dozing when the door swung open suddenly. He lifted his head against the sudden light, his eyes squinting. He knew that the tall form filling the doorway was not his usual guard. The figure didn't speak or move. Finally Max's eyes adjusted. Reinhard Heydrich was watching him. His arms were behind him in the correct posture Max had seen a hundred times.

"This is your . . . home, Maximillian?" he asked pleasantly.

"I'd offer you a chair if I could, Reinhard."

Heydrich turned slightly to a man waiting behind him. "This is a stinking place. Bring him out."

Heydrich left and two men grabbed Max roughly by each arm and led him from the cell.

Heydrich led them down a corridor, up a flight of stairs, down another corridor. While Max didn't like the rough treatment, he welcomed the men at his side. He hadn't done this much walking in so long, and his legs felt incredibly weak.

They entered a room approximately the size of two cells. Two chairs, two high windows, one suspended lightbulb. They shoved him into the chair.

"Send the captain in."

Heydrich strolled along the perimeter of the room until the door opened and a thick-set, greasy-haired man entered. He wore a worn-looking army uniform. He stood with his back to the door.

Heydrich sighed and took off his hat. He assumed his pose in front of the prisoner. Max was watching the sunlight pour in through the rectangular windows.

"You are looking a little pale these days, Max. You need to get in the sun more. . . . In Spain or Italy, boating like you used to do," Reinhard taunted.

Max said nothing.

"When you were first incarcerated here, you were investigated by the Gestapo. I'm afraid I don't put much faith in them. So I've come this afternoon, Max, to handle the questioning properly ... and on the strength of our friendship that goes so far back." He smiled.

"Now you've been in your tidy little home for six months. Six months. You were supposed to sit there for a full year before you were questioned again, but ... Eric came to me, pleading." Reinhard shrugged. "So, I decided after these months you would be more inclined to talk."

Still Max said nothing. He was hardly listening to the arrogant man posing in front of him. He was talking to himself, telling himself he could survive what he knew the man who stood at the door was going to do. They would try to break him, but they wouldn't kill him.

Reinhard was irritated by Max's silence. He was accustomed to Max's flippancy.

"So I will speak slowly and give you time," he said patronizingly. "You did not come by the SS uniform you posed in or the timetable for

Jewish arrests or transfers by accident. You got the information from SS headquarters. Your information was very precise."

Max was composing a piano piece in his mind.

Heydrich's hands formed fists behind his back. He waited. He nodded to the man at the door. Max was sent sprawling to the cold stone floor by a single blow to the side of the head. With the world suddenly spinning, he gasped for air. He hardly felt the pain or the kicks to his side. The man jerked him back into the chair.

"You haven't . . . changed . . . Reinhard. Only now you have someone to do your bullying for you."

Reinhard's slap brought blood spurting from his mouth and nose.

"What was the name of your contact in Geneva?"

The minion applied the same swift treatment. Max was on the floor again, thankful for the momentary blackness that swallowed him. He was thrown back into the chair.

Heydrich waited until he had Max's attention. His boot was propped up on the opposite chair. Relaxed and confident.

Reinhard snapped to attention. "You are a fool, Max. If you don't rot in this prison, you'll die from your torture. You can make things a little easier if you answer my questions."

Max slowly shook his head. The man moved forward, but Reinhard held up his hand. Max had closed his eyes, waiting for the blow.

Reinhard's voice was low. "You are stronger than I thought. That is your Farber blood asserting itself. But every man has a weakness. All right. Let's talk about something far pleasanter. Not about the SS or your contact in Geneva. Let's talk about your wife."

Max couldn't keep his head from rising painfully. Now he wanted to plead with Heydrich.

"Ah, I have your attention." He started his casual circuit of the room. "I saw Emilie just last night. Last night . . ."

The footsteps in the room pounded in Max's brain.

"Emilie is very beautiful. She was even more beautiful to me last night."

Max held on to the chair with effort.

"She is staying at your estate. I have taken the *liberty* to *insist* she stay there instead of Berlin. It's safer with the air raids. I felt you would want her to be safe."

He came to stand before Max, his arms crossed over his broad chest. He was typically a man who came to a decision quickly, and once made he didn't waver. But he couldn't decide what would inflict the greater pain to Max—knowing his wife was pregnant—or telling him later at the end of the summer. Watching Max bleed, he decided to hold his tongue and keep the little secret.

"I am expecting a very . . . pleasant summer."

The man at the door laughed obscenely.

Max lurched up, his arms swinging the wooden chair toward the towering Heydrich. If he had not been battered and weak the chair would have struck the SS chief's head. Instead it caught him against his arm.

Max felt the warm gush of blood as the world darkened and spun and enfolded him.

● ● ●

"How are you feeling?" she asked.

"I'd feel much better if I knew where I was. This . . . this nurse who has been hovering over me is as mute as a statue. My nurse Helga was never like that."

"Helga wouldn't tell a patient something they didn't need to know," she laughed.

"Not if the patient was a doctor!"

"You had me very frightened, Uncle Josef."

His voice was contrite. "I'm sorry, Emilie. But you do look blooming. The baby?"

"Everything is fine. The doctor says two more weeks."

"Where are we?"

She watched his face. "This is the home of Irwin Farber, Uncle Josef."

Percy had come to the bedside and was standing on his hind legs. Josef reached out and stroked him for a long time.

"You were so weak, and I didn't know what to do. I was afraid . . . you were dying. I called Irwin and he got a doctor and sent an ambulance. He felt it would be better for you and for me—away from the raids and with access to better food and everything."

He could hear the need for approval in her voice. He smiled. *This place is quiet and safe and good for both of us. So why am I suddenly afraid?*

Emilie found Irwin in his study. She had been waiting, and, just as the servant had said, it was nearly midnight before she heard his car. She met him at the bottom of the staircase.

"May I speak with you, Irwin?"

He nodded and led her to his library. He tossed down a briefcase, loosened his tie, and poured himself a drink. He leaned against the edge of his desk.

"Have you found everything satisfactory here, Frau Farber?"

"Oh yes, that's what I wanted to tell you. Everything has been more than I expected."

"You are feeling well and rested?"

"Yes."

He allowed his eyes a brief scan of her stomach. He drained his glass. She knew he must be tired. *But . . .*

Her hands were clasped in her lap, and sitting there, Irwin Farber knew exactly why his brother had married this woman. The tenderness evaporated as swiftly as it had come.

"Was there something else?" he asked with just the slightest trace of curtness.

"Yes . . . yes . . . everything is perfect here. I do feel safe and Josef is being cared for. All as you said."

He crossed his arms. "Yes?"

She wondered what his face looked like when he smiled.

"I'm safe and I'm fed and . . . and I'm happy because I'm going to have my baby soon. But . . . it doesn't change the fact that my husband is in prison. I—"

Irwin grunted and shoved himself away from the desk. His hands were jammed in his pockets. His pose was defensive as he stood before her.

She spoke hurriedly. "I'm not asking you to change one whit of what you feel about what Max did or . . . didn't do . . . or anything. I'm asking you if there isn't something you can do for him in even a small way. And if . . . if there could be any way I could see him."

"You must think I have tremendous power, Frau Farber."

"I think you can do anything you want to do."

"The SS is in charge of your husband. He is in a prison."

"I think you can do anything you want to do."

"I will look into his condition. As for you seeing him, I will consider it."

He didn't want Max to know his wife was carrying his child. Not yet.

Emilie stood. "Thank you, Irwin. That is all that I ask—that you try. Good night."

Alone, Irwin Farber poured himself a drink and smiled. His sister-in-law possessed more than beauty. He would have to tread very carefully.

* * *

They threw him to the floor of his cell. As though from the end of a tunnel, he was aware of someone saying that Herr Heydrich would question him again. "Maybe he'd feel more like talking." Then there had been a final kick in his side.

For most of a day he laid there, not feeling the cool stone floor on his back—only the pain. He was sick and sweaty. He could feel the blood drying on his skin. Finally, crying out in pain, he pulled himself up against the wall. His right eye was swollen shut, his nose was broken, his ribs felt as if they were broken. His breathing came out in gasps. A gash ran along his hairline. His face was a mass of bruises. Both his top and bottom lip were split. His hands were cut and bruised.

"I made it," he whispered. "I'm alive ... I'm alive." He painfully moved to the corner and dug up his watch. Its presence comforted him. Then he spoke his name out loud. There was something reassuring about the sound of his own voice. He closed his eyes painfully. He thought of Heydrich's questions. He was relieved this man of immense power was still groping, still without a clue as to how the charade had been pulled off. *It must stay that way. I will die before I tell Heydrich the name.* Ever since his capture months earlier, he had fervently hoped his source would be safe. *If Heydrich learned who had betrayed him ...*

His cell door creaked open and he tensed. Had the madman returned so soon?

"Farber."

Max opened his eyes slowly. It was his guard.

The man came to stand over him. Max had never seen this man so close. He was older than he had thought—and as gray and colorless as the place he worked. *What a job . . .*

"I hope you're not bringing me another visitor. I'm a little under the weather today."

"Farber, they're moving you. You'll have to get up and follow me."

"Moving me?" Max rasped. "I don't think I can stand."

There was a moment of stillness. Max looked at the ground, his head throbbing. Then the guard reached out his hand. Concealing his watch from the guard, Max reached for the guard's hand, suddenly feeling he would cry. *This man . . . where will they take me? Could there be a worse cell? I won't have this friend any longer . . .*

July 2, 1942

Irwin had worked from his downstairs office, locking the door so no one could see him pace. On this day, anything the German army did—of triumph or tragedy—paled. This day, with a cry that penetrated the cavernous house, a new Farber came into the world.

Irwin had sent a maid to interview the nurse. Yes, mother and baby were fine. Dr. Josef had held the baby and placed it in Frau Farber's arms.

The business magnate could not conceal how this affected him. So again he sharply told the staff not to bother him as he locked himself back in the office. He poured himself a drink with trembling hands and lifted it for a moment in some personal tribute.

Yes, a healthy new Farber. A son!

16
The Price

The mistress of Adolf Hitler was an unremarkable woman with a very small handful of personal friends. Hitler liked her inaccessible and remote persona. The German public needed to think of him in only the highest moral regard. He had said many times that his calling to lead the German nation precluded any personal luxury such as romance and marriage. Only his closest circle of advisors and the upper echelon of Nazi society knew what the mysterious Eva Braun looked like. So it was a great surprise that Hitler held a dinner party in honor of Eva's thirty-fourth birthday. It was an unexpected, unusual, magnanimous gesture for a man who had been consumed and enraged by the misfortunes of his war this summer.

Katrina Farber hadn't wanted to come to this party at Herman Göring's. She knew a little of the fuehrer's mistress to recognize an ally of sorts—a woman overshadowed and dominated by the man she loved. Eva was timid at times, almost hysterically nervous at others. Still Katrina didn't desire a closer relationship. She did not like the pompous, absurd Göring or his arrogant new wife. She didn't really enjoy the society of any of the Nazi wives. But she came because she knew Irwin preferred it. She knew he liked these gatherings even less than she did. But he knew what it took to be a successful businessman.

They would mingle briefly, give birthday greetings to Eva Braun, then leave. They both had their own unshared motives for wanting to hurry back home. Katrina had retreated to the perimeter of the laughing party when someone touched her elbow. She turned.

"Hello, Katrina."

The woman who greeted her was a classic Ayran beauty, although not the robust type Hitler said truly typfied German maidens. She was tall and slender with a smooth, flawless face and deep-blue eyes. Her blonde hair was piled high in a French twist. She wore glittering jewels at her throat and wrist and ears. Katrina couldn't conceal her surprise. It had been so long since she had seen Reinhard Heydrich's sister.

"Elaina!"

She reached out and they gave each other a long hug. "I didn't know you were going to be here."

"I didn't either until the last moment." Her eyes swept the room. "I suddenly wanted a dose of this . . . for a nice long laugh."

Katrina's eyes blinked in confusion. "Is your husband, the count, here with you?"

Elaina Heydrich turned her glacier-blue eyes on Farber's subdued wife.

"You really are isolated out there in Dahlm, aren't you?" she returned sarcastically.

"I . . ."

Elaina's eyes softened and she took her old schoolfriend's hand. "I'm sorry, Katrina. You must not keep up on the gossip grapevine."

"No, I don't really. I find it as offensive as you find this party amusing."

They looked at each other and smiled as they relaxed.

"My husband remained in Milan. He has decided our marriage isn't working." She shrugged and turned away to the party. "He was right. It wasn't working."

"I'm sorry, Elaina."

"I'm a little sorry at times too," Katrina sighed. "I know what it's like to be in a house with . . ." She couldn't finish.

They stood watching the party surging and pulsating in front of them.

The corpulent Hermann Göring was attempting the tango across the floor. They could not see his dance partner. The two woman cut eyes at each other and laughed.

"Since I've only been back in Berlin a few days I don't know all the latest. Is Max in Tegel?" Elaina asked casually.

Katrina's voice was low. "He is in Tegel. I don't know much news either."

Elaina reached for a glass of champagne on a tray held by a passing waiter. "Max was always too impulsive and independent for his own good. It simply got him in to trouble this time. It makes me a little sad for him."

Katrina was surprised. Because Elaina and Max had been close friends since childhood, then courted as adults, she had thought there was love there, not just a tinge of regret. Suddenly she wanted to see if this was merely a woman's ruse.

"Speaking of Max, we have his lovely wife and her uncle living with us now. Percy too. I must say, he is a well-trained animal."

The perfect mask did not flinch, falter, or drop.

"How charming. I met her once. She was pretty in an American sort of way."

Katrina smiled to herself. She knew she shouldn't tell the secret she hugged, oh but how she wanted to!

Elaina Heydrich embraced her own secret. But unlike Katrina Farber, this one brought her nothing but fear.

● ● ●

Great joy had come tempered with sorrow. Emilie looked at this small and perfect gift and saw her and Max's love. *Max was taken from me so quickly, but now God had given in His swift and generous way.* She had come to realize in her heart that she might never see again the man she had fallen in love with. Not in this life. But she had more than his fortune and his name and their sweet memories. She had his son.

She heard a whining and saw a nose pressed under the sitting-room door. In all these hours of labor, Percy had been forgotten. Laughing she left the bed and opened the door for him. Typically he bounded in, but some canine instinct told him they were not alone.

"Come on, it's all right. Hurry or you'll get me in trouble."

Percy crept up on the bed.

"Look, Percy," she said in a hushed voice.

A perfect small head with wisps of blond hair. She unwrapped him. *He was smooth and pink and perfect.*

"He has blond hair, Percy, already like Max ... his father."

She leaned back with the baby pressed in her arms. She closed her eyes.

"Like his father ..." she repeated softly.

• • •

If the Nazis had been out of power and Max free, Josef Morgan's happiness could have been complete. What seemed like a lifetime ago, he had told Max Farber he needed to marry and provide him with children to enjoy. Let him be a grandfather as he had not been a father. *Now! Now at last there is this blessed baby to hold in my arms.* He still felt weak from emotion. He had comforted Emilie through her labor, taking a surrogate role that should have been Max's. Emilie had instructed the doctor to place the infant in Josef's hands first. Together they sat for hours watching the baby. They smiled and laughed and felt as if they were suddenly very rich.

With each day, his color and his appetite improved. He grew stronger. He could walk short distances with the aid of a cane. The staff had taken to helping him out of doors once a day, where he would watch Percy frolic. Since their meals were brought to their rooms, Josef never saw Irwin Farber and only rarely and briefly, his wife. From his window he watched her working in her lush garden. *Such a huge house for two,* he thought.

One afternoon he left Emilie's bedroom where she and the baby were resting. Percy was trotting at his side. He was a little curious about the closed doors off the hall. He watched as a maid unlocked and entered a closed room. He strolled toward the room. She hadn't closed the door completely. He pushed the door open, looked inside, and stopped in shock.

The maid was humming with her back to him. She stood across the room arranging long-stemmed roses in a glass vase. Josef's mind worked quickly. From Emilie's balcony he had seen Katrina Farber cutting the flowers. His eyes widened as he stepped into the room. It was a large room with thick carpet and beautiful furniture, and accents in pastels.

Shelves of dolls and bears, boats and books, a lustrous wooden rocking horse. He had entered the Farber nursery.

The maid turned, startled.

"Doctor Morgan! I didn't hear you!"

He bowed. "I'm sorry. I didn't mean to startle you."

"It's all right."

Josef stepped farther into the room. "I love fresh flowers in a room, don't you? Frau Farber has that special touch with growing things. Never had it myself." He leaned and smelled the flowers. "Lovely. They add to such a lovely room."

"Yes," the maid admitted slowly.

"Nice that the room doesn't have a stuffy smell for being locked up."

"That's because it's my particular duty to come and open the windows each morning. And bring the flowers."

"How thoughtful of Frau Farber."

The maid nodded. "Frau Farber loves this room. She selected every piece."

Josef was strolling around the room. "I can see that." He picked up a toy soldier.

"That was from Herr Farber's boyhood. And the dolls and the horse come from Frau Farber. Isn't it nice that they kept such things?"

Josef nodded. "Nice. How long have you been airing the room and bringing flowers?" he asked calmly.

"Oh for months and months."

Back in his room Josef sat weakly on his bed. He couldn't let fright or worry push him into a relapse. He suspected Emilie Farber was going to need him now more than ever.

In the weeks that Emilie had been in the Farber house, she knew that to find Katrina Farber you simply went to the garden. If she wasn't working in it, she was reading there. Emilie had observed her from her window and had speculated that this wealthy woman was very lonely. And very sad.

Emilie felt she had to get out into the fresh air to start a normal recovery. So leaving the baby with her uncle, she ventured out around the house and grounds. She ended up in the garden. Katrina Farber was there, a large hat shading her face. The full heat of summer had arrived. The garden with its trees and pools was the coolest place on the grounds.

"Good morning," Emilie greeted her brightly.

Katrina smiled slightly. "Good morning. You're up and about."

Emilie nodded. "As nice as the room is, I didn't think I could stay there another moment. I needed the fresh air and it is such a nice day."

"I know. I try to stay out here as much as possible."

"I've walked some of the grounds. You have a beautiful home."

Their eyes met. Katrina was cautious by nature, yet there was some sympathy in this young woman's eyes. She would listen; she would understand.

"Yes, thank you," she said without enthusiasm. She leaned back on her heels. "I thought it was the most beautiful place on earth years ago. I thought it was what would make . . . him happy . . . make me happy too. I filled the rooms with the finest, the most expensive . . ." She looked back to the earth and her little trowel. "I'm happiest out here working, watching things grow."

Emilie brushed back her hair, her head tilted. "You haven't been to see my baby, Katrina, your nephew."

She didn't see the other woman flinch. Katrina didn't look up from her work.

"I didn't want to impose. I wanted to wait until you were ready."

"That's very thoughtful, but you wouldn't be imposing," Emilie laughed. "I confess I'm quite ready to show him off! He's only the most beautiful baby boy in the world!"

Katrina stood up suddenly. She tossed the trowel aside. "I have to . . . I have an appointment. Please excuse me."

"I can't figure out what suddenly upset her."

Emilie and Josef were having dinner on the balcony of her room.

"It was so odd. She was talking and I felt we could become friends. She's so lonely and then all of the sudden she was gone!"

Josef was bent over his food. "Katrina Farber is definitely lonely."

Emilie waited for further observations from her uncle, but he was silent. She sat back in her chair thinking.

"Irwin's kitchen certainly has fine cooks. These are excellent cabbage rolls," Joseph allowed.

Emilie frowned. "You don't think her behavior was odd?"

Josef shrugged. "A little, perhaps. Now, more importantly, Emilie, the doctor is waiting for you to give him the name to put on the certificate and make little Farber all official. Have you decided yet?"

Emilie stood up and went to the bassinet. She scooped the infant into her arms and carried him to the table. She was smiling as she straightened his nightgown.

"He is the most beautiful baby, isn't he Uncle Josef?"

"I have delivered quite a few. He is by far the handsomest of this generation or any other!"

They laughed but her smile faded, her voice low. "How strange that I must christen this child without his father's suggestions." She stroked the downy head. "I've thought and thought about what Max would like, what he would want."

"He would like and want whatever you choose," Josef said gently.

"Yes ... well, then." She propped him up a little higher in her arms. "Uncle Josef, meet Morgan Farber."

Katrina Farber knew her sister-in-law's daily routine. A walk in the early morning and a walk in the evening. She stood at the library's French doors until she saw her pass with Percy dashing in the lead. That meant that Josef Morgan might be with the baby, or he might be in his own room. She would just have to risk it. She knew why she chose this subterfuge rather than simply going to see the child as Emilie had invited her. *Perhaps if Emilie saw me looking at the infant she would somehow know. ...*

Katrina's nerves were stretched taut these days.

She hurried up the stairs, but paused at the entrance to the corridor. A maid was coming toward her with a stack of linens.

"Where is Frau Farber?" she asked.

"You just missed her ma'am. She went out for her walk."

"And Dr. Josef?"

"I just took him the morning paper in his room."

"Fine, fine."

She went to Emilie's room, drew a breath, and opened the door.

A maid was tidying the room.

"Oh, Frau Farber."

"Good morning, Marguerite."

Katrina approached the baby bed. He lay on his stomach, two creased legs with white booties, a dimpled hand by his pink cheek.

"See how the light catches his hair?" the maid said with wonder.

Katrina leaned forward. His eyelids fluttered for a moment.

Emilie didn't exaggerate, she thought. *He is the most beautiful baby in the world.* Katrina nearly ran from the room.

• • •

Elaina Heydrich went to her bedroom dresser and opened the small box she kept hidden there. She retrieved something and carried it back to her chair. She held it out to the column of sunlight that poured through her French doors. It was a silver necklace with a sterling heart. She opened it. Max etched on one side, Elaina on the other. She clicked it closed. He had given her this when she was fifteen. They both thought it had sealed their future together. She swung it from her fingers. *It had sealed nothing. It was only a memory of ... of when we both were free to do as we pleased.*

She began to cry. She faced east where miles away in the distance she knew Tegel prison lay. *He was there. If only I could help him ...*

"There is nothing I can do, Max. I'm sorry," Elaina said mournfully.

• • •

Young Morgan Farber was one month old. Emilie had sent to Berlin for a stroller for him, and now she and Josef pushed him around the many sidewalks of the estate. Emilie had never felt stronger, and Josef privately thought she had never been lovelier.

"I keep going back and forth on this, Uncle Josef, and I just can't decide."

"Hmm?"

She stopped and searched his face. "Something is bothering you. Are you feeling all right?"

"I'm feeling fine. Nothing is bothering me."

He had been thinking of the nursery. *Emilie hasn't discovered the locked room with its fresh flowers and old Farber toys. The room that was waiting ...* He had seen Emilie give the request for a stroller, but he had overheard Katrina Farber specify the design, the color, and the store for the maid to shop at.

"Actually, Emilie, I suppose there is something that's on my mind."

"I knew it. We can't hide much from each other," she laughed.

"I've been thinking that in another two weeks, when you're fully recovered, it would be a . . . a good thing to return to the estate—Max's estate."

She stopped and looked at him.

"But why? Why would you want to leave here? Everything is perfect."

He steadied his voice. "How long were you thinking of staying here with your brother- and sister-in-law, Emilie?"

"Frankly, I hadn't thought into the future much. I've just been enjoying right now."

"Yes, of course."

"I hope that isn't selfish."

"No, no, you're exactly right."

"You don't like Irwin, is that it?"

"Well, he doesn't bother us."

She held his arm. "But you can't forget how he hurt Max in the past."

"I can't forget that his brother is sitting in prison, and he won't try to help him."

She tightened her grip on his arm. "That's just what I was trying to tell you earlier. I've been thinking about this. I talked to Irwin once before the baby came about me seeing Max." She looked around a moment, then down to the stroller. "Josef, it's breaking my heart that he doesn't know he has a son."

Josef nodded, but said, "If he can't be freed from there . . . it could break his heart to know he does."

The tears tracked slowly down her cheeks as she studied her sleeping son.

"Then you think I shouldn't have Irwin get a message to him."

Josef gripped his hands behind his back. "I don't think you should trust Irwin Farber with that message, Emilie. Not with how he feels about Max."

It was the same scenario it had been the first time she had sought him out. Late at night she waited for the sound of his car. Again he led her to the library.

He seated himself behind his desk, and Emilie had the uncanny feeling she was involved in some kind of business deal. They both sat warily, waiting for the other to be the first to speak.

"How is the child?" he asked finally.

Emilie wanted to laugh. *Couldn't he say "my nephew"?* But she held her thought and replied in an even voice.

"Morgan is doing very well. He's gained seven ounces."

She wanted to ask why he hadn't come up to see him, but she didn't dare.

"Morgan Farber," he repeated, staring past her head. "That is a good strong German name."

"I think his father will like it."

"I can tell you that your husband has been moved to a different cell. He is doing better."

She sat forward. "Doing better? Has he been sick?"

He looked at her steadily. "He was interrogated by the SS. He received some injuries. He's recovered from them according to the report I saw."

"Heydrich did this!" she said passionately, jumping up. She paced the room.

She swung around on him, her eyes blazing. "Your friend did this to Max!"

"Reinhard Heydrich is not my friend," he replied coolly.

"Aren't you the least disgraced that your precious Nazi party acts like such absolute brutes! Not just to the Jews, but to your own brother, Irwin Farber?" she asked condemningly.

She was saying things she had never planned to say. At least not this evening. But she couldn't help herself.

He watched her in stony silence. She sunk back into her chair.

"Heydrich will kill him."

Again Irwin said nothing. And even in her emotion she knew his silence was his agreement. Finally she looked up.

"Please, Irwin. Heydrich hates him as much ... as he wants me. He will kill him. Please, isn't there something you can do?"

"I was responsible for having him moved to a better wing of the prison."

"Irwin, I'm talking about more than that."

"You said any small thing I could do, Frau Farber. When the war is over, the SS may be willing to bring your husband to trial."

"He's more than my husband, he is your brother!" Her voice had risen. She didn't care who in the house heard them now. "And when the war is over could very well be too late! You told me you were bringing us here for your little brother! Where is your heart now?"

"What do you want from me, Frau Farber?"

"I want you to keep my husband—your brother—from being tortured or killed by Reinhard Heydrich or any of his thugs by whatever means you can." She swallowed with difficulty and her voice was barely above a whisper, "I want to see him, talk to him . . ."

He gripped his knees so she wouldn't see his trembling hands.

"I can bring Max out of Tegel, Emilie. I can give you a future with him. I could get you both to Switzerland."

Her hand went to her mouth. "Irwin . . ."

He leaned forward, his eyes dilated.

"I protected you from Heydrich. I got a doctor for your uncle. I improved Max's conditions. I can keep Heydrich from him. As you said Heydrich will kill Max with great pleasure. But the means to rescue Max will not be easy." He watched her with a look that suddenly chilled her.

Something was tolling in her mind, demanding attention. But she brushed it aside. This was too important. *Max could be free. They could be together.*

"The means will not be easy," he repeated, and Emilie felt his voice was almost hypnotic. "We cannot have children, Katrina and I. But more than anything we want a son. A son to continue the Farber name. You and Max can have other children."

She stood very slowly and felt herself sway into blackness.

17
Block Seven

Max woke up terribly sore and stiff but without the searing
pain. It had been ten days since the beating. This was the first day he
could think clearly through the racking pain that gripped his entire body.
Something warm was striking his face. He sat up slowly, blinking, his
heart pounding at what might have wakened him. His smile was crooked.
A shaft of warm sunlight had pulled him from sleep. His new cell had a
window! He got up as quickly as he could and staggered across the room.
This room was essentially the same: a metal cot, a thin mattress, a bucket
in the corner. But it also contained a crude wooden chair that held a pail
of clean water and a box that held an extra blanket. The door to the cell
had a barred opening across the top half. He dragged the chair to the wall
and stood on it. He was twelve inches too short to grab the ledge to lift
himself up. But if he was stronger he could. When he was stronger, he
would! This luxury was too great to be disappointed.

Each day after the beating had been a struggle just to breathe and
drink and eat and try to move in his agony. He knew the longer he laid
perfectly still the more his muscles would ache from disuse.

Max had come through the first step of imprisonment—the shocking
loneliness, the total separation of comfort, coping with the bare essen-
tials, being totally dependent on oneself for everything, including sanity.
In desperation Max had reached out to the One who had created him,

though he knew so little of Him personally. All his life he had heard of God, he had believed in His existence, but what did God have to do with Max Farber personally? With only gray walls to speak to and to hear him, he was going to find out.

Now he passed through and survived another grim reality of imprisonment: torture. The thought of the Heydrich's henchmen's return made him cringe and sicken. *How can I stand this pain again? Can I keep from crying out the things Reinhard is demanding?*

Heydrich was unleashing years of hatred. Max knew for business or pleasure, the SS leader would come back to Tegel prison. Even if he told the man his secrets, he would continue the beating until it finished him. Looking down at his swollen hands, he wondered if he would ever be able to play the piano again. *I won't speak to Heydrich,* Max Farber determined. *Death would come anyway, perhaps my silence will hasten it.* That was his future. He had to face it squarely.

So he sat back on his bed and let the sunlight hit his face.

"Just like lounging by the river at home," he chuckled to himself. While this discovery was precious to him, he had yet to find the cell's greatest asset.

To think of Heydrich's interrogation made him wince. But he felt he had to think back over everything the gloating man had said. *Eric had gone to see Heydrich.* Max smiled at the thought. *His brother cared. His brother was trying to do something for him. His brother had not forgotten him. His brother was not too ashamed that he had tarnished the Farber name.*

He stood up impatiently and stalked around his cell. Then he leaned against the wall, his arms outstretched, pushing against the wall in frustration. He could hear the mocking voice clearly.

"I saw Emilie last night. She was more beautiful to me. I have taken the liberty to insist she stay at the estate."

Max turned and slid down the wall, his body screaming at this treatment. His head lowered and his arms encircled his knees.

"I'm expecting a very pleasant summer," Heydrich had teased.

He felt like sobbing. *How* ... All his confidence at surviving this ... *Emilie.* ...

"God, I don't know You ... really. But I'm asking You to help her. Protect her from this evil man ... God!"

A long black car drove into the purple shadows of Tegel prison just as the lights were coming on against the evening. A man emerged from the backseat. His hands were shackled together in front of him. He wore tan trousers and a white shirt. He stood for a moment looking at the buildings before he was motioned toward a door. He had a pleasant face and kind eyes behind gold-wire glasses.

He was processed in silence and without incident. He was assigned a number and a cell. His hands were freed and a small leather case was returned to him. They led him down the corridors lit in intervals by a single light bulb. It became darker and fouler as they progressed into the interior. For all his face revealed he could have been taking a tour of a museum. Finally they stopped before a door and unlocked it. He stood in the hallway a moment longer, looking up and down. He looked at the two guards at his sides, but they were staring into the cell. He stepped inside. The key grated loudly in the lock. He counted their hollow sounding steps down the hall. Thirty-five.

He walked to the bed and placed his satchel upon it. He examined the walls and window and table and chair. He stood in the center of the room for several moments, hands in his pockets, his face upturned. Then he went to the bed and sat down. He slowly pulled off his glasses and polished them with a handkerchief from his pocket. He placed the glasses in his pocket and a took a long breath. Then the newest prisoner of Tegel lowered his head.

The light in his cell was turned off promptly at nine each night—from some master circuit in the guard's quarters he assumed. He knew it was nine from his watch that he had salvaged from his old cell. It was now tucked carefully between the mattress and cot frame. The first night that he was aware of after his beating, he discovered what made this new cell priceless. The light had been off for five minutes. Max was standing on the box on the chair watching the stars come out in the night sky. *It's the first night sky I've seen in almost a year.* His throat tightened with emotion. He gripped the ledge like a lifeline, doubting that he would want to leave this spot even for sleep. There was so much to see.

First he determined that this prison wing faced north. From his window he could see the dirt courtyard where prisoners were permitted to exercise. He could see the corner of a guard tower and yards of barbed wire. From growing up near Berlin, he knew the prison compound lay at the remote end of an industrial section. He had been overjoyed to hear the sliding and screech of a train shunting somewhere in the distance. He knew somewhere beyond his vision lay a forest. He had eighteen inches of sky. He couldn't wait for sunrise in the morning—or for a thunderstorm. He had awakened from his beating in the world!

A guard entered with his evening meal. "You can go out in the courtyard twice a week for thirty minutes. Your turn tomorrow. Showers once a week."

He was gone.

Max jogged the perimeter of the cell, ignoring the pain, his arms pumping the air. *I get to go outside tomorrow!* He laughed aloud. *Fresh air!*

He was so absorbed at the window that he didn't hear the routine of block seven's "nine o'clock" news. Finally, he heard them. *Voices. From the hallway.*

He jumped off the box and bounded to the door. He hadn't bothered with the door earlier because he thought it had been like the old cell— looking out on a gray, dank tunnel.

"Five?" someone shouted at the end. The light in the hall had also been turned off.

Voices in the dark.

"Six?"

"Seven!"

Max almost jumped when a voice somewhere to his right responded to the voice at the end.

"Seven here."

"Eight!"

"Eight here, and wishing he weren't."

Laughter erupted from the blackness. Max gripped the door bars. He was sweating with excitement. *Prisoners were talking, others . . .*

He listened while the roll call continued down the other side of the corridor to sixteen. Sixteen cells in this hallway.

"Give us the date, number ten."

"Thursday, August 2, 1942."

Max took a breath. "Say! I . . . I think I'm number six!"

The laughter erupted again, and Max received the greetings of fourteen men. When it had died down the "leader" took charge.

"I'm three. Give us your name, number six."

Max's voice was shaking. "Max Farber."

"Well welcome to block seven, Max. We heard them bring you in almost a week ago."

"They roughed you up a bit, Max?" one man asked.

"A bit."

Again the good-natured laughter.

"This is the only time we have that the guards leave us alone. Which explains why some of us sleep late in the morning."

"The guard told me I get to go out for thirty minutes tomorrow!" Max said eagerly.

And a few of the men, hardened as they were, were stirred by the youthful eagerness in the newcomer's voice.

Max spent the night talking, listening, and watching the moon.

It was a pendulum life for a prisoner—times of hope and determination to survive, to beat the Nazis, against times of despair and deep anguish. Many knew in their hearts that this home would also be their graves. Max was no different. He wanted to emerge strong and whole from this pit. But reality loomed as real as the metal bars and the guards that he might never leave this place. He would never see the world outside his eighteen-inch panorama. He'd never see Emilie or Josef. The hopelessness of it threatened to overwhelm him at times. You could hear it in the voices at night, in the darkness, the kind of day each man had had. Hope or sorrow.

But for Max this twice-a-week trip outside was of great encouragement. He stayed out until the guard had to roughly command him in. The others wagged their heads in amusement. Max had run and shadow-boxed nearly the entire time. The guards mocked him. The prisoners were not allowed to speak to each other in the courtyard. But the first day Max had learned through a few raised fingers which faces belonged to which nine o'clock voice. Some days the guards were lazy and indifferent and looked the other way, then the men would hurriedly whisper to each other.

"Just heard. Hitler sacked Rommel."

"Sacked the Fox? Why?"

"Messed up in Africa. Brits took El Alamein."

"If the little corporal keeps firing his generals, the Allies have a pretty good shot at winning this."

"Then for our sakes, I hope he puts that bucket of lard Göring in charge of things. We could be out of here by Christmas!"

It was the fourth night of his twilight conversation.

"Five."

A moment of silence, then, "Five here."

The hurrah went up. Max leaned forward, as if he could see into the gloom. This man was his closest neighbor.

The man cleared his throat, then his voice became firm.

"My name is Pastor Dietrich Bonhoeffer."

A hushed silence fell on the hallway. No one stirred or spoke. Then number eleven cursed. They didn't have to say it; they all felt the same. The Nazis had succeeded in imprisoning another good German—and one who, to many, was the greatest German alive. He was here with them. They felt a mixture of elation and pride—and sorrow.

Max was stunned. He had been to church to hear this man now less that six feet away from him. He had been Max's model of courage. Emilie had been so impressed with him. What had she said? *My father called him a lone voice of truth in Germany. I found him a great man of courage.*

Max was the first to find his voice. "Welcome to block seven, Pastor Bonhoeffer. We . . . we are all deeply honored to have you here among us. I'm Max Farber."

"Thank you, Max. But please call me Dietrich. And it is for me an honor to be among all of you. I think . . . we will all be good neighbors."

If the beating he had suffered from Heydrich had somehow brought about a room with a window, the liberty of outside, and now a great man beside him, he could be grateful for the pain. *Could this be the answer to my prayer? Or is someone else praying for me?* Max felt almost giddy with joy.

Because Max was only released to his time in the courtyard with other even-numbered cells, he was never able to walk with or speak face-to-face with Dietrich Bonhoeffer. Their once-a-week time at the shower never coincided either. It was a pathetic little ruse the jailers used to discourage interaction—and plots—between prisoners. So Max depended on the nightly conversations, standing for hours at his cell door developing a relationship with this man he so respected.

"I have met your wife. She is a lovely young woman," Bonhoeffer said.

"Tell us about her, Max!" someone called out.

"Yeah, tell us. Didn't I read in the society page that she's an American?"

"Max is married to an Ally!"

Max laughed. "She's an American, but by birth she's German. Her father served in the German diplomatic service in the States for many years. She's a photographer."

"But what does she look like?" a voice persisted. "Blonde or brunette?"

"She's brunette. Average height, blue eyes." He thought of her as she had been that night in Munich in her white gown.

"Any kids, Max?"

"No, no kids."

A long silence.

"Dietrich, have you seen her recently?" Max asked in a strained voice.

"No, I'm sorry, Max. It's been over a year." He then recounted for Max the last conversation they had had in her apartment. "She is a godly, courageous woman. You are very fortunate. Germany is fortunate."

"Yes ..." Max responded slowly. He leaned back into the cell, his eyes closed. There were no such things as private conversations here.

"Are you all right, Max?" Dietrich asked softly.

"I'm a little tired. Good night, Dietrich."

"You'll see her again, Max!" the voice of number eight called out encouragingly.

Max stretched out on his bed and stared up at the ceiling. *A godly and courageous woman ... I know so little about her. Will I ever know more?*

September had brought the autumn rains. Max sat watching the rain streak the window, his frame of the world a square of melted gray. The cell was damp. He knew the men in the prison were dreading the coming of winter. They had spoken of it the night before. They would be issued a cast-off jacket and an extra blanket to fend against the German winter. The cells would be frigid. Coughing and fevers would stalk the prison corridors. Some of the cells would become tombs. But none would be vacant very long.

After he exercised, he went through his geography lesson, naming every country and capital he could think of. He finished the morning humming the complete Nutcracker Suite. It made him think of another old friend besides Josef Morgan, his first friend—Elaina Heydrich. She loved the Nutcracker so he had taken her to Vienna to hear it when they were nineteen. They had been very happy and innocent in that brief time in the Austrian capital. There was no shadow of his father or Irwin or Reinhard. He never knew Elaina secretly had pretended the tall, broad man beside her was her young husband.

Now these years later, Max Farber couldn't help but wonder what life today, September 4, 1942, would be like if Elaina had accepted his marriage proposal. If she had not been afraid of her brother and acceded to his pressure, they would be married. He stared at the ceiling.

Marriage to Elaina. Would we have been happy? Would there be children now? Would I still have helped the Jews? If I had married her, would I be sitting in Tegel prison?

"You helped the Jews, Max? Why?"

"I felt I should."

"If you knew you were going to be caught and imprisoned, if you had known that for a certainty, would you have done what you did? If you hadn't, you would be with your wife tonight. You would be a free man listening to the rainfall."

Dietrich had put a question to Max that left him silent for several moments. He knew every ear strained in the darkness to hear his response. Every man had shared the circumstances of his arrest and captivity. All in block seven knew that Max Farber had aided in the escape of Jews.

"I feel very small tonight, Dietrich. I ... I had to help them; I couldn't turn away. But I'm here now, and if the SS doesn't kill me first, then I may be in here ... forever."

"I understand, Max. Every man here understands."

"In two weeks, I will have been here a year," Max continued slowly.

"Think on this tonight, Max: 'Deliver them that are drawn unto death, and those that are ready to be slain; if you say, "Behold, we knew it not," does not He who weighs the hearts consider it? and He that keeps your soul, does He not know it? And will not He render to every man according to his works?' That's from the book of Proverbs.

"Put it as a pillow under your head: Rest on it, let it invade your sleep. You helped the Jews at great risk to yourself because you felt you should. You felt it was the right thing. You responded to that voice of God in you.

Your own self would have told you to do nothing in order to protect your flesh. Now you are here, separated from the ones you love, and your flesh is speaking. That is entirely understandable. Our flesh and our spirit are always at war. I would prefer not to be here. I'd rather be teaching and preaching. But God has given me this pulpit. This is hard, Max, very hard, but we must die to ourselves to live truly as free men. Honor and decency and integrity are very expensive. Nothing Himmler nor Hitler nor any other man does can enslave us when we're in the truth of God. And if He can see our hearts, isn't it best He see honor and courage and kindness there?"

"But Dietrich, I don't understand God the way you do, the way you know Him. This is all new to me. God has been in the church, speaking through the pastor, through men like you. All my life He has been real but in a very distant way."

"He is here with you now, Max, in Tegel prison—just as He is with me." Max turned away thoughtfully.

The men of block seven responded with one unified voice when the two leather-coated Gestapo agents came for the prisoner of cell five.

"Cowards! Cowards!"

When the lights were extinguished at nine that night the men were subdued. Bonhoeffer had not been returned to his cell. There was little conversation among them. Max paced and spent a restless night. Mid-morning the following day, the hallway door swung open. Each man in eagerness and in dread hurried to his door. Two men were dragging someone between them. They opened the cell door. But first they stopped and swung him around for the horrified eyes watching.

"Gentlemen! Here you have your esteemed pastor! Look at him!"

It was a long, silent day. Max took his courtyard time with little joy. When darkness fell, a palatable tension hung in the wing. Cell five had been eerily quiet. Had the pastor died during the day?

"Number five?"

The sound was a moan that cut them all. "Number five ... here."

"I have been praying for you, number five," Max said firmly.

Silence.

"I have been praying for you. Is ... He with us ... number six?"

Max gripped the bars tightly. "He is with us."

18
A Greek God

Canadian Wilderness

The photos were barely forty-eight hours old when they were spread across the rough pine table. A team of six men, all in civilian garb, were examining them with magnifying glasses, comparing them to books about Czechoslovakia. Two other men and two women wove among them, causing animated discussion as they studied the photo then went to the long, nearby table to build a model of the house in the photo. Still another team of four men commandeered a corner of the barrack for their own discussions. They were studying a detailed map of Prague. A Czech citizen who had been smuggled from the country was among them, giving them all the local nuances of the city and surrounding environs that the map could not provide. He was the most important member of the team. In a smaller room, three men examined men's Eastern European clothing styles, railway timetables, and currency. Though the surroundings were primitive, this organization of men and women was impressive and calculated.

The leader at the photo table straightened and stretched and motioned to an aide.

"We need coffee, Jim."

The man nodded and hurried from the barracks.

"Our boy is a very busy man," someone mumbled.

The leader nodded. "Reinhard probably gets around more than any other Nazi henchman. He makes Boris Karloff look like a choir boy. Yep, he gets around."

"How'd he manage to get himself set up in a castle acting like a king or something?"

"Sources say he had Hitler pack off the other guy on sick leave and appointed himself protectorate of Moravia and Bohemia."

"Man, I'd make my sixth-grade geography teacher proud with the places I know now!"

Laughter.

"With all this power-grabbing it looks like Heydrich is gunning for Himmler. Can't stand being deputy to a chicken farmer."

"That's what they say."

"Mankind wishes he'd stayed a chicken farmer."

"Okay, fellas. Did London send us a good shot?"

"Looks good."

The leader stretched again and dropped a calendar on the table. He motioned the others to join them. All jesting was gone. He surveyed their faces.

"I've let you guys gab this over, but the boys who are dropping won't know till that night who the target is. So again I warn you to utmost secrecy. Our target has been labeled the 'Greek god.' " He pointed to the calendar. "We have four weeks to get this exactly right. A lot depends on this. We have to make this place as real as if it's our hometown back in Missouri. Four weeks."

He jabbed at the photo of the country villa.

"Four weeks and the Greek god falls."

"Heydrich" and "Hitler" laughed. "Himmler" was chewing furiously on his thumb.

Spring 1942
Country Villa Near Prague, Czechoslovakia

Heydrich didn't particularly like this unfamiliar place where he didn't know the language. But it was a satisfying place, a change from Berlin for a season. He could work from this place of great beauty like the medieval king he felt like. Even Lena and the children had taken to it. And Prague, only fifteen miles away, afforded him new and interesting diversions after his work hours at the castle. Everything should have been idyllic.

He strolled on the terrace, grateful that Lena had taken the children swimming. He looked over the vast panorama of forest and was stirred. Yes, this could be a perfect place this summer. All he could want was here. He turned back and gazed at the huge house. *You could live in one wing of it and never know who lived in the other.* His lips curled into a faint smile at the thought.

Reinhard Heydrich in all his ambitions had not forgotten Emilie Farber. She haunted his sleep many nights when he lay in the arms of other women. She entered his thoughts at work at times, something triggering her face in his mind. Invariably his hands would clench.

A trusted aide entered the terrace from the house. He clicked his heels together and saluted. Heydrich motioned him to sit.

"Himmler has been looking into your office while you're away," he said bluntly.

"What do you mean looking into my office?"

"You told me to watch him watch you. At first, I thought he was just generally trying to keep tabs on you. But then, after I . . . did a little persuading—"

Heydrich laughed and nodded.

"I found out who he was talking to and what he was asking. He's looking into the Farber thing again. He's trying to find out who leaked information to Max Farber from your office. As soon as he has it, he'll go straight to the fuehrer."

Heydrich burst out in a rare display of genuine laughter.

"So he's snooping in my drawers, asking my people about this leak! Well, the idiot should know I've already purged the place. How can he expect to find something I didn't?"

The laughter turned into a glower. He waved the secretary away. He pulled back a chair and slumped into it. He had spoken the truth. Himmler couldn't find this information because he couldn't find it.

Max Farber had to have had help in his little charade. Someone very close to the top. Someone close to him. The thought made him seethe. *Someone he trusted, someone he probably worked with daily had helped Max.* He had tortured several people in headquarters he suspected were involved. They had told him nothing.

If after all these months, Himmler is still after me on this, I must be equally determined. I must find the traitor first!

He shouted for the secretary. The man returned breathless.

"Yes, Herr Heydrich?"

"I want you to go back to Berlin. I want all the phone records that went to my office in that time period. Everyone traced. Every call in the building traced and accounted for. Do you understand?"

"Yes, sir. Shall I bring them back to you here, sir?"

Heydrich had cooled. His confidence returned. A brilliant stroke. Business and extreme pleasure.

"No, no, Herman. I'm coming back to Berlin in ten days on business. But it will be a very short stay. And I'll be returning with a ... companion."

1943 Canadian Wilderness

It took well into May before the winter loosened its grip on the upper reaches of Canada. So the training for Operation Strike Lord went on in deep snows and biting wind until the third week in April. The team of nine men had perfected every element of this mission—parachute jumps, the language, train timetables, the geography of Prague were imprinted in their minds.

The leader assembled the two dozen personnel who had worked on this project. The team would be leaving for Europe just after midnight. They were all solemn in this final hour. They had worked hard and melded together in their common purpose. And they would very likely never see each other again. They had been brought together for this one plan, then they would go their separate ways.

They shook hands all around and the leader voiced the words they were all feeling.

"Our thoughts go with you. You will be ridding this world of a terrible menace. All of mankind—Jew or not—should be grateful to you." He smiled a wobbly smile.

"We expect to get the report in four days ... that you were successful."

• • •

They had hoped for heavy cloud cover even though the moon was in its last quarter. They got both. It was a good beginning, and it infused them with renewed optimism. The Royal Air Force plane glided through the night sky heavily trafficked by Nazi bombers, on their way to England; support planes; Allied bombers over the Reich. It skirted the dangerous border of Germany by flying over Poland. It reached its target over Czechoslovakia at two in the morning. It swung down low over a field of wheat, then went up again. The side door opened and without hesitation two men parachuted into the darkness. They had penetrated fortress Europe. The silver plane banked and began its return trip.

In three minutes the two Czech patriots had landed, cut their parachutes, and were scanning the darkness. Their nervousness increased. They bounded toward a band of trees. They huddled there. Reports had indicated that Nazi patrols did not typically come out in this remote region, but if they had spotted the plane ... or if some farmer up with a sick cow had seen, or a Nazi sympathizer ...

Then a light, one flash, to their right. Once again. They must take the risk that this was their contact. They hefted up their packs carefully and jogged toward the light, desperately hoping they were right.

• • •

Emilie and little Morgan went to Josef's room. She knocked and entered. He was sitting at the window reading. He turned when he saw her and smiled. She crossed the room with the baby reaching out to the old man in the wheelchair.

She sat on the edge of her uncle's bed. The child sat in Josef's lap, reaching for the old man's glasses. He managed to pull them off and immediately began gnawing on them. Emilie and Josef laughed.

"You shouldn't let him do that," Emilie said smiling.

"He prefers me without them," Josef answered. He took the glasses from the baby and little Morgan became still. He snuggled into the man's arms, his cheek against the chest, his little dimpled hand patting the chest. It was a familiar gesture. Josef closed his eyes in ecstasy.

Emilie stood up and crossed the room. Turning away she felt like crying. Why she hid this emotion she didn't know. Of course Josef knew. Something had happened to her. She knew it. He knew it. Even the silent, emotionless staff of the house detected it.

Emilie Farber was slipping into some kind of apathy. As if her will and spirit had been drained away. She knew when it began. That horrible night eight months ago when . . . when Irwin had said . . . she could have Max in exchange for the baby. After her initial shock she had told him he was crazy.

That had been the last time she had spoken to him.

Then the first anniversary of Max's imprisonment had come and gone.

I haven't seen my husband in a year and a half. I don't know if he knows he has a son. I don't know if he is still alive. His memory is becoming so distant . . . So much has happened since the last time I saw him and heard his voice, she reflected sadly.

Heydrich. Irwin and Katrina. They all want something. I must make a life for the three of us—Morgan, little Morgan and me—a life that doesn't include Max. And the thought was heartbreaking. Her determination was slipping under the steady determination of this house.

"Emilie," Josef called.

She turned and they looked at each other across the room. The baby had fallen asleep against his chest. He motioned to her.

"We have to talk." He glanced toward the door.

She reached out and stroked the baby's soft blond hair, then the wrinkled hand.

"You have such a way with your namesake."

"He has a way over me. Now, Emilie we have to talk."

"About?"

"About you and Morgan. This . . . this can't go on."

"What can't go on?"

"Living here. Emilie, I know what Irwin and Katrina are trying to do. They are trying to wear you down, one way or another. They want you to give them Morgan."

She covered her face in her hands.

"Emilie, Emilie, child . . ."

"Josef, I don't know what to do. I've spent hours on this. I can't find a way out of this and Irwin knows it."

"There is a way. I've spent hours thinking on this too. There is a way."

She wiped her tears, watching him. And his heart swelled for the love for her. She was his daughter.

"Tomorrow night is Hitler's birthday. Göring is throwing him a big party at the Kaiserhof Hotel. I read that in the paper. I overheard the maids saying both Irwin and Katrina are going. They were getting her dress ready. So they will be out of the house until very late."

Emilie's eyes widened. He held up a hand.

"Now hear me out. I have puttered about and know the schedule of the staff in the evening. I know what most of them will be doing after you settle in for the night with a headache, and I go to bed, and the Farbers leave for their party."

"But—"

He held up his hand again. He reached in a sweater pocket and held up a key.

"Here's the key to the car that Ivan uses when he goes to town for supplies. It's all the way down at the stable. You can drive off and you won't be heard."

"Josef—"

"Emilie, you and Morgan must leave this house tomorrow night. You must."

"Morgan and I! Josef, you can't think I'm going to leave you here because I won't!"

He leaned forward, holding the child close. "Emilie, you must. You have to think of your son in this. I can't travel in this chair. It would give the whole thing away. The staff knows you are supposed to stay on this property. If they caught us leaving I'm not sure what they would do. They'd try to detain you. Their loyalty is with Irwin and Katrina. They don't want to suffer that man's wrath if you escaped."

"Escaped," Emilie moaned.

Josef was shaking his head. "That man . . . I knew he could never be trusted. If his father could see the disgraceful way—"

Emilie took his hand. "Josef, this won't work."

"It will work. You will drive straight to the Swedish embassy. You still have your American papers. They will give you temporary refuge. They will contact Geneva. You have to try, Emilie. You have to try this. It may be the only way of saving your son."

She was crying. "I can't leave you."

She had leaned into his lap, and he was stroking her hair. "Emilie . . . Emilie, my daughter, how I love you. We have been through so much together. You have told me about God, Emilie. We have to trust Him now."

But Emilie Farber was afraid. She and her son were as much a prisoner as Max in Tegel.

• • •

"I think this is the break we've been waiting for," the aide said excitedly. "I just have a feeling it is."

"I rarely go on feelings, myself," Heydrich returned smoothly. "But tell me what you have."

The man pushed the phone records across the desk. "Here are all the records you requested. It took a lot of time and work to get them."

Heydrich gave the man a reptilian smile. "If there is anything here— or in your feeling—you will be amply rewarded."

"I have found out that a man left the SS supply warehouse two days after Farber's arrest."

Reinhard slammed the desk and cursed. "Why didn't we see this the first time?"

"Because someone altered the records. He was working with the supply of officer uniforms, but the records showed he was working in the medical supply."

"I will have someone's head for this!" Heydrich shouted.

"I think the man was paid off and is in Berlin. I'm on his trail now." Heydrich stood up abruptly, his finger jabbing at the man.

"You will contact me by ten o'clock in the morning in my office in Prague with everything this traitor has. You will see him buried. And if you don't get me what I want this time, it will be your head in a noose. Do you understand?"

"Yes, sir."

Heydrich glanced at his watch as he pulled on his dress jacket. The phone list went into the inside pocket. "I'll pay my respects to the fuehrer, then be off. The plane is waiting?"

"Yes, sir. I told the pilot to expect you between ten and eleven."

"Between ten and eleven," Heydrich nodded. *Just a little longer . . .*

• • •

Katrina Farber was nervous, but she didn't know why. She knew she didn't want to go to the fuehrer's birthday party, but that didn't explain her emotion. She knew Irwin was waiting for her down in the library. Drinking. *If only ... if only we could forget the party, perhaps spend the evening in the nursery.* She hesitated outside her bedroom door as she looked toward Emilie's wing. She must see him once more before she left.

He was not in the nursery. She hurried across to Emilie's bedroom, knocking peremptorily.

"Come in."

Emilie and the child sat on the carpet in front of the bedroom's enamel fireplace.

"I ... he wasn't in his nursery ..." Katrina mumbled. Emilie didn't bother to look up.

Katrina knew what was happening to this pale young woman. In a way, the same thing had happened to her years ago. This house had killed her. Then her eyes traveled to the little boy. This child had given her back life. Any guilt or sympathy hardened at that moment. She went and scooped him into her arms.

"There, now, was dinner nice, hmm? Another tooth, what a boy!" She lowered him back to the floor. She really didn't want to go to this party.

"Are you feeling ill, Emilie?" she asked with a trace of the old kindness.

"I've just had a terrible headache all day. I'm going to bed as soon as Morgan gets sleepy," Emilie answered flatly.

"I could stay and help with him. I could give him his bath and read to him and put him to bed. I really don't want to go to this party anyway."

Emilie closed her eyes.

"Katrina, we're going to be late." Irwin Farber said, as he stood in the doorway, his eyes fastened on the baby crawling toward him. He took a step backward.

Katrina laughed. "Irwin, you look like you're afraid of our ... of Morgan."

Irwin hadn't seen him in weeks. He looked so much like Max.

"Herr Farber, do you have any baby pictures of your brother that I might have?" Emilie asked.

Irwin was shocked at the deadness of her voice. He shook his head almost angrily.

"Irwin, why don't you go to the party without me? Emilie isn't feeling well, and I'd like to look after the baby."

Emilie felt they must hear her heartbeat. His eyes must see the two little suitcases under the bed.

"No, not tonight, Katrina. This is the fuehrer's birthday."

• • •

Heydrich gossiped with the party hacks and listened to Hitler for thirty boring minutes. Then he excused himself for a drink. He took a place behind a group of men. Then the Farbers arrived. He smiled and drained the glass. He turned and slipped from the room. The Mercedes was speeding from Berlin. He had traveled this road alone the last time.

• • •

They held each other a long time.

"I love you so much, Emilie."

She clung to him. "I'm afraid of what they'll do to you when they find us gone."

He smiled. "What can they do to an old man in a wheelchair with a weak heart? They won't do anything. Katrina Farber is still decent underneath all that Irwin has put her through. You must not worry about me."

She pulled back. "But I will try to get someone to help you."

She was surprised at the strength of his grip on her arm. "Emilie, getting you and the child safe is the purpose here. Everything else is secondary. Now promise me you'll be safe before you contact me."

She nodded.

They looked at each other then at the baby. Neither of them felt they could say something cheerful like "We will see each other again." They didn't feel that way.

"I feel like whatever . . . heart I have left is breaking."

She turned at the door and he lifted a hand and smiled.

"God go with you, child."

"And you, Uncle Josef."

• • •

The car had just emerged from the Farber estate and onto the road to Berlin when a car pulled from the shadows and blocked it. Emilie gripped the steering wheel in horror as a man emerged and walked toward her. Tall and straight and in an SS uniform. *Reinhard Heydrich.*

He bent down. "Well Frau Farber, what a pleasant surprise!"

She looked straight ahead. "Reinhard, please . . ."

He clicked on a flashlight and swept the car. A sleeping baby. Two suitcases. He straightened up and turned off the light. She could see him turn and stare toward the house a moment. His voice was amused. "Ah, a mother and babe running away."

"Reinhard . . ."

"It pleases me that you call me Reinhard. Now, Emilie, gather up your child and your things and get in my car."

"Please, no."

"You have no choice."

Finally she looked up, pleading with her eyes. He smiled down at her. "I was coming for you."

One hour later Emilie Farber was leaving Germany for the first time in seven years—and beginning her first trip to Czechoslovakia.

19
Heart and Flesh

Winter had been as hard on the men of block seven as they had expected. Fevers and dysentery had gripped the prison as severely as the bone-chilling cold. Four bodies had been carried from block seven before the spring thaw had come. In their weakened, malnourished condition fighting off any illness or injury was an enormous battle. It was the time of lowest morale among the captives, and hope seemed as bleak as the cold, gray walls. The "nightly news" was apathetic and cheerless. Often only a few voices sounded in the frigid gloom. Each man was fighting in his own way a host of unseen enemies.

But Dietrich Bonhoeffer always spoke in the darkness. He could not imagine how the men looked forward to the sound of his calm, steady voice. *If he hadn't been there* . . . Those among them who had entered the bowels of Tegel without any faith hung on to his comforting words like a lifeline. Some nights he would laugh and tell them he was going to repeat an old sermon or try out a new one. No one ever objected. They knew that the Nazis had allowed the man paper and pen and that he spent his days writing. Sometimes he read to them from the pages he titled, "Letters from Prison." They sensed he was a private man, but for them he gave whatever he had. Some nights his voice was weak or hoarse, then he would simply pray for each man by name and their families. And each night one of them would privately hope that if only one man could survive Tegel, it would be Dietrich Bonhoeffer.

Max had felt the dwindling attention along block seven. He had been in charge of the nightly courses and debates in literature and astronomy. But he too had grown listless. Still, in the days when the sunshine was diluted through his window, he jogged and exercised. He couldn't stand the thought of emerging from this place looking flabby. He laughed at himself and told himself he was vain. Vanity or not, Max was hardly sick at all in that longest winter of his life.

He had memorized long passages of Bonhoeffer's book that the man had given him orally. And, wrapped in his blanket on a particularly cold afternoon, Max Farber counted on his calendar and found that he'd been a guest of the Nazis for a year. The pastor had remembered because, facing the risk of punishment, at midmorning he called out a gift to Max.

"Number six!"

"I'm here. Just relaxing, Dietrich. It's been a tiring morning, you know."

Bonhoeffer chuckled. "Just don't relax too much, Max. I have a Scripture for you. You need to think on *it* today, all right?"

Max smiled and nodded. It was kind of his new friend to want to cheer him. How right Emilie had been in her swift estimation of this man.

"All right."

"This is from the book of Psalms, seventy-third chapter. 'Whom have I in heaven but Thee? and there is none upon earth that I desire beside thee. My flesh and my heart fail, but God is the strength of my heart, and my portion forever. For, lo, those who are apart from thee will perish. But for me, it is good to be near God; I have made the Lord God my refuge.' Tonight I'll tell you about another psalm writer named David. He had a few troubles over the years . . . yet he was a man after God's heart."

"Thank you, Dietrich."

• • •

"You must tell me where she was going, Josef Morgan!" Irwin shouted loud enough for the entire house to hear.

"I told you, Irwin, she was going to the Swedish embassy for refuge," Josef answered calmly.

"And I told you she never made it to the embassy. Her car is just out on the road. And there are tire marks of another car!"

"I can only hope the other driver was a nice, caring person," Josef returned easily.

The staff tried to stay out of sight because Herr Farber looked like he would fire anyone on the spot. Frau Farber had been hysterical, and the doctor summoned. Only the old doctor in the wheelchair had been unperturbed. Yes, very strange goings-on in the big house in Dahlm.

Midmorning of the following day, Irwin came from the library at the sight and sound of a taxi drawing up to the house. He rushed to the hallway. A staff member was helping Josef down the stairs. A maid carried two suitcases and led Percy on the leash. The butler was white with fear and guilt at the sight of his master.

Irwin stood, his veins bulging in his neck, his face a cast of purple. In some ways, this old man had been his nemesis for years. *Imagine a crippled old doctor,* he thought disgustedly.

"Stop, please. I'd like to speak with Herr Farber," Josef said carefully.

Irwin and Josef looked at each other a long moment.

"Many years ago you told me you were the heir of the Farber fortune," Josef said. "And so you were. You have multiplied that fortune many times over from what I see and read. You have made the Farber name widely known. You live in a great house—a lovely house—with a lovely, sad wife. Everything you've grasped for, you've gotten. You could force me to stay here, you could keep hunting for Emilie and what is not yours to grasp. But I say to you, Irwin Farber, you never inherited from your parents what was most important. *Honor,* Irwin, honor. Max and Eric got that."

He motioned for the man to take him to the waiting taxi. Percy growled as he passed the big man.

• • •

The society matrons of Berlin imagined that a woman in the throes of a ruined marriage would want their constant traffic and gossip. After all, Elaina Heydrich was the sister of a very powerful man. She was a woman with a sterling family history and was still very wealthy. So it came, unsought, along the currents that wove through dinner parties and café luncheons, that Katrina Farber was in a maternal fever. *And it wasn't even her child! Such an unusual situation!* they pondered. It stirred the gossip well deeply. Bringing the wife of traitorous Max Farber into your home and taking his baby! *How could the mother stand that? Had Irwin bought her off?* They wanted to see Elaina's reaction as Max's old flame.

Elaina Heydrich played the role to a credit. She didn't welcome her old acquaintances with any real interest or enthusiasm. She wasn't intrigued by the news of Katrina. She felt only genuine sorrow for her old friend. She didn't display any emotion at the rumors, and her friends went away a little piqued and disappointed. Marriage, or a failed marriage, had changed Elaina. She was more aloof than ever now.

But alone in her room, Elaina could think without pretense. *Max had a son* . . . She spent a long time thinking about that. *How could the American girl possibly consent to give this child up? How could you part with your own flesh? What leverage had the cold Irwin Farber used?*

Her hands went to her mouth in silent horror as she guessed the truth. And in that moment, Elaina Heydrich was able to see beyond her own pain, her own loss, and her own heartache. *I can't help Max anymore. But can I help his wife?*

● ● ●

With their worn Eastern European clothes, their native language, their familiarity with the area, they slipped into Czech society easily. Two men passing through Prague, staying with a friend on their way to the fruit harvest farther south. They shouldn't have attracted attention. But they did.

And the local Nazi commandant was informed. Two strangers were in the area. In less than two hours, the farmer who had given them refuge had been questioned—then buried. The SS and Gestapo were alerted. Another report suddenly surfaced. Three nights previous a plane had flown very low south of Prague. Two parachutes dropping from an ink-black sky. Two strangers.

The hunt intensified.

Country Villa
Near Prague, Czechoslovakia

Fear had exhausted her; anger had revived her. For hours Emilie had lain across the vast bed in a kind of stupor, only vaguely aware of Morgan crawling over her, pulling her hair, poking her eyes with his chubby fingers. She had fed him then slipped back into this waking coma. When her son tumbled to the floor and cried, she sat up, disheveled and blinking, then scooped him up and soothed him. Then she wandered into the huge and elegant bathroom and bathed him. She locked the door and bathed herself. When she returned to her room, a tray of food was waiting.

She ate. Then, carrying Morgan, she pushed aside the drapes and stepped onto the balcony. She was amazed, then felt herself wanting to laugh. She whispered into Morgan's ear. "Well, I suppose if you have to be held captive, it's the scenery that counts."

She looked over a vast forest, and she could see sparkling lakes. She went to the bedroom door. It was locked. She sat down on the edge of the bed, at last able to clearly assess her situation.

A beautiful room with a beautiful view. Only the finest. I've fled one captivity for another.

Her anger flared to life. Emilie Morgan Farber was feeling more like her old self. The old self who had confronted Max Farber with his Nazi associations. And she was with her son.

"I'm a kept woman," she said aloud. She went back to the French doors. "Wouldn't you be surprised, Bess Bennett, if you could see how things have turned out for me? I've turned into the tragic heroine of a film we saw at the Metro."

She turned and looked at the locked door. Her captor would come through it sometime. He had flown her to this place where Irwin couldn't reach, where nothing could disturb his plans. He would come.

She went to her suitcase and pulled out her Bible. She drew Morgan into her lap. She flipped through it with uncertainty. *I need help,* she noted. *I need comfort. I need strength for what is coming.* Suddenly she thought of Dietrich Bonhoeffer.

She had read with sadness of his arrest. Another voice of reason silenced in her adopted homeland. She remembered the time she had heard him at the evening service of a Berlin church that first winter she'd been in Germany. He had read some verses from Psalms. He had said it was his favorite book in the Old Testament. She turned to Psalms. After an hour of reading, with Morgan falling asleep in her arms, she knew why it was Deitrich's favorite. She scanned a few pages until her eyes riveted on a few lines. They were written for her.

Whom have I in heaven but Thee? and there is none upon earth that I desire beside thee. My flesh and my heart fail, but God is the strength of my heart, and my portion forever. For, lo, those who are apart from thee will perish. But for me, it is good to be near God; I have made the Lord God my refuge.

She stroked Morgan's silky curls. "You are all I have, Lord. You are my refuge. In this place be my refuge . . . no matter what happens."

Berlin

Her bedside phone ringing shrilly brought her instantly awake. Her heartbeat raced in her ears. *Who would call at this hour? The count calling to say we must try again? That he missed me?* Elaina pushed herself up in her bed and turned on the small light. Two o'clock in the morning. The voice was hurried and obviously upset. It didn't identify itself.

"They got to Stephan. They killed him. I'm leaving town. I'm just calling because he's on your trail."

"But—"

"I can also tell you, if you care, that he took that American girl to Prague with him."

American girl?

Elaina gasped. "You mean Max's wife, Frau Farber?"

"Yes. I got the pilot to talk. Well, I've got to go."

"Yes, yes," Elaina said slowly, trying to comprehend. "You must—"

"You are not safe either." The phone went dead. An ominous silence.

No, I'm not safe. I'm in terrible danger from the hand of my own brother.

• • •

At twilight of her first day, the maid entered with her supper on a tray and a white box. Emilie sighed. *The white box again.* The woman handed it to her wordlessly. Yet their eyes met and lowered in womanly understanding. Twilight deepened and a curtain of rose fell over the forest.

Emilie expected him to come. Morgan drifted to sleep and would sleep through the night. Finally she opened the box. She lifted out a long, white, silk-and-lace nightgown. *The finest quality—probably from Paris,* she realized. *Something like what Max would have given me. Max . . .*

Max was gone. *What we shared had been brief, like one night's dream. But this is reality. The reality that I can't afford to anger this man,* she thought bitterly. She slipped into the nightgown. It fit perfectly. She turned off the lights and sat in the moonlight that came in from the balcony. *I'll submit my body but not my spirit. What other choice do I have? I'll survive this way. Morgan will survive. Then perhaps, when the war is over . . . perhaps then God would prepare a way for me to escape.*

"And I will leave Germany," she said to herself. "I'll go back to America. I'll raise my son with the joy he brought and with the heartache of the past."

She prayed, and a calmness descended over her. *Whatever happens, I have a refuge.*

But he didn't come that night and finally, exhausted, she went to bed.

Morning came, sunlight streaming in warm fragrance through the French doors. But a shadow blocked the sunlight. She stirred, blinking, disoriented but knowing it was still early.

"Max?"

The shadow moved. "You are very beautiful as you sleep, Emilie."

A smooth, cool voice. Not Max's. Her heart raced. She brushed back her hair. She glanced over at the crib. Morgan was still sleeping. He followed her look, then back to her.

He came to the edge of the bed and sat down. She pushed herself up into a sitting position. He reached out and fingered the gown.

"I am glad to see you didn't reject my gift this time."

He was wearing brown pants and a white shirt open at the throat. She looked down at her lap.

"Sudden business detained me last night," he said.

Still she was silent. He watched her a moment. "But I will go late to the office this morning."

She looked up at him. "I have only one thing to ask you. Please, Reinhard."

"What my American beauty?" He moved closer to her. He took her hand in his.

"Could you summon a maid to take Morgan away for . . . awhile? To another room."

Reinhard blushed an angry red. He liked to strike at Max Farber whatever way he could—even through a child. He was tempted to tell her no.

"Please," she repeated.

He would agree to whatever suited him. It would profit him to have this woman in a more relaxed condition.

He stood up and went to the door. He was gone for a moment. Emilie watched the maid wheel the crib away.

"He'll wake up soon and be very hungry," Emilie called.

"Yes, ma'am. I'll take care of the young one."

Emilie closed her eyes in gratitude for this unexpected kindness.

Heydrich returned to her side. He appraised her a long moment, the same look she remembered from the first time he had seen her—undressing her with his eyes.

He pulled her into his arms with authority. "I have waited a long time for this, Emilie Farber."

He buried his face in her neck. Emilie closed her eyes and repeated her psalm.

. . .

Heydrich's aide reread the information for the third time. This was not the kind of thing you could afford to misunderstand. He knew the man was expecting the answer to this long, nagging mystery of Max Farber's contact within the SS. *But . . . but is he expecting this?* He looked down at the papers again. Then he looked at the Czech countryside without seeing it. He glanced at his watch. It was very early. Too early to go to his boss?

But the man had wanted to know immediately. This will be either a crown of my career . . . or . . . He shook his head against the thoughts. He gripped the steering wheel nervously and pushed down on the accelerator.

. . .

The two Czech agents in pay of the Allies had hidden under the bridge culvert for nearly six hours. They had seen the sudden activity of

SS vans with soldiers. They knew instinctively they were the hunted. All these months of planning—they couldn't fail! In the mud under the bridge they buried their maps and anything that could possibly betray them. They kept only their forged papers, the clothes on their back, and one small pack. They inspected it in the night, then rebundled it. They checked their watches. Four more hours and they would move to the target area—which would mean walking through town.

"They are looking for two. We'll split up and approach the park from east and west."

"But, Jan, that isn't according to the plan. We're supposed to stay together."

"It wasn't according to the plan for the Nazis to get on our trail, but they have."

"We don't know for sure they are looking for us."

The older man shook his head. "They know. Somehow they know. Nazis are part bloodhound. So, we split up. I'll carry this." He hefted up the cloth pack.

"That means you have to make it to the spot."

"Yes, I'll be there at nine-forty-five. Set your watch with mine."

The younger one leaned back against the earth. It was nerve-racking, this waiting. Jan patted his knee. "Relax. I have a good feeling about this. I think we are going to be successful."

He nodded, but it was little comfort knowing a city full of SS was hunting you like wounded prey.

• • •

He pushed her firmly back onto the bed. He leaned over her, looking at her as if he could erase her husband from her mind and imprint himself. She could see a blend of passion and triumph and anger in his blue eyes. She stifled her revulsion. He leaned closer to kiss her.

There was a knocking at the door that he tried to ignore. Then cursing he stood up, pushing back his hair. "Come in!" he shouted.

His aide entered. He took in the bed and paled. Heydrich spoke through gritted teeth.

"This better be good, Herman."

"I . . . I . . . I . . ."

"What do you want?" Heydrich shouted again.

The aide's hands were shaking as he stretched them forward with the papers.

"I knew you wanted this information very much. I didn't think you would want me to wait."

Heydrich's breathing returned to normal as he snatched them. "Go wait in the hall," he commanded roughly.

Emilie pulled on her robe, watching the tall man as he moved with a bent head toward the French doors. He spoke aloud, forgetting her presence entirely.

"The phone records show the calls came from . . . from my residence. The man says a woman paid him to steal the uniforms . . ." he read aloud.

He sat down in a gilded chair suddenly, his mouth gaping.

"Of course . . . she was living there until she married. She stole into my home office; she had access to everything. She loved him . . ."

The papers fell and scattered from his hand.

He looked so stunned, so out of control. For the first time to Emilie Farber, this man looked human. He sat speechless for a full minute and Emilie's fear mounted. *This had something to do with Max. His terror would flame and then . . .*

He looked to the papers on the floor. Then he remembered her. He looked up. She was watching him. In his weakness. He stood up.

"Herman!"

The man entered instantly. "Bring my beloved sister to my office." He glanced at his watch. "By eleven. I want her there by eleven!"

"Yes, sir."

The door closed and Heydrich looked at the open French doors. He didn't see the beauty. He spoke through gritted teeth.

"I will kill her with my own hands, and it will be a pleasure."

He swung around. Emilie was standing beside the bed. He pointed at her.

"Your husband has come between us for the last time, Frau Farber, for the last time." He came to her and roughly grabbed her hair. He pulled her forward, against him. "So you have a little reprieve."

She winced in pain and he smiled. He stopped at the door. "You will wear that again tonight."

Then he was gone.

• • •

Elaina Heydrich spent a restless day trying to determine her options. Finally she settled on returning to Milan. Her former husband would shelter her. For all his faults, he was not cruel. She packed hurriedly and ordered her car. Descending the stairs, the front bell started ringing. She stopped, her knuckles turning white on the banister. The butler looked up at her with questioning eyes.

"Let them in," she said in a choked voice.

She should never have imagined she could pull this off without him learning. *All my life he has bullied me, tormented me with my secrets. I could never call my soul my own. Just that once, though, I had the courage to defy him. And now, now, I'm going to pay the terrible price.*

The two SS officers stepped into the tiled foyer. They saw her on the stairs.

"Herr Heydrich wants to see you. We have come to escort you."

"My brother is in Prague," she stuttered.

One of the officers bowed. He was delivering her death warrant, but his voice was flat.

"We have come to escort you."

• • •

Jan Kubis and Josef Gabiek had escaped from their homeland when the Germans overran the country two years earlier. They had found refuge in England and become part of the free Czech army there.They had been waiting for an opportunity to strike at the Nazi invaders. Finally they had their chance. To live or die, they had done what they could. They were crouched in some shrubs that paralleled a main thoroughfare in Prague. Their sources had told them Reinhard Heydrich passed this way each morning at ten o'clock on his way to his office in the city.

They slipped the bomb from the bag. There was no turning back now. Five minutes till ten.

• • •

Heydrich pushed aside his personal chauffeur and jumped into the Mercedes convertible. He roared from the villa in a comet's trail of dust. Two women, at opposite ends of the winding house watched his departure. Lena Heydrich wondered what had infuriated her husband to this temper, what had sent him storming through the corridors. Emilie sat and wept, knowing her husband was certainly doomed now. Heydrich would order his execution within the hour. She would suffer another heartbreak.

She fell to her knees, weeping. "How much more, Lord, how much more can I take?" But after a time her weeping stopped and she thought beyond her own pain.

"I don't know how much he knows of you, Lord, but please, in some way let him know that I love him and want to be with him."

• • •

Though Jan had alerted him at the corner by raising his hat, the car came so swiftly around the corner that it almost took him by surprise. It was supposed to slow at the corner where the train tracks bisected the road. But it was still speeding. Josef Gabiek ran from the shrubs, the timer pulled from the bomb. Jan, seeing the car was going too fast, ran toward it.

Heydrich slowed at the sight of the man coming toward the car. It momentarily confused him. The sunlight blinded him for a moment and the last thing he saw was another man coming close, his face intense, his arm outstretched as if appealing to him.

The bomb exploded on target and under the screen of smoke the two strangers in Prague slipped into the nearby park.

• • •

Two weeks had passed before the news swept Tegel prison. A prisoner who cleaned the guardhouse saw a discarded paper. No rumor, it lay before him in black and white. Whispered throughout the prison compound, by nightfall most had heard it and were privately celebrating. Block seven could speak of hardly anything else.

"'Hangin' Heydrich blown to bits. . . . Well, it's about time one of them tumbled."

"Been nice if Adolf had been sitting with him, chatting. He'll be with the devil by mornin'."

Max listened without comment. Then he retreated to his window. He looked out on the beautiful spring night. *Reinhard Heydrich assassinated*. It was difficult for him to grasp. *The man had seemed invincible. Is Emilie safe now?*

He sat down on the cot cross-legged. He didn't feel like sleeping. Then he returned to the window as if lured by the moon. The shining orb was surrounded by a halo of light. Max felt peaceful, the beauty of the night infecting him. He felt no joy at Heydrich's death, no sense of triumph, apart from that it may have helped Emilie. Most likely Heydrich's death would change nothing. He was still considered a traitor of the Reich. Would Hitler or Göring or Goebbels show compassion? He smiled.

He lay back down, the moonlight illuminating his face. *Emilie.* He had given her up. He had no expectation of ever seeing her again. He had come to the realistic terms of his life.

If only I could say one last thing to her. If given the chance, what would I say? He spent the night composing it. At morning he was eager. The guard was a pockmarked-faced youth who always regarded Max sullenly. Max would take his chances.

"You know who I am," Max said without preface.

The man looked over his shoulder and shrugged.

"Then you know my family has money; I have money. I need a message taken to my wife."

The man said nothing, but he didn't retreat.

Max held out his watch. The skinny arm reached for it. Max smiled faintly as it dropped into the man's pocket.

"It has a paper attached to it—a message to my wife. You get it there personally and it tells her to give you or your messenger some money. You can make more than you make here in a year by doing me this little favor. And no one will ever know."

The man retreated without a backward glance, the door swinging shut, then the turn of the key.

"And I will never know," Max smiled sadly.

• • •

They were in the garden together again. Josef lounging in the shade; Percy racing after a butterfly and barking. Morgan with unsteady steps was trying to follow. Emilie came from the inside of the house hurriedly.

"Josef!"

He looked up, alarmed at the sight of her sudden paleness. She was laughing and shaking and crying.

"Emilie, what is it?"

She sunk to the grass beside him. "I . . . I was coming out . . . and the front door rang and a man was there. He handed me this." She held out the envelope to him. "Emilie, please give the carrier of this five hundred dollars."

"It's Max's handwriting!" Josef nearly shouted.

"I know, I know."

"Who was the man?"

"I don't know. He must work at Tegel or something. He smuggled this out for Max. I paid him and he left like he was frightened."

She held it in her lap. "Uncle Josef, I'm almost afraid . . ."

He squeezed her arm. "Our first word from him . . ." He began to cry.

Emilie, there is so much to tell you, but only space and time for two. I am not the same man who entered this place months ago. They can only kill my body. One thing remains unaltered—my deepest and strongest love for my beautiful bride.

Max

PART 3

Wilhelm and Natalie
1942

Do not fear, for I have redeemed you; I have called you by name; you are Mine! When you pass through the waters, I will be with you; And through the rivers, they will not overflow you. When you walk through the fire, you will not be scorched. Nor will the flame burn you. For I am the LORD your God, the Holy One of Israel, your Savior.

—Isaiah 43:1,2 NASB

20
A Gathering of Secrets

Spring 1942, Munich

The young man who sat calmly drinking his beer at the sidewalk cafe wasn't really surprised at the few army personnel he had seen, either at the café or on the streets. It was a quiet, somnolent afternoon. The soldiers and officers of the great German army were off taking care of the fuehrer's business. *I'm among the enemy,* he thought quietly. *But it isn't survival that brings me to this German city, this mecca of Nazis.* He smiled to himself. *I've lowered myself into a pit of snakes. It would be so much safer if I'd remained hidden in the country, hiding in little rural hamlets with sympathetic folk or the Jewish resistance. But that isn't my life—even if it would be safer.*

A German officer with a pretty fraulein on his arm approached the cafe and selected a table nearby. *A snake coiled at my left arm.* He counted to one hundred. He took a long drink and turned slightly, deflecting any chance for this man to take the advantage.

"Excuse me, would either of you happen to know where," he consulted a thin black notebook, "a music store called 'Goldstein's and Picard's Fine Instruments' is located? I'm new to Munich."

"Yes, it is on Zellerstrasse. You can take the tram," the fraulein answered pleasantly, pointing at the corner stop.

The burly officer was pleased at the interruption. He had been wondering about the young man. Any man not in uniform drew attention in the Reich these days. Especially a young man. The youth of Germany were like a river flowing both east and west from the nation. What right did any man have to stand without some sacrifice to the Nazi colossus?

"It is on Zellerstrasse, she is right. But it is no longer Goldstein's. How could a Jewish business still remain in Germany?" he laughed easily.

"Of course. I was wondering the same thing," the young man returned with a smile.

"Old Goldstein would be in a camp, if not molding in his grave by now." The officer said as he yawned and stretched. "It does a man good to think that he has helped the poor swine to his next stage. Who knows, maybe old Goldstein will come back as a general next time around!" He laughed deeply, a disharmony with the earlier quiet.

The young man glanced at the woman. She looked down at her own glass, as if a little embarrassed.

"Excuse me, what exactly do you mean 'help the fellow to his next stage'? I have never heard of that."

The officer wagged his head. "I was in Berlin only two weeks ago. I heard this in a speech by Himmler himself."

The young man nodded.

"Himmler said that when we eliminate the Jews, we open the door for them to the next life. We are helping them with their karma—into the next step in the evolutionary process."

"Helping them on to the next stage," the young man repeated softly, nodding.

"You said you are a visitor to Munich."

"Yes." The young man smiled to himself. *I expected this. Better to expect, than to be surprised,* he remembered. "It's been years since I was in Munich. I'm from Berlin originally. But my work takes me all over the great Third Reich these days." He lifted his glass and peered at the contents as if speculating over his good fortune.

"Yes, I noticed you were not in uniform," the officer continued pointedly. "Your work?"

"I'm in medical recruiting. I work with the SS and the army. I administer Nazi policy concerning physicians. The army is always looking for good medical personnel and the SS is always . . . concerned with unhappy ones." He smiled knowingly.

"You have an exemption then?" the officer continued.

"Yes, unfortunately. I'm blind in one eye." He tapped his heart. "And weak here. Total reject for the army. So they send me around. I'd like to be on the front lines though. Lost a brother eight months ago to the blasted Russians. It would please me to take down a few commies."

The officer was clearly impressed. "And to Picard's?"

The young man almost laughed aloud. *Such a nosy Nazi. Typical. Always on the prowl.*

"A gift for a friend who loves music."

"Ah . . ." The officer finally turned back to his own table.

The young man drained off his beer. He was ready to leave, to find the music store, but he didn't want to leave with this curious Nazi at his back. The couple soon left with a nod. If he relaxed, it was imperceptible.

Quiet again. This encounter with a Nazi had gone smoothly. That was rarely the case. Yet if the man had demanded to see his papers, he could have shown them with confidence. The papers were impeccable. And thoroughly forged. A neat little folder of lies; a passport of desperate survival. He was rather proud of his ability to lie so effortlessly—something that would have horrified his aged parents. But he thought of them rarely these days. The mind must be honed to select ambitions with little tangent distractions. Distractions could lead to disaster.

This passport gave him the third identity he had assumed in the last eight years. *Assumed identity. What a crazy world,* he mused, *that some people can't declare their own names.* In this land designed by Nazi architects, disguise was common and nearly as real as the truth. *When the madness is over, will the survivors have forgotten their own names?* he wondered. *When will I proudly give the name my parents gave me? No artifice, no pretending.* He looked forward to that day. He never pulled the papers from his inner pocket that he didn't think of his young American friend who had secured them. They were priceless, and men would kill to get them.

Finally he tossed the coins on the table and began his walk to the nearest corner. Besides his instinct for survival, the young man was driven by another ambition. And sometimes, alone, especially at night, he wondered why the drive was so strong. *Why am I so determined? Why am I really taking these risks? To find one young Jewish girl, one of the hunted, in this city of thousands when there is no certainty she still . . . lives.* He had not seen her in over five years. *Five years. Is this a dream*

I'm chasing? Is this part of the painful past and best left to memory? Shouldn't I get on with my future, whatever that will be?

But late at night, staring up at the ceiling, feeling frustrated and terribly lonely, he would think of her face, tranquil and content as she had played her violin. They had shared no intimacy, only a brother and sister role. *Why can't I forget her? Why this connection?* He questioned himself a dozen times a day on this topic with no satisfaction.

He settled into the tram for the short ride, giving a swift perusal of the other passengers. There was always the remote chance he would literally run into her. *What a surprise that would be for both of us!* He knew it would shake him out of his usual cool composure. *Would I recognize her after five years? She would have passed from girlhood to young womanhood. Would she recognize me? Glasses don't do much to alter a man's face,* he thought.

He had come to Munich two days earlier, renting a modest hotel in a middle-class district. He had immediately consulted the telephone listings for the name "Weisner," the first, most obvious lead. Two days of calling had been fruitless. Few Germans welcomed a stranger questioning them over the phone. The Gestapo used a myriad of methods to uncover subversion—even an innocent search for a long lost cousin. Suspicion and self-preservation were vapors the citizens inhaled daily.

Now on his third day in the city, he was ready to pursue his second lead. A slender thread really. Goldstein's and Picard's, one of Munich's dealers in fine musical instruments. Or rather just Picard's now, as the officer had generously pointed out. The young man was accustomed to such bluntness. Savagery was no longer politely gloved in the Third Reich. She might have maintained some contact with her old skill and pleasure. That would mean a changed identity, a gentile identity ... like himself. Both concealing who they were in their homeland. The thought made him inwardly seethe. *What has reduced Germany to such stupidity? A life of deceit was a fragile facade. Could Natalie have maintained it all these years without discovery? She who had been so sheltered?* When he thought about her chances of survival, it seemed foolishness for him to look for her. Foolishness. The facts were as brutal as the officer's statement on Jews. All he knew for certain was that she had escaped the roundup of the Jews of Nuremberg five years earlier in the protection of a German gentile. He remembered what he had learned: *They had fled to Munich. Hardly a safe haven,* he thought. *Without papers, with her inex-*

perience, they could have been easily spotted and taken away. If they had made it, could they survive on their resources? Improbable, he conceded. *Impossible,* his old friends would say. *Foolishness.* Then he would think of the eyes of the old rabbi, trusting him. *Perhaps the memory of the old rabbi's approval and determined affection is the real impetus to my search. I'll continue the hunt until ...*

For his second approach, he visited each music store personally, making discreet inquiries, hoping for just a word.

"A young woman, twenty-one, dark brunette. An accomplished violinist, a quiet girl ..."

"Her name?"

A hesitation, a feigned embarrassment.

"I don't know her name. I have admired her from a distance."

"Ah, young love," the clerks would say, winking knowingly.

"Do you have a customer that fits that description?" *Hoping.*

Still there is another possibility. What if the Gentile Weisner and the girl had both realized the danger in that game of masquerade. If so, they could simply be hiding. And if the SS or Gestapo hasn't found them in all these years, can I expect to? Reason told him it was absurd and ridiculous—as impossible as Adolf Hitler appearing in front of the German people wearing a yarmulke. Another voice told him he must be certain; he must try until he knew she was gone. He would have to be very determined, very patient. But his money wouldn't last forever.

The tram slowed, the passengers gathered up their packages and their children. The babbling increased. He stood also. He could see the green-and-gold facade of a music store just to the left. A plate-glass window with instruments on display. *Picard's.* He frowned and disembarked, Wilhelm Mueller, actor, Jew ...

• • •

Rain was falling in quiet melody from a canopy of deep gray, coming down from a benevolent sky upon a sleeping city peaceful in the early hours before sunrise. The woman who stood watching this melody from the bedroom window of her apartment decided a rainfall like this was gracious to any city, no matter how coarse and ugly that city was in the light of day. Especially Munich. Having spent most of her twenty-two years in Nuremberg, this German city seemed ugly and harsh to her with its sophistication and big-city brashness. A city so thoroughly Nazified. And she knew it was, to her, a hostile city. It would be a beautiful morning when the skies cleared—a fresh and fragrant day. It was Passover. For the Christians, Easter. She couldn't celebrate Passover, and now she barely kept it in her heart. But it would never fade entirely—no matter what happened around her.

Hitler had destroyed both Passover and Easter. Such a powerful man, she mused with a certain detachment. *With a stroke of his pen he erased centuries of tradition. Was there anyone left in Munich, in Germany, to care that the sunrise should have brought the Jewish and Christian holiday?* She shook her head slowly, answering the question inwardly. Although in her isolation she didn't know it, she was part of a remnant.

She turned from the window to watch the man who was sleeping across the room. He was on his side, his face away from her. The street-light through the curtain caught the gleam of his gray hair. She could hear his breathing. He was a heavy, deep sleeper. She was grateful of that. So many nights she lay beside him until he was asleep, then she would slip from their bed and go to the apartment's front room. She rarely turned on a light, but sat in darkness that was a concealing and comforting veil around her. After an hour or so, she would return to bed. And though she kept this nightly ritual, he had never awakened to find her gone. Besides the twice monthly weekends when he traveled to Berlin, this time was truly her own.

She pulled on a light robe and went to the front room and opened the curtains. She opened the glass just a fraction. She quietly made herself a cup of tea and relaxed as she sipped the warmth and listened to the rain. She surveyed the darkened room and allowed herself a slight smile. Hugo had insisted she decorate the entire apartment, sparing no expense. She had chosen everything. He had enthusiastically agreed with every purchase she had made—and inwardly wished for the hundredth time that he could make this lovely, prudent, young woman his wife.

Her eyes rested on a wooden chest that sat under a window and her smile faded. *Beautiful wood—Hugo had been delighted with my choice. It was a perfect place to store fine linen and wool blankets.* But sometimes, like during these vigils, the wooden chest appeared as a coffin to her. It always drew her eyes when she entered the room. Tonight she stared at it, as if it would speak. And it did. Underneath the blankets lay a box, and below that, a violin case. Hugo knew nothing of its existence;

he had never looked beyond the first blanket. But she knew it was there. It was her box and her violin. And it was her secret.

She went to the window to avoid looking at the chest. But the rain had cast its spell and stirred the memories as it soothed the soul. She glanced at the closed bedroom door. Slowly she walked to the chest. *Why not tonight?*

First, the box. Slowly she lifted the lid. *A pair of ice skates.* She could explain those easily enough to Hugo if he came upon them. Unless he gave them more than a superficial glance, and saw they were not her size. They were men's skates. She fingered the metal blade. *He had seemed so glad to see me that day on the ice in Nuremberg. For that brief space of time, less than an hour, we smiled and laughed together. We were free. We were just two people out skating. Then, the Nazis had come ...* She closed the box.

She stared into the chest. *Why not pursue this painful remembering a little farther. Maybe the pain could purge my soul ...* So she pulled the violin case from beneath the blankets and cradled it in her arms. The leather felt cool under her fingers. She could remember the day she had chosen it from the shop in Vienna. Her grandfather had spared no expense. She should have the finest violin in Europe! But she hadn't opened the case in nearly six years. Six years. Of course she could remember the last time she had played it, her command performance, a concert for her grandfather. Though they had not known that at the time. She could see his face in her mind, smiling and proud, nodding.

She gazed at the case a moment more before returning it to its hiding place. She hadn't opened it. That would be too much, too tempting. She had closed and hid her violin case with as much finality as she had closed and hidden her past. *I won't open it this night. It is buried with the old Natalie Bergmann ... Jew.*

• • •

Wilhelm knew nothing about music beyond what he liked and didn't like. His time in America had given him a taste for jazz, and in this proper, elegant store he could hardly imagine the climbing notes of a saxophone. A man was playing something obviously classical on the grand piano at the front of the big store. *Imagine the raised eyebrows and shocked looks of the proper patrons if the sounds of Benny Goodman suddenly filled the place.* The thought made him smile.

"May I help you, sir?" a voice asked at his elbow.

"You have any saxophones?" Wilhelm asked casually.

The man's eyebrows knit together. "No, we don't carry that instrument. But we can order it for you. Picard's deals primarily in stringed instruments and pianos. We have the finest selection in southern Germany. We also carry a large selection of sheet music."

"Yes, I see."

"Were you wanting a saxophone?"

"Hmm? Oh, no, no, thank you anyway. I'm just browsing." He glanced around the store, spotting an elderly man at the piano.

"That Goldstein or Picard?"

"Neither. We're just Picard's now," the clerk replied, his voice clipped.

"I used to live in Berlin," Wilhelm returned easily. "I saw a package of sheet music once. It belonged to a friend. It had Goldstein's and Picard's on the return label." The memory had come to him suddenly, like the opening of a forgotten box. "Violin music," he said slowly.

"We specialize in violins," the clerk returned. "It was Herr Goldstein's instrument."

Wilhelm could not miss the tenor in the man's voice. He looked at him, but the man was looking at the piano. Wilhelm knew he was getting detoured, and detours could be dangerous but he couldn't help himself.

"What happened to Herr Goldstein?" he asked.

A long silence followed, the clerk's eyes were still fastened on the piano. "He died. May I help you with something besides saxophones?"

"I'm trying to find someone," Wilhelm blurted, instantly angry with himself. His carefully planned lie would not leap to his lips. The man was looking at him steadily, yet with something else. A sadness hung in the blue eyes. As if . . . as if he would understand anything Wilhelm poured out.

The clerk seemed to be measuring him, looking him up and down.

"Let's go to my office for coffee," he said, clearly after a mental decision had been made.

Wilhelm tensed. His guard had momentarily slipped. He could not afford to let that happen.

"Well, I . . ."

"Honey cakes too. I ordered them in from Jensen's. They're the best in Munich. Come on."

Wilhelm followed as if pulled, but he couldn't ignore the inward protest.

"I'll be in the office if you need anything, Rolf," the clerk called over his shoulder to a man polishing a small organ.

"Yes, Herr Picard."

Wilhelm stopped in the threshold of the back office. This slightly rumpled, sad-faced man was the owner?

"You're Picard, the owner?"

The man smiled and nodded.

"Please sit down."

He poured two coffees and brought over a plate of pastry. He sat behind a massive, cluttered desk. Wilhelm still stood, his eyes sweeping the room. *This was not the plan. Adapt and take advantage,* he reasoned. He relaxed slightly and took the chair.

"You're the owner?" he repeated.

"Yes, I'm a Picard. But I'm not the Picard on the sign. That was my grandfather, then my father. I only ... recently took up this work." He sighed. "And know precious little about it." He leaned back, sipping his coffee. "You are new in Munich?"

"A few days, yes." His eyes continued their sweep of the office. He needed to see some sign of this man's Nazi sympathies. But the only photographs appeared to be family ones. No party photos, no badges, no swastikas. He looked up and found the music store owner watching him with a slight smile.

"You said you were trying to find someone. How can Picard's help you in that?"

"This ... young woman was, is, an accomplished violinist. It has been several years since I've seen her. But she was moving here when I last saw her. She ... she was sixteen then, so she'd be twenty-one now. She was pretty then. Dark brunette, blue eyes, slender."

Picard nodded. "You have her name?"

Wilhelm hesitated. "Just Natalie." It was the first time he had said her name out loud in years.

"Natalie."

"You see, I thought perhaps she would come here to your store."

"Yes, I see. Well, off-hand, no customer of that description comes to mind. I'll ask Manfred when he comes in tomorrow. He handles all the violin orders. He may recognize your description."

Wilhelm stood up. "Well, thanks. I better be going now. Thanks for the coffee. Maybe I'll stop back in tomorrow."

He was suddenly nervous. Picard remained seated, his eyes still locked on Wilhelm.

"Is there any other way I can help you?" he asked gently.

Wilhelm had lived by fine-tuned instinct most of his life. He knew this man was not referring to musical instruments—or even to finding someone. He was looking at him with compassion. Wilhelm had not seen that in years. Hatred had been the dominating expression.

I can't trust this man, he reminded himself. He shook his head and turned for the door, but the voice behind him stopped him.

"If you need anything, ask for Thomas Picard."

• • •

For this event Hugo had insisted on dressing her. The dress had come from Paris, from a fashionable shop on Champs Elyées. Natalie pulled it from the box and tissue slowly. *It really is beautiful—even if it isn't something I would have picked out,* she thought. Silver satin caught the light and glimmered.

"It is beautiful, Hugo."

He stood behind her. "And you will be beautiful in it." He pulled back the satin dressing gown and kissed her shoulder.

She turned around, a hand going to his chest. "You're ready. Now go wait in the living room and let me dress."

He kissed her hand. "I'd prefer watching you dress."

She shook her head. "I'm a little . . . nervous tonight. Why don't you go put something on the phonograph while I finish. It will help me."

"As you wish. I have a few new records in fact." He left the room.

Natalie fingered the garment in her hands for a long moment. Finally she began to dress. Then she stood before the full-length bedroom mirror. Still, after all these years, the transformation still had the power to shock her. She hardly recognized herself.

She was just entering the living room when the music started. She stood in the doorway, stiff and unsmiling. At first, he didn't notice because the dress distracted him.

"Natalie! I knew the dress was perfect for you the moment I saw it. You will be the most beautiful woman there, and I will be the most envied!"

Natalie couldn't hear him. Only the violin. *It is Vivaldi's Concerto Number 6. I've played that so many times,* she remembered. *I won my first music medal in Vienna playing it.* It paralyzed her.

"Natalie? My dear, you're suddenly so pale! Are you all right?"

"I'm fine."

He took her by the shoulders and looked into her eyes.

"Natalie? What is it? Something is wrong."

She tried to smile. "The music, I ... I haven't heard that piece in a long time."

His look was puzzled. She pulled from his grasp and went to the phonograph. She lifted the needle. He was still watching her.

Finally, she smiled. "I'm all right, really. I'll listen another time."

He came up to her. "Natalie, all over the Reich people are celebrating the fuehrer's birthday. You shouldn't be nervous about this party."

There will be so many people there, so many important people,

"We're just going for a short time, I promise.

She was silent.

"And how can I resist wanting to show you off?" he smiled, then kissed her cheek. "You have nothing to be afraid of Natalie."

• • •

She was a portly, gray-haired woman whose bakery in this southeastern corner of Munich was becoming increasingly known for its huge and delicious pastries. And it was a growing attention that the cheerful woman didn't welcome. The shop bell over the door announced a thriving business—a merchant's dream. And it set off a tolling of anxiety in her.

She had been a resident of Munich for almost three years. Her appearance had been sudden, her manner brisk. She had bought the shop at first sight and in two short weeks was churning out fragrant coffees and sweet delicacies. Her reputation of kindness and generosity rippled through the neighboring streets like the aroma of bread and cakes that wafted from the ovens in the back room. The children soon found their precious coins could buy a huge cookie and maybe even a second one tucked in for the sibling ill at home. Tradespeople came for their morning coffees and snacks. In the evenings it had suddenly become a social gathering point for young adults. Situated a block from a city railway terminal, it drew commuters. In all her hard work the store could make Hilda Jensen a prosperous woman. But she really didn't care about that anymore. To make a good, sustaining living had been her first ambition. She had been a hard worker since she was eight years old working on her father's dairy farm. But that ambition had gradually changed after the initial months of opening the bakery. The new ambition had evolved quite abruptly. A matter of life and death had literally been thrust into her floury hands. She had taken only a moment before she made a decision and acted upon it. Now daily that ambition, her "after hours' sideline," put her in the path of the Nazi boot.

The bakery closed at eight. It took Hilda and two of her employees forty minutes to tidy the tables, wash the dishes, sweep, and prepare the dough for the next day. Then Hilda said goodbye and locked the front door. She lowered the green shades in the front windows. One final look, then she climbed the narrow stairs to her suite of rooms. Off with the apron, soaking her feet in a tub of warm water, she'd settle in to read the evening newspaper though it did nothing but disgust her. She read it only to understand what her customers might be chatting about the next day. She longed to tell them the truth. So many times she thought she would burst if she didn't tell them that Goebbels' newspapers were lies from front to back. But of course she couldn't say that.

Hilda Jensen listened to the outlawed BBC each evening from nine till ten. She listened in the bathroom with the parlor radio playing opera and her second radio turned low. Perhaps it was an unnecessary precaution since she was the only one in the red brick building, but one didn't take chances these days. All she wanted her neighbors to know was that Fraulein Jensen closed her shop punctually at eight and took a bath and listened to opera from nine to ten. A hardworking, loyal, pragmatic German. Very commendable.

But this evening Hilda's routine altered a bit. She was soaking her feet and rejecting the lies as the rain fell in the background. It had been raining since before sunrise. It hadn't deterred business however, and she was a little fatigued. She had perused the front pages and was about to toss it into the trash when she flipped to the society pages. It always made her smile. *What silliness were the Nazi leaders doing now?* She had seen an American film with two men called *Laurel and Hardy*, and since then, she invariably thought of the fuehrer and Göring as "L and H." She stared in disbelief. Her past looked back at her in a black-and-white photo. She hurriedly read the text accompanying the pictures. She didn't really need to. The face was too familiar. It didn't need the name. She knew the beautiful young woman in the photo—the woman on the arm of an army officer at the fuehrer's birthday party. She folded the paper slowly.

How a few years could change the details of life, Hilda reflected. *A life that had been moving in one distinct current, then abruptly altered. Only a few years ago, I was an employee and not an employer,* she thought quietly, *back when I lived with the elderly rabbi and his granddaughter. But no, the current had really changed before that. Years before, when I was a happy bride and then, seven short months later, a widow. That's when the current changed,* she decided. *Friedrich and I were going to have a big family. We were going to farm my father's land. We were going to grow old together. But then Friedrich had taken that terrible fall from a stallion and died in my arms.* Tears came to her eyes as she remembered the past. *Our farm outside of Nuremberg had to be sold to pay off debts.*

She had packed one small, battered, wicker suitcase and trudged to the city. "Nuremberg will be my home now," she'd told herself. She found work the first day in the city—she had found the rabbi. *Or had he found her?* Hilda mused.

There on the bench in the park, disheveled, tired, and discouraged they had met. He was feeding pigeons he said and mentally composing a book of prayers. Suddenly she had poured out her sadness to this middle-aged stranger. He had nodded, and she tried to think of what she knew about Judaism—it was very little. But he was so kind with her. Come with him. He would give her work. Without fear or suspicion she had followed him. She had followed him for over twenty years.

She went to the mantel. She picked up her silver-framed wedding picture. Then she picked up the frame beside it. The rabbi, his daughter, herself. Smiling and happy, content and safe in their tranquil routine. She had cooked and cleaned and modestly bossed the rabbi and mothered the girl. *It had been a happy house. Then the Nazis came.* The current became stirred, then turbulent, then churning, then changed course altogether.

She took the photo back to the chair where she had been sitting. She turned to the society paper again. She lay the framed picture beside the newspaper photo. The same face only older.

"Lovelier," Hilda said aloud.

A rare visitor to the upstairs apartment might notice the similarity. Hilda sighed as she placed the old photo in a drawer.

21
The Almond Bun

He was deep in thought as he turned the final corner before his hotel. His head was lowered—he could have passed inches from Natalie Bergmann and not seen her. Suddenly the crowd on the sidewalk formed an impasse. His head went up. It had the eerie feeling of a waking dream, a repetition of another time.

Four SS were leading a dozen Jewish men down the street. The yellow star stood out vividly on their dark jackets. They were prodded with rifle butts; they were kicked and spit upon. A few who stood around Wilhelm were nodding and laughing. He felt a hollowness in his stomach. *I can't watch this.* He pushed his way through to the street and hurried to the entrance to his hotel. As he stepped on the curb, turning his head from the scene, he caught a glimpse of someone. He swiveled around to look. One man had turned to look over his shoulder. Their eyes met. He was young, dark-haired, and bearded. An ugly red welt marred the pallor of his face. Then he was jerked forward. Wilhelm stood watching a second longer. *I'm one of them. I should be in that line, abused and captive.* But he was free, and at this moment his freedom was painful. He hurried to safety.

He slammed the door to his room. He stood in the center, scowling. *Why do I have to witness such scenes? Do I have to be reminded who I am, what is really happening to my people? My people.* He sat down tiredly on the bed. His father and mother and sister had made it safely to Switzerland three years earlier—thanks to Max Farber. He knew where they were but making contact was simply too dangerous. Maybe after the war, but if the Nazis won the war . . .

His brother, Walther, had been sent to Dachau by the hand of Reinhard Heydrich. They had never heard a word from him. Walther was a gentle, passive soul. Wilhelm couldn't imagine him being able to survive the harsh brutality of a concentration camp. *So I'm alone, without friend or family in Germany. No ties, no identity. Except Emilie Farber.* The thought of her made him relax. He stretched out on the bed, his hands behind his head. If he had ignored the pull of true identity those years ago in America, he could have married Emilie Farber now. *Likely they would be living in her Georgetown home, playing cards on Friday nights or going to the Gary Cooper films she loved. Or visiting with her witty friend Bess Bennett. Maybe I would be working for a newspaper as a reporter? Emilie would take her pictures and raise our children.* He closed his eyes. *Three. Two girls and a boy. Just right. We'd row on the Potomac on Sunday afternoons. He'd carry their little boy on his shoulders and read the inscriptions around the Lincoln Memorial. And they would read about the European war from a newspaper. They'd be safe. It could have been that way,* he thought. He fell asleep with his daydreams.

• • •

Hilda Jensen had become as skilled in this dangerous passing of information as she was in turning out her delicious pastries. Initially, it had made her nervous. Now it was merely an automatic reaction. She hardly thought of it anymore, like some of her recipes that she put together mechanically. There wasn't time to worry if this little man with the pencil-thin mustache and shiftless eyes was merely nervous for the danger he was in or because he was, in fact, a Nazi plant. There was always that chance. And every time the call came, Hilda Jensen took that chance.

A middle-aged man helped her with the baking. A younger woman helped her with the orders and clearing the few tables. A boy, too young for the Hitler Youth Corp, worked parttime in cleaning the shop. Hilda trusted all of them. She had listened carefully to their conversations as they relaxed between customers. She had casually questioned them about family—and learned their feelings toward the Nazi order. All of them were against the regime. But Hilda wouldn't involve them in her extra work. Too hazardous for them. Too hazardous for her. Every form of resistance in the vast Reich empire embraced the creed: fewer involved, fewer risks.

Hilda never saw a dark-haired young girl enter the shop that she didn't think of Maria Goldstein. And when she thought of Maria, invariably she felt a stab of sadness and guilt. Maria hadn't returned to work one morning and, by discreetly inquiring, Hilda had learned the father and son had been taken away by the SS. Maria and her mother had disappeared a few days later, the house abandoned. Hilda knew the SS had taken them, swept them up like the ones she occasionally saw on the street in guarded convoys. Maria with her beauty and subdued wit. She had come inquiring for work. She boldly told Hilda she was a Jew. Standing there, obviously nervous, Hilda had been reminded of the other Jewish beauty, Natalie Bergmann.

She had hired Maria on the spot. In unspoken agreement, Maria had stayed in the back, washing dishes and mixing dough. Hilda often saw her wistful looks past the parted curtain to the front counter and the laughing young people. Once she had seen her turn away, her hands clutched together until the knuckles turned white. Holding herself in. Hilda had turned away in pain as well, a blessing for this tortured girl on her tongue battling with a curse at the Nazis.

Hilda had meant to speak to her privately, to see how her family was faring. She wanted to find out if there was anything she could do. Then Maria was gone. Hilda had wept all evening at her failure. She vowed— no matter the cost—that it would not happen again.

The air of the shop was a melody of cinnamon and citrus and apple. The coffee was steaming and fragrant. Hilda was bustling and commanding and chuckling all at the same time. Her gray hair never stayed long imprisoned in the bun she coiled each morning. Already by ten, the tendrils had rebelled and escaped so that as she bustled, they waved like flags around her blushed face.

A woman approached the pastry case, appearing absorbed in a struggle between sesame buns and cinnamon swirls. She shook her head when Hilda's helper tried to assist her. Only when Hilda had scurried past did she give a meaningful look. Hilda slowed and brushed back her wings of flight.

"May I help you, fraulein?"

"One almond bun, please. It is my husband's favorite."

"Perhaps an apple tart, too?"

"All right."

"Just one?"

The woman nodded. "One."

"The apple tart is my favorite," Hilda said, passing the bag with a smile. "One almond bun, one apple tart."

The woman paid for the treats, gave her a brisk nod, then turned away.

Hilda hurried to a cluttered table. The coffee urn needed refilling and the sugar had spilled on a corner table. And one almond bun this evening—the most important order of her day.

●　●　●

Wilhelm stood looking out the hotel window for a long time. He watched the line of Jews until they disappeared around the corner. He thought about the last Jew in line and his look of appeal. Wilhelm understood it. The Jew didn't expect Wilhelm to do anything, to affect any kind of spontaneous rescue. He had been looking for a shred of compassion—that someone witnessed this atrocity, that someone might care. Even if silently.

I must care. I am still free. I'm not in line marching toward the concentration camp. I have to try to do something because I am a part of them. Wilhelm went through this evolution of thought and purpose swiftly. And he returned to the same conclusion he had reached those years ago in New York City. *This time, this time I won't look back. This time I won't waver,* he vowed. *I will work for my people just as the row of men were marched steadily toward their destruction. And if I am destroyed in the process—which will most certainly happen—I'll die with an honor I know my father would be proud of.*

Searching for Hilda Weisner had proven fruitless. If she had changed her name, then his search was impossible. He had no beginning point, no reference. Remembering her role as cook in the Bergmann household, he had tried a circuit of green grocers. He recalled she was almost fanatical about the fresh quality of her produce. His inquiries produced nothing. No one knew of a middle-aged woman named Hilda. He didn't linger long because of the clerks' inquiring looks. A young man out of uniform. Wilhelm knew it was only a matter of time before he drew attention that would not be easily deflected. Some SS or Gestapo brute would stop him. In this vast, thriving city, he would be spotted. His mission had an expiration date whether he liked it or not.

When he left his hotel room he taped the city map he had marked to the back of a dresser drawer. He pulled a wine-colored carpet thread from his room's carpet and tucked it under the crack of the door to alert him if he had had an unwanted visitor in his absence. He carried no paper of addresses on him, but committed everything to memory. The small black notebook was empty. He had lived like a criminal for years. *I wonder if there will be a time when I won't need these skills—when they won't be automatic*

There were seven music stores in Munich. He visited all of them. He had asked questions discreetly; he had appeared absentminded. No leads. No one could tell him of a young, dark-haired violinist fitting his description. A few possibilities had proven false. There remained "Picard's." He could return there as he said he would. But there was the man, the owner, who looked at him so intently. Wilhelm could trust no one, another instinct of self-preservation. He would not go back to the music store. It was a long shot anyway. Perhaps he would saunter past the store on occasion in the very remote chance he would see the young girl.

For two days he visited the museums, the libraries—places Natalie Bergmann would like. Nothing. He scanned the sidewalk cafes. He strolled past the middle-class clothing stores. Nothing. If he found her, it would be purely by accident. *I wonder if it's time to give up my search*, he wondered quietly.

• • •

Hugo von Kleinst, wanting to put his mistress in a romantic mood, had purchased wine and a huge bouquet of red tulips. He lit the tall white tapers on the mantel and helped her set the table with the white linen cloth and the good china. He smiled as she removed the apron over her pale yellow dress. Her hair was shining in the candlelight. He pulled back the chair for her and then sat across from her.

"Everything smells wonderful, my dear. As usual."

"Thank you, Hugo. I was at the market just as they were unloading the cod, so it's very fresh."

He took a bite and groaned in satisfaction. "I have never had it like this before, it's delicious. What is the spice?"

"Coriander seed."

"Your own invention?"

An innocent question yet it prodded her past. She pushed her potatoes around on her plate, her eyes downcast. "I just came up with it while experimenting."

Though Hilda Weisner had never formally trained her in cooking, Natalie had watched her enough to have picked up a few of her trade secrets. With a little practice, she had become an accomplished cook. And she rarely cooked that she didn't think of the woman. *She would be proud and pleased of how I can cook,* Natalie reflected. *And that is all.*

Hugo chatted about his work, his frustrations. Natalie tried to listen.

"The army is suffering great losses in North Africa. We have taken Tobruk, but at a great price. And of course the British will try to take it back." He shook his head. "This war is extracting a terrible price from the German people."

"You sound like you are a little uncertain about the war." Natalie rarely asked such a probing question.

He swirled his wine in his glass, looking toward the window.

"Perhaps, I am. But, I'm not alone. Over coffee, in the office, with the military men, you hear the same concerns. Has Berlin become greedy? Does it know when to stop reaching for more land, more prize? When is enough?"

"Yet the fuehrer says the German people need more living space."

He raised an eyebrow and smiled. "You do read the newspapers."

She returned the smile. "A little."

"Well, as for needing more living space, the more you have the more you must administer. That can be very burdensome. Very heavy. In a way, like amassing luxuries, the possessions—or captives—capture you. I don't want that. I have no desire to be a feudal king."

Again he gazed out the window. Natalie studied his profile. *Hugo von Kleinst, at fifty-two, is still a handsome man. He is athletic-looking and powerful. And in our time together he is nothing but sensitive and gentle. He's not like the proud, arrogant Nazis who dominate the party. This man, despite his loyalty, still has compassion,* Natalie decided.

She had wept many nights in silent gratitude that he expressed no violent contempt for the Jews. She had questioned him about this in such a delicate way that he didn't know he was really questioned. He viewed the Jews as unfortunate targets the Nazis had chosen. And, as a loyal German, he must abide with the laws. As for persecuting personally, he avoided that and considered it with distaste. He wanted to do his work efficiently and competently. Then he would retire to his country estate to take up his love of gardening and painting.

He turned back to Natalie. "That brings me to a rather unpleasant subject, Natalie. I was called to a meeting with my commanding officers this morning. It was long and thoroughly boring and wasted my time. But at the end, at the very end, they mentioned that I may soon be transferred from Munich."

Natalie was puzzled. "A transfer from Munich?"

"He gave me no specific details of the work itself, beyond the fact that it will be administrative duty. Of course, I'm hoping nothing will come of it."

"Where would you be transferred to?" she asked slowly.

Hugo instantly regretted mentioning the topic. He knew this young woman's face well enough to see her struggle with fear and distress. He didn't want anything like that on this lovely spring evening.

He sighed. "Poland. Warsaw, Poland."

"But why you?"

"Because I'm fluent in Polish. Because my records show that I spent a summer of study there years ago. Because everyone else is turning it down."

"Can't you?"

He smiled. "Natalie, please don't start worrying about this. I'm sorry I brought it up. It won't affect us—what we have together—I promise."

She got up and came to him. He pulled her onto his lap. She snuggled in the shelter of his arms, knowing this was not a promise Hugo von Kleinst could keep.

• • •

If he could not find Natalie Bergmann, he still had a goal—help the Jews however he could. That meant the resistance or the Jewish underground if it still survived. Now Wilhelm faced an equally challenging hunt—find the resistance in the Munich area. Find men and women who didn't want to be found. From his experience in the Nuremberg resistance, he knew some areas of the city where he might find contacts. It would take weeks of listening and watching. It could involve money in exchange for information or a slender lead. It could take weeks or months. But time was about the only thing Wilhelm Mueller had much of.

• • •

It was the rainiest spring Munich housewives could remember. It brought up the kitchen garden, but farmers were lamenting the flooded fields, especially with Berlin constantly demanding higher production to feed the troops. The rain was in its dual personality of blessing and curse. Hilda eyed the weather with the same conflicting speculation. Did it make a delivery more difficult or easier? It provided a cover, but it drew attention to anyone venturing out in such a downpour.

The five o'clock rush was not diminished when a man stopped Hilda as she bustled back to the counter. She had been refilling coffee cups and trading jokes with a young man and his girl at a front table. The shop was packed to standing room only as many late shoppers and workers on their way home dashed in for refuge. Then a man was at her elbow, literally dripping water from his soggy homburg onto her shoulder.

"Frau Jensen, I've come for the almond bun and apple tart."

Hilda nearly skidded into an ungraceful stop. Her eyes flew wide and protest formed instantly on her lips. *It is five o'clock. He is four hours early!* But he was looking at her intently. *He's frowning as if he can read my thoughts.* She sighed. This was the way of business; things did not always run smoothly and on schedule. Humans were involved here.

She turned and he followed her to the counter. Her voice was steady and lowered.

"The almond bun."

He nodded. She scanned the case. "Well, ah, they really are best when warm."

"Yes. They would certainly not taste as well if they were rained on."

Her eyes widened again, now in alarm. The package was out in the rain! She overcame the urge to swat this courier for his stupidity.

"I felt I had no choice," he stammered. "The people around me wouldn't . . . like the looks of a messy almond bun."

This exchange was almost unnecessary for the din of the shop. Still, one never took too many precautions.

So the package was obviously Jewish. And standing out in the rain near her store. She had to think fast. *I could refuse this package. It is too risky. How can I bring it into the backroom with my staff present? There is no choice.* She could only hope someone in another building was not watching the progress of the rain or the man standing huddled in a doorway. And that no one was asking why he was being led around the back of Jensen's bakery.

"Your fresh tarts will be ready in five minutes. I'll give it to you at the back of the shop."

He nodded and left. Hilda gave a brisk order to Gretl then hurried to the kitchen. Olaf was pounding out the stollen dough vigorously to the tune of a Russian folk song.

Hilda's mind raced for an excuse. She knew there would be a knock at the door any moment.

"Olaf, I want you to go take a quick inventory of the flour and sugar for me."

The big man's eyebrows knit together. "The bin is full and there—"

"I may go to the warehouse when this rain quits, and I need to know exactly."

He lifted up his dough-covered hands.

"Yes, please hurry for me, Olaf."

He shrugged and mumbled as he shuffled to the storeroom. Hilda knew it would take him a minute or less. The back door opened.

Wordlessly she grabbed the black-coated figure and shoved him to the open basement door. Olaf appeared.

"Three flour, two sugar, Frau Hilda."

She ignored his peevish voice. "Thank you, Olaf."

He looked at the huge puddle at the back door. He looked at her then back at the pastry table.

Olaf Swensen was not unacquainted with the strange ways of women, but he knew to hold his tongue. Frau Hilda was certainly acting odd.

She pulled the shades though the summer night was calm and pleasant.

"If one must be taken into hiding, I think a bakery is the very best place to be," the young man ventured with a shy smile. He ladled the final spoonful of his third bowl of soup.

"Our world is a strange and sad place, Isaac," Hilda said from the stove, "that people should have to be in hiding."

He nodded. "My father would say the same. But he would also say as Jews we should expect this." He rubbed his full, dark beard. "I only wish we had understood this a few years ago and cleared out then, left Germany. If we had, we might still be together."

"Your family?" she asked gently.

He sighed and stared down at his cup. "You don't recognize me then?"

"No, I'm sorry."

"I grew up a few streets over. On Blumenstrasse. I've been in your shop a few times . . . ." He gave a little nod and sad smile. "I'm the middle son of Aaron and Sophie Goldstien. I moved to Bonn and married. We lived with my wife's family. They were captured in a raid six months ago. I . . . I would have tried to join the partisans or try for the border, but . . . I was driven by this need to find out what happened to my family. I shouldn't have taken the risk coming to Munich. A man at the train station saw me and rescued me. He went to Blumenstrasse for me while I hid. He told me the house was closed and locked. It looked like no one had been there for months. He couldn't find out anything else. The neighbors acted afraid. My risk gave me nothing." He shook his head. "A coincidence that he should bring me here to you."

Hilda sat down across from him. "I don't believe in coincidences, Isaac." She moistened her lips. "I wish I had better news of your family."

He leaned forward eagerly. "You know of the Goldsteins of Blumenstrasse?"

She hated to see the pain in his eyes. "I knew your sister Maria briefly."

"Maria," he fell back, closing his eyes. "Did they take her? Please tell me."

"Maria came here two summers ago to work for me. I could tell she was a smart, vivacious girl not really suited to this work. But I could also see that she needed something. She worked with me in the kitchen— never went up front. My staff asked no questions, but I think they suspected. Then one day she didn't come to work. I waited a few days and then I went to your street. She had told me where she lived. I knew your father was a violinist. I knew she had three older brothers."

"What happened? What did you find out?" he choked.

"Only that your father and oldest brother were taken away by the Gestapo. Your mother and sister disappeared a few days later. It would appear they left on their own."

Isaac was staring at the table.

"I overhear a lot of gossip here in the store—most useless, some helpful. I will tell you Isaac, that there was a . . . story that a woman was taken in your mother's place by the Gestapo. That is, they thought they had your mother, but they didn't.

"What? How?"

"A woman posed as your mother. It was said the neighbor woman went, saying she was Sophie Goldstein. This woman never returned from the Gestapo."

Isaac was stunned. "How . . . how . . . could this be true? Who would do such a thing?"

Hilda shrugged.

"Frau Picard?" he stammered. "That would mean . . ."

Hilda returned to the stove.

"Why would she do . . . that?" He began to cry unashamed. To cry for his lost family, for his wife and son, for his friends.

Hilda came to stand beside him awkwardly.

Finally he could speak. "If that . . . if that is true about Frau Picard, then with people like her, like you . . . there is hope."

She nodded. "Yes, Isaac. There is always hope."

22
A Princess and a Pariah

Hugo von Kleinst loved to look at what he considered Natalie's classical beauty. Sitting across from him in the mellow sunshine, against a background of potted flowers, she exhibited that composed elegance he found so attractive. There were hundreds of young and lovely German girls, but not many could claim this innate dignity he prized. It was this quality he had first noticed in the young woman behind the pastry counter. It was more than just shyness—he thought of her as royalty in the humble rags of disguise. In his mind he thought of her as his princess. In his travels, in his position, he had the power to enjoy many women. Natalie had been the first woman he had formed a relationship with beside his wife. Every other young and lovely woman looked dowdy in comparison.

How had she acquired this quality? Was it something she was born with? In random moments, he wondered about her past. She told him very little. He knew she was guarding the past, but he didn't press her too much. Still, it didn't entirely quench the curiosity. *She was living with her friend, the owner of the bakery,* he reflected. *She told me she had been orphaned as a young girl, and the bakery woman and taken her in. She was originally from Darmstadt.* His princess had a very scant biography.

"Are you enjoying our little vacation in Dresden?" Hugo asked as they strolled the old cobbled streets.

She nodded. "Dresden is a lovely city." It seemed conspicuously absent of swastikas.

They finished their lunch and continued their tour. Arm in arm, Natalie in her white linen dress and matching hat, Hugo in his spotless uniform, they looked two paragons of Aryan perfection. She shook the image from her mind.

After an hour walk, Hugo hailed a taxi and left for a meeting with local Nazi administrators.

"You're sure you don't want me to drop you at the hotel?" he asked.

She shook her head. "The square is so quaint I want to keep exploring. And it's so nice outside."

He got out of the taxi and smiled down at her. "I don't know, fraulein. You're a little too pretty to be out by yourself. I see the looks you get."

She shook her head again.

"You have plenty of money if you see anything you want?"

She nodded and he kissed her cheek. He climbed back into the cab with a wave.

It was a beautiful old square. A fountain bubbled in the center and flower-and-fruit vendors sold their wares from colorful canvas-topped carts. Natalie surveyed the scene with pleasure. *It is so calm and peaceful here, so ... timeless. It doesn't seem to reflect the changed face of Germany.*

She stood on the curb, her hands holding her little black purse in front of her. Her face was shaded by the hat. Her eyes traveled across the square. A wooden hotel sign was squeaking on its post. She chewed her lip in thought. *What would it be like to register under my own name? To truly lead my own life. Without Hugo's generous provision? How could she earn a living? The violin ... foolishness.* She started walking again.

Thirty minutes later she came to a narrow, cobbled lane. Huge chestnut and linden trees shaded the way, and roses were climbing along the old brick walls. Wild violets grew in grassy patches. Such a beautiful old street. Hugo would have been delighted with it. Several women passed her. She watched them. They were entering a church at the end of the lane. Natalie started toward it. It was obviously of Armenian origin and, like the street itself, beautiful. She couldn't see far into the shadowy entrance beyond the iron gate. She turned around and looked back down the way she had come. It was totally empty. There was only the sound of birds in the trees that paralleled the path. She looked back. She had never been in a Catholic church.

Natalie stood on the sidewalk, suddenly feeling her own fatigue, the summer heat, and something else. *How long ... how long has it been since I've been in a house of worship? It's been so long since I've felt holy communion with God. But certainly God wouldn't want to commune with me. Not now. Not when I—not who I am now.* Tears filled her eyes and she almost choked. It had been years since she had cried. Crying belonged to the past.

The sanctuary was smaller than she expected. Nor had she expected that it was nearly filled with worshipers. She hesitated until a woman motioned that there was a place at the end of the aisle. Natalie went and sat down, looking at her lap and realizing she had made a terrible mistake. She knew nothing about their traditions and order. It was too late to leave.

An organ was playing somewhere to her left, in the shadows, and she found it soothing. She lowered her head and the tears came again. Perhaps no one would notice.

She heard the words of the priest, but didn't really listen. She had slipped into this foreign place of worship and found her thoughts returning to her memories of familiar worship. *How could I have thought I could ever forget the synagogue? The same quiet, somber atmosphere. A place to seek God.* Movement at her elbow. The women were rising. Natalie stood also, not thinking what this might mean, only wanting this tranquillity to not be disturbed. With a bowed head, she followed them to the front altar. The priest was administering communion and speaking in a low, soothing monotone. She knelt with the other women. She couldn't stop weeping.

The priest came to her right, but she didn't look up. He was extending something to the woman beside her. Then he was in front of her and Natalie understood. He was giving her a communion wafer. She reached and took it in her hand. Before she could place it in her mouth she heard gasps all around her. The gasps sounded magnified in the small church. The priest had hesitated only a moment before he went to the next woman. She leaned forward and accepted the wafer on her tongue. Natalie's eyes widened. She could feel every eye upon her. *I've committed a terrible sin. A sin. To come here.* She stood up shaking. She turned. *Everyone is looking at me. Every accusing face.*

She stumbled down the center aisle for the entrance. A woman to her left in the congregation stood also, her voice acidy. "Did you see what she did? She's a Jew, I tell you!"

Natalie froze, her heart pounding. She turned white. The nightmare of discovery had happened. This was her punishment for entering this holy place as such a sinner.

The congregation stirred. The priest was coming from the altar behind her, his voice pleading.

"Please, please, no, let her be."

But Natalie heard no more. She was running, bursting through the heavy doors, then gates, to the sunlit path.

• • •

Hilda Jensen had never been a woman to mince words.

"I think it's dangerous, Isaac," she said handing him a plate of steaming eggs.

He looked up, his dark brows holding the faintest suggestion of his mother, Sophie.

"Since my life is in your hands, fraulein, I'll do what you say," he replied softly.

She sat down in the chair across from him, glancing at the kitchen clock.

"I have to go down and get things going. Olaf and Gretl will be here shortly." She watched him eat a moment. He was as ravenous as he had been the night before. She knew this was the way of a hunted creature who existed on sporadic meals, never knowing when he'd eat next.

"I understand you're wanting to make contact with someone who could give you information on your family," she said at last.

"If I shaved my beard—"

She wagged her head. "The SS are always stopping men on the street, demanding identity papers. I see it everyday from my window. No, Isaac, it's too dangerous."

"Yes, of course, you are right."

She dumped the remainder of the eggs in his plate. "I'll take care of it myself. I'll go to see Herr Picard."

Isaac looked up, his eyes brimming with gratitude. "Thank you, Fraulein Hilda."

• • •

Von Kleinst knew something was wrong the moment he entered the hotel room. Natalie was not smiling and brimming over with the pleasure of her day. She was pale and withdrawn. She would tell him no more than she had gotten too much sun and was very tired. He unknotted his tie and studied her across the room. She sat curled up in a satin chair looking out the window on Dresden's most fashionable street.

"Shall I summon a doctor, my dear?"

She smiled wanly. "You are very kind, Hugo, but no. I'll be fine in the morning."

He wondered if she would ever fully trust him. Did it matter? His family in Berlin was his own private place.

"I'll order dinner up here." He squatted before her. "Then I'll draw you a nice bath and give you a massage, then you'll have a nice long sleep."

She reached out and touched the gray hair at his temples. It was one of her rare moments of voluntary affection.

After her bath, she dressed in his thick robe. He stood behind her and combed out her long hair.

"I was offered some things today by the SS chief here."

"Hmm . . ." Her eyes were closed.

"He's a man who likes to give gifts, sort of a prestige thing with him, I suppose. I was going to politely say no thanks when he showed me. I thought they would look fine in our place—that is, if you like them. One is a beautiful Oriental carpet. It would look perfect in our entrance way. Very expensive. The other is a silver menorah. I wouldn't have given it a second look except it's very lovely. I thought as much as we like to eat by candlelight, it would be nice on our table."

Natalie's voice was low. "Where did these things come from, Hugo?"

"I didn't ask. Some officials take those liberties when a Jewish family is taken."

"Couldn't . . . couldn't someone . . . I mean, the SS and Gestapo are so suspicious, think . . . seeing the menorah you were . . . Jewish?"

"They could think that, I suppose. But I wouldn't worry about it. They say Göring's house is filled with paintings by Jewish artists. I think everyone in Berlin has something from a Jewish house."

He stopped brushing and came to sit beside her, searching her face.

"Is there a problem, my dear? Would you prefer I didn't take these things?"

She was so tired, so drained, yet she must think clearly to reply.

"I'm sure they're beautiful pieces." She looked at her lap.

"But you don't want me to take them."

"I would just feel strange having other people's things in our place. I'd feel almost like . . . like a thief. Hugo, I'm sorry."

"Don't be sorry. I understand. Now, off to bed."

The deep, even cadence of his breathing told her he was asleep. She rolled on her side and watched him in the dimness. *There was so much to be grateful for in this man,* she decided. *He doesn't care for Nazi functions and rarely takes me to them. He is so generous, so sensitive. He could have pressed me about the gifts. Would I have broken down? Tonight I was that fragile. A little pressure and I might have told him the truth. What would he have done? Abused me? Drug me to the nearest SS station?* She couldn't imagine that, yet . . . he was a loyal man. He had said so many times.

She reached out a tentative hand and touched his chest. She could feel the steady beat of his heart. *Does he love me? Does a man love his mistress . . . or does he simply use her?* If she woke him now and said she was a Jew, would he kiss away her tears and hold her?

"Hugo," she whispered. But he didn't stir.

● ● ●

It was unprecedented. Frau Jensen was leaving the shop entirely to her staff as she went out on errands. She had given them thorough instructions and briskly told them she'd return within the hour. Even in her briskness, they could see she was nervous. Pulling her hat down on her hair with a gesture of finality and purpose, she sat off without a backward glance. They exchanged a look and shrug and returned to their work.

Hilda Jensen had made a vow to Isaac Goldstein and she was going to keep it. She would ignore the risk. Picard's music store was only three blocks over. The walk would give her a chance to revolve her options. She knew only of Picard's from their twice-weekly request for pastries. She supposed she had seen the man Isaac described as Thomas in the shop, but she could recall no clear impression of him.

"But if he was a pastor, would he be at his store?" she had quizzed Isaac.

"I don't know. With Herr Picard gone, and if what you heard about Frau Maria is true, who else would manage the place? At least one of the clerks could tell you something. It might be better than going straight to the house."

"Yes ... but, we don't really ... know ... what his feelings may be toward a ..."

"A Jew in hiding, I know. But Thomas has been my family's friend for many years. I'm not going to worry if he has Nazi-thinking now. He can tell me about my family."

"All right."

Isaac had slumped, looking down at his hands. "We lived by each other for years."

The practical, realistic Hilda made no response. She knew that didn't always matter. Wives had been known in this new Third Reich to betray their own husbands, children, and parents. A friendship stretched by Nazi pressure could easily snap.

At the last moment, before she had left him locked behind her apartment door, he had grasped her hand. "Frau Hilda, I'm sorry, don't do anything that will put you in danger, please. I ... I was being selfish. You are part of the network that helps Jews; I shouldn't put that in danger."

She had smiled and wagged a finger at him. "Stop worrying, Herr Goldstein."

Now she stepped through the etched glass doors with a confidence that belied her anxiety. She adjusted her hat as she looked around the large room. A violin was playing somewhere. A clerk was instantly at her side.

"May I help you, ma'am?"

"Well, I ... where is that music coming from?"

The clerk smiled. "Frau Berta is playing for a customer, just over here."

Hilda followed him to the counter where a woman was playing the violin. A young girl and her parents stood smiling and listening.

"I would just like to listen," she said to the clerk.

He bowed and moved away.

It had been so long. She had stepped into this Munich music store and stepped back into the rabbi's home in Nuremberg. Natalie was playing and her grandfather had closed his eyes in ecstasy. Natalie's music always seemed to knit them together. Even when the trouble came.

What was the piece she played?

"Could you play a little Mozart?" she asked when the woman was finished.

She smiled and nodded. Hilda forgot entirely what she had come to this place for. Then the music ended.

"Thank you." She turned and found a man in the aisle behind her.

"Welcome to Picard's, Frau Jensen."

Hilda was terribly startled. *How does he know my name?* He smiled.

"My clerk recognized you. He always fetches the pastries for us."

"Oh, oh, I . . . see."

"I'm glad we get to meet at last so I can thank you for the wonderful things you send over here. I'm Thomas Picard."

Hilda's eyes closed briefly in a silent prayer. "Oh."

His hands were behind his back. "Did you come about buns and cookies today or pianos?"

"I . . ."

"You enjoyed Berta's playing?"

"Oh, yes. It . . . it reminded me of someone I used to know, an old friend who could play the violin. It's been a long time since I heard such music."

He nodded with understanding. "There are some melodies . . . once played . . . that are never forgotten. And the artist . . . who plays them."

A sadness had crept into his eyes and Hilda knew he was remembering someone else, just as she was. Then he refocused on her.

She spoke quickly. "I thought we might work out an arrangement for me to send you your order rather than have you spare an employee. I've just hired a delivery boy. Other businesses around are doing the same thing."

"Yes, that would be splendid, Frau Jensen. Thank you for suggesting it."

She glanced around the store nervously. She looked back at him and he smiled. And nodded slightly. Somehow he knew there was more. She relaxed slightly.

"I've also come, Herr Picard—"

"Thomas, please."

"I have made the . . . acquaintance of an old friend of yours. He . . . cannot come here."

It was a sentence, she hoped, with only one meaning. She was admitting to harboring a Jew, an enemy of the state. It shifted her from a sympathetic bystander to a potential victim. Most Germans had read the newspaper stories of Jews discovered in hiding. Their rescuers had perished with them. A white star of David had been designated for the concentration camps, "Friend of Judah." Hilda had heard the shrill voice of propaganda minister Goebbels on the radio.

"You help a filthy Jew, you become a filthy Jew." A succinct judgment from a man who loved the manipulation of words.

So she was telling this stranger with the kind face she was a criminal. He could turn very casually and summon the Gestapo.

Thomas felt a momentary confusion that his face didn't reveal. He understood the baker's words. But who could she mean? Like Hilda Jensen, only moments earlier he had breathed a quick prayer. *This woman doesn't look like a Gestapo plant. But then, who does these days?*

He glanced around the store. If he put himself in danger, who would care for Gretchen?

Then calmness descended over him. As it had with the stranger asking about a saxophone.

"Well, Fraulein Jensen, I'm always pleased to hear from old friends. When shall we meet?"

She had already weighed this. *Move Isaac to this store or have Picard come to the shop after hours?* She made a swift decision.

"Come to my shop just before closing, Herr Picard. I'll have some fresh, hot almond buns for you."

Thomas absently tended to his office work. Finally he could stand the confines of the store no longer. He could think better as he walked. In the "old" days he had prepared sermons this way or worked through a problem with his congregation. *In the old days.* He told his staff he was going home early. They could lock up.

He decided he would walk home and spend an hour or so with his little sister. He would pray as he walked. Thomas Picard had become more of a man of prayer than ever before. Old Professor Begg had summed it up: "Pain or sorrow or age always makes a man a better prayer. He quits looking at God's hand so much and looks at His face."

Isaac Goldstein knew what to hope for. He didn't know what to expect. Thomas had been a good friend for so many years. In many ways, he had been like a brother. Now, these years later, what would Thomas Picard do with the sudden appearance of a friend from the past?

Hilda contained her anxiety with a scrupulous cleaning of her bakery kitchen. Then the evening crowd had come and for several hours she forgot about the presence of the young man upstairs. In fact she forgot about the meeting entirely until she glanced up and saw Herr Picard taking a table in the corner. She took him a cup of coffee and a bun. They exchanged a smile but no words.

Finally the store was closed, the employees gone, the lights exstinquished. Hilda led Thomas up the narrow steps and into her apartment. The two men stood transfixed for a breathless moment. Then Thomas hurried forward, his arms sweeping Isaac into an embrace, slapping his back. At the sight of Isaac's face, Hilda turned away and fiddled with the lamp.

"Isaac."

Isaac Goldstein was weeping. So many months of strange faces, hardship, and uncertainty, of living as a hunted animal, hatred circling around him. It was not quite the same as seeing the face of his brother, Maria, or his parents—but it was close.

Finally they stood apart. "I had no idea it was you, Isaac," Thomas laughed. "No idea."

Isaac was smiling and nodding.

Thomas pumped his hand again. "It is so wonderful to see you."

For Thomas it was a reminder of the past that had been free of shadow. When everyone had laughed and loved—a simpler time. They couldn't return to it. But this, this was a fragile gift.

They sat down on the sofa, each taking a moment to study each other. Hilda hovered in the background.

"We've both added a little gray to the roof," Thomas said.

"These are times that will gray any man's roof," Isaac returned, and they both were able to laugh.

"I remember the time Frau Sophie came bursting into our house and told my mother she had found several gray hairs that morning!"

Isaac nodded. "I remember. They went out and got some kind of hair wash—"

"And her hair came out this terrible red!"

Isaac was laughing.

"I remember your papa went around quoting 'Vanity goes before a fall!' "

"Like the time Maria cut her own hair when she was twelve or something."

"She had Jacob do it," Thomas corrected.

"That's right. Jacob tried to copy some style in a movie magazine. Papa would look at her head and tell her the floor needed mopping!" Isaac chuckled.

Hilda had sat across from them, relieved to see the two men laughing. It returned youth to both their tired, lined faces. She watched the animation in Thomas' face, his eagerness, his constant reaching out to touch his old friend. *I didn't have to be anxious for a moment. This is a good man.* She breathed a prayer of thanks.

They had to be sober soon enough. Maria's name had brought them crashing back to the reality that Isaac was the only survivor of the Goldsteins of Blumenstrasse.

Isaac told his story first.

"I only had letters from Mama to tell me what was going on here. I was forced to leave my work in Bonn. Britta—"

"Your wife?"

Isaac nodded and stopped; his face blanched in pain. His head hung. "We were able to hide for a time. Britta and I, her older sister and parents." He looked up. "I . . . I have a son, Thomas."

"A son!" Again Thomas was hugging him. Then he frowned. *A baby, a Jewish baby.*

Isaac read his thoughts.

"I suppose that is the only part of my story that is good. The hunt for Jews in the city became so intense we were afraid for him. Britta's older sister, a good woman, knew of a Christian family in Cologne who was willing to shelter a Jewish baby. A family we could trust. We . . . we sent little Aaron there. He is safe."

Hilda watched Thomas Picard. His shoulders had become progressively hunched as Isaac's narration proceeded. His hands were laced together, his face riveted on the floor. She suspected this man carried burdens that no man should carry. The joy of the reunion was bittersweet.

"I thank Jehovah for providing a way for my son, for Britta's son. I was out looking for a contact who might smuggle us to Switzerland when the SS came and found my family. They were all taken. The last I heard they were sent to a camp called Buchenwald." His voice returned to its factual tone.

"I waited about five months in Bonn. The last letter I had from Mama was about Papa staying at home and your brother Rudi killed."

Thomas nodded. "Jacob left a few weeks after that," he said softly.

Isaac nodded. "I guessed that. Well, Jacob is tough. I think if any Jew can make it, he can. I was able to meet up with a resistance group. I stayed with them for almost a year. Then ... then I simply couldn't wait any longer to find out what had happened here in Munich to my family. Mama was always so stubborn about staying on Blumenstrasse." He shook his head. "As if Blumenstrasse was a fortress against the Nazis. I think Papa should have left Germany. He shouldn't have listened to her."

Thomas knew this feeling of listening to someone against that inner, better judgment. He felt wrenched under Isaac's words.

"I started back here even though I knew it was dangerous. I had to know. In a way, what do I have left? I found our house empty. I made contact with the underground and they brought me here to Frau Hilda's."

Both men looked up and regarded her for the first time. She smiled.

"Thomas, did you know Maria worked here for a time?" Isaac asked.

"I had forgotten that. I was ... very busy with my church work then."

"What has happened with the church?" Isaac asked gently.

Thomas sighed deeply. "The church became part of the government. I ... I was part of it for awhile. Then I was graciously allowed to see the truth. Seeing the truth, I couldn't be a part of the Reich church. I'm ... ashamed that it took me so long." His voice trailed off and he stood and went to the enamel fireplace. A heavy silence hung in the room. Finally he turned, tears streaming down his face. "It took me so long, Isaac."

"The God we both believe in is a forgiving God."

Thomas nodded. "And thankfully so."

"Thomas, what can you tell me of my family?"

"I'd give anything to tell you better news, Isaac. While I was in Berlin disentangling myself from the church everything went crazy on Blumenstrasse. Another shame I must tell you ... my Uncle Otto brought the SS to arrest Abraham and your father. I was in Berlin trying to rescue Gretchen when ... my mother tried to save Sophie and Maria."

"She went in my mother's place," Isaac said softly.

Thomas nodded. This memory stabbed as sharply now, two years later, as it had in the first shocking moments. It kindled so many regrets.

"A few days later Sophie and Maria disappeared. I could only guess they were trying to follow your father. He was sent to Poland."

"Poland." Isaac leaned back and closed his eyes.

"I planned to follow them . . . to try to help somehow. But Gretchen became terribly ill. She was having seizures nearly every day. The doctor told me it was very unwise to move her. She needed rest and stability. For several weeks I was able to make contacts through old church associates. After three months, I found out Sophie and Maria had actually made it to the Polish border. I lost their trail after that. Gretchen still asks when we're going to find Maria. I've been working on getting the store in order so I can leave and go to Poland."

Isaac's eyes opened. He sat up. "You would do that, Thomas? You would go to Poland?"

"I . . . I would want to do no less, Isaac. Your family is mine now."

23
Decisions, Deception, Discovery

Every city has its underbelly, a society within society that city fathers lamented and travel brochures tactfully did not describe. This underbelly was mainly comprised of smoky, all-night taverns, card rooms, and brothels. Wilhelm found the basement taverns easily enough. He sat on the stools, slowly drinking his beer, listening intently in the din of raucous laughter and cursing, and hating the putrid smoke that clung to his clothes. He appeared bored though he was watching for quickly opened doors and muffled conversations. Anything that indicated some resistance to the Nazi regime. He did not expect to find any Jews gathering for an underground meeting. He knew that the Jews who remained in Munich were carefully hidden, almost buried alive, helped by Gentiles. *Helped by Gentiles* ... He stumbled in his mind over this; it brought something faint, yet demanding to his attention. Something from his recent past.

Summer was fading in a new coolness in the evenings and mornings, fading with as much certainty as Wilhelm's money. Calmly he assessed the roll of marks Emilie Farber had given him so long ago. He counted out his hotel expense and the one meal a day he was living on. He had one more week. *Then* ... He went to his hotel window and looked out, frowning. He wouldn't go begging to his one friend in Germany, to Emilie in Berlin. He would start stealing.

After three weeks of nightly vigilance, he finally had a slender measure of success. An SS officer, a low-ranking man, talkative, unhappy with his work and his home life, found Wilhelm's company on the stool companionable. Wilhelm was a good listener. He offered the well-timed question and sympathy and paid for the drinks. In low voices, they could both talk about the absurdity of Göring, Goebbels' obvious lies in the paper, and Hitler's foolishness in running the war.

"You'd think there would be a little more . . . I don't know, resistance to all this. But I guess you SS guys keep the lid on pretty good," Wilhelm said as he tipped back his glass.

His companion gave a grunt and a sideways smile. "You think so?"

"I've been here about three weeks, I haven't seen one anti-Nazi thing. I sort of expected to at least see an underground newspaper laying around. Something."

"They smashed the presses years ago. Those guys are already in a pit."

"Yes, I . . . can imagine. Well, like I said, for all their faults, the Nazis are tidy in their work."

"Not so tidy. . . . Things are still going on—"

"That's just rumor I'm sure."

"Last month an army warehouse in Stuttgart was burned to the ground. Arson. The railway is the usual target for partisan groups. Someone in Dusseldorf made a bonfire using *Mein Kampfs*. Good riddance, I say. You don't read those stories in Goebbels' rags." He leaned closer. "There's an organization here in Munich that smuggles Jews or other dissidents to the next city in the network. They try to get them across the pass into Switzerland."

"Here in Munich? That's crazy. There's an SS on every corner! Bartender, another beer!"

"My young friend have you forgotten I'm SS—"

Wilhelm smiled. "I haven't forgotten."

"I'm telling you this network exists. They exist all over Germany. Have you forgotten the attempt on the fuehrer's life at his headquarters in Rastenburg? Not every one is plodding along with a smiling face and 'Heil Hitler.' "

"This is dangerous talk," Wilhelm countered smoothly.

"You think I'm afraid? I've heard the talk from the men I work around. In the last few months they caught two men who were in this network.

They found someone they could bribe for cigarettes and brandy and he talked. They found the two had forged papers for Jews."

Wilhelm waited, then said, "And they wiped the thing out. There you go."

The man gulped a long drink, wiped his mouth with the back of his hand, and belched. "They stretched 'em. They didn't talk. Their secrets went with 'em."

Two men "stretched" for a package of cigarettes and a bottle of brandy. Wilhelm tried to ignore the mental image. His fists clenched under the bar.

"Not that I'm all that cozy with the Jewish vermin, but you have to at least admire these Germans who are willing to stir the pot," the man winked.

Wilhelm looked around uneasily. As crowded as the bar was, there was little chance of being overheard . . . unless someone was deliberately listening—like he had been earlier. This intemperate man was making him nervous. Wilhelm eyed the door. This would be the final night he came here. He needed to disappear into the city again.

"Wonder how they found the two in the first place?"

"I told you, someone ratted."

"That intrigues me. How do you find a rat?"

The man laughed. "Rats usually smell. You come to places like this and put your nose into the air . . ."

"Hmm . . ."

The man leaned closer again, and Wilhelm winced at the body odor.

"I do know they think this little Jewish traffic flows through the southern part of the city. I've been on patrol there myself. They think businesses are involved. You know, transfer information during working hours and no one notices. Very clever."

"But it won't last, not with the bloodhounds of the SS," Wilhelm chuckled as he patted the man's back.

"Personally I think we should just focus on the war, stop this hunting around in our own cellars." He shrugged. "But they don't consult me."

"They don't consult any of us," Wilhelm finished.

Later Wilhelm lay in his darkened hotel room. The man's words were comforting in that opposition and help for the Jews existed, no matter how weak, against the tide. But it provided him no real lead. *How can I observe an entire section of city and expect to see anything? Impossible!*

He rolled over feeling small and loney, wishing desperately he could reach out in the darkness and call his brother, Walther. As a boy, on those rare times when he had been afraid or confused, he talked to Walther or reached out and felt the slender arm after the breathing told him he was asleep. It had comforted him. *Comfort. How long has it been since I've felt any shred of comfort? I must leave Munich. I've failed to find Natalie. I've failed to find any Jewish resistance. Failed ...*

• • •

Alone in their apartment, Natalie waged a personal battle as the one between the armies of Germany and Russia. She was a Jew, and she was hated. The hatred had turned to hunt. The hunt meant imprisonment and death. She stared at the opposite apartment wall but she saw her grandfather being taken in the open truck. Her last sight of him. He was gone now.

After the first shock—the sorrow, the apathy—the desire to survive, even in this cruel world, had come. She knew her chances were slim. She had to lose what she was and become what she wasn't: a Gentile. She had something—her looks. She didn't feel entirely safe with Helga Weisner. Then the day had come when Hugo had come into the bakery. Hungry and kind, asking her opinions, making her smile with some little joke she had since forgotten. He had come back the next day and a few days later. He had lingered. Then he had asked her to dinner and she was shocked. She had fooled one of the hunters. If she could fool one, she could fool many. She would survive—and ignore the cost.

The struggle had raged in her, not only that she was no more than a prostitute, but also that she had forsaken the faith of her grandfather and her past. The day in the Catholic church had mocked and reminded her. And, after weeks, steeled her to a new resolve. The past was dead. Natalie Bergmann was dead. By her own hand she had buried her. No more guilt. No more tears. There were only two things to be done, and the personal funeral would be complete.

• • •

This was his final day in Munich. In the evening, he would take a train west toward the border of France. He had heard Jewish partisan groups in Vichy, France were very active. Hopefully he could meet up with them. Keep going a little longer. Carve out yet another identity, a new life.

Train terminals were the worst place for avoiding SS inspection of papers. He knew he was taking a great risk besides using up his small reserve of money. For the resourceful Wilhelm Mueller that was the least of his concerns. His forged papers, with medical stamps from Dr. Morgan, had gotten him this far, he would take another chance.

He ate a heavy breakfast then began walking. It was a mild, cloudless, autumn day. The streets were full enough for him to blend in. He walked without any real direction or purpose. He had no expectations of any kind. This was just a final look at Munich. Midmorning found him on a street watching a military parade. The crowd on the sidewalks was not enthusiastic and cheering. They were largely still and silent. Many of these men would not march back. The glory was gone.

After four hours of strolling, Wilhelm recognized he was hungry again. He watched part of the crowd cross the street after the parade. They entered a bakery. Wilhelm could smell something warm and sweet. His mother's strudel. He squinted into the sun. "Jensen's Bakery."

A cup of coffee and a slice of strudel. His mouth watered. His last meal in Munich. But his fingers curled around the few cold coins and his resolve stiffened. He turned and continued toward the train terminal.

• • •

Hugo knew Natalie wouldn't appreciate bribery in the form of flowers or jewels. She would expect directness. And he must tell her quickly to give her time to adjust.

They sat on the couch, Hugo reading the paper—or pretending to— and Natalie at the opposite end reading a novel.

"Natalie."

She looked up instantly.

"I was called into the commandant's office two mornings ago. I'm being transferred to Poland. I have to be there in three weeks."

She sat very still, almost unblinking. "All right."

What does this mean to us? She wondered. Her heart was racing though her face was impassive.

He came closer and took her hand. "I've thought this through carefully. I must go back to Berlin ... to my family. I'll stay there two weeks and finish the paperwork. Then I'll come back here and we'll leave for Warsaw."

She said nothing.

"Natalie, do you understand? I want you to go with me. I don't want this transfer to separate us. I need you."

I need you. The three words reverberated through her mind.

"Natalie, please say something."

"Warsaw. I . . . I don't have papers to travel, Hugo."

He kissed her fingertips lightly. "You think I can't take care of that? That should be the least of your concerns. You should have no concerns beyond where you want to live in Warsaw—a hotel or an apartment."

"For how long?"

"Perhaps a year, no longer."

"I know nothing about Poland," she lied. Geography had been one of her favorite subjects. She had taught herself many Polish phrases.

"I will help you with the language," he murmured as he pulled her into his arms.

The trees were losing their leaves in a shower of red and gold. Munich could boast of several impressive parks. Hilda Jensen had never been to this park, however. She couldn't properly enjoy it with this eagerness tempered with anxiety. She was grateful it was such a cool and lovely day. There were people everywhere: mothers pushing carriages, boys tossing balls, couples strolling arm in arm with the intensity that comes with a prized weekend army pass. Hilda fit right in. She glanced at her watch. Ten-thirty at the zoo entrance. It was ten-twenty.

Hilda hated that she was pacing, but she didn't know what else to do. It had been nearly two years. She fingered the note in her coat pocket. It was real. The boy had brought it to her during the morning rush. It had caused her to pour sugar into a customer's coffee thinking it was cream. She had laughed as heartedly as the others, but her mind was reeling. The two hours since then had crawled by.

She watched a group of boys playing soccer across the way. She glanced back at her watch. Ten-thirty. She looked back to the zoo entrance. A young woman was approaching her. She wore a dark skirt, white blouse, and camel-colored coat. Her hair was loose around her shoulders.

Hilda's throat constricted. *All she needs is the ribbon in her hair,* she whispered to herself. She moved forward, stiffly, surprised that the sight of this young woman could have such an affect on her. She could see the girl was smiling. Only then did she see the violin case the young woman carried. A few feet from each other, she gave a small cry and ran to Hilda's outstretched arms.

"Natalie, Natalie, my girl . . ."

Natalie's resolve to not cry collapsed immediately. Hilda was already weeping. Finally Hilda straightened.

"Here, here, let's walk. I passed a bench just over on that path."

With their arms around each other they walked to the bench. Spread before them was the park, a saucer of yellow-green grass bordered by chestnut trees. They were alone.

"I . . . I hadn't meant . . . to cry," Natalie finally smiled.

Hilda brushed back the girl's dark hair with the same gesture she had used for years.

They looked at each other.

"You look well, Natalie. You look happy," Hilda allowed with no resentment.

Natalie squeezed her hand. "I am happy, Hilda." She glanced across the park.

Hilda watched her, amazed again at the young woman's beauty. She firmly put the rabbi from her mind.

Natalie turned back. "Hugo is a very kind man. He is very good to me."

"I am glad you're happy . . . and safe," Hilda said softly. "Truly I am."

Natalie looked in the older woman's eyes, and the tears pooled up in hers again.

"You have been so good to me, Hilda, so faithful." She took a plunging breath. "My grandfather was so wise to bring you home to us. You have been a faithful blessing to . . . to the house of Bergmann."

Hilda's tears came again. She shook her head, and they sat together in silence several moments.

"We must stop this weeping," Hilda said with a shaky laugh, "we'll attract attention. Not to mention what my staff might think!"

"I . . . I contacted you because I'm leaving Munich, Hilda. I wanted to say goodbye."

"You're leaving Munich?" the baker blinked rapidly.

Natalie nodded. "Hugo has been transferred to Warsaw."

"Poland! But, but Natalie . . . that's so far . . . I mean . . . Do you want to go? Natalie, if you don't I have a place for you, you know that."

Natalie smiled. "I know, dear Hilda, I do know that. Hugo is a good man, Hilda."

Hilda turned away, thinking, praying, guarding her tongue from the hasty things that were leaping to it.

"Does he know you're Jewish?"

The question cut through the crisp air.

"Hilda, I know that this is . . . is difficult to understand. But that is in the past. I can't . . . I brought this to you. I wanted you to have it." She extended the violin case toward her.

Hilda was shocked. "No, Natalie! You can't part with that! Please. Why did you want to see me? I'm part of your past. You can't deny me anymore than you can—" She stopped. "I'm sorry, Natalie. Please forgive me."

They stood up and hugged again, but something was different now. Hilda took the case.

"I wanted to see you, Hilda, to thank you again. And to tell you I love you."

"And I love you, my girl."

• • •

He was walking when he recognized the street. He looked up. The sun glinted on the broad sheet of glass. "Picard's Fine Instruments." He stopped and busied his attention with the books displayed in the window of the bookstore opposite. In the reflection he watched people enter and depart. After several minutes he realized he was going to attract attention. He was too obvious. He turned and looked at the store and walked up the opposite sidewalk. *There is no point in going in that place. There would be no word about a brunette violinist. The owner . . .* Wilhelm slowly walked away from the store, a strange and sudden sadness settling on him—an overwhelming sense of defeat and resignation. He recognized it immediately. Resignation was what happened when Jews gave up and meekly submitted to the slaughter. He had always vowed vehemently that it wouldn't happen to him.

"Your stubbornness can be your strength or your downfall," his mother had once told him. "I know, Wilhelm, I need never worry about you fighting on the wrong side for the wrong thing."

"Still, maybe you wished I took the right side a little less often, eh, Mama?"

She had tousled his hair. "You have caused me all my gray hair and extra mending, yes."

Wilhelm paused again on the sidewalk as he thought of this conversation that reached back in the years. He could see his father placing his wrinkled, gnarled, trembling hand on his head. His father's eyes were squeezed together, yet tears escaped.

"You have given me life, Lord, let my beloved son have life as well."

"I don't know if I can go on . . . much longer, Papa," Wilhelm whispered.

He should have been shocked with himself, but he was too tired. To stop on the street was an open invitation to curious scrutiny. *If my aged parents are still alive, are they still praying for my wayward soul?* he wondered. He looked up and turned for one final look at the music store, as if drawn to it.

The door had opened and Thomas Picard emerged. Wilhelm stood rooted. Picard was starting down the street at a leisurely pace, his hands in his pockets. He called out some greeting and a wave for a shopkeeper sweeping his front steps. He disappeared around the corner. Wilhelm turned and followed.

He couldn't say why he was following Picard. He didn't like it that he didn't have a reason, that he was behaving irrationally without a plan. Yet he continued one block, two, three. Picard never turned. He was back on Brennerstrasse. And then he was entering a shop. "Jensen's Bakery." Wilhelm ducked into a cafe. He stayed close to the front window.

"A table for one, sir?"

"Hmm? Oh, ah, no. I'm fine here. Just waiting for a friend. Then we'll take a table. Thanks."

Less than five minutes later, the music store owner emerged, a white box in his hands. Wilhelm turned to the waiter.

"Well, looks like I've been stood up—"

The man was clearly puzzled. "Stood up?"

Wilhelm was horrified. American slang. It had been years since that had slipped into his speech. *Things are getting bad; all my defenses are shaky. I'd better get out of Munich fast.*

"Friends not coming, thanks."

He was behind Picard again, still on the opposite sidewalk. He would follow him back to the music store then steadfastly continue his way with no odd impulses or weakening sentiments.

Thomas was nearly to his store when he glanced in the plate-glass windows across the way. Even at the distance, in the blur, he recognized the uncomfortable man. He slowed his steps. The man slowed. Thomas smiled. *I'm being followed.*

For one brief moment, Thomas considered the possibility that this man was an agent of the Gestapo determined to find some final crime on a former minister. Well, there was only one way to find out. No cat and mouse games.

He turned and looked at Wilhelm. Wilhelm was tempted to turn when he saw he had been seen. *Yet the man was smiling. Well, it would just take a moment.*

He crossed the street.

"You never came back," Thomas said without preface.

"I suppose I felt it ... there wasn't much chance with the slender description I could give you."

Thomas looked at him a long minute. That same look he had given in the office. He nodded at the box in his hands. "I've just fetched the indulgences. Come on in and we'll talk it over."

So he was going to get a Jensen pastry after all.

Through the walls and frosted door he could hear the violin and the piano.

"Like a concert every day, I guess," Wilhelm said with a mouthful.

Thomas nodded. "I don't know much about the business, but I do know about beautiful music. I'm fortunate in that respect. My staff is very talented."

"You haven't run this very long?"

Thomas put a testing finger around the lip of the cup. "A little over a year. My father and mother, and Herr Goldstein, ran the business. They ... were the heart and soul of it. My grandfather and Herr Goldstein's father began it."

Wilhelm tried a little offense. "What did you do for a living before you did this?"

Thomas leaned back, relaxed his hands behind his head. "I was a pastor here in Munich."

He could see the question leap to the young man's eyes. He smiled.

"I quit before I was fired. I wanted to preach the gospel. They wanted me to preach *Mein Kampf*. One of us had to go," he chuckled.

Wilhelm didn't have to ask who they were.

Thomas leaned forward, his arms on his desk, his fingers laced together.

"You didn't come back."

"As I said, I didn't have much hope you could tell me anything."

"I asked but didn't come up with anything, true. Can I assume you haven't found your young brunette violinist?"

Wilhelm smiled in spite of himself. "I hadn't really thought of her ... as my violinist. No, I haven't found her."

"I'm sorry. I too am a little acquainted with looking for someone who has disappeared. It's very discouraging."

Wilhelm nodded. "I'm leaving Munich this evening."

"Oh?"

"There's no point in staying. My work here is finished." Wilhelm looked around the room. The silence lengthened and felt awkward to him.

Wilhelm swallowed and licked his lips. "That time before, when I was here ... you said, you asked if there was something else you could help me with."

Thomas was rubbing his forehead, his eyes closed. He nodded.

"Why did you ask me that?" Wilhelm asked bluntly.

"I am always interested in trying to help Jews."

Wilhelm knew he should be shocked. But he wasn't. He didn't even feel afraid. *I could jump up and rush out the door. This man wouldn't try to detain me. But I don't want to. Not at all,* he decided.

Thomas opened his eyes and smiled. "I would like to help you—"

One last hesitation. "Wilhelm. My name is Wilhelm Mueller." And he suddenly laughed. He had said his own name!

"Why don't you tell me your story, Wilhelm Mueller, while we polish off this strudel."

One of the staff knocked and was politely sent away. Picard was very busy.

Two hours later Wilhelm was finished. The strudel was finished to the last crumb. He had told him everything. He had gone back to the days in Nuremberg where he'd met the dark-haired violinist. He told him of his time in America and of Emilie Farber. From his false shoe sole, he pulled out a pamphlet in waterproof cloth. It was his writing from his underground days. He wanted this man to see he had some meager talent beyond mere survival.

"That piece of paper would be my death warrant if the Nazis ever found it, but somehow, all these years, I just wanted to carry it around, you know? Something I did, something I could be proud of."

Thomas nodded. "Yes, it is very good writing."

Wilhelm glanced at the clock on the wall. "I'd better be pushing off for the station."

"May I see your papers?" Thomas asked.

Wilhelm nodded and Thomas studied them.

"I'm sure you know the SS and Gestapo patrol train terminals pretty heavily. They stop everyone boarding and look them over."

"Yes, I know that."

Thomas sighed. "I don't think these papers will help you, not with the scrutiny they give them. Especially a young man out of uniform. You want to leave Germany, correct?"

"I don't feel I have much choice."

"Why not make for Switzerland and your family?"

Wilhelm studied his trouser leg a moment. "I'd thought of that. But Switzerland is safety. In France, I can . . . try to help . . . my people."

My people. It was the first time he had said the words out loud. It startled him, yet sent a warm feeling coursing through him. *My people, even with the persecution, I belong with them.*

"I want to do something against the Nazis," he said firmly.

Thomas nodded. He liked this young man.

"I don't think you should use these papers."

"But—"

Thomas held up a hand as he stood up. "I think we need to go to the bakery and thank Frau Jensen for her creations, don't you agree?"

Wilhelm stood slowly, surprised at this sudden change in conversational direction.

"Well, I . . ."

"You don't need to leave Munich tonight. We need to talk with Frau Jensen first."

Then Wilhelm understood. He smiled as Thomas patted his back. Wilhelm paused at the door. "How did you know I was Jewish, Thomas?"

Thomas laughed—a genuine laugh of inner joy. "God told me, of course."

Hilda wanted to scream at the thought of the violin case she had put into her closet. The joy in seeing Natalie had turned into a sorrow. Her heart was broken as it hadn't been since Natalie's first defection. *How could the young woman deceive herself to such an extent?* she wondered. She couldn't shake the face of the beloved rabbi from her mind.

She pulled the shades and locked the door. Someone knocked, but she ignored it. She went to the kitchen and banked the stoves. She would regret this in the morning, but she would wash the dishes then. She'd get up extra early. It would be a new day. She doused the lights and turned for the stairs. The knocking, impatient and incessant sounded at the backdoor. She hesitated. She was too tired. They were supposed to send a message first. The almond buns were always preceded by a message. Unless this was a trap ...

Another hesitation, another knock.

Reluctantly she went to the door.

Thomas stood there with an apologetic smile. Another man stood behind him in the shadows.

"You closed early," Thomas said amiably.

She nodded, then said, "Come in, Herr Picard."

She turned to remove her apron. When she turned back, she didn't see Thomas. The other man had come into her kitchen.

She clutched at her throat. He was like ... someone from the past. Someone from long ago. No ...

Wilhelm had started forward as shocked as she. *It couldn't be ... but ... yes, it had to be!*

"Whoa—Wilhelm! Catch her, she's fainting!" Thomas cried.

They lowered her to the floor.

"Lock the door," Thomas commanded.

Wilhelm stood nearby uncertainly. He had paled. Thomas looked up, a quizzical smile on his own tired face. "Can I assume you two know each other?" He looked back at the woman who was stirring.

"The rabbi's housekeeper?" he asked incredulously.

Wilhelm nodded, his voice hoarse. "Hilda Jensen, Hilda Weisner."

24
When the Laurel
Is Sorrow

Hugo von Kleinst didn't want this assignment in the Polish capital. He didn't want to leave Germany. He didn't want to be so far from his family in Berlin, even though he saw them infrequently. And he didn't want this position that others had refused. The job description had been curt and cryptic—administrative duties in the army headquarters of Warsaw. That could be interpreted in a multitude of ways. But he didn't have the will to refuse what others had. A loyal German did his duty despite the discomfort and unpleasantness. He could only hope it wouldn't be too unpleasant—especially for Natalie's sake.

Hugo entered the apartment, his fine wool coat over his arm, his face flushed from the exertion of carrying down the last few bags.

"Natalie, the cab is waiting to take us to the station."

She turned and smiled. He knew she didn't want to go any more than he did. He suspected she was afraid. But with her smile, he also knew she was trying to be brave and cheerful for him.

Natalie reached for his hand. "I'm ready to leave now, Hugo."

• • •

The autumn dusk had fallen and with the shifting of wind and scuttling of dark, heavy clouds the night had turned harsh. At the northern edge of the horizon, lightning threw gnarled, grasping fingers into the purple blackness. Thunder rumbled under the tossing clouds; the wind raised its voice in a high treble and shook the glass. It was not a night to be out.

Thomas and Wilhelm helped Hilda, suddenly weak and trembling, up to her apartment. Then Thomas started the coffee and called home. Wihelm paced the room while Hilda sat in her armchair for several minutes with her eyes closed. The only sound that reached them was the orchestra of the storm. Finally Thomas knelt down to her.

"Frau Jensen? Here's the coffee."

Her eyes fluttered open, the color slowly returning to her ashen face. She accepted the cup with a shaky hand.

"Are you all right? May I get you anything else? Any medication?" Thomas asked.

She shook her head. "It's just been too much ... for one day." She patted her chest.

She took a drink of coffee and wagged her head at Thomas. "Stick with violins and pianos. I'll do the coffee." She patted his arm in sympathy.

Thomas laughed deeply and Wilhelm stopped pacing. Hilda drank, then lowered her cup. They stared at each other across the small room.

"I guess we gave each other a scare," Wilhelm smiled shyly.

She nodded. "It's been seven years," her voice still revealing the disbelief that he stood in her apartment.

Wilhelm sat down, his elbows on his knees. "Yet suddenly it really doesn't seem like that long. You look, you sound exactly the same, Frau Hilda."

"But much has happened in seven years." She took another drink of the strong brew. She pushed herself up in her chair, assuming her natural dignity. She smoothed her loosened hair bun. Then she took a deep breath and smiled.

"It is good to see you, Wilhelm Mueller."

He smiled and nodded, pleased to hear his name from her lips. Hilda looked at Thomas.

"You brought him here."

"Because I thought you'd be the one to get him better papers. He wants to leave Germany."

Hilda refocused on the young man. "You want to leave Germany? You have been in Germany since you left us in Nuremberg?"

He shook his head. "I went to America for two years. I've been in the Reich since then."

"Hilda, would it be all right if Wilhelm stayed here tonight? I need to get home to my sister, and I figure you two have a lot of catching up to do."

"Of course."

Thomas stood, pulling on his coat. He smiled.

He doesn't look so tired now, Wilhelm thought.

Thomas stuck out his hand. "I'm glad to be a small part of this reunion of old friends. One doesn't get to do that much these days. Thank you for trusting me earlier, Wilhelm. I value that."

Wilhelm stood, feeling awkward with this sudden thrust of security and kindness into his barren life.

"I'm thanking you, Thomas," he said.

"I'll come by tomorrow. Between the three of us, I think we can come up with a better plan for you. Well, goodnight. No, don't get up, I'll lock up after myself."

Wilhelm listening to his retreating steps repeated his final words, "The three of us will come up with a better plan."

Helping Gentiles . . . Now he knew. Now he believed.

"If my memory is anything at all, you have quite an appetite," Hilda said briskly, restored to herself.

He smiled. "That much hasn't changed. But I haven't had any meals to equal yours in seven years."

She brushed past him, chuckling. "And the old charm hasn't faded. I'm going to put us something together."

He followed her. "May I help?"

She turned surprised, knotting her apron.

"Peel potatoes or something," he shrugged.

"Just sit. Now what did Herr Picard do with the coffee?"

Wilhelm laughed. A little grayer, perhaps a few more pounds, but the same Hilda. So he sat in the warm, cozy kitchen and closed his eyes. He relaxed. *I could be in my mother's small kitchen back at the Farber Estate, the kettle hissing in the background, the sizzle of something turning over the open fireplace—and mother's steps on the wooden floor,* he contemplated. *It's the sound of dependability. Just like Hilda.* He opened his eyes.

She was setting a steaming bowl of dumplings in front of him. She sat down across from him and poured from a new pot of coffee.

"I remember a time when you fell asleep at the rabbi's house—and woke with all of us staring at you." She laughed briefly at the memory. She wanted to engage in the good memories now. Just the good. But his face, across the table, the line that creased between his brows. She had seen it before.

"Frau Jensen, I ... this looks delicious; I'm certain it is. But I have to know whether Natalie Bergmann is alive."

He won't let me bask in the memories. Impatient youth. From the first shocking moment in the kitchen downstairs, she knew this moment was coming. With it, new agony. She had hoped to forestall it a little longer. She pushed her own bowl away and calmly folded her hands in front of her.

"Natalie is alive."

Three simple words. Wilhelm slumped back in his chair. Maybe this was even more of a shock than finding Hilda. The hope that had driven him, then dimmed, then finally turned to cold ash was revived. He felt a surge of vindication. His purpose had been worth it—for the old rabbi's sake.

He wet his lips. "Is she here in Munich?"

Hilda had a strict code about lying. She had the wild impulse to tell Wilhelm she was suddenly feeling weak again, and they would talk in the morning. But she had seen this young man's determination more than once. He would not have allowed such a retreat.

"She's not here in Munich. But she is safe." She pushed the bowl toward him. "Eat."

Wilhelm ate with a relish that pleased her. She sensed relief emanating from him. Perhaps her few words had been more nourishing than the food he took in. She ate slowly and plotted her strategy with as much care as the generals on the Russian front.

Since Jensen's was only four blocks from Blumenstrasse, Thomas Picard didn't have too far to walk in the inclement weather. Though it tore at him, turning his collar up and his hat brim down, he didn't mind it at all. It was better than stillness. The stillness would make him feel the loneliness that was like the oppressive summer humidity. This was savage weather—and it matched his emotions. He knew the exertion against the wind and blowing rain would do him good. He needed a release from the energy and emotion that churned in him like the thunder and lightning that churned the heavens. He was roiling inside.

He felt the deep relief of finding Wilhelm Mueller. Here was someone to help. He felt the gladness and thankfulness of seeing him reunited with Hilda. The key had fit the lock, and he was able to smile at the thought of the two people he had put together.

He turned on Blumenstrasse, now drenched in darkness and rain. *Home.* Many times he had thought of selling the place and moving to something smaller. It housed so many painful memories and frustrations. But Gretchen needed the security of the familiar.

He had Gretchen. There would be no reunions for him; he had come to face that. But ... but tonight had reminded him ...

He hurried up the steps. "I have you, Lord. I have enough," he said to the raw wind and rain. And he was able to smile.

• • •

Hilda held a slender hope that a full stomach was some defense against shock. *Wilhelm Mueller looks thinner than I remembered,* she reflected. *He's not going to like what I have to tell him.* They finished their meal in silence then she allowed him to help her wash up. Her own day, the meeting with Natalie, was dragging at her body, clamoring that she could go to bed and shut all the unpleasantness out for awhile in the storm-shrouded darkness. But there was Wilhelm Mueller, stirring up the coal fire in the living room with an eagerness that was eloquent. He was ready to make a night of this.

She settled into her deep armchair and watched him. Finally he turned and smiled that boyish smile that had been hibernating for too long.

"We each have ... a story to tell. You go first, Wilhelm, and let me rest a bit."

He shifted and eyed her speculatively. "Why do I get the feeling you're putting off telling me something?"

She shrugged with casual indifference. "Now, Wilhelm, you know very well Herr Hitler has made many things unpleasant in Germany these days. For a baker trying to get supplies, everything is a trial!"

"You're doing more than baking strudel these days," he pointed out. "We are starting with you."

He nodded. This woman had commanded the rabbi and his daughter with affectionate tyranny. Wilhelm could see it was easy and effortless for her to reassume such a role.

He began his story from the July night of 1936 when he had left the rabbi's house. A seven-year sojourn was reduced to thirty minutes. Hilda interrupted with a few questions.

"After I left Berlin I met up with a Jewish underground group in Frankfurt. I stayed with them for nearly six months. Then most of them were taken one day on a general roundup." His face darkened. "I was out literally looking for food for us. I was the only one not taken. I left Frankfurt and headed south. I was able to make contact with a partisan group. I stayed with them for a time. But some in their midst had very strong feelings about having a Jew with them. They said it was too great a risk." He shook his head. "As if they weren't at risk themselves. It completely baffles me how they forget we fight the same enemy."

"Two hands working together instead of two working apart lightens the load," Hilda said.

He nodded. "Exactly. I don't know ... It's strange sometimes. I wonder if the Nazis are ever defeated and a few Jews survive—will we work together to make Germany better? Or will it be the same old story of hate?"

He watched the flames of the coal fire, and Hilda watched him. Finally he looked up.

"That's pretty much it. I went back to Nuremberg and found out you and Natalie left for Munich. I had some money from Frau Farber that I saved. I had always ... planned to try to find out if you made it all right." He looked down at his hands a moment and smiled faintly. "I felt like I owed it to the old fellow."

Hilda nodded and turned to look at the flames herself. The old fellow. The old fellow had loved this young man like a son. Hilda knew that, though it had never been spoken of. *He would have given his grand-daughter's hand in marriage to this boy—even with all his worldly ways and lack of material substance—if Wilhelm had approached him. Their bond had been brief but it had been strong. Strong enough to bring Wilhelm to this dangerous city on a nearly impossible task. Yet ... the impossible had happened.*

Still not looking at him, Hilda spoke. "You are a survivor, Wilhelm." Her voice was gentle. And sad. Wilhelm felt that stirring of apprehension he had felt earlier. She didn't want to tell him about Natalie.

Yet she turned and faced him squarely, her brown eyes quite alert, her posture correct. The time had come.

"I know this is difficult for you," Wilhelm said gently.

The insight startled her a moment but she nodded slowly.

"But you have a right to know. The Bergmanns were your friends. You have ... shown great courage and persistence to find them. I know the rabbi would have been impressed with that."

They both looked away. They had both loved the old man. And they knew he was gone.

Hilda cleared her throat.

"I remember the night you left, right after the Nuremberg rally had ended. The city was wild and dangerous, like ... like a pack of wolves the Nazis were, roaming the streets as if they smelled the blood of the wounded."

"They did," Wilhelm nodded.

"We had gone to the synagogue to comfort those who had gathered there. They wanted to see Rabbi Bergmann. He could calm them. I was afraid of course—a Gentile woman in the company of a rabbi." Her eyes snapped, her voice momentarily fierce. "But they would have had to climb over my dead body before I let them touch the rabbi!" Her fierceness died away as swiftly as it had flamed. "I was so thankful we had not allowed Natalie to accompany us, yet I was afraid for her in the house alone. All the Jewish houses were marked and the rabbi's especially. But then we came in and you were there with her." She reached out and patted his hand.

Though that night was seven years old, Wilhelm could remember it vividly. Natalie had clung to him, wanting to be brave, yet so terribly afraid. And rightly so. He had been afraid. There was a price on his head that night. He would have made a perfect bonfire for some Nazi's career if he had been caught that night.

"What happened after that night?" he asked.

Hilda sighed. "For several days the city stayed in a ferment. Jews hid; Jews were hunted. It was simply too dangerous for them to go out. Any day we all expected them to come to the house. So I went out and did all the shopping. The Bergmanns couldn't go out. They stayed behind their locked doors and drawn curtains like prisoners." She shook her head sadly.

"How did they take this confinement?"

"To the very end, even as they tossed the rabbi onto the truck that night, I think he was hopeful, optimistic that the persecution would end."

"And Natalie?"

"She became even quieter. I tried to get her to talk, but she wouldn't. She played her violin all the time as if . . . as if she wanted to be playing when they came for her. I found her one day writing, and she told me she was keeping a journal. But it was at night and she was sleeping when they did come."

"Were there, didn't any of you make any kind of plans to get out of Nuremberg? To escape?" Wilhelm asked with sudden bluntness.

"I'm sorry," he said at the look on Hilda's face.

Her smile was patient. "The rabbi was so reluctant. I tried to persuade him to do something for Natalie at least, to try to send her away. She said she wouldn't desert him. I wanted to do something, Wilhelm. I thought about it constantly. I—"

"I'm sorry, I . . . I'm sure you tried. You were a better friend to them than I was."

"We lived like this for many, many months. Then one night in February the truck came to the house. I awoke instantly and went to the window. I knew. Though it was dark I could see people huddled in the back of the truck. I can only tell you . . . that the Lord helped me that terrible night. He gave me a clear mind and a swiftness I have never had before. I ran to Natalie's room, woke her, and sent her to my room. I made her bed and straightened her room. I went to my room and had her lay at the end of my bed in the pile of rumpled covers. I told her to be very still. She . . . she didn't say a word the entire time. By the time I reached the stairs the rabbi was on the way down in his robe, and they were beating on the door. Then the glass was smashed . . . that beautiful glass. Have you ever noticed how Nazis love to break glass?"

Wilhelm closed his eyes a moment. He could see the glass in his mind; he had estimated its cost many times.

"I had been so bold as to tell the rabbi to allow me to do the speaking. They came in very triumphant looking. I knew . . ." she stopped a moment, looking down at her lap. "I knew I couldn't save Rabbi Bergmann." Her voice wavered. "But I was determined I would save his granddaughter.

They demanded to know where the girl was, and I spoke up and said that an anonymous friend had warned the rabbi and he had sent her away on the train that afternoon. 'Where?' they asked. I told them she was sent to Vienna. They searched the house anyway. They didn't find her. Then they pulled the rabbi out the door. He was ... he was thanking me for all my years of service. They took him away."

She refilled her cup. "The Nazis came the next day and told me the house would be going to an SS officer and I must vacate by the end of the week. All of those family treasures—everything would go into their hands. I truly hated that. Natalie seemed to come out of her shock for a time, though she was so pale and thin. She chose a few things to take in her suitcase. She lingered longest in the library. She took a few photographs—I don't know what else. She took her violin, and we left one afternoon for Munich. We stayed in a hotel while I got us this place. I had saved up, and Natalie had given me money from the safe. Because we were making a new start together, I felt I should change back to my maiden name. Natalie became my niece. Natalie deeply grieved for her grandfather. She knew she would never see him again. She stopped playing the violin."

Wilhelm was rubbing his forehead, trying to imagine all of this. The young girl thrust onto the stage of a terrible drama, to grow into a woman, to choose her own part to play.

"Such was our life as the war started."

She stopped, and Wilhelm watched as the knuckles went white in her clasped hands. His own stomach tightened. He knew they had come to the difficult part.

"One day I left the shop to go for supplies. Natalie was here alone. Olaf was doing the baking, but she had the front of the shop. It was the slow part of the day, and, I thought, even in her shyness, she could handle anyone who came in. An SS officer came. Apparently he struck up a conversation with the very quiet ... very lovely shop girl. He came a few days later. For several weeks he came at least twice a week. He ate very slowly. He was charming. Suddenly Natalie realized he couldn't tell she was Jewish. And he obviously thought she was attractive. She must have seen him as an escape."

Wilhelm stood up abruptly, his face flushed. "What are you trying to tell me?"

Hilda's mouth compressed into a thin line. Her voice was clipped.

"She went with him. She has been with him for nearly two years."

He braced himself against the fireplace.

"I don't think I want to hear anymore, Frau Hilda. I can't ... not tonight. Can I just bed down here on your sofa?"

His back was still to her. She felt the tears that had come to her that afternoon threaten again. She stood up, feeling if this day alone had aged her beyond the last ten.

"Yes. I will get you a blanket. It has been a long day."

The thunder scraped in the sky to underscore her words.

She stood up, her hand going out to him, but still he stood rigid at the fireplace.

"I understand, Wilhelm. Goodnight."

His paleness, his haggard appearance told her he hadn't slept any better than she. He was sitting on the sofa, dressed yet rumpled when she came from her bedroom the next morning. He was staring into space. Though her heart went out to him, her tone was crisp.

"Good morning, Wilhelm. When was the last time you had a bath, shaved, and had your clothes cleaned and pressed?"

He found he could still smile. "I don't remember."

"Well, a man who looks like you are looking this morning immediately calls attention to himself when he's on the street." She waved a hand at him. "And I don't mean from frauleins. Now, you go get a bath, toss your clothes out, and I'll get breakfast. I have to be down to the shop in an hour."

He knew it was useless to protest. He sank into the steamy tub of hot water. He smiled. Maybe he should just let Frau Hilda decide everything for him, plot out his life. It would be a change, a relief. He pulled on the trousers and shirt that Hilda kept hidden for almond buns that needed their clothes cleaned.

Hilda frowned as Wilhelm picked at his breakfast. She pushed her plate aside and refilled their coffee cups.

"You'll be fine here. Don't worry about walking around, we can't hear you downstairs. I'll come up and fix you something at noon."

"You don't need to do that. I can get something myself. It isn't like sitting will give me much of an appetite."

He sighed, leaned back, and crossed his arms. She looked at him—a young man with too much lifetime in his years.

"We have to talk before I go down, Wilhelm."

"Yes, I suppose so."

"I've had many months to think about what Natalie chose. I don't like it still, but I've had time to understand it better."

"She was safe here with you," he blurted.

She was glad of his passion. It was better than apathy.

"She was safe to a degree. But there was always the chance someone would look into my story and discover I didn't have a niece. There are a hundred ways she could have been discovered."

"And being with a Nazi, an SS officer, is safer? I don't see that, I'm sorry."

"She ... she has told me he is not like many of the SS, not at all. He—"

"I don't want to hear about him. I want to ..."

"What do you want, Wilhelm?" she asked with unexpected gentleness.

"How could she ... how could she," he broke off, shaking his head.

Hilda smiled tolerantly. "Natalie grew up in seven years, Wilhelm, remember that."

"I know she did."

"Yes, think about that. To grow up, Wilhelm. She was a young girl becoming a young woman who only wanted the chance to grow, to have a normal life like other German girls."

Wilhelm's voice was drenched with frustration. "Things aren't normal in Germany! And you don't, you don't ... It isn't normal to go with a Nazi to try to make things normal!"

"Sadly no. But life still flows through a girl. Hope still burns in her heart. She felt he could give her freedom and safety. One day she was gone. She left a note telling me not to worry, telling me how grateful she was for all I had done. And please don't try to find her."

Wilhelm sagged into the chair. "But ..." He shook his head. "Freedom and safety in the arms of a Nazi." Wilhelm lowered his head into his hands.

"She came into the shop about six months later. I had given up hope of ever seeing her again. She looked so well, so cared for and, in a way, happy. She is a brave girl. She told me everything. She wanted me to know she was safe. She insisted I take some of her money. I sickened at the thought of taking the Nazis's money . . . and then I reasoned, well, if it could be used against them . . ." Hilda lifted her shoulders.

"She can't allow herself to think of what her grandfather would think," Wilhelm said slowly.

"I cannot find it in my heart to judge her," Hilda said as she stood.

Wilhelm studied the table with a frown. Hilda studied him. The room was silent several minutes.

She went around the table to him. She touched his shoulder and he looked up.

"Wilhelm, I'm sorry. I know you're disappointed. But don't hate Natalie."

"I don't hate her, Frau Hilda."

"You're going to have to work through this yourself, as I did. You will have to do a lot of searching of your own heart."

"You sound like my mother. She told me once I needed to enlarge my heart, have more compassion." He ran a weary hand through his hair. "I don't know . . ."

The apartment was quiet. Painfully quiet. Wilhelm sat at the table. He was warm, safe for the moment, full of good food. In many years this was the best situation he had been in. So why did he feel so utterly miserable?

25
Gentiles and Jews

Otto Beck was not a man to forget insult or injury. And the Nazi world afforded men like Beck plenty of opportunity for revenge. It was a quality the fuehrer himself appreciated and frequently employed. Beck blamed Thomas Picard for his sister's insane sacrifice for Sophie Goldstein. It was not that Otto had the greatest filial feelings for Maria, but a sense of honor—the Beck name—had been tarnished by the action. And Otto didn't mind the thought of striking out at his nephew.

Only Thomas could have infected Maria with such Christian stupidity that would make her pose as a Jew marked for destruction, Otto decided. *Thomas is guilty of a multitude of offenses. My nephew's true loyalty was seen when he resigned from the Reich church. That told flagrantly of his anti-Nazi feelings. Thomas isn't just a personal irritation, he is an enemy of the state. And my work with the Gestapo is to ferret out and destroy enemies of the Reich. It will be a pleasure to capture this nephew of mine.* For that reason, the shadow stood sentinel each day across from the Picard home on Blumenstrasse and the music shop. Thomas Picard didn't make a move that his uncle didn't know about. And now these personal trips to a bakery . . .

Hilda didn't come up to her apartment until the end of the day. She flailed herself as cowardly—she couldn't face his disappointment and his anger yet. She thought he needed the hours alone to struggle through this sorrow, to come to his own conclusions. When she walked through the door as evening fell she found him asleep on the sofa, an open book sprawled across his chest. She stood looking down at him a moment, relaxed and at peace. And it was in that quiet moment that Hilda knew she loved this young man as a son, as she loved Natalie as a daughter. Her heart had broken for Natalie; her heart was breaking for him. She turned and went to the kitchen to prepare their meal.

She remembered how he had always eaten her bratwurst and cheese blintzes with such enjoyment. She tied on her faded floral apron and went to work. She was very tired from the long day and sleepless night, but cooking for one she loved filled her with renewed energy. She could remember setting the steaming platters and tureen on the Bergmann's elegant table and seeing Wilhelm's eyes light with eagerness, the rabbi's with amusement, and Natalie's with shock. And her heart went out to him again. *Seven years later he was still struggling just to eat. Of course he must be disappointed and angry, and now his searching for Natalie had come to this.*

And what had it come to? Hilda stirred with vigor. He was too wounded to work through this alone. She was going to have to help him. By the time the first warm, savory odors drifted into the living room, he had stirred and was yawning in the doorway.

"If I ever get a home of my own," he said, "I want it to be above a bakery." He sat down at the table; there was no point in trying to help.

Though he was clearly trying to be cheerful, she could see the shadows in his eyes. It had been a lonely day for him.

"Or better, you could try to marry a woman who knows how to bake."

The brief smile went from his face. He shook his head. "Years ago . . . Rabbi Bergmann showed me, very . . . diplomatically of course, that I don't have much potential for marriage."

"I was rarely in the room when you were with him, but I cannot imagine him communicating that to you, either diplomatically or not. Why in the world would you think he felt that way?"

"If the daughter you loved brought home a man who was wanted by the police and didn't have a job—no way to support a family—how would you feel?"

"I'd feel she must see things in him I couldn't, and I should look closer."

Wilhelm leaned back and laughed deeply.

She shook a spoon at him. "You can laugh if you want, Herr Mueller, but I think I knew the Rabbi's mind on this matter a little better than you."

Wilhelm's laughter died away as he shrugged. "It doesn't matter now anyway."

Hilda held her tongue. She glanced at him. He was slipping into a moody, frowning silence. She whipped off her apron. She went to the front room to turn on the radio. A stilted German opera filled the room. Wilhelm looked up, still frowning.

"You like that?"

"As a good German, yes."

She laid the table, but before she sat down she went to the closet and carefully brought out the concealed radio. She brought it to the table and turned it on low. The clipped tones of the BBC spoke into the little kitchen.

"As a true German, I like this."

Wilhelm relaxed and smiled. They listened throughout the meal.

"I haven't done anything all day—I'll wash." He imitated her finger wagging. "You sit."

"I shall be happy to, thank you, Wilhelm."

She was tempted to tell him that dishwashing was a very adequate beginning for being a satisfactory husband, but again she held her tongue. She sensed he didn't like this indirect reference to his future.

"What did you think about today, Wilhelm? Besides living above a bakery?"

He didn't turn immediately from the sink. Finally he said, "I thought about a lot of things. Then I got very tired of thinking." He sighed. "I considered just coming downstairs and ... and slipping out and leaving Munich as I planned."

"That would have been foolish—not to mention ungrateful and rude. I honestly didn't think you had those things in you, Wilhelm."

His tartness matched hers. "Look, I'm sorry." He tossed aside the dishrag. "I don't know what to do, Frau Hilda. I don't know what to do. This ... I gave up that she was alive. It would have been better ... it would have been better if I thought her dead."

"You're speaking out of hurt. You don't really mean that."

"I'm not just talking about going to this SS officer as ... as protection. I'm thinking beyond that. Think of the house she grew up in! Think of what the Rabbi thought she was. Pure in heart, devoted to the faith. Think of how proud he was of her! Doesn't that haunt her?"

The German woman spoke in measured tones. "Well, if we are going to talk of faith, what about yours, Wilhelm?"

"What do you mean?"

"If I recall our days in Nuremberg, you were raised in a home by God-fearing parents. You are as Jewish as your father, and his father, and a long line of Muellers. As Natalie Bergmann is."

Wilhelm sat down and shifted in his chair. His voice was sullen.

"My parents also embraced Christianity when I was a boy."

Hilda nodded. "And which have you embraced?"

He looked away for several moments, then back to her.

"You should have played chess with the Rabbi back in those Nuremberg days, Frau Hilda," he said sullenly. "You would have been a formidable partner."

She stood up, her voice accepting his jest.

"I am going to bed. The BBC says we may have bombers tonight, and I need my rest." Now she lingered at the doorway. "I am confident, Wilhelm, that you're going to find the answers to all of this as you need them. You will find the right way."

But staring up at the ceiling later, Wilhelm Mueller was not so confident.

"You listen to the BBC, Frau Hilda. Herr Picard expected you to be able to get better forged papers for me. You're doing more than just baking pastry," Wilhelm said without preamble the next morning.

Hilda was preparing to leave. She eyed him critically. He was going to push aside this problem with the rabbi's daughter. She could see that from the hard glint in his eye, his scowl, his blunt tone. So be it. Perhaps it was better this way. How could she untangle everything? This world the Nazis had made, yes, maybe as Natalie herself had said, the past belonged buried. It was over. Looking back, maybe that was where the pain and danger was. All she should focus on now was this young man's safety. The present—with some hope of a future for this Jew.

"What are you asking me, Wilhelm?"

"Just what you're involved in. I'm curious. You help Jews escape from the Reich?"

"I try to help Jews, yes. I try . . . to help anyone who needs help."

Their eyes locked across the small kitchen. Wilhelm exhaled loudly. He leaned against the door frame, sagging, his head back and eyes closed.

"You need a haircut," she said. "I'll give you one this evening. I close the shop at four in the fall and winter months."

His eyes opened and he smiled. "I suppose I do need help, body . . . and soul."

Hilda hadn't expected his words. She didn't expect the tears that came suddenly to her eyes. She took a deep breath. "I will help you. I will be glad to."

Strangely, Wilhelm wasn't restless with this unexpected inactivity and personal reflection for a second day. His life had been a diet of infrequent cheap meals, snatched sleep, energy expended in walking and running and hiding. This interlude was a welcome thing. And of course it was an interlude. He knew that. As much as Hilda Weisner would help him, this arrangement would not last forever. He would resume his efforts to leave the Reich or join up with some resistance group somewhere.

The apartment was quiet. The morning had dawned under a flat, colorless sky. He could hear the thin, muted voices from below, and of course smell the wafting odor. Carefully concealed, he stood and watched the streets, the traffic, the customers. Then he would turn back to the room and hear Hilda's voice. He was not going to think about Natalie Bergmann. That was over. But he couldn't ignore the challenge the German woman had put to him the night before. *What is my own faith? I didn't grow up in a godless home. I'm accountable for what I know. Like it or not I do know.* And Wilhelm Mueller knew he had to face that one. This safe haven had to be the place. No distractions; danger at bay.

So he spent the long morning pacing the carpeted room. Pacing and thinking. And after an hour he was wishing he had his aged father beside him. They could talk.

"I would listen now, Papa. I would." He said out loud. He thought of the old man again. How he loved him. He sat down on the sofa, and for the first time in a very long time, he began to cry. Thirty minutes later he still sat with bowed head. He didn't hear the apartment door open.

"Wilhelm."

The kind-sounding voice, not his father's, pulled at him. He raised his head.

Thomas Picard stood before him, gently smiling.

Wilhelm looked away, clearing his throat with embarrassment. He looked back up.

"Well, I suppose if ... if you're going to be caught praying and crying, it's best that a preacher is the one who catches you."

Thomas came forward and shook his hand.

• • •

Munich, Nuremberg, Leipzig, Potsdam. The train sliced through the darkness at the Polish border just after midnight. They had been traveling for four days. A trip that should have taken less than half that time had lengthened with countless delays from troop movements, supply trains, and destroyed tracks. Even Hugo's rank couldn't make the journey faster or shorter. So far the trip had been without incident—until Nuremberg.

"They say we have three hours here. Let's go stretch our legs and find a place to eat. Nuremberg is pretty."

Natalie had tried to demur. "Are we on this same train the entire way?"

"We change at Leipzig. At least according to the schedule."

"Well, let's just stay on. What if they can leave early? We'd be blocks away."

He laughed. "I assure you, they won't leave us."

Still she hesitated.

"Natalie?"

"I suppose I'm tired. I know it's silly, since we've been sitting ..."

"Natalie? You're looking afraid."

"If you want to go, we will."

The day had been bright blue with a slight wind that stirred the leaves that embroidered the streets. It was a day like her grandfather had loved. He loved this old city. She smiled at Hugo and clutched his hand. She banished the thought of her grandfather from her mind.

"The porter said there's a place just over a few blocks. We'll get a good meal there." He directed the cabby. "Krowenstrasse, please."

Natalie was looking toward the square. A Nazi banner fluttered in the breeze. "If you take Vaderstrasse, it's shorter. And the bridge is nice—" she said absently.

She stopped, her heart beating erratically. She couldn't look at Hugo. His voice was unruffled calmness as he redirected the cabman.

He didn't mention the incident, yet Natalie knew he would wonder. She had told him she had never been to Nuremberg.

• • •

Thomas Picard had swiftly decided he liked this young man. They could be friends. Perhaps in the future, they would be. They sat across from each other in Hilda's front room.

"I'm sorry I couldn't come by yesterday, Wilhelm. My sister took a fall and I wanted to stay with her."

"That's all right. How old is your sister?"

"She's twenty-three. She has epileptic seizures."

Wilhelm Mueller decided he liked this tall, academic-looking man. His face displayed some unspoken testimony of great grief. It had tempered him and left him a kind and gentle man. Wilhelm felt he could trust Picard. In this brief interlude, they could be friends. It had been a very long time since he could call someone friend.

"You have other family?"

Thomas shook his head. "Just my sister Gretchen."

"And you're not married?"

This made Thomas smile. "No. A disgraced pastor doesn't draw crowds of frauleins in want of a husband."

"Yet with the war," Wilhelm smiled too, "you should be a prized commodity."

Thomas shook his head again, "It's better this way. What I do, and with Gretchen, it makes life . . ." But his words fell away and he looked to the window. *Easier. Lonelier.*

Wilhelm understood. They were graduates in the same class.

"Your family?" Thomas finally asked.

"Have you ever heard of a Berliner named Max Farber?"

"Of course. Everyone in Germany read about his case. He was accused of helping Jews escape and aiding the Allies in Geneva. It made headlines for weeks."

Wilhelm nodded. "Some of those Jews were my family. They worked for the Farbers. He helped my parents and sister escape to Switzerland just before the war. It's been several years since I had a letter from them. I don't keep a permanent address, you understand. My brother, Walther, wasn't . . . so fortunate. He was taken by 'Hanging Heydrich' himself. He was sent to Dachau." He shrugged. "We never heard ... but Max Farber, he's in Tegel Prison last I heard. But he ... he is a helping Gentile. I ... I see I've been fortunate to run into a few of them in my life." He stopped on that thought.

"We might part in agreement on that point, Wilhelm," Thomas smiled.

"What point?"

"That you've been fortunate and merely run into these people. That would imply coincidence. From my own life, and what you've told me of your experiences, I would think it's more than coincidence."

So they came to the question of faith as swiftly as Hilda had the night before. Wilhelm smiled to himself. There was no getting away from this.

"You would think it was?" Wilhelm prompted.

But Thomas shook his head and leaned back, his hands behind his head.

"You tell me what you think it really sounds like."

"Well ... like ... like I've been protected. That ..." He stood up abruptly and walked around the room.

"When you came in, you caught me considering all of this." He looked at Thomas a moment. "All right. As if God is caring for me. I don't know how else to say it."

"That's a pretty good starting point, Wilhelm. That says a lot. Another way would be that He who created the universe created you, loves you, and sees you now."

"Somehow," Wilhelm laughed shakily, "I don't like to admit this. It means I'm not in control anymore."

"You've never really been in control, not entirely."

"No, but if I acknowledge that ... that He is, then I'm accountable."

"Whether you acknowledge Him or not doesn't change who He is, or what He has planned, or that He will love you one bit more or one bit less. But if you think you can see He has put these "helping Gentiles," as you call them, in your life, if He has protected you, then you have to decided what your response should be."

Wilhelm stood at the window for several minutes.

Thomas' voice was gentle at his back. "Was there ever a time, Wilhelm, that as a boy growing up, you did something that ... grieved your father?"

Wilhelm, standing with his hands in his pockets, didn't turn. He laughed shortly.

"There was rarely a time when I wasn't grieving him."

"Did that bother you much or were you able to ignore it?"

Wilhelm's throat tightened. He could almost feel the warm hand of his father on his head.

"It bothered me," he replied simply.

"And what did you do?"

"I tried. I wanted to make it right."

There it was. To make it right. Wilhelm stood another minute before he turned. He found the music-store owner, the former pastor, his new friend, bowing his head.

Wilhelm sat down, feeling more at peace than he had in years.

•   •   •

His office was a shabby little room on the third floor. The sleek black car had delivered the man to the building, then the two SS men had escorted him up the stairs. There was no name on the frosted glass of the office door, and Olaf Swensen was sweating and shaking. He couldn't conceal these tremors, and he knew the SS guards were smirking at him. But a midnight call from the Gestapo was enough to send the strongest, bravest man into some manifestation of anxiety.

By the time he sat in the proffered chair, his lower lip was trembling and his hands were leaving damp prints on his thighs. He didn't recognize the pudgy-faced, unsmiling man behind the desk. And the man did not offer his name.

"You don't need to be nervous, Herr Swensen. You have only to answer my questions and my men will return you to your home."

Olaf nodded eagerly. "How can I help you, sir?"

Otto Beck smiled. "Tell me about Frau Hilda Jensen, your employer."

Olaf blinked rapidly. "Frau Hilda?"

Beck leaned forward and consulted his paper. "That is correct. Frau Jensen."

"But, but what would you want to know? I mean about Frau Hilda?"

"The faster you can come to those answers, the faster you'll be back in your bed. Otherwise, it may be a long night for you."

Olaf licked his lips. "I . . ." He shrugged. "I can only tell you she is a very fine baker. She is a kind employer." He shrugged again.

Beck leaned forward again. "You have a brother who is a communist."

"He was many, many years ago. I haven't seen him in a long time."

"A pity."

"Frau Hilda has done something? I mean . . ."

"Tell me about the customers to the bakery."

"I know very little about them, nothing. You must know I'm simply the baker. I stay in the back in the kitchen all day."

"I know you have two eyes and two ears. I know you see and hear more than just the dough you knead. Unless of course, there is nothing but dough between your ears."

The two guards snickered.

"Hear and see what? I mean, I'm sorry, I'm confused."

"Have you ever seen anything strange at the bakery, anything not connected to the sale of pasty?"

"Well . . . no. Frau Hilda is a respectable lady."

"Have you ever seen her speaking with anyone about something other than her business? Think, you simpleton!"

Olaf was thinking hard. Frau Hilda had been acting . . . a little strange lately. As if there was other things on her mind. And that day she had sent him upstairs to the storeroom . . . . .

Olaf related these things quickly.

"You didn't see who she let in the back door?"

"No, no, I can't be sure that she let anyone in. I mean, I think it was opened, that's all."

"And what do you think she was preoccupied with?"

"I have no idea, sir."

"Has she ever had anyone upstairs while you worked there?"

"Upstairs? No, she lives alone."

"You are certain?"

"Well . . ."

"She has had frequent visits from Herr Thomas Picard lately."

"I don't know. He has been in the shop to pick up his order. He stayed late after closing one night. I suppose they were chatting."

"Up in her apartment. What do you suppose an older woman, a baker, and a younger man, a music-store owner, have in common to chat about?"

"I'm afraid I don't know, sir."

Otto Beck stood up abruptly, his chair screeching against the tile.

"I'm afraid you have told me very little."

"I ... I ..."

"Understand this little meeting won't be discussed with anyone. Understand that we are watching you. Understand that you will bring anything about Frau Hilda that seems strange to you. Understand that we can find your brother."

• • •

As much as Hilda liked to bake for her customers, she preferred to cook a meal for people she knew and cared for. She enjoyed seeing their enthusiasm for her food. So watching the two bachelors, Thomas and Wilhelm, eat was a great pleasure. Whatever they had been discussing over the day had left Wilhelm looking calm and relaxed. The angry lines between his eyes had smoothed. After dinner, they took their coffee to the front room.

"We need to make plans for you, Wilhelm," Thomas stated. "We need to start tonight."

He nodded. "Well, whatever we plan, we have to take into account that we're being watched."

Hilda's cup stopped in midair. "What?"

Wilhelm grinned. "There's been a guy out there all day. I saw him yesterday too."

Thomas and Hilda exchanged a look, then looked back to Wilhelm.

He shrugged. "You kind of get ... trained in looking for those guys. They stand out to me."

Thomas was frowning.

"Maybe you two should tell me what you're involved in so we can understand why he's out there," Wilhelm said.

Hilda spoke first. "I knew that I wanted to help the Jews however I could after I had gotten the bakery established. I listened to customers, I asked a few discreet questions, and soon I met a man who came to the shop. We were able to talk one evening. We had to trust each other. He told me he was part of a Christian group that tried to smuggle Jews out of Germany or, in the worse case, to simply hide them in safe homes. He was responsible for the forged papers. We worked out codes. And then they started coming. I keep them for a few nights until the next contact is made. There have been a few occasions where I've had to escort them to the safe house personally. Thankfully nothing has ever happened. Things have gone smoothly. I don't know the man who contacted me first or the people I go to. We never exchange names."

"Except with you having a business, he knows who you are. You would be the most visible of the group," Wilhelm pointed out.

Hilda's chin went up. "I suppose so. But that doesn't frighten me."

Wilhelm smiled. He couldn't imagine this woman being afraid of very much.

"That might explain the man outside. I was told a few nights ago, by the SS, that the SS knows some kind of network exists for the Jews."

"Then Frau Hilda and you, Wilhelm, are in danger," Thomas said. "There might be another explanation though. I'm watched too. I'm just not sure why. I have an uncle in the Munich Gestapo. He has a few grievances against me. I imagine he'd like to take care of that one way or another."

"Then, to use an American expression, we're all sitting ducks."

"Well, perhaps," Thomas conceded. "But we have to plan our response carefully. Frau Hilda has a network depending on her. I have my younger sister. You see, Wilhelm, Frau Hilda and I have been working in the same group for about a year, and we didn't know it. I'm one of the people who scout for safe houses. I can take my piano tuner with me and have a look at houses and folks and try to find contacts. Some have been placed in my home."

"Then we're sitting ducks with the scope hairs on us," Wilhelm said with sudden grimness. "They know Thomas is up here, maybe me too."

"Wilhelm, your talk is beginning to make me a little nervous," Hilda sputtered.

"If they only have the front watched, then we have a chance. We can find that out easy enough."

"I agree we have to be especially careful now, but let's not be alarmed yet. I have a few details to work out to make sure my sister is safe. Give me another day or two. Frau Hilda, you need to get the word that Wilhelm needs papers. I brought money with me tonight. And you need to ask for papers for yourself."

"But, but . . ."

Thomas smiled. "Just as a precaution." He looked back to Wilhelm. "Next order of business is figuring out what you want, Wilhelm. Where do you want to go?"

"An easy question," Wilhelm snorted. "I've been thinking about that ... among other things." His eyes met Hilda's. "I don't have any reason to stay in Germany. I'm not ready to join my family in Switzerland. I know a little French. I thought about trying to get to Vichy, France, and joining the resistance there." He shrugged. "I know it isn't much of a plan."

All three were silent for several minutes.

"Do you know any Polish, Wilhelm?" Hilda suddenly asked.

"Polish? A little. Why?"

"Just curious," she said unsmiling.

"I think we'd better break up for the night. I'll go out the front door and you give me a sack of stuff to carry. It may not be the best ruse, but it's the only bluff we have right now. Wilhelm, you watch from the window and see if our man moves off. But first, we pray."

26
Once the Polish Capital

Warsaw, Poland

Natalie was frightened. She had never seen Hugo like this before. He had entered their hotel suite, closing the door with a little more force than usual. Natalie was in their bed, but she could see clearly into the sitting room. While her room was in darkness, she had left a light burning in the outer room. Now she could see him as he strode into the sitting room. He was pacing for several minutes, his posture rigid, his hands behind his back. She had seen this parade in other men, but never her Hugo. She could only see his unsmiling profile. His chin was raised, and she could sense a hard cast to his face. Finally he stopped and yanked off his hat. He tossed it into a chair. Usually he laid aside his uniform with care. He unbuttoned the uniform jacket with abrupt, jerking fingers. He flung it off and paced again. Natalie pushed herself up in the bed. Her heart was racing.

Hugo entered the bedroom. He stood in the splash of moonlight at the end of the bed.

"Hugo?"

"I didn't know you were awake," he said in a clipped voice. "I'm sorry if I woke you."

Her fear inched forward.

"It's all right, I wasn't asleep. I was waiting up for you."

"You shouldn't have. I told you I would be late."

Still she couldn't see his face in the darkness, but she knew he was regarding her, unsmiling and silent. Coldly. *What had happened?*

Yesterday, their first day in Warsaw, they had lounged in their room most of the day. Hugo had teased and laughed and pampered her. Then they had rented a cab and driven around the city at dusk. It had been twenty years since he had been here. On the trip from Germany he had told her it was a beautiful old city. Now entire blocks lay in ruins. Hugo had made no comment.

They had come back to their room for dinner, and Hugo had tenderly told her he was glad he had brought her.

This man, in this brief time, was sounding, even standing, like a stranger. Natalie could hardly control her rapid breathing.

"Hugo, you sound upset. Are you all right?"

He didn't answer. He stood in the same stiff posture for a full minute. Then he began pacing, his voice still foreign.

"Duty is paramount to me. Other feelings may come and go, but duty remains. Duty remains even as governments change, as leaders rise and fall. As . . . as leaders are wise or foolish. Every German understands this. It is what keeps empires strong. Duty."

She had the chilling feeling he was reciting some long-ago lesson. She sensed he had forgotten her presence in the room.

"Hugo, I don't understand."

His step and voice didn't falter. He walked and turned like a puppet.

"I have been brought here to . . . to administer the Jewish ghetto. Hugo von Kleinst is to administer the Warsaw ghetto. With all my military skills, my abilities I . . . I have been brought here to this, to listen to a bunch of haggling Jews! To be their landlord, their, their schoolmaster, their commandant!" he said tightly.

Now Natalie understood. Hugo was furious. He didn't want this work. It assaulted his dignity.

Still he didn't turn. "To administer the Warsaw ghetto . . . a ghetto."

He stood before the long windows that looked out on Krulewska. He rocked on his toes. She could hear his voice grow even and steady. Five minutes passed. What should she say? What did this mean to them?

In her resolve to bury the old Natalie, she had to employ the new ways. Even when she was afraid, she had to take a few risks.

"Hugo, please come to bed. I'm cold."

The voice in the darkness took a moment to penetrate his thoughts. He turned, and again she could feel his look on her. She wanted to cover herself and slip further into the bed. But she didn't.

"Hugo."

He walked to the end of the bed. He sighed and she could hear his weariness, his disappointment. He gripped the footboard and leaned forward slightly. His voice was calmer, even, but still hard.

"I have my duty. I understand that. They may think I'll make a bigger mess of this, that I'll shirk my duty like the others, but they'll be surprised. They'll see a ghetto run tighter and more efficiently than any in the great Third Reich. They give me this nasty little mess and they chuckle behind their sleeves at Hugo von Kleinst."

He straightened, removing his shirt and boots. "We shall see."

He stalked to the bathroom. Natalie was trembling. He climbed into their bed, not speaking, not touching her gently as he always did. And now she was terribly afraid.

•   •   •

David Szmulewski and this group of ten had been living in the basement of the funeral home for over two years. For basement living quarters, the eleven considered themselves very fortunate. The place was dry, warm, well-ventilated, and gave them an abbreviated view of the world and weather. It was large enough to conduct their limited activities and afford all of them occasional periods of privacy. Above all it was safe. As safe as it could be in Nazi-occupied Warsaw. They watched SS trucks pass on their street all the time.

But in the two years they had never had an occasion to use the hidden second entrance at the back of the building as a sudden escape. The only other way out was up the winding stairs to the first floor of the funeral parlor. The door to the basement was in a false closet of cleaning supplies. Two large bottles of greenish yellow embalming fluid sat noticeably on the center shelf and had a disarming effect for anyone who might be tempted to curiosity. The entire building had that effect. It was not an attractive place. It stirred up morbid sensations. For hiding Jews it was perfect. Thus the funeral home became the headquarters for the Jewish underground of Warsaw. Only a very select group knew of its existence— the Jews in the basement, the owner of the funeral home and his wife, and one member of a Polish resistance movement that operated in the city.

This was the one tenuous link the Jews had to others who were fighting against the Nazis with matched, if not entirely the same motivation, intensity.

The middle-aged couple who owned the funeral home were Christians and had taken the command to help the least of these quite literally. They had offered their basement to the Jews. They had offered their very lives by the act. Their one helper in their grim business was a man they trusted implicitly, in some part because he was deaf. So the couple had conducted their work with the eleven living underneath them. They supplied their food, which had proven to be the most difficult task of all. How could they explain shopping for thirteen appetites when there were only two of them? They had solved part of the dangerous problem by having the families of their "customers" pay partly in food. With the hardships of war and occupation, this was often easier than ready cash. It was an arrangement that had worked for two years. They brought news with the one daily trip of food.

The small group was busy despite its confines. The members kept track of the real war news through the BBC. They published pamphlets telling this truth about the German invaders and distributed them every few weeks. They kept in touch with other resistance groups throughout Poland by courier. They knew they were not alone in the struggle. They were responsible for contact with the underground inside the closest concentration camp, Treblinka, barely fifty miles northeast of Warsaw. And perhaps more vital, they were the only Jewish link with the ghetto underground. While David worried over the prisoners of Treblinka, he knew the road to the concentration camp began a mere six blocks away in the Muranow district.

David Szmulewski, or DS as he was known, was a thin, little, balding man whose courage and physical strength was mocked by his stature. He looked very absorbed in the boot sole he had been mending most of the morning. It was his turn to slip out at midnight with the pamphlets. Each time one of them left, it might be the last time he was seen. There was a finality about any casual goodbye. Each knew the great price of this excursion out: If caught, torture must be chosen before betrayal of the rest of the group. A great and terrible price indeed. Life on a tightrope.

But he was not absorbed in the work in his hands or the dangerous outing he would take in eight hours. He was thinking of Treblinka. He thought a lot about it. More than he let on to others. And not for the obvious reasons. If they were caught and not killed in torture, they would be sent to the camp. No, he was a gentle man, a compassionate man, and he could not help but think of his Jewish brothers and sisters in that place. In the twilight of 1942, David and his comrades knew the terrible truth— these were not work camps for Jews as Berlin loudly defended. These were extermination camps. The courier had breathlessly told them all the details. The ovens, the pits, the stench of twisting smoke that spiraled up to the sky night and day spoke over the Nazi propaganda.

David tried to understand how people could hate this passionately. He couldn't do it. He gave up trying. Now what mattered was how to tell the rest of the unbelieving world about this atrocity. If only they knew . . .

"David!" one of the group called.

He ambled over to them. They were unloading the food basket.

"Here is yesterday's paper. Look." David leaned forward and read quickly.

"Well, well, they have another rat-catcher, huh?"

"The Nazis have an endless supply, that is the tragic part."

David straightened and stretched. "Commandant Hugo von Kleinst, new protector of the Jewish quarter."

"Jewish quarter," someone snorted. "Jewish ghetto. Even the Poles call it that. Who do they think reads this foolish rag and is deceived?"

"Hugo von Kleinst," David repeated. "Sounds very proper and German."

"Can't you see him strutting like a king? And his kingdom is over thousands of starving Jews. What an honor!"

Silent frustration clamped over the group. The Nazis did seem to have an endless supply of masters.

David looked around. "This new king is marked by the resistance. They would like nothing better than to take out a new pompous Nazi. It's been a while since they've had such an effective strike."

They all looked at him intently.

"A car bomb," he shrugged.

Treblinka

He was keeping the Sabbath in his heart. In this place that was nearly the only way to keep it. The men around him were shuffling to their bunks, talking in low, tired, apathetic voices. He didn't listen. He sat cross-legged at the end of his bunk space, which was slats covered with a thin, lice-infested blanket. But it was his space, and he would not be bothered. He kept this vigil with his sanity every evening. The others around him had given up their teasing and ridicule. It was a very simple outcome to this place—one was driven into the arms of God or away from Him. Men and women came out atheists or strong in faith. It had never occurred to this man to do anything but seek God. Certainly he had enough time to think. Thinking was the only distraction to pain and suffering.

He had meditated on Scriptures that he had known since boyhood. He was now a man of thirty-four. And strangely enough, he still looked his age—beyond the thinness and paleness. Then he systematically thought of his father, mother, brother, and sister. It seemed so much longer than two years since he had seen them. He prayed for them with an intensity that made him weep. If only he could know that one of them—even one would survive this . . . this holocaust. That would make it easier to bear. Then lights flickered once. The barracks went dark. The men crept into their beds with sighing. A few precious hours.

But the young man stayed on the end of his bed, still in the same cross-legged position. He counted off twenty minutes. Then he crawled out. No one spoke to him. Each man's business was his own. He went down the center aisle, paused, and counted to forty while the camp guard passed. Then, hugging the shadows of the building, he crept forward in the autumn gloom. Abraham Goldstein was going to the underground meeting.

• • •

Driving through the pale sunshine, Natalie's first impression of Warsaw remained the same for her entire stay—it was a ravaged but still beautiful city. There was something about it that reminded her of Nuremberg. There were classical lines to the buildings that remained standing: the gothic churches, the opera house, and the magnificent Royal Castle. There were parks along the Vistula River that bisected the city. The biography she had read boasted of Warsaw's cultural sophistication. As real as the pock-marked roads, shredded trees, skeleton buildings, that sophistication was gone. This was a city of conqueror and conquered.

Natalie rented a cab the next day after Hugo had left for his office. He had been withdrawn as they breakfasted together, asking her absently about her plans for the day, making no reference to the scene the night before. Natalie pretended it hadn't happened.

As the cab negotiated the capital, Natalie craned forward to see better and her horror and indignation mounted in the unflattering light of day. There were no military installations in the center of the city. There had been no reason for the Germans to burn and pillage this city. She shook with rage to think of the civilians who must have died. The Munich papers had reported the German army had moved with decisive authority. They had respected the Polish citizenry, though the Poles had fought savagely. Natalie had suspected the lie even then. This place gave a terrible testimony. And this would be their home for a year. She leaned back and sighed.

"New to Warsaw, eh?" the cabbie asked in patchy German.

"Yes, just the day before yesterday. I think it's a lovely city, I mean . . . what is here."

She felt awkward. "You have lived here long?" she asked.

She could see he hesitated, mentally preparing his answer. "All my life. Warsaw's been my home all my fifty-four years."

Their eyes collided and skidded away in the mirror. There was so much more to his words and they both knew it. But she'd get no more from him. He understood that if she was new to the city she was one of them, one of the masters. She glanced away frustrated. How she would have liked to talk easily and casually to someone who didn't care about her past. Just talk.

She wanted to tell him she wasn't really one of them either, and she hated what they had done to his homeland too. She returned to the window.

"That area there, to the left, what is that? It doesn't say in the guidebook."

"You can toss that away. Most of what is in there is gone. And that isn't in there either."

"It's fenced." As soon as she spoke the two words, something clutched at her and she knew.

His voice was laconic. "It's the ghetto for the Jews. Crammed all the city in there nearly, and they ship in more each day."

The car came to a stop at an intersection. She watched a line of women and children under escort entering through the barricade.

The cabbie yawned and shifted in his seat. "In they go."

"They are allowed in and out as they please?"

He yawned again. "For now. They have a curfew at night. But the rumor is they're about to clamp down, shut them in there. They won't go out except on the cattle cars. The trains come up on the northern side."

The cab was stalled as yet another military truck disgorged a dozen personnel.

"Cattle cars?" she asked in a hushed voice.

He shrugged. "North to Treblinka, south to Auschwitz. Or a dozen other ones around. The Jews don't seem to know or understand, but the rest of us do."

"I'd like to go back now. To my hotel, please."

In less than five minutes he pulled up to the entrance of the hotel. His eyes were fastened forward, eager for her to leave. She could feel his contempt. Coming before this hotel merely confirmed what her accent and questions had told him earlier. *Here was a German invader. A wife or a mistress.*

She hesitated, her hands twisting her purse handle.

"I don't like what they've done to your homeland either," she said hurriedly.

Again their eyes met in the mirror. And again the cabby held his own thoughts.

As the newest officer of the Reich in Warsaw, Hugo von Kleinst must be feted by his fellow officers in proper style. And in the Polish capital there was much spoil to fete with. Commandant von Kleinst was hosted at private dinner parties and theater parties and in clubs for nearly every night for the first few weeks. Hugo detested these drunken orgies, but he knew he must politely attend them. Each invitation required the careful consideration of whether to take Natalie with him. Everyone knew of her presence; she was, after all, a strikingly attractive woman Hugo would naturally want to display. Yet Hugo knew her loathing of these affairs matched his own.

He asked her to go no more than twice a week. He made sure she wore a new dress to each occasion. There was no question the commandant was proud of the brown-haired beauty. When they entered the room, heads turned, voices dropped in whisper. There was something . . . almost regal about the young woman. She would smile, her head held high. She rarely spoke unless spoken to. Yes, she was a cool one, but those who did engage in conversation found her approachable and easy to talk with. She was reserved but not haughty. Soon Hugo discovered he was the most sought after guest in Warsaw—because of his mistress. Natalie never disappointed.

Natalie endured the outings with theatrical composure. She hated the German arrogance that swirled around her. *They are thieves, nearly all of them. But Hugo is different. Hugo is different,* she told herself.

This dinner party was hosted by Hugo's junior officers. They had taken over the huge ornate dining room of one of the few surviving Warsaw restaurants. Natalie thought every officer in Warsaw, connected with Hugo or not, had come to the party for the free drinks and food. The place was a crush of uniforms under a vault of cigar smoke. With the strident laughter, the smoke, the heavy, cloying smell of liquor, Natalie was developing a colossal headache. She wished desperately that Hugo would look at her and raise his eyebrow. She would return the gesture with a smile. It had always been their private signal that it was time to leave. But he was sipping champagne, laughing, and relaxing, appearing as if he would go with the last reveler to sunrise.

She studied his face. *He was the same; he was different.* In the two weeks they had been in Warsaw, she had felt an abrupt departure from their old relationship. First, he was gone longer—early in the morning till late at night. Clearly he was keeping his vow of doing a good job in this new responsibility. When he did come back to their room, he was quiet and preoccupied. In these short weeks he was already looking haggard. On the rare evenings he came back early, he would lay on the sofa, staring up at the ceiling, with the phonograph playing something soft in the background.

He spoke to her without really seeing her. He displayed the old protection, even if the tone of gentleness was absent.

"You must be very careful when you go out, Natalie. This isn't Munich. Warsaw is an occupied city and as such there are violent elements still present. Not to mention attacks from Allied planes. I'd rather you not venture out too far from the hotel."

He rarely held her or touched her. Natalie spent hours trying to interpret this. *Is he angry with me? Does he regret bringing me here? Is it only his loathing of this job that has changed him?* She stared out the window over the city changing from leafless fall to winter. *Do I care that he rarely caresses me anymore?*

She left the gilded chair she had been sitting in and returned to the circle of men and women around Hugo. He took a sip of his champagne and looked at her. He smiled. And for a moment Natalie felt reassured. It was a look that went to her eyes, a look like he had given her in the past.

"So, Commandant, what do you think of this Jewish district you're overseeing? It's an embarrassment if you ask me."

The voice was sneering and drunk. Natalie looked at the man. A captain in the army.

"I have to detail men over there every day for escorting the vermin in and out. Then of course there's the whole smuggling problem. It's a mess." He belched loudly and a few tittered nervously around him. Yet they were looking to Hugo.

Hugo took another slow, deliberate sip of his champagne.

"I plan to tidy up the little mess, Herr Metz," he replied smiling and cool.

"How, Herr Commandant?" another in the crowd asked.

"You must not have observed the changes we've already been making. The Jews will stay inside the ghetto to work on specific assignments like the uniforms. We have about completed the transfer of machinery to the inside. This will be much more efficient."

"Well, that's good! It's about time for a little of the famous Berlin efficiency!" the drunken man bawled.

No one around him laughed.

"The ghetto will be sealed by the first of next month," Hugo continued placidly.

"Sealed? As in, no in, no out?"

Hugo smiled. "As in, no in, no out without a pass. Exactly. The first way to clean up a mess is to contain it."

The leader of the Warsaw Jewish underground had finally come up with a plan. It had come to him as he perused a six-week-old Jewish newspaper that had been smuggled into fortress Europe through Switzerland. It had come from the World Jewish Refugee Agency in London. To the undergrounds scattered around the Reich, this was a precious paper. It was their fragile bond to the other world, the world of sanity and safety. By the time it reached the hands of David Szmulewski, it was ragged and worn. Several pages were missing. But the second page contained an article that caught and held his attention. "Reports of Nazi concentration camps and atrocities in occupied Eastern Europe are receiving increasing attention in international press and radio. The Red Cross has investigated camps under the careful escort of the Nazis. The camps they saw were work camps, nothing of these extermination rumors. So what really is happening in the camps in the Reich? Are the terrible rumors true or exaggerated fabrications of hysteria? How could the safe world know the truth?" the article asked. The world must know the truth and not through Nazi editing. If only the world could see ...

David closed the paper slowly. *That the world could see. There it was.* Like most Jews, he felt each day of freedom could easily be his last. But with all his strength and might, with his very life, he would help the world to know.

Natalie hadn't intended to disobey Hugo. For several weeks she stayed on the streets near the hotel. She had her favorite shops and cafes. The weather was turning colder, yet she went for walks along the Vistula and tried to ignore her deepening loneliness. Warsaw was not a happy place. They had left Munich for a vast prison complex. Hugo had retreated into his work, into a personal place he had barred her from. One afternoon, when the blue sky was to lovely to ignore, the air crisp, she walked farther than she intended. She turned a corner and came upon a young boy. He was pale and his dark eyes darted nervously. His spindly legs stuck out below a ragged coat and too-short trousers. His voice sounded raspy and older than his years. He thrust a basket toward her.

"Lady, want a cat?"

"What?"

He looked over his shoulder, then past her. She followed his look. *Who is he looking for?*

He pushed back a dirty cloth to reveal one crouching kitten.

"A kitten, see? Want him? I can give you a good price today."

Natalie leaned forward. Then she looked back to him. She smiled. She wanted to reach out and push back the lock of hair from his eye.

"You're pretty," he said abruptly.

She laughed. It felt good to laugh.

"How are old are you?"

"Seven."

"Where do you live?"

Again that look past her, behind her. He frowned.

"Want a cat? Good price today."

She reached out a finger to stroke the gray-striped animal.

"You want him? He's little, see? Thought I'd drown him if I couldn't sell him."

"Oh, no, I wouldn't want you to do that."

"Got plenty of cats to sell in there. Can't give them any food. There isn't any." He jerked his head behind him. "They think I can't find anything to sell, but I can always find something. You want him?"

"He's very handsome."

"You didn't ask how much."

She was looking past him, finally seeing the wall topped with barbed wire. She looked back at the small figure. A child from Hugo's ghetto. Her throat tightened.

"Help me think of a name for him," she said softly.

He shrugged. "He's not really special. Just a kitten I'd have to drown."

"Then I think Moses would be a good name, don't you?"

For the first time a smile lighted his strained features.

"You're a good German. You'll take good care of him for me, huh?"

She nodded, unable to speak.

"He likes his stomach scratched like this." She could see tears forming in the dark eyes. Then he was craning around her again. "There they are. I have to hurry."

She turned. Two SS sentries were coming up the street.

She dug into her purse and handed him a wad of money. His eyes widened. He shoved the basket toward her before he bolted.

"Well, shalom to you lady!"

He darted between a loose board of the fence with feline agility.

She couldn't keep the words from her lips. "Shalom to you little one."

She bathed him, brushed him, fed him—then sat back on her heels feeling very pleased. She had a pet at last, one that needed her as she had needed him.

"Little Moses," she sighed. She took him to the sunny window seat of their parlor, and the kitten curled in her lap and purred contentedly. Her own little something to care for, her little Jewish cat. She couldn't help but smile a little. The hotel suite door opened.

Hugo was carefully pulling off his hat, placing his gloves neatly in them. He loosened his top jacket button as he crossed the room.

"You're early," Natalie said easily.

He nodded. "I . . . I just got tired of it for awhile. I thought I'd come and take you to lunch. I've been neglecting you lately. I'm sorry."

"Hugo, I understand."

"Well, well, what have we here? A drowned rat?"

She laughed. "A kitten, of course."

He sat beside her. "He's pretty small and scrawny."

She brought him close to her face. "All the more reason he's perfect for me."

Now Hugo smiled and reached out and touched her cheek. "This doesn't mean I've been replaced does it?"

She shook her head.

"Where did you get him? If there is a pet store in Warsaw, I'd think they'd be ashamed to pawn off such a little beggar," he chuckled.

"Off the street. A little boy was selling him."

Hugo's eyebrow raised. "What street?"

Natalie didn't meet his eyes. "I don't really know. Some street nearby. I didn't see the sign. I'm not sure I would know anyway. Speaking Polish is difficult enough without trying to read it also."

He nodded, watching her in silence a moment.

"Have a name for him yet?"

So this little cat would be truly her own, they would have a secret name between them. She smiled. "Well, how about whatever is Polish for cat?"

"We'll ask when we go for lunch."

Their eyes held a moment. Munich was over. So their time in Warsaw was not going to be a time of growing closer.

Neither could imagine that their time in Warsaw was going to change everything. Forever.

27
The Truth About Lions

He had been dreaming. Many nights his dreams were merely mirrors of his day: impossible chases, hiding, near-death escapes. But always he survived. He was never captured. He knew it meant nothing, still, it gave him some boyish sense of triumph and a little comfort. But this night he had dreamed of a far different setting.

He was in a vast auditorium. He was looking very dapper in a black suit and tie. He was happy, actually raising up on his toes and whistling some tune. He greeted people, waving a folded program. Then he took his seat. None of the faces in the audience were familiar. He tapped the program nervously on his knee. Then the house lights had dimmed. The heavy drapes opened and there was an orchestra. The audience was clapping, but he wasn't. He was looking at the third row, the string section. Her hair lay in smooth brown waves against the plain black dress. Her head was lowered, her face in rapt concentration. The conductor raised his baton; she looked up. He was stunned at her poise, her beauty. Then her face had turned back to the music stand as she drew her bow. Natalie Bergmann was playing her violin.

Wilhelm sat up, breathing hard. He was tense in the unfamiliar setting. *It is . . . it is only Hilda's apartment. Yes.* His breathing grew easier. *It had all been a dream. Such a vivid dream.*

The door to Hilda's bedroom opened. Her head appeared.

"Are you all right?" she asked.

"Why, yes. Why?"

"I thought I heard you call me."

"No . . . no . . . I was having a dream. But I didn't know I called you. I'm sorry I woke you, Frau Hilda."

"It's all right, Wilhelm. Good night."

The door started to close.

"Frau Hilda?"

"Yes?"

He hesitated. He looked down at his hands a moment.

"Is she in Munich?"

His voice sounded very small. Hilda's head disappeared and for a moment Wilhelm thought she hadn't heard him. But she had heard him very clearly. It was a question she had long expected—no matter what route it took for him to reach it.

She reappeared, drawing a heavy robe around her. It seemed undignified to her to appear this way, at this hour, but she must forsake a little dignity for this cause. She sat across from him.

"Is Natalie in Munich?" he repeated.

"No, Wilhelm, Natalie is no longer in Munich."

He leaned back with a sigh. "I had this dream. It was so real, you know. I was in the Berlin opera house at a concert, and she was there. I mean, I know she's grown up, but I saw her as she was but even more beautiful. And she was playing the violin, of course." He laughed a short nervous laugh. "You should have seen the suit I had on."

"So it was a pleasant dream?"

He shrugged. "Yes, I guess so." His brow furrowed. "I just remembered something. I had another dream about Natalie years ago when I was in the States." He shook his head. "She was sledding and she was afraid. I woke up and decided I needed to stop hiding out in America. That's when I returned to Germany."

A long silence.

"How long has it been since you saw her?" he asked slowly.

Her hands were pressed tightly in her lap. The igniting question had come. No more evasions. He had been through his struggle.

"I saw her five days ago."

He bolted up to his feet. "What?"

"I saw Natalie five days ago here in Munich. We met at the park."

He ran an unsteady hand through his hair, standing it up on end. He was pacing in front of her, and she couldn't help but smile a little in the darkness.

Finally he stopped, his tone a little crisp. "Why didn't you tell me that first day?"

"You didn't ask me," she returned calmly.

"I . . ." He stared at her, then laughed. "Frau Hilda, you are forever a surprise."

He stood before her, hands on his hips. "Well."

"Well."

They both laughed now.

"All right . . . five days ago." He started pacing again. Finally he sat down, leaning forward. He couldn't see her face clearly in the darkness.

"I can't believe it." He scratched his head. "All right. So . . . all right, where is she now may I ask, Frau Hilda?"

"Poland. Natalie has gone to Poland."

Again he was on his feet. "Poland!"

"You're going to wear yourself out jumping up like that, Wilhelm."

"Poland. Why in the world did she go to Poland?

But Hilda didn't answer. He peered at her in the gloom, his heart racing.

"The man she's . . . with?"

Hilda nodded.

He slumped down again. He remained hunched over for several minutes.

"Please tell me." His voice was subdued.

"Apparently he was transferred for duty in Warsaw. He wanted Natalie to go with him. It's that simple."

"Did she say . . . did she say how long, I mean, is it a permanent assignment?"

"She didn't say. She didn't really give me any details about it."

The silence lengthened. Wilhelm was having great difficulty with Hilda's words—the girl in braids and plaids whom he had known had grown to be an independent young woman, a mistress. The girl who he had searched for.

His voice was barely above a whisper. "Can you tell me about her, Frau Hilda?"

Hilda Jensen could barely conceal her emotion. She did love this young man.

"We met at the park. She had sent me a note saying she would like to see me. It had been nearly two years since I had heard from her. I went to the park. It was a lovely day. She ... she is no longer a girl of sixteen, Wilhelm. She's twenty-two. She's very lovely. She has a grace and poise about her that long ago I suspected would come but has fully blossomed now. We sat on a bench, and she told me she was leaving Munich the next day. She said she was happy, Wilhelm."

Now it was Hilda's turn to fall silent. Wilhelm's mind was in high gear. He had been in the city with her the entire time. They could have passed on the street. He could have been in the park. Only five days ago.

Hilda's voice was firm. "I told her she could come back to me here at the bakery if she didn't want to go to Poland ... with him."

"But she wouldn't come back with you," Wilhelm finished in a flat voice.

"True."

He stood up again and faced her. "Would you have told me about her, I mean, if she was still here in Munich?"

"I don't know, Wilhelm. It would be painful for both of you."

He exhaled slowly. "Yes, you're right."

"This way ... this way the past is ... past. You both have a future before you."

A future. Wilhelm turned the words over in his mind. *She had chosen a life for herself. A very deliberate choice. What right did he have to ... interfere?*

"What are you going to do, Wilhelm?" she asked gently.

He sat back down. "Well, Frau Hilda, I'm going to do something I haven't had much practice at." He gave the short, deprecating laugh she knew well.

"I'm going to pray."

• • •

Otto Beck had questioned the Picard's employees. Now they all looked at Thomas with a puzzled, inquiring look. Why was the Gestapo interested in their boss? It made them all a little anxious. Putting food on the table depended on this job. The war years had trimmed luxuries like buying instruments. Times were tight. No one could afford an employer hauled off to some interrogation—or worse, the whispered camps. And certainly not the kind Thomas Picard. What could he possibly be guilty of? He had so much personal grief in his life, why should he incur the wrath of the Gestapo? So they went about their work silent and watching, and hoping the Gestapo was very wrong this time.

Otto hadn't risen in the ranks of the Gestapo by personal magnetism or even bribery. He had comparatively little personal wealth. He had risen principally because he was hardworking and willing to put in long hours since he had no family at home. But Otto was also shrewd. He was willing to make conclusions based on his own guesswork, on his own twisted thinking. He was convinced Thomas Picard was involved in resistance work. He also suspected Hilda Jensen's involvement.

"You will watch both Herr Picard and Frau Jensen. They go nowhere and make no move that I am not told about immediately," he said to his two subordinates. "There better be no foul-ups in this."

It would be a pleasure to capture both of them. Perhaps a commendation from Himmler himself, Otto thought, pleased with himself.

• • •

He stood in the doorway of the kitchen, momentarily distracted by the smell of coffee and sausage. Hilda's back was to him at the stove.

"Frau Hilda."

She turned. "Good morning, Wilhelm."

But in that swift look she knew something was different—or perhaps it was the old Wilhelm. She had seen this pose before in the Bergmann foyer. Something of brashness and confidence and boyishness.

"You have to get word to Thomas this morning. I've changed my plans. I'm going to Poland."

She almost dropped the pan. Her mouth fell open. Finally she could sputter.

Wilhelm was openly laughing.

"But, but . . ."

"I'm going to Poland," he repeated as if she had not heard. "I'm going after Natalie Bergmann."

"What do you mean going after?"

"Just that. Going to her and showing her what a mistake she's made and that I'm willing to help her out of it."

"Wilhelm, it's hardly that easy." She sat hard on the chair.

"I know it won't be."

"It will be terribly dangerous."

"I know that too. What isn't dangerous these days?"

"He is a Nazi. Poland is the Reich. The travel . . . everything!"

"I know all that. I don't have all the answers, but I have thought it all out."

"Wilhelm, it's . . . it's impossible."

He smiled for an answer. Then he went to kneel in front of her.

"I think I can persuade Natalie to leave this life she's chosen. I don't know why, but I feel I can. She's a good girl at heart. She made a mistake, and she'll see that. She's worth my effort. I may die trying, Frau Hilda, but it will be worth it. I'm no hero, but this is what I want to do."

The woman ordered two coffees and pastry. She gave Hilda more than money in return.

"Sugar for your coffee?" Hilda asked with a smile.

"No sugar, thank you."

Hilda's smile dropped a fraction. "No sugar?"

"Sugar always slows me down, causes problems. Thank you. Perhaps next time."

They were having trouble getting papers for Wilhelm.

"All right, well, enjoy your pastry!"

Hilda watched the woman go. Her eyes stayed fixed on the front window. *Was the man still out there Wilhelm had spotted from upstairs? Thomas said we must move cautiously but quickly. Each day Wilhelm remains hidden in my apartment is one more day of danger. But Thomas had decided he would no longer come to the shop. How can she contact him with this newest problem? The phones could be tapped I. . . . And there was Wilhelm's change of plans.*

She turned to Gretl. "Box up the Picard order for me. I'll take it personally on my way to the warehouse. Our ration of flour is almost up. How do they expect a baker to bake I ask you?"

"It's a lovely morning," Thomas said cheerfully.

Hilda didn't feel cheerful. She set the large white box on the back table of the store. With no customers in the store, the staff flocked to the table. Hilda fiddled with the box and rearranged the napkins. Only then did Thomas see her agitation.

He called out to his pianist. "I'm feeling like a little Chopin this morning, Rolf."

The man nodded and began playing. The store was filled with the rich melody.

"I'll walk you to the front," Thomas said. "What's wrong?"

"Only that both of us are being watched and there's a delay with the papers."

Thomas reached out to dust off a shelf with his handkerchief.

"How long a delay?"

"They didn't say. I feel nervous with him there."

"I understand. But there's no place to move him yet."

"That's not the only problem. He's had a change of plans."

"A change?" Thomas asked quickly.

"He wants to go to Poland," Hilda said lowering his voice. "I'll have to tell you the specifics later."

"Poland."

They had reached the front of the store. Hilda was pulling on her gloves.

"He's very determined. He wants to go to Warsaw. He does have a plan, sort of."

"Might I guess that this involves looking for someone?"

"You are an excellent guesser, Herr Picard."

Thomas was frowning out the window. Hilda was adjusting her hat.

"That does present some complications. The travel . . ."

"Exactly."

"But I do understand about being determined to find someone. I'm sure he prayed about this."

Hilda nodded briskly. "I hope you'll enjoy the strudel."

He smiled. "We always do." He patted her back. "Don't worry. I'll come up with something. Have him sit tight."

Olaf had looked up only briefly when Frau Jensen came down the stairs with her hat and purse. He had nodded at her instructions. He had lumped the dough with several hearty thumps. He had iced the tray of buns. He checked the dough that was rising and the wheat loaves that were baking. He had seven minutes. He leaned against the doorframe that led to the front of the store. Gretl was wiping the counter. There was only one couple at a table.

He affected a yawn. "I'm going to step out back for a few minutes and get some fresh air," he said to Gretl. "I'm watching the ovens. You have the front all right?"

She nodded.

He closed the curtain that separated the two rooms. He glanced at his watch. Frau Jensen would be gone at least another hour. He dusted off his apron then went to the storeroom. Frau Jensen had shown him a spare key to her apartment long ago when he had first gone to work for her. But there had never been a reason to use it. There was a reason now.

He found the key and quickly climbed the narrow stairs.

Now that Wilhelm had made a decision, he could hardly contain his excitement. He felt that old surge of energy at the prospect at being back in the chase. But he also felt something else, something novel, something new. He felt at peace with himself. He felt an inner confidence in what he was doing. He had bathed and shaved and thought and planned. And he thought what it would be like to find Natalie at the end of this decision. There were miles and dangers between them, but all he could think of was that he had been so close. No, life was not a series of coincidences.

He was in the kitchen cleaning the morning dishes, so deep in thought that he didn't hear the key turn in the lock. When the door opened, he turned—expecting Hilda.

They regarded each other in heavy silence for several seconds.

Wilhelm rinsed his hands, his tone pleasant. "You must be Olaf!"

Olaf nodded uncertainly.

"I can smell your creations up here all day. You're an artist, if my nose is any judge. We could use you in my division."

"Who are you?" Olaf said abruptly.

Wilhelm affected a startled look. "Wilhelm, Wilhelm Jensen." He tossed the rag aside. "Hilda's nephew."

"Frau Jensen didn't speak to me or Gretl of any nephew," Olaf spat out.

Wilhelm shrugged and laughed. "Well, I didn't think Aunt Hilda was ashamed of me, but you'd have to ask her."

"I will."

Wilhelm was leaning against the counter, his arms crossed, his head slightly tilted. He looked as if he was speculating on what kind of species this baker was. He made Olaf shift uncomfortably.

"What are you doing here?" Olaf asked.

Again, Wilhelm smiled. "Well, I'm here because I'm on three-day leave. But the better question would be why are you here, Olaf, unlocking a locked door?"

It was only then that Olaf Swensen thought of what Hilda Jensen was going to say about this. For all her kind and generous ways, he knew the woman could wield a tart tongue. He didn't want to be without work.

He licked his lips nervously. "I . . . I thought I heard a noise."

"Ah . . ." Wilhelm was staring at the key that dangled in his hand.

"You are in the army?" he asked curtly.

"I understand why my aunt has you in the back and not waiting on customers. Yes, I'm in the army. I'm waiting for posting. And you? How did you get an exemption? You look fit enough."

"I have a bad heart."

"Ah . . ."

Olaf didn't like these "ahs."

His eyes swiveled around the room. Wilhelm knew he was looking for a uniform or mess kit.

Wilhelm turned back to the sink, plunging his hands into the water.

"I'm the sound you heard. If whatever you're cooking is too burned for the customers, you'll send it up here, won't you? I don't mind at all."

Olaf turned with a scowl and hurried down the stairs.

The late afternoon shadows had fallen in purple diagonals across the cobbled street in front of the bakery. From behind the lace veneer of curtain, Wilhelm watched the street. All day, motionless and expectant, rigid with tension. Now he stared morosely at the building opposite. *It reminded him of a crouching hawk. Waiting. Waiting for him to emerge from the bakery.*

He derided himself for the sentiment he felt. It was the only explainable thing that had held him. As soon as Olaf had retreated he had put his few things together in the small leather bag and prepared to leave. He had wanted to scratch a note to Hilda, but he didn't want Olaf or anyone Olaf might bring with him to find it. What seemed the reasonable thing to do was to hurry down the stairs, through the kitchen, out the back door almost behind the startled Olaf. Of course, it would confirm all the obvious suspicions. But it would put him out on the streets with slightly better chances. But something had spoken to him against that impulsive, familiar plan. Instead, he had waited the long afternoon in Hilda's front room. They were, he later reflected, some of the longest, trying hours he had ever spent. How could all his struggles, his hopes, his new decision crumble because of some impudent man's nosiness? He had never been in a worse trap.

And a trap was certainly what it was. The black car had not moved. Olaf hadn't left the bakery. There was the phone however. With every car that turned at the corner, Wilhelm expected a van of SS or a patrol of black Mercedes with the Gestapo. Neither had happened. He had seen Hilda's return, but she wouldn't be coming up until the shop was closed.

Wilhelm had reasoned that the oafish Olaf would be too cowardly to confront his employer with what he had done. Since the Gestapo or SS had not come yet, that meant the baker was still hesitating, still wondering if he had made a foolish misstep. He would know in the morning by Hilda's reaction. Or he would decide that the young man had been bluffing. Either way, Wilhelm wasn't going to stay in this trap any longer. As soon as Hilda came up, he was leaving.

• • •

Gretchen Picard had a fragile, pale beauty that would have pleased her mother had Maria Picard lived to see her. Her large green eyes were luminous, her hair, which she wore coiled at the base of her neck, was the color of ripened wheat. She was as tall as Thomas and strongly built. Yet she moved slowly and gracefully. She had practiced this grace for hours at a time. Thomas had been amazed at her determination. Her explanation had been brief.

"I will be like Maria. She will tell I can."

Maria Goldstein. Thomas smiled sadly. His sister wouldn't forget her best friend. The most betraying feature of her condition was her stilted speech. But even that had improved over the years. Thomas had worked patiently with her and now she was largely self-sufficient. She could cook. But what she did best no one had taught her, and again Thomas was amazed at how God worked. Over the years Gretchen had listened to her father and Aaron Goldstein playing their instruments. She had sat still, hour after hour, as they played, listening more intently than any of them had suspected. She had never attempted to even touch the instruments though Michael Picard had encouraged her. She had watched and listened. And when the men died, she began to play.

Thomas entered his home on Blumenstrasse to the sounds of the piano. He smiled and stopped. It was one of his father's favorite piano pieces. He looked down at the carpet. Even the smell of mushroom-and-barley soup drifted from the kitchen. He should find his father at the piano, Gretchen listening, Rudi stretched on the floor reading the sports page, his mother setting the table. The lights should be burning in the Goldstein's house next door. He slowly pulled off his hat and coat. He felt old and tired. He entered the front room.

Gretchen didn't hear him at first. She was bent over the keys, smiling. In her own world. Thomas went to the kitchen and ladled up the soup she had made. He reentered the living room.

"I'm home, Gret."

She didn't look up as she closed the piano. "I know."

"Your Brahms sounded very good. Just like father playing."

"I know."

Thomas shook his head and smiled. "Let's eat in here tonight; it's warmer."

"Don't get anything on the carpet."

"I won't."

They pulled a table up before the fire. Gretchen went to pull the front blinds.

"Hager home." She nodded at the neighbors. "Army man."

"Yes home from the front," Thomas replied absently. "Soup smells great, but of course you know that."

She laughed. They sat across from each other. He sighed and looked into the fire before he prayed.

"Your hands cold," she said.

Again he nodded absently as he began to eat.

"Good day, Thomas?"

"It was all right. You?"

"Good day."

"Good."

Her hands were clasped in her lap. She was leaning forward, frowning.

"You got a bother, Thomas? What?"

He leaned back and studied her and smiled. "You know me too well, little sister."

"Too well. What's the bother?"

He laughed. "You won't eat till I tell you, will you?"

She shook her head.

He drew a design on the table. "Well, I do have a bother. I'm trying to help some people and I'm not sure how to help them. They need help quick though."

He went back to eating.

"You help them, Thomas, just ... take care of it."

"It isn't that easy, Gret. There are people who want to hurt my friend.

"The Nazi people?"

He was always startled at her perception. He nodded.

"Like the Daniel people," she added.

"The Daniel people?"

"Sure. You told me before, Thomas. They wanted to put Daniel in the lion's den. The Nazis did."

He laughed and squeezed her hand. "Wouldn't your interpretation go over well from the pulpit!"

"God saved the Daniel. He did."

Thomas sobered. "Yes, He did. He protected him and He protects us."

Again, he ate. But Gretchen persisted. She wouldn't relax until her brother looked less anxious.

"God will watch your friend."

"Yes."

Thomas leaned back. He closed his eyes. He had been praying all afternoon since Hilda had come. He had always relished a problem, looking forward to seeing the unique way God would solve it. *But this ... this needed a solution fast.* Everything he had thought of had run into a wall. *Wilhelm Mueller is in danger—and now this desire to go to Poland. How can I help him?*

"You praying, Thomas?"

"Yes, I'm praying, Gret. Now you go ahead and eat before it gets cold."

Wilhelm was in the den. How could he help him with all the circling lions? he pondered.

"How do you help a man in the lion's den?" he said barely above a whisper.

Gretchen Picard carefully placed her napkin in her lap as she had seen Maria Goldstein do a hundred times. She slowly picked up her spoon. Her voice was almost singing.

"You become a lion."

Thomas opened his eyes. "What did you say?"

"Oh Thomas, you hear. You become a lion."

"A lion . . ."

He stood up and paced. He walked to the window and raised the blind. He could see no car along Blumenstrasse that might contain the Gestapo. He chewed his lip in thought.

"Hager came over, and he heard me play. He said I was good. Said I was good. He's a nice boy, Thomas."

"Who, Eric Hager?"

She nodded.

"He came over?"

"It's all right?"

He turned back to the window. "I suppose…"

His eyes were drawn to the Hager home by some pull. *Avowed Nazis . . . lions.*

He swung around to his sister, smiling.

She smiled back. Thomas was all right now.

● ● ●

"We have to stay calm," was the first thing Hilda said after Wilhelm hurriedly told her the story. Then she said, "That sneak!"

Wilhelm managed a smile in spite of the tension. "Remember, he's a good baker."

Her voice was haughty. "I can only see that I trusted the man! How dare he!"

"Frau Hilda, we have to get ready."

Only then did she see he was dressed, his suitcase at his side. She pressed her fingers against her temples. "We have to stay calm," she repeated.

"Frau Hilda, he went home or he's gone to the tavern and gotten a few under his belt to make him bolder. He's thought it out and he'll take the chance that he's right. He may be thinking of some kind of pay-off, a reward from the Gestapo."

"Like cigarettes or cognac," Hilda returned disgustedly.

"Exactly. I can't stay here any longer. I have to move out now. Our shadow is down at the corner, but the back alley is clear, for now. If I—"

"We have to contact Thomas. He said to wait on him."

"There isn't time!"

Hilda stood up, wringing her hands, pacing.

"Wilhelm," she said, slumping into a chair. "I don't know . . ."

"Did Thomas ever give you a plan in case of emergency?"

"No, no, he . . ." She jumped up. "The key!"

"What key?"

"He gave me a key to the back door of his office."

"Then I'll go there for the night."

"He has said they are watching him too."

"I'll have to take that chance. Sitting here they know where I am, going there, they don't. Besides, if he's at home, which he probably is, they are watching an empty building."

"But what if I said you were my nephew."

"I don't have any papers. If they do come and I'm gone, you say I've left, caught the train. It will take them awhile to track it down. And it will give you some time."

"But on the street."

He laughed. "Frau Hilda, I've been on the street most of my life, remember? I'll be all right. I can get into Picard's if it's clear. I'll wait for Thomas tomorrow. Then I'll leave Munich. I have to go now. I want you to lock up behind me."

Hilda couldn't conceal her tears.

"I'm afraid for you, Wilhelm."

He knew then that this Gentile woman loved him. *It has been so long.* He reached out and put his hand on her shoulder. He couldn't speak.

"I will bring the order tomorrow, to see . . . you. Please don't leave Munich yet," she whispered.

"You mustn't come if you know it isn't safe, Frau Hilda."

She nodded, then he was gone into the night.

● ● ●

If he had discussed the plan with anyone, they would have laughed. He could even imagine Hilda's shocked expression or Wilhelm's disbelief. Yet he hurried up the Hager steps with nervous confidence. He had passed Eric's parents on his way home. He didn't know how long he would have with the young Nazi. He would have to be blunt. There was no time to parry or preface this gamble.

He pushed the front buzzer. "Lord," he breathed. "Please close . . . the lion's mouth."

The door opened almost immediately. Twenty-three-year-old Eric Hager stood in the entrance. He wore his uniform without the jacket. He stood in his socks, a book in one hand. He was very surprised; Thomas Picard had never been to his home.

"Herr Picard."

"Good evening, Eric," Thomas replied pleasantly. "I'm sorry to bother you, but may I come in?"

"Yes, of course."

He closed the front door. "My parents aren't here I'm afraid. They went to a memorial service. They—"

"I came to see you, Eric," Thomas smiled.

"Oh . . . oh, well, please come in."

He led him to the front room. "Please sit down, Herr Picard."

Eric was quickly putting on his shoes.

"We are neighbors, Eric. It's just Thomas."

The young man sat down, nodding, but visibly nervous.

Thomas leaned forward slightly. "You are home for a few days?"

"Yes, until Saturday."

Thomas nodded.

"If this is about coming over to see Gretchen, I apologize to you. I should have asked you first. I saw her at the piano through the front window. My mother has told me she plays beautifully."

"Your mother has heard her? Through the window?"

"Oh, no. Gretchen came over and asked her if she would like to come over. She, ah, she said she thought my mother looked lonely and would like the music."

"That sounds like Gretchen."

"I hope you don't mind."

"No," Thomas said slowly, his mind revolving around the idea of Frau Hager in his house.

"I wanted to hear her . . . and, honestly, Herr Picard, it wasn't because of . . . of how she is."

"What do you mean?"

"Her condition, I mean. It wasn't like I wanted to see if someone like that could play. I just . . . I've seen her on the steps . . . and she reminded me . . . of what, well, like a little sister. I felt like I might be . . . like a friend." He shrugged and looked away embarrassed.

Thomas looked away also. His eyes fell on the hat that lay on the chair. *A Nazi and an officer in the army. And he has been gentle with my sister. A contradiction.* He looked to the floor, praying.

Eric turned and watched him. Then their eyes met. *Well, we'll have to trust each other.* Thomas drew a deep breath and plunged forward.

"What rank are you, Eric?"

"Captain."

Thomas nodded. "Gretchen told me . . . many months ago that your mother wanted a piano. I had a lot on my mind, and I didn't think about it much. Being a seller of pianos, but, I thought if your parents were really interested in an instrument, they would come to me. As I said, I didn't give it much thought. Until tonight."

The young man looked confused. "I . . . my mother has wanted a piano for years. We had one long ago. But with my father and the war, there hasn't been extra money."

"I understand. Yes. Well, Eric, I've come over tonight to put a proposition to you."

"A proposition?"

Thomas smiled. "Yes. I'd like to give you a piano to give to your mother. You can say you've been saving for it and that you and I have worked out an arrangement. You would like to give her a piano, wouldn't you?"

"Yes," he said slowly. "But I . . ."

"Eric, you're a smart young man. So you're going to have to . . . weigh out what I'm proposing. I would like to exchange a piano for one of your uniforms. And I need military passes and stamps."

Eric stared. His mind worked fast and he understood perfectly. But still he was shocked. *What is this man involved in? Didn't he realize the danger?*

Thomas stood up. "I'm not usually so blunt, Eric. You understand what I'm asking."

Eric stood up slowly. "Yes, sir, I do." His eyes flitted to the front window, to the darkened Goldstein home.

He looked back to Thomas, and his young shoulders suddenly sagged. "You . . . understand, don't you? That's why you came to me tonight."

"Gretchen trusts you. I find her judgment pretty reliable."

"I . . . wanted to . . . like her."

Now Thomas was puzzled. "Who? Gretchen?"

He shook his head, still looking out the front window. "Maria. Maria Goldstein."

Thomas turned to look at the silent house.

"You see, I just haven't been able to swallow all of this. For my father—but, in me, inside, it isn't who I am."

In that moment Thomas Picard understood the terrific pain and price other Germans—lonely like this young man and forced into bravado and cruelty—must face. It gave him encouragement.

He put his arm around the young man's shoulders.

Will you take the piano?"

"Yes, I would be honored."

They looked at each other a long moment. "I'll get you my spare uniform. I'll make some excuse."

"The stamps and passes?"

"That will be a little tougher. When do you need them?"

"No later than tomorrow night."

"Tomorrow night! I thought I'd have a few days at least."

"I need them tomorrow night."

"All right. I'll have them," he said firmly.

"I have to go. Eric, the Gestapo watches my house, so don't bring them over. Late tomorrow afternoon I'll send the piano from the store in a big box. You get your parents out of the room and put your payment in. It will be brought back to the store."

"Yes, yes."

Thomas lingered in the doorway. "God bless you, Eric Hager."

• • •

The appearance of the Gestapo or SS could not have startled her more. She was expecting them. She didn't expect this stranger—who was not entirely a stranger. This was not Herr Wilhelm Mueller, yet, it was.

But in a captain's uniform. Standing very correct and unsmiling. Finally he smiled. She opened her mouth to speak but instead swayed. Thomas hurried a chair underneath her.

"I'm getting too old for you pulling this kind of prank on me, Wilhelm," she said in an attempt at severity that made both men smile.

She looked back to Thomas with a look akin to wonder. "You've pulled it off."

He shook his head. "This is just the beginning. We've gotten through the opening measure; we have the whole concert now."

Hilda knew better than to ask any questions. She looked back to Wilhelm. He was fingering the wool sleeve.

"I made the army, huh. Well, what's my new name?"

Thomas spread the papers on his desk and all three leaned forward.

"These look clean," Wilhelm said after a moments perusal.

"They are. These didn't come from the underground."

Both Hilda and Wilhelm looked up at the tall, slender man with new respect. He glanced at his watch, then he pushed over a train schedule.

"You leave on the six-fifty."

"Just an hour," Hilda said in a moan. "It will be dark . . . at least."

Thomas nodded. "You leave here and go straight for it, Wilhelm. Here's the ticket but board late. I think the rest you can understand. If you're stopped . . ." his voice trailed away uneasily.

"I'm on my own. I understand."

Thomas straightened. "If any of us are questioned, we all . . . are on our own."

The words hung heavily in the office. Hilda's hands clenched around her purse handle.

"I should shove off in about fifteen minutes then," Wilhelm said calmly.

"You should leave first, after we check the back," Thomas said.

But in the shaded light of the room, all three half in shadow, they knew that none of them was really quite ready to break this bond that had been forged so suddenly—and so completely. They would likely never see each other after this night.

Hilda stood up, her voice once again confident and commanding.

"Let me see your suitcase, Wilhelm, how you packed."

He smiled and winked at Thomas, but made no protest. The small satchel on the table looked pathetic in the drab light. She scanned the contents.

"Well."

She turned to the shadow of the doorway and pulled out a bigger, stouter leather case. Neither man had noticed it when she entered. And at the sight of Wilhelm, she had momentarily forgotten it.

She laid it across the desk, her hand protectively on the lid. She made no move to open it. Her eyes searched his face with such intensity that he shifted a little uncomfortably. He was surprised at the slowness of her speech.

"I thought this bigger case would look a little better. It's one I had."

"Thank you, Frau Hilda."

"I put in some extra clothes and provisions. There's no telling what the food will be like along the way."

"You didn't need to go to that trouble, but thank you again."

Again she was staring at him. Finally her eyes lowered. He could see she was struggling with something.

He touched her arm. "Frau Hilda?"

She opened the suitcase slowly. For a moment, he didn't want to follow her gaze. Her look was so sad. He looked into the case.

A violin.

Her voice was hoarse. "I've scolded myself that ... that this is too impractical for you to have to carry."

Wilhelm was stunned. He finally drug his eyes away. "She ... gave you this?"

Hilda nodded. "The day I saw her in the park. I would like you to give it back to her. I think, I think when she sees you she will accept it."

Still Wilhelm didn't know what to say. *Natalie's violin.*

Thomas drew closer. "I'm sorry but you need to leave in about five minutes Wilhelm."

Wilhelm nodded.

Hilda touched the violin case with her finger. "You know she was in love with you," she said with a trace of a smile.

"What?" Wilhelm gasped.

"Yes, she was in love with you. Surely you could see that."

"Surely I could see nothing of the kind! She was fourteen when she last saw me!"

"She was sixteen."

"Why do you imagine this absurdity?"

"Well . . ." Hilda looked momentarily embarrassed. Her voice was a little saucy. "She forgot her journal, and I forgot to return it to her."

Then Wilhelm folded her in his arms, his head dropping to her shoulder.

Thomas came up to them, a tremor in his voice. His hand was on Wilhelm's shoulder.

"Lord, You are our refuge, You are our shelter. Hide us in the shadow of Your wings. Go before us, Lord, please go before us."

28
Stalking

Warsaw

In a huge room of the city palace, Natalie stood resplendent in a long glittering gown of royal blue. Her hair was twisted up into a French swirl, diamonds dangled from her ears, her neck was slender and inviting. She was easily the most beautiful woman in the gathering. She walked to a long window that stood looking over the ruined palace garden. The trees along the Vistula were leafless now. The river was a sluggish steel-gray current. With the wind that roared from the Russian steppes to the north, winter had gripped Warsaw. Everything looked colorless and cold. The sky was a moving canvas of dull pewter with an occasional dimension of cloud—but always in some shade of gray. She and Hugo had come to a dying city, and they both knew it. Each day of gripping, slicing cold she thought of what it must be like in the crowded, starving ghetto. She tried vainly not to think of it. Yet it had proven nearly impossible. Few lights shone in the city. Less than one hundred miles north, the German and Russian armies were locked in battle. Warsaw was crowded with military units hurrying to the front.

"You look very melancholy, fraulein," a smooth voice said at her elbow.

It wasn't Hugo. Hugo had called the hotel suite to tell her he was working late. She had asked him if he minded if she went to the party alone. He hesitated only a fraction, then told her to go. She hadn't missed the forced cheerfulness in his voice.

The man handed her a glass of champagne, which she accepted with a smile.

"Lieutenant von Kleinst is a very hardworking man."

"Yes he is," she said, smiling.

"He has won the admiration of all of us; that is the truth. Berlin did right to send him. He has brought order to chaos."

Natalie sipped her drink.

"Of course, all this hard work leaves you lonely," he continued easily.

He had cornered her at previous socials. She knew why—and she couldn't ignore the personal magnetism emanating from him. He was young, handsome, and charming. And he wanted her. Well.

Natalie had never considered it before. Never. *Hugo ... Hugo was her protection. I belong to him.* She didn't need to seek other men. *But ...* The thoughts and her racing pulse made her turn away from him, back toward the window. But he had seen the blush that colored the lovely neck. With a well-trained eye, he had seen it. He leaned forward.

"This party can do without us, don't you think, Natalie?"

It was the first time he had called her by name.

Temptation. It shook her and flamed the old struggle in a new way. *I'm already on the path of ... sin, what does it matter a little more? He will see me, speak to me, treasure me—if only for a few hours.*

She turned around, giving him the full strength of her eyes.

"I don't think Lieutenant von Kleinst would approve, Herr Major."

She turned and walked away, hearing his low chuckle at her back.

She found a chair at the perimeter of the party and sat down listening to the laughter and voices, a part of them but not a part. She stared into her lap, collecting her thoughts. The major had returned from the failed conquest to the social circle. He stood opposite, and when she finally looked up he winked. She knew he would try again. A very bored military man in a cold foreign city didn't give up pursuits easily—especially one so lonely and lovely. And vulnerable.

She looked back to her lap. *I should leave soon ... before my own loneliness melts my defense against him.*

"Look here! The Poles ran off and left everything just laying around!"

Natalie looked up with the rest of the group. The man held up a violin.

They had all drawn up their gilded chairs around the huge fireplace. The patina of the wood caught the glow of the fire. The man grabbed up the bow and scratched it across the strings. The group laughed.

"Give it up, Boris. Stick with machine guns."

He laid the violin carelessly back on the recessed shelf. The talking resumed. One of the partygoers had gone to the grand piano, playing now with far more relish than finesse.

Natalie stood up with pounding heart and strolled to the long table laden with food and drink. But her eyes sought out the shelf. She could see it there. She had recognized it immediately even from the distance. It was no cheap instrument. A Stradivarius—an obvious testament to the haste the Polish royalty had left with the Germans in pursuit. There hadn't been time to protect the precious instrument.

She took another glass of champagne and wandered to the shelf. She leaned against it. No one was really paying attention to her. The major was in some absorbed conversation. She turned and picked up the violin. She wanted to run.

But slowly, still sipping her drink, she strolled to the piano.

"You play very . . . energetically," she smiled at the SS man at the keys.

He winked. "You play that?" he asked nodding at the violin.

"Oh, no. It's just such a beautiful instrument. Look at the wood."

He shrugged. "I know nothing about them."

Natalie turned, still walking slowly, still casual. She slipped from the room. She looked up and down the hall. *Deserted.* Across the hall were a dozen doors. She went quickly across and pushed open a door. She peered inside. It was a huge ballroom. Vacant of furniture. *Another Warsaw tomb,* she thought. She stepped inside, her steps hollow on the tile. It was very cold, but she hardly noticed. She went to the end of the long room, to the French doors that looked out on the same garden she had seen earlier. She sat her glass down and pushed back the drapes. Enough moonlight.

She looked inside the f-hole. A Strad, just as she thought. She smiled and touched the instrument with her fingertips, almost reverently. It felt so good in her hands—like the caress from an old, trusted friend. *So right.*

She looked at the bow. *Why am I doing this?*

She lifted the bow and began to play very softly. She closed her eyes and then the tears came.

She didn't hear the ballroom door open. The major stood in the cold shadows.

She played from her heart. She played for all the years the music had been locked inside. She forgot all impression of time.

The door opened and still she didn't see or hear.

Hugo von Kleinst saw the major first. He was lounging against the wall, smiling. Their eyes met and Hugo turned. Natalie at the windows, playing a violin. He had expected them together. He hadn't expected this.

He looked back to the major. The man lifted his shoulders eloquently and slipped from the room.

It was nearly half an hour later before the violinist lowered the bow. The tears had dried on her face. Her breathing was even again. She felt like laughing. *The music hasn't died inside me! My sin didn't kill the music. I can still play!*

Only then did she hear the steps coming toward her.

He stopped only a few feet from her. She expected a hardness in his voice. But it wasn't there.

"Natalie," he said.

She just stared.

"Why did you keep this from me, that you could play?"

"I . . . I don't know, Hugo."

"It is a part of your past."

She swallowed. Now the hardness was there, leaping up, mocking her. "Yes."

The minute stretched to feel like an hour to Natalie Bergmann. He was watching her, waiting.

"And does the major know you are a Jewess?" he asked quietly.

The room, already dark, deepened and tilted, the floor and walls shifted to impossible angles. The violin was slipping and now she felt the coldness, a cold that was rising up around her like a tide. And the tide was roaring in her ears.

• • •

Olaf was haggard and petulant with worry. He had spent an evening in the tavern, followed by a sleepless night. At sunrise he staggered up and tried to form a plan. He ridiculed himself that he had thought of spying on Frau Hilda in the first place—she who had always been so good to him. What business was it of his who she was keeping in her apartment? But now that he had blundered in, he was committed. Face Hilda's wrath or the Gestapo's. There was really no choice.

The light from the bakery threw out warm yellow beams into the street, still robed in the darkness before dawn. The street stirred awake to the light and smell from Jensen's Bakery. Short of receiving bomb damage, the people of this district of Munich couldn't imagine a morning without the comforting presence of Jensen's. Gretl was bringing out the tray of crockery when she heard the car pull up to the curb. She glanced up. Olaf was emerging from the backseat. *Olaf!* She turned to hurry to Frau Jensen who was up to her elbows in flour in the kitchen. But they were already pounding on the door.

Hilda heard immediately and her hands stilled. Her eyes closed in swift, silent prayer. *So Olaf had found the courage.*

"Frau Hilda! There are—"

"Yes, yes, Gretl, open the door before they break the glass." Then lower, "The brutes."

She emerged through the curtain, wiping her hands, her face a classic picture of annoyance.

Four men in their dark leather coats stood regarding her. *And Olaf.*

Her eyes widened in surprise. "Olaf? What has happened? Are you all right?"

The Gestapo chief swung his hand out, grunting one word, "Upstairs."

Two of the men brushed past her roughly, through the curtain, up the stairs with pounding boots.

"What is the—"

The door to the apartment was kicked in. Her hand went to her chest. Otto Beck regarded her coolly. "Sit down, Frau Jensen."

"I, Gretl, please close the door."

Gretl was pale and weeping, and casting furtive glances at Olaf. Olaf couldn't meet the eyes of his employer.

The silence was broken with the sound of smashing furniture. Hilda's heart was thudding in her ears. She felt light-headed.

"Why are you doing this? I . . . I have a business to open."

Otto snapped his gloves at Olaf. "Ask your baker why we are here, Frau Jensen."

She blinked rapidly. "What has happened, Olaf? Why are these men here?"

Olaf's head came up. "You know why." His voice was hoarse.

"If I knew why, I wouldn't waste my time asking you," she snapped. She turned her eyes on Otto. "I want to know the meaning of this outrage. What right have you to be here?"

But Otto said nothing. He stood with folded arms. Still the rampage continued.

Hilda stood up.

"Sit down!" Otto snapped.

"I have things in the oven," Hilda retorted. They locked eyes. "I'm sure you wouldn't want a German business to burn down. That wouldn't look very good." She swung around to the kitchen.

Otto hadn't been prepared for this woman.

The two Gestapo had come down, red-faced and swearing. Hilda didn't look up from her table. They tore into the storeroom, dumping things over. They came into the kitchen, and Hilda looked at them with dripping contempt. They hurried for the basement. Hilda returned to the front room. She stood beside Gretl. Her voice was steely calm.

"My apartment, my shop is being torn apart, my business interrupted, and I would like to know why."

"You know why, Frau Hilda!" Olaf shouted.

Hilda gave him a withering look. "Have you been drinking again, Olaf?"

He looked to the floor, muttering. She turned back to Otto, her hands on her hips.

"Tell me."

He strode past her to the coffee urn. He poured himself a cup of coffee then calmly sat down. He crossed his legs and regarded her with a stiff smile.

"Your baker claims you are hiding a Jew."

The two Gestapo returned, breathless. "Nothing. Nothing."

"She's gotten him out, I tell you. They had the night! He was there! He said he was her nephew. But he was a Jew!"

Otto didn't bother to turn. "If that is true, then his escape rests entirely on you, Herr Swensen."

Olaf felt faint. His mouth had gone dry.

Otto motioned for the two men. "Take Herr Swensen out to the car."

"She's lying, she's lying. He was here!" Olaf yelled.

The Gestapo chief sipped his coffee. "It would be a shame to put this place out of business by your arrest, Frau Jensen."

She nodded. "Yes, I would find it a great shame."

Otto was startled. He laughed nervously. Her look didn't flinch.

"I tend to believe that fool, you see. I think you were hiding a Jew. I think you have been hiding Jews in the past."

Hilda had turned to Gretl. "It's all right. Go in the back and get things ready for the morning rush." She patted her arm. "And be thinking where we might find another baker."

Hilda sat down across from Beck.

"You employed a Jewess named Maria Goldstein," Olaf said steadily.

"Yes, some years ago. I didn't know she was a Jew. I needed help and she applied. She disappeared after a few months."

Otto's eyes narrowed. He leaned forward menacingly. "A woman will not make a fool out of me, Frau Jensen, understand that."

Hilda held her tongue.

"Your baker saw a man in your apartment yesterday."

"My former baker saw no one in my apartment yesterday. He does drink, you know."

Otto's fist came out like a lashing whip that caught her mouth and chin, and sent hot coffee across her. Hilda doubled over in pain and whimpered.

"You put on an act! We have been watching this part of town for months! We know the underground is at work here. You are part of them!"

She was huddled and shaking her head. "You have fallen for his . . . lies," she whispered.

"He has no reason to lie!"

"If you promised him some reward, a man like that has a reason. Gretl saw and heard no one."

"I have asked her. She heard and saw no one because you are smarter than your imbecile employees!"

He paced in front of her. "Hiding Jews is punishable by death."

Hilda looked up, blood trickling from the corner of her mouth, an ugly bruise rising on her jaw. Her hands were burned from the coffee. Tears of pain filled her eyes.

"You are wrong."

He stopped. This woman unnerved him. Even now she was calm.

He spoke in a measured tone. "You have had meetings with Herr Thomas Picard."

She blinked and frowned. "He buys pastry here."

Otto laughed curtly. "There is more going on than buying pastry. He stayed after closing. On two occasions."

Hilda didn't speak. She only stared. He was sweating.

"Why did he stay late?" he demanded.

Hilda looked down at her lap a moment. "He found out I employed Maria Goldstein. They were neighbors and she disappeared. He ... thought perhaps I could tell him something. We were sad about her disappearance. That is all."

His nephew interested in a Jewess? Yes, that much was believable. Otto strode to the door. "Don't think for one second I am finished with this, Frau Jensen. Now go sell your bread," he smiled thinly, "like a good German."

• • •

Wilhelm Mueller in his uniform felt relatively safe and comfortable—apart from the indignation of wearing the conqueror's bloody robes. With his passes and stamps, his kit and uniform, the clipped hair, he had very smoothly become one of the enemy. He smiled to himself as he stared out the train window. *If a partisan or resistance group took action ...* He laughed out loud at the thought. *To be maimed or even killed while posing as a Nazi!*

The exodus from Munich had been uneventful. He had slipped into his seat, pulling his cap over his face, and shifting into the posture of fatigue that didn't invite casual conversation. It was, however, more than a defensive ploy. The last forty-eight hours of anxiety and decision, of parting, had drained him more than he expected. Now if only the miles would pass uneventfully in the rhythmic swaying of the train. He would be one man, among hundreds, bleary-eyed and war-weary, dutifully reporting for the next assignment.

His thumb peeled open the passport held against his thigh. He wanted to see again who he was now. Friedrich Epp, originally of Frankfurt. He was twenty-eight years old. The one-inch, square, black-and-white photo had been carefully pasted from the old papers Wilhelm had carried. Thomas had been thorough.

"Your stamps get you food and lodging, but questions too. If you want to take the risk ... Since no one has a report of your posting, you're going to have to do a lot of bluffing and hope that no one is too curious. Stay on the train as much as you can. Crossing into Poland will be the greatest test. That's when they'll look closest, when they'll want to see your posting orders."

He had looked intently at Wilhelm. "That will be the toughest. Hopefully you can blend in."

Blend in. Wilhelm had no plan for when that greatest test would come. It would be reactionary, as much of his daily living had been. He slumped lower in the seat as the miles of Germany slid past.

He roused long enough to push his cap up and yawn, take note of his hunger, then slump back into cramped sleep. When he finally awoke it was to the acrid smell of cigarettes. Someone had pushed his kit on top of his feet and was pressing his arm against him. He straightened and found the empty seats were no longer empty. Two army officers sat opposite and an SS officer sat beside him. They were eyeing him with amusement. Wilhelm's heart went into double beats: *This is an unpleasant way to wake up!* The smoke veiled his traveling companions for a moment.

One of the army officers addressed him amiably.

"Where are you headed, soldier?"

Wilhelm had sat up, removed his hat, and combed his hair with his fingers. He picked up his kit, visibly annoyed.

"I guess this is what you get for sleeping through a stop."

The army officers smiled and nodded, but the SS man, with his crossed arms and granite features, didn't flinch.

"Warsaw," Wilhelm ventured with a stab at the truth.

The two exchanged a glance. "You must have messed up somewhere royal to get that." They laughed in obvious pity.

Wilhelm shrugged. "If there are women and vodka, the winter will pass all right."

They laughed knowingly.

"I'm going to Warsaw," the SS man spoke abruptly.

The army men shifted, looking at each other with covert looks. No one should imply that this senior officer had messed up.

"I've been in Munich for ten days. I didn't really bother with the papers. So what's the news on Warsaw? Why are you ... gentlemen pitying me?" Wilhelm asked smiling.

They didn't appreciate Wilhelm's question. Not with the superior officer in their midst. But Wilhelm knew no better way to squelch their curiosity.

"Well, ah, we've heard that the resistance is pretty active around Warsaw. Snipers, bombings. There was even a bank robbery last week. Jews broke in and stole the payments they had made to . . . us."

Wilhelm snorted derisively. "You must have had a few too many, friend. Whoever heard of Jews robbing a German bank? Next you'll tell me Göring has sworn off pork!"

They laughed at this. But it was an uneasy laugh. *If only this SS would go for a stretch.*

"Believe it or not, it's what happened. Warsaw is a battleground at times. The Jews will pay for their boldness."

"What Jews are left," Wilhelm yawned. He leaned on the glass. "What's our next stop?"

Friedrich Epp had played the first act very well.

• • •

He took Gretchen on a long walk through the park and then window-shopping along the streets. After a circuitous route, they arrived at Jensen's. Gretchen had been excited to meet a her brother's new friend. Thomas eyed the street casually. Several parked cars, one at the end of the street, but he couldn't see clearly. He didn't have the practiced eye of Wilhelm Mueller.

"Closed, Thomas. A sign, see?"

He turned. A neat white sign declared the bakery was closed. The shades were drawn.

Thomas' stomach tightened. *In the middle of the week, in the middle of the morning. Something was wrong. If they had come for her . . . if they had taken her away . . .*

He looked across the street. "Come along, Gret. Let's see what we can find."

"Frau Hilda gone, Thomas?"

"I hope not."

He stepped into the printer's shop. A little man greeted him from behind the long front desk.

"May I help you?"

"Well, I was going to Jensen's Bakery with my sister, but I find it closed. I've never seen the place closed during the day."

The man shifted a large tray of type. "Just closed, like the sign says."

The man was afraid.

"Well, I hope it isn't long. I don't know if I can do without Frau Hilda's rolls," Thomas smiled. "I hope Frau Hilda isn't ill."

The man didn't rise to the bait. He turned aside. But his wife was sweeping across the room.

"The Gestapo came."

Three words. Thomas was instantly chilled.

His mouth had gone dry. "You mean? They—"

The printer gave his wife a withering glare but held his tongue. She wagged her head at him.

"So I can't talk? I see things and I can't even say! Well! I saw it all. It made a ruckus, I'll tell you. They smashed things up." She shook her head. "As if Hilda Jensen could do anything . . ."

"Did they take her away?"

"No she's there. But she hung out the sign and closed the door yesterday. I saw her for a moment." Again the ominous head shaking and drawn brows. "Her face . . ."

"Hilda hurt?" Gretchen piped up.

"Well, I'm sorry to hear that. I hope she can reopen soon," Thomas said slowly. He turned to leave.

The woman was not finished with her venting. "They even questioned us. The whole street. They've been spying on her. What a shame!"

"Yes. Thank you. Goodbye."

Out on the street, Thomas studied the silent, closed building. Every window was shaded.

"The lions again," Gretchen said.

He nodded. If the lions had moved on Hilda Jensen, they were moving toward him as well.

"Let's go, Gret. We have a lot to do now."

"I think so too, Thomas."

Warsaw

He had vowed he would not sleep through another stop. The army officers had disembarked at Leipzig. The SS major had shifted to the vacant seats, now spreading his kit and bags across to discourage any crowding. It was a little too cozy for Wilhelm's comfort. The man was so quietly assessing. But Wilhelm felt it would be too suspicious to leave. Still, he didn't want to enter Poland close to this man. As the border loomed in the blackness of night, Wilhelm had no choice. An entire division joined the train, crowding on. Wilhelm was virtually surrounded by the German army.

It felt like a trap. He had already determined he would throw himself off the train before he was taken. *They can't trace me—or anything— back to Thomas. I'll just be one suicidal soldier left along the tracks of the frozen Polish countryside. No one will mourn me. Hilda will never know what happened. Thomas will never know if his aid had been successful. And Natalie Bergmann will never know a friend from the past had tried to rescue her.*

Trap that it felt like, the advent of the army on the train had precluded any scrutiny at the Polish border. Now Warsaw was only a few hours away. Wilhelm decided he would wait in the corridor. He adjusted his hat and reached for his bag.

"What's your posting in Warsaw?" the SS major said abruptly.

He hadn't spoken or moved for hours. Wilhelm had thought him sleeping.

"They didn't tell me specifically. Something with the general staff. And you?"

"SS duties," he replied cryptically. "Curious that you're traveling without a unit."

Wilhelm shrugged with eloquent practice. "I know a bit of Polish. And, as you know, Berlin is anxious to put these resistance attacks down. Maybe I'll see some action after all."

"Maybe." The man lit a cigarette.

Wilhelm stood up. "Could you keep an eye on my kit. I need to use the . . ."

The officer shrugged and looked out the window. He pushed through the crowded car. Men were sitting in the corridors, some in huddled groups playing cards. He stepped across them with various mumbled excuses. He entered a second car and strode down another swaying companionway. Finally he found what he was looking for: A soldier deep in sleep off in a corner by himself. Wilhelm leaned against the wall, watching him with narrowed eyes. The man's kit lay carelessly beside him. Wilhelm looked up and down the corridor. He swiftly lifted the bag and slung it over his shoulder. He wouldn't have to return for his own kit. Let the officer think what he would.

He made his way to the last car of the train, gathered the case that Hilda had given him, then found a space near the exit. Perhaps he had acted rashly and drawn more attention to himself. He would take the chance. Like always. He leaned against the wall and closed his eyes.

Someone down the corridor spoke. "Warsaw."

Wilhelm pressed near the grimy window. As the suburbs of the city came into view, he was startled. The land looked flattened and frozen. A skyline of a great European city—mounds of rubble and shredded trees, bleached or blackened buildings like claws reaching in a leaden sky. It gave him the eerie feeling of waking and walking into a lifeless place. The Germans had shown their contempt quite graphically. And now the resistance had made it another battleground. A place then of violence, dying, and death.

And he had come to rescue Natalie Bergmann from this dead city. He gripped his bag tighter and instinctively knew every challenge before was prerequisite training for this one. He hoped Thomas and Hilda were praying.

29
Now a Lion's Den

Thomas Picard was having trouble sleeping. Finally at three in the morning he got up, dressed, looked in on Gretchen, then padded down to the front room. Tangerine-colored embers still glowed from the fire of the night before. He stirred them up, then fixed himself a cup of coffee. He would regret this intrusion in his sleep later in the day, but now there was nothing he could do about it. He simply couldn't sleep.

He stood before the fire and thought of his mother. He thought of her the last time he had seen her—troubled and sad. And so heavily burdened by guilt. He had not suspected the intensity of her sorrow for what the Nazi way had done to her, the way she had compromised—and lived beside that compromise. The Goldsteins. He sat down and began to pray.

Thirty minutes later he was still not sleepy. He began pacing. He felt an odd, unexplained nervous energy in the dead of night. As if ... as if something was coming. *Beck.* He went to the window and peered past the blind. The car was a black object at the end of the street.

Thomas shook his head. "In this cold, poor fellow. What a job."

He turned back to the room. "Lord," he whispered, "show me ... I feel so ... I don't know!"

His eyes fell on the small table where Gretchen had put the day's mail. He'd forgotten to look it over last night. He picked it up and squatted before the fire. Only three envelopes. Nothing very interesting.

The third envelope . . . He drew closer to the light of the fire. He had seen this handwriting before.

He turned it over and looked at the front again. He suddenly laughed out loud with joy. He was holding a letter from Sophie Goldstein.

• • •

He didn't personally have the stomach for the torturer's role, but he found it a highly effective tool in his trade. The break had come at last. He had known his patience would pay off eventually. And the crowning success had been two leads in one day. An employee of Picard's Music store reluctantly admitted, under repeated threats, that Herr Thomas had been very distracted of late. More importantly he had given instructions on what to do in the event of his prolonged absence. He had turned the manager position over to another trusted employee. And he had made an unexpected trip to the bank. The bank teller had gruffly conceded that Picard had made a substantial withdrawal. Otto Beck knew what this little tidying up meant. Then the report from the victim had been handed to him. The underground had been moving Jews through the southern part of the city. No, he had had no contact with any women. Only one man— a tall, slender man, brown-haired and blue-eyed. Around thirty. They hadn't exchanged names of course. He was known to them only as Mozart. Beck had laughed uproariously at this. He had despised Michael Picard's love of music. It represented weakness to him. And now that weakness was about to hang his nephew.

• • •

The Munich station was always most congested at early morning. Travelers always hoped such early-hour vigilance would pay off in beating the delays caused by the troop trains and cattle cars. It rarely made a difference. Trains throughout Germany had become notoriously late and unpredictable. A train schedule caused a bitter laugh among them. Still, there was always hope that the connection could be made in some reasonable time frame. Thomas was hoping and praying it would happen quickly on this cold, sunny morning in late December.

He paused to scan the terminal. Of course there were SS and Gestapo everywhere. But no one had seemed to notice this party of three. He glanced at his watch. Their train was due in seventeen minutes. Seventeen long minutes. He made his way to the huge pillar where Hilda and Gretchen waited.

He smiled nervously as he handed Hilda the paper cup of coffee. "It won't be as good as yours of course, but it's hot."

She accepted the coffee with equivalent nerves. Hot coffee stirred her memory. She felt Thomas' eyes above the rim of his own cup.

"I'm sorry," he said again. "It shames me when I look at you, to see what my uncle has done."

"He thinks he is being faithful to Germany. We'll have to forgive such men after the war. That will be the hardest part," Hilda returned calmly.

Thomas stopped. He hadn't thought into the future like this sacrificing woman had. He looked at her with a deeper respect. Her bruised face testified to what this forgiveness would be about.

"Gretchen, dear, are you warm?" Hilda asked. She placed an arm around the young woman's shoulder.

"Hilda, dearest, I'm warm, thank you."

Thomas smiled at Hilda above his sister's head. "Gret remembers her best friend Maria very well. She picked up more of her ways than any of us imagined." He looked at his watch and frowned. "It's late."

Hilda followed his eyes across the terminal. He was watching the two SS men who stood beside the gate. No telling how many plainclothes Gestapo informers were interspersed through the bustling crowd. He turned back to Hilda.

"Now Frau Hilda, I need you to understand. You board with Gret, the first car if you can. I'll be on a later car."

"I understand, Thomas. Please stop worrying, you make me nervous."

"Well, we're so ... exposed out here, and now it's late." He leaned forward, his voice intense. "If anything happens, anything, you keep going. Get to Dachau. You'll be expected."

"The little yellow farmhouse at the end of the lane across the field from the church."

"Yes, you can't see it from the road unless you're looking."

"All right."

"You understand about Gretchen's medication?"

"Yes, yes."

"You going where, Thomas?" Gretchen asked, pulling at his arm.

"I'll try to stay with you, Gret. But if I can't, you must do exactly as Frau Hilda says. Exactly."

He leaned over and kissed her forehead.

"Yes, Thomas, yes, absolutely."

"There's a cafe just past the train depot. Wait for me there as the train leaves, to see if I'm on. Hopefully, I'll be able to take you to the Schillers."

Hilda's tone was brisk. "I will guard your sister with my life, Thomas."

He smiled. "I know you will Hilda, thank you."

She looked away a moment. He was surprised at the sudden tears in her eyes, though her tone was still formal. "Thank you for coming for me this morning."

"I—"

His words were silenced in a sudden scream. They were caught up in the crowd that surged forward to the glass windows. His hand instinctively tightened on Gretchen's. Hilda's grasp was firm.

The empty tracks gave them a starkly graphic view. The SS had found their prey. A man was running across the tracks wildly. The SS calmly took their positions on the platform.

Thomas pulled Gretchen away with effort against the press of passengers. The shot rang out.

He met eyes with Hilda. She had paled, the bruises as patently a witness as the gunfire to Nazi brutality.

It gave Otto Beck a good feeling to stomp through the Picard house—like a warrior. Never mind, for this brief satisfying moment, that the quarry had flown. *This is mine now. I told my sister that years ago. It is very simple to men like me. Men of vision.*

"The house is empty, Herr Beck. He is not at his place of business. He is on the run, certainly."

"Yes, certainly."

Beck was distracted by the silver-framed photograph of his sister on the fireplace mantel. Her eyes seemed to bore into him.

"He's not here. He escaped," he repeated dumbly.

Two of his men exchanged a quick glance.

Otto ran an unsteady hand through his thinning gray hair. "He will have gone to the bakery."

But an agent had entered the house breathless.

"We have been to the bakery, Herr Beck. Picard isn't there. The Jew lover is gone as well! We should call the stations from here, put them on alert for the two of them."

"What? What?" Otto was like one coming from a dream. *She shouldn't accuse me. I'm only doing my duty, Maria,* he whispered.

The man snatched up the phone to make the calls. Otto watched then pushed past his men.

He shouted to his driver, "To Hofgartenstrasse! Hurry!"

Those behind the curtains watched in shock as the big black car squealed in a whirlwind of flying leaves. And then Blumenstrasse was quiet again. Now with two silent houses.

The porter was already short-tempered at eight in the morning. He too often was the recipient of the commuters' frustrations. He was not responsible for the train delays. And now there was a dead body on the tracks. His answer to the tall, harried-looking man was curt.

"They told me twenty minutes, but that was thirty minutes ago. I can't tell you anything else. Your train is late."

Thomas turned away with an almost churning anxiety. He now understood what Wilhelm Mueller had called "being a sitting duck." German or America phraseology, it came down to being caught in a trap. And with one look at Hilda, he knew she felt it too.

His hand was sweaty on the leather handle of his bag. Had he acted too rashly in the night, taking the long-delayed letter from Sophie Goldstein as the wrong message? Had it been a case of overworked nerves after sending Wilhelm off that made him feel like his uncle was breathing down his neck with barely restrained vengeance? Now in the light of day, in this place, he wasn't sure what he had felt the night before.

Hilda seemed to read his thoughts. "Thomas, if our train doesn't come soon, I think we'd better come up with another plan. He'll know we're both gone by now. He'll have men at every station, at every gate."

Thomas looked to her. He had to protect Gretchen at all costs. That she was his niece meant nothing to a man like Otto Beck, Thomas knew. That she was handicapped also meant nothing to a man like him. He was equally determined to protect this older woman as well.

"You're right. He's looking now. If the train's not here in five minutes, we'll hire a cab."

But less than a minute later, the high shrill of an incoming train sounded. The porter shouted above the din.

"Dachau, Nuremberg, Dresden!"

Thomas restrained Hilda. "It's going to take them at least fifteen minutes to load. Stay by that pillar then get on at the last call. If ... he came he'd have you sitting there." He looked at Gretchen. *If Hilda is spotted, she will be taken as well. If only she was self-sufficient enough to get to Dachau. But she's already looking nervous and confused. If she has a seizure ...* Thomas felt a surge of desperation.

Gretchen Picard felt Thomas' tension. She looked up at him. His face was hard-looking. She really didn't like it when he looked like that. She followed his gaze. He was watching the men at the gate, the men in their dark leather coats. They were harder-looking than her brother.

"Thomas, them?"

He nodded absently. "We need to get past them." He looked at her, then pulled her close.

"God help us," he whispered into her hair.

She laughed suddenly. "Oh, Thomas, of course."

He smiled. "Yes, of course." He motioned Hilda forward while he turned to disappear into the crowd.

Otto Beck had the choice of three train terminals to look for his nephew. The fourth Munich station had been heavily damaged by Allied raids. One terminal had trains leaving for the south of Germany and Austria. Another terminal had only afternoon trains for civilians. Morning trains were reserved for troop movement. That left the Hofgartenstrasse station. He would go there; as a safeguard he would send men to the others. Only as he raced across the city did he feel the full force of rage against Thomas Picard. *His disappearance declares his guilt. And now he has eluded my men and slipped from the Blumenstrasse house. The only hope I have is that the first train has been delayed. If not, there will be a warrant speeding across Germany. There will be Gestapo agents at every station. A piano seller and a baker! They won't get far.*

Thomas saw two Gestapo agents at the boarding gate. Examining papers, they were clearly looking for someone. It could be him or some other poor soul trying to flee. The line inched forward; the train was boarding, tendrils of smoke curling from the undercarriage. It would be pulling out soon unless the police force stopped it.

A third Gestapo agent came hurrying up to join the two at the gate. He spoke to them rapidly; the line of passengers shifted nervously. Thomas appeared to be absorbed in the morning paper, but he was watching the back of Hilda's head. They had reached the gate and the agents. He saw her submit the passports. Gretchen swiveled around, trying to find Thomas in the crowd. She saw him, but he shook his head imperceptibly. She smiled broadly and he groaned to himself. Then he heard his name.

"Again? Who?"

"Thomas Picard."

The agents were discussing him.

He heard Gretchen's voice. "Thomas?"

Thomas turned to hurry away, when someone in front of him screamed. *I can't see,* Thomas groaned. He heard Hilda's commanding voice.

"She's having a seizure. She's an epileptic. Please."

"Clear off, clear off, she's sick!" and agent shouted. "Give them room!"

The passengers in front of Thomas were processed quickly.

"Someone get a doctor!"

"I'm a doctor," Thomas said hurrying forward, folding his paper.

"She's having some kind of seizure," the agent said, his own agitation and nervousness showing.

Thomas bent down. "Yes." He looked up at the agent. "She needs to be moved. Let's put her on the train so she can have room."

Hilda was fumbling with her bag. "I have her medication here, I—"

"Give it to her on the train," Thomas commanded. "Here, help me," he motioned to the Gestapo who stood by wide-eyed.

"She—"

"She's not going to bite you. Come on man, help me."

Gretchen was twitching and jerking as they carried her to the train. Hilda followed, weeping. The train released its departure whistle.

"Here, stretch her over these seats."

Hilda huddled over her; Thomas stood in the aisle.

"I'll help you," he said.

"Yes, please, I'm shaking so."

Thomas turned to the Gestapo. "Thanks."

The man nodded and backed away. The eight o'clock train began to chug forward.

Warsaw

Wilhelm Mueller was having an easier time entering Poland than Thomas Picard was having leaving Munich. He had been processed in the long line of soldiers as they disembarked in Warsaw. Wilhelm was stunned at the SS personnel who filled the shabby terminal. There were hundreds, all-grim faced with rifles slung over their shoulders.

Wilhelm asked one of the guards, "What gives? There are more guys here than we have up in Stalingrad!"

"High alert. We captured a partisan who said there are plans to blow up the station soon."

Wilhelm shifted his bag. "Not today I hope."

The man grinned. "The general staff is all in a stew over it."

"Welcome to Warsaw, huh?"

The man laughed and waved Wilhelm through. For hours, Wilhelm had been considering his options once he arrived in Warsaw. Natalie was here in this gutted place of German invaders, Jews, and Polish slaves. He felt a surge of excitement that he was so close. But first he had to establish himself here. He had to have a safe identity before he approached the mistress of a German officer.

• • •

Hilda Jensen was scolding herself that she had been so unprepared for Gretchen Picard's sudden seizure. She herself had trembled as she dug for the medication, tears spilling down her cheeks at the sight of the struggling girl. But Thomas had taken over calmly. The other passengers had politely kept their distance as the train moved through the Munich suburbs and into the countryside.

Thomas had sat down, Gretchen's head rested in his lap. "There, yes, just one." He helped his sister up a little. "Here, Gret, take this."

Her eyes were clamped shut, her body stiff. She opened her eyes, clear and unconfused.

"Don't cry, Hilda, don't cry. Gret's fine."

Her hand closed over Thomas'. She shook her head against the pill he offered.

"Oh, Thomas," she smiled.

His eyebrows shot up. "You . . . you're all right? You didn't have . . ."

She barely suppressed a giggle.

Hilda looked up. "Your sister is an actress!"

He nodded. "And she got us on the train!"

• • •

Otto Beck arrived at the station twelve minutes after the train had departed. He was in control of himself now. He pushed through the crowd to the gates.

"Anything?" he shouted before he reached his men.

"Nothing, Herr Beck. He could have caught the train last night."

"Maybe," Beck growled. He scanned the commuters. He turned back on his men.

"Where have the morning trains left for?" he snapped.

"One for Mannheim; one just left for Nuremberg. That's it."

"You checked every passenger?"

"Yes, yes, Herr Beck, there was no Thomas Picard."

"And the Jensen woman?"

"The Jensen woman?" The two agents exchanged a nervous look.

"You fools! Weren't you looking for the Jensen woman, the baker?"

"We only heard the report was for Picard."

Beck cursed. "She could have been on that train!"

"We . . . we didn't see Picard. It was normal, sir. Except for the sick girl, there was nothing. He could be hiding—"

"What sick girl?"

"The . . . the . . . girl that . . ."

"She was having some sort of seizure."

"Of course she was not alone!" Beck said with mounting fury.

"I . . . I . . . she . . ."

"An older woman was with her, Herr Beck. But it was nothing, and the doctor helped her." The agent's voice trailed off at the sight of Beck's reddening face.

"A doctor helped her on the train. About thirty, brown hair?"

They nodded mutely.

He cursed again. "Tell me again where this train was bound," he said tightly.

"Nuremberg, Dresden."

Beck was scratching something on a paper.

The other agent spoke up eagerly. "And a stop at Dachau."

Thomas was thankful for the bright sunny weather. Though it was cold; it was a fine day for walking. They had disembarked at the station with a wave and finger across his lips to the old station master who nodded behind the grilled window. It was good to see Pastor Picard back in Dachau. Carrying their three bags, they took a road away from the city—a winding road that Thomas remembered well.

"I'd walk this way from the church when I came to the station," Thomas said cheerfully.

"Preacher Thomas, Thomas," Gretchen piped as she walked between them, swinging Thomas' hand.

Thomas smiled at Hilda. "Gret, you're pretty proud of yourself, aren't you?"

She nodded and laughed.

The road took them away from the small village of Dachau and into the country.

"As soon as I get you two safely installed at the Schillers', I'm coming back to get the next train."

"Leaving?" Gretchen frowned.

There with not a soul in sight, Thomas stopped. He was still holding his sister's hand.

"Gret, I have a surprise for you."

"Yes?"

"I had a letter from Frau Sophie. They are in Warsaw. Gret, I'm going to go find Maria and Frau Sophie and try to help them."

Her eyes widened, then she threw herself into his arms.

He couldn't speak for several moments.

"You'll bring Maria back?" Gretchen whispered against his chest.

He nodded. "I'll try." He put her at arm's length. "But that means you are going to have to be very brave. Uncle Otto is trying to find us. Find me and you and Frau Hilda. You are going to have to listen to Hilda and do what she says. I may be gone for quite awhile. But the people here in Dachau are expecting you. They're good people, and they'll take care of you."

"You'll come back?"

"Yes, Gret, I'll come back."

"If only your letter had come sooner," Hilda spoke up, "you and Wilhelm could have traveled together."

Thomas smiled. "Guessing his skills, I probably would have slowed him down. Hopefully we can meet and perhaps help each other."

Hilda nodded. "Gretchen and I will pray you can find him—that you can help each other."

Thomas nodded as he looked out over the flat, sunny fields he remembered. *Hunted and heading for more danger. Still, I haven't been this happy in years.*

• • •

Wilhelm had been in Warsaw for ten days, and it had been the most dangerous time of his life. Twice he had been told to stop and show his papers, once a shot had rung out after him. Their surprise had saved him. He had thrown away the hated uniform. He was a civilian now. And being young, his presence meant only three things to the occupiers—a Polish slave, an escaped Jew, or a partisan on reconnaissance. In this city of high tensions, the order had gone out: Shoot first, ask questions later. He was a marked man, far more than he had been in Berlin or Munich.

Still he was determined to play this survival game the way he knew it best—surveying the city, learning its altered geography and the location of army camps, SS and Gestapo headquarters, and labor camps. He walked the entire perimeter to understand where roads, which could be used for escape into the forests and countryside, led. He found hiding places both north and south of the city. And one evening at dusk, sitting on a hill that overlooked the eastern districts, Wilhelm saw the Jewish ghetto of Warsaw. He sat for a long time and thought of Rabbi Bergmann. He thought of his aged parents and sister. They could have been in a place like that.

Even in the cold gloom and shadows, he could see the thin tendrils of smoke from fires. This city within a city would be freezing. And starving. Among his army companions he had heard the truth. *The Germans were killing the Jews. There was no plan to merely exploit them for slave labor. Empty the ghetto.*

The night mists rose up between him and the city floor, and the cold began to creep over him.

Empty the ghetto. What hope do they have down there?

The memory came to him strong and clear. He remembered the voice of his father, speaking quietly when he thought Wilhelm was asleep. But he was only pretending. Wilhelm spoke out loud to the night mists.

"The Lord is my shepherd I shall not want. Yea though I walk through the valley of the shadow of death ..."

He was so absorbed in the haunting scene below, in the memory of the comforting words, that he didn't hear the sudden steps behind him until it was too late. A horrible pain on the left side of his head and down his shoulder, the warmth of blood dripping into his ear, then the mist swallowing him into the valley of the shadow.

PART 4

Reunion
1943

Put me like a seal over your heart, like a seal on your arm. For love is as strong as death.
—Song of Solomon 8:6 NASB

30
By a Single Thread

When she thought of them, they were the Americans, not just the Allies—and certainly not the enemy. So each night, regardless of the law, she turned to the BBC sputtering from London to hear about the Americans. She now knew of Patton and Montgomery and Eisenhower as much as the German papers told her of Rommel and Keitel and Paulus. Her favorite time was to fix herself a cup of tea in the kitchen, pull Morgan on her lap, and listen to Churchill.

"Even though large tracts of Europe and many old and famous states have fallen or may fall into the grip of the Gestapo and all the odious apparatus of Nazi rule, we shall not flag or fail. We shall go on to the end; we shall fight in France; we shall fight in the seas and oceans. Let us therefore brace ourselves to our duties, and so bear ourselves that, if the British Empire and its commonwealth last for a thousand years, men will say, 'This was their finest hour!' "

She hugged the eight-month-old boy and smiled. "Now that, young man, is a statesman! This bombast from the chancellery is pitiful nonsense. One day you shall memorize the prime minister's words." She laughed at herself, adding, "And some of Roosevelt's too, of course."

She had discovered the attic with its dozens of trunks and boxes filled with letters, photographs, army uniforms, and medals. In the quiet hours spent up there, Emilie learned a little more than Josef or Max had told her about the Farber family. She was a Farber now—a wife and mother—and as lonely as Max's mother must have been when her husband had gone off to war thirty years ago. A new stone monument had been placed in the enclosure, the grass not yet growing over the rectangle of brown earth. The wars had come, and still raged, the house stood. And now Emilie Farber was mistress of the place.

Tegel Prison

It would have galled Adolf Hitler and his cabinet to know the inmates of Tegel prison learned of the German army's surrender at Stalingrad a mere six hours after they had. The network in block seven was perhaps more efficient than the Nazi bureaucracy of Berlin. A handful of guards sometimes held their duties with a little less zeal and commitment than they had years earlier. What was so terrible about whispering a little war news to the poor souls in the dark, stinking cells? How could they possibly pose a threat to the war-lords? They were prisoners and powerless; they were men waiting to die.

The voice sounded hollow at the end of the dark corridor.

"Max?"

"Yes?"

"I was in . . . the infirmity yesterday, you know. While I was waiting I saw a newspaper."

"Yes?"

"I . . . ah . . . well, do you have a brother named Irwin?" The man knew the answer to this already, but he didn't want to be quite so blunt.

"Yes, my oldest brother is Irwin Farber."

"The paper . . . the paper said he died, Max. Hitler even went to the funeral. I'm sorry, Max."

A pause.

"Yes. Thank you."

He couldn't get over the shock of it. Like Reinhard Heydrich, Max had held the childhood conviction that these two men were somehow invincible. Another brother he hadn't been able to reconcile with. And to the new Max Farber, prisoner of the Reich, this was the greatest sorrow. *If Eric has died in some battle, I could be the last Farber.*

He closed his eyes, praying for his brother.

● ● ●

Emilie flipped past the broadcast from Berlin. For days it had been the same—the communiqué from army headquarters announcing the defeat, followed by the roll of muffled drums and the second movement of Beethoven's Fifth Symphony. Göring or Goebbels would then spend an hour extolling the bravery of the German army and condemning the treachery of the Russians. "Germans shouldn't be discouraged. The defeats in Africa, Stalingrad, and the Allied landing in North America were not doom, merely setbacks."

Emilie was washing up the supper dishes with the BBC in the background. Morgan was teething madly on a knotted dishtowel from his high chair. Percy was stretched blissfully in front of the fire. Her mind was neither on the radio, the baby, nor the dishes. She thought of the box of letters she had gone through in front of the library fire that afternoon. She supposed she should feel a little guilty for this, but the letters were old and what did it really matter now?

Except a letter that had been stuck in a stack of old magazines. It was a letter to Max Farber from Elaina Heydrich. Emilie estimated they had both been college age. It had been a brief, newsy letter on lavender paper largely devoted to what she had done on a recent vacation. The signature had been with a flourish. It was the two closing words penned with obvious care that kept her thinking: "Always friends."

Always friends ...

Morgan squealed, drawing her attention. He had dropped his towel and Percy was mauling it.

"Percy, leave off." She ruffled his ears. Then she scooped the baby into her arms. "All right my little man."

Pushing a little tea cart, she left the kitchen for the parlor she had converted into Josef's bedroom. He was too infirm now to climb the stairs.

The bedroom lamp was low as she entered. Propped up in bed, Josef was reading. He looked up, a smile wreathing his face.

"My favorite time of night."

She smiled and poured him a cup of chocolate.

"Is it raining?" he asked.

She was stirring up his fire. "Just the wind."

"Awfully cold out."

She nodded. "But you're warm aren't you, Uncle Josef?"

"Yes, quite toasty. You pamper me, Emilie Farber."

She kissed his forehead. "No more than you deserve."

"Humph."

She settled into the chair opposite the bed with her own cup. Morgan guzzled a bottle in her lap.

"I think our boy has gained a pound since I saw him this afternoon," Josef said, smiling.

She laughed. "I can't deny that this little Farber isn't so little! He's outgrowing everything—besides chewing on everything. I caught Percy with a bone in front of him and Morgan reaching for it."

"They're the best of friends," Josef said. Their eyes met. "As it should be."

The baby reached out a chubby hand for Josef. The old doctor took it in his and smiled.

"What did our British friends have to say tonight?"

"I admit I was hardly listening. I think they were talking about Italy as the next Allied prospect. A spring campaign. Josef, how serious were Max and Elaina Heydrich?"

"Serious?"

"I mean in their relationship."

"Well, they grew up together. They were friends. Then as young people, I suppose, everyone assumed they would marry. But Max took to the bachelor road for a long time. Until a few months before you came to Germany. Then he asked Elaina to marry him."

"Obviously she didn't. I wonder why? I mean, it sounds like she adored him."

"I think she did. But I think she could see, perhaps better than Max at the time, that they could be friends but not really husband and wife. They were too different. And Reinhard wasn't for it. I'm sure he wielded pressure for her to refuse him."

"And now he's gone," Emilie mused aloud.

Josef's head was cocked. "Why were you wondering?"

"Oh, I don't know. Just like you said, it seemed like they were destined to marry, being so fond of each other and comfortable with each other."

"Well, I would guess that Elaina Heydrich has regretted her refusal more than a few times."

"Now why do you say that?" Emilie smiled.

"Can you imagine turning loose of a man like Max Farber?"

Now Josef was regretting his words. Emilie's face had blanched.

He cleared his throat awkwardly. "These times at night, you bringing the hot chocolate reminds me of our nights together at Tiergarten house ... the three of us."

Emilie studied the top of her son's blond head. Josef studied her.

His voice was very soft and gentle. "Have you lost hope?"

She looked up. "Some days ... I can't ... I can't quite remember the sound of his voice or his laugh, Uncle Josef."

"I understand, but Emilie, for my sake, for Morgan's, please don't give up hope." His voice rose and she was surprised at its strength and intensity. He had released the baby's hand to take hers.

"No matter what happens, until ... until you know he can't come back, don't stop hoping. Don't stop praying, Emilie."

• • •

He stood very tall and straight in the morning sunshine that brought the precious warmth to his cell. For these few morning hours the cubicle would be comfortable. He would stand this way all morning, going through his exercise routine and thinking and praying. Though the clothes were worn and dirty, they didn't conceal his still-broad frame. His thick blond hair hung to his shoulders; the beard he kept raggedly trim with a coveted pair of scissors. While his face wasn't tanned as it had been in his days of freedom, still with his outings in the prison courtyard his pallor was not a pasty white. Where Dietrich was their spiritual leader, Max had become their physical trainer. He had made each of them a personal regime based on calorie intake, guessed weight, and age. He exercised with each of them, and they all felt that if they emerged from this place Max would be the most fit. It had been Max they appealed to in a plot to overcome the guards and attempt an escape. Max had gently refused. There was no hope in that plan, no real chance of success.

"Max!"

Max turned and went to the door. It was unusual for the men to talk during the morning. The guards, depending on their mood, could penalize the talker with a sudden, unplanned beating.

"What is it, Kurt?"

"Manfred is ... dead. You heard them take him away. He kept telling us to have hope. You said it the other night, and Dietrich has said the same thing. There is no hope here, not in this place. Look what happened to

Manfred. Hope! If we aren't starved or killed by sickness or disease, then we'll freeze to death. If not that, then the bombs will kill us when they fall!" he said savagely.

"I understand how you feel Kurt. You can't want out of here any more than I do. But without help, inside help, and help waiting on the outside, there would be no chance at all. We'd be gunned down."

"Max is right."

"Don't you fools understand?" Kurt shouted hoarsely. "They will shoot us anyway. They can never let us out. They can't face what they've done. And if the Allies entered Berlin, the guards are under orders to kill us before they escape. Do you see? The Allies will enter Tegel and find one vast tomb!"

Dietrich spoke up. "Kurt, this is no way to be talking. All it produces is despair. We must conserve our strength—our thoughts for good thoughts, for hope, for encouraging each other, for trusting God."

"You trust Him, Bonhoeffer! Not me! I will not trust in a God who lets a man rot in prison when he is innocent. And what of the poor Jews! They are called His 'chosen people.' If that is what happens to chosen people, no thank you. I will make it or die on my own."

"Kurt, you have spoken thoughts that we have all had. You are angry with God. I have been angry with Him as well. But I know such anger is wasted. His ways are so often higher than our own. And for us here, we truly must exercise only the best qualities and emotions, just as Max has us exercise in the flesh. We don't have the luxuries, but we don't have the distractions either. All is pared down to being alone with the Creator of the universe. There is nothing else. We either cling to life and hope and trust in Him—no matter what happens—or we cling to death and darkness. I have so little here, but I do have Him. He is worthy to be trusted; I do have Him. The Nazis cannot take that from me, no matter how hard they try. And if you trust God, Kurt, they will not take Him from you, either."

Kurt's voice was subdued, broken, and weeping. "I just ... don't know how much longer ... I just want to walk, to walk for miles. I want to be warm and eat. I ..."

Max waited a few moments before he spoke. "If it's any consolation to you, Kurt, I had a dream about chocolate last night—and strudel."

There was relaxed laughter along the corridor.

"Now if you want to be able to walk when you get out," Max continued cheerfully, "really hike those miles instead of being bent over and weak like an old man, get up and start your laps. Manfred would have wanted us to keep going."

• • •

Emilie looked out on the back lawn of the estate. The night had dropped a blanket of frost, and now everything looked like rippled yards of fine lace. She could see the blue gloss of the river from the window. Her eyes traveled to the fenced cemetery and she thought of Irwin Farber. She rarely thought of Max's oldest brother without thinking of Reinhard Heydrich.

She had returned from Czechoslovakia on Heydrich's personal plane. She would never forget the day Heydrich's secretary had entered her room. He was ashen and nervous. His tone and words gave no clue to any emotion.

"Herr Heydrich has been killed on the way to Prague."

Emilie had sat down slowly in the bedroom chair, clutching Morgan to her. Then she started crying, a sobbing kind of cry, the cry of relief. The secretary, privy to all of his master's world, knew the reason. This woman was free. He had just delivered the news to Frau Heydrich in the opposite wing of the great villa. But this woman's quiet weeping unnerved him more.

"Frau Farber, I . . . will secure you a flight back to Berlin within the hour."

She had barely nodded through her tears. Now, these months later she could remember that overwhelming sense of God's protection for her and her son. He was worthy to trust. She had wanted to ask Heydrich's secretary if the plane could fly to Geneva . . . to freedom, but there was Josef. She had left the mountain retreat that Heydrich had brought her to within the promised hour. She sat in the same plane, in the same seat she had occupied only forty-eight hours earlier. Then Reinhard had mixed drinks and smiled and been confident of her eventual submission. But he had been cut down. Suddenly, so suddenly this powerful man. He was mortal.

Back in Berlin, Emilie had found Josef at the Tiergarten house. Irwin hadn't punished or pursued him. He had tried to care for himself. With the near nightly raids on the capital, Emilie decided it would be safer for all of them if they returned to the country estate. She had expected the Mercedes in the drive, Katrina and Irwin Farber at the door. If they had been willing to bargain for a child, she expected they would be willing to simply demand him. And with his power . . . But the car had never come. They had not appeared on her steps. Only a phone call three weeks after she and Josef had installed themselves told her that Irwin Farber had died of a massive heart attack. The car finally came. Now, however, it held only Katrina, dressed in black and saying very slowly that her husband should be buried in the family plot. Emilie had made no protest, and the following day a Farber son was brought home.

Heydrich was dead. Irwin was dead. At last, there was a measure of safety.

Carrying the breakfast tray, she went to check on Morgan sleeping in the nursery. She bent over the crib. He was stirring, but not yet awake. His fat, dimpled hand lay near his blushed cheek, his blond hair curling over the back of his neck. She reached out and touched his hair, amazed for the millionth time that she and Max had made this beauty. Lying there so peacefully, she saw her husband in her son. She slowly turned away, not really seeing the nursery she had decorated with Max's things from the attic. She was thinking of Josef's words the night before.

"Can you imagine turning loose of a man like Max Farber?"

She held herself. "I have turned loose of him, Uncle Josef. I had to."

She quietly left the nursery and went back down to Josef's room. She knocked, then entered with the tray.

He was not in his chair as usual, waiting. He was still in bed. The blinds still drawn. She set down the tray and stirred up the rusty embers of fire.

"There, now . . ." But she spoke with an odd, chilling premonition before she reluctantly crossed the room. She stood at the foot board, gripping it. *Josef has gone in the night. Now it is me and my son alone.*

It had been a long, dreary day with the sky slate-gray and a stiff wind blowing with a purpose that suggested the grip of winter would not be easily loosened. Yet spring was, by calendar design, only a few weeks away. Emilie noted the changes on the estate by the land, the days that were longer and warmer, and the trees budding. Life continuing.

She sat before the library fire folding diapers. Her thoughts returned to the morning trip she had taken into Berlin. The city was becoming pockmarked with Allied bombing. Huge flak towers had been built around the zoo.

Emilie had driven Max's car slowly with the feeling that she was seeing the defenses erected for a great battle. She could imagine the still-standing proud buildings becoming more piles of rubble. *The Berlin that had been Josef's city and Max's was gone. It's no longer my city—if it ever had been,* Emilie reflected. *And now, now, what is there to keep me here?*

She had driven to the home of Elaina Heydrich, drawn a deep breath, whispered a prayer, then climbed the steps to the fashionable townhouse. The maid who answered the door said the mistress was away. She didn't know when to expect her. Did she care to leave her name? Emilie had hesitated a moment, filled with an alloy of relief and disappointment.

"Yes, tell her . . . Emilie Farber came to see her."

Now as she sat in the Farber library she pondered again what she would have said if the woman had been home. She had rehearsed the words, but she suspected that one look from Max's former girlfriend and her planned speech would evaporate. And of course, this whole sudden idea had come from reading someone else's letter. *If they had been friends, good friends, almost husband and wife . . .*

The library doors opened; Emilie looked up and smiled. God had sent her help when she was once again in need. A middle-aged woman entered carrying the tea tray.

"You read my thoughts, Berta, thank you."

"On a day such as this, fire and tea are the very thing. And with the last of the flour, I made two loaves of bread and a batch of cookies."

"Well, let's hope our ration coupons come today so we can shop Friday."

"Heinrich has Morgan in the greenhouse, puttering about. He clapped his hands when Heinrich picked him up."

Emilie laughed. "My son is a social fellow like his—" She stopped and busied herself with the tea. "I'm so thankful for how he's taken to both of you. I know in his own way he misses Josef." She looked to the fire. "I only hope he will remember him when he gets older. Josef loved him so."

Berta reached out and touched her hand. "You can keep Josef alive to little Morgan, you know."

Emilie nodded. *Just like his father. I'll tell my son of these two men.* She looked at the woman.

"Berta, I can't tell you what it means to have you and Heinrich with me here. Not only for Morgan's sake, or for the house that's too big for me to keep alone, but for me."

"Oh, Emilie, it's our pleasure and blessing. That we saw the notice in the paper—well, I believe God brought us here. Heinrich is convinced of it. He had been praying."

It had happened so suddenly, like Josef's death. The couple had seen the obituary in the paper and the notice for the funeral at the Farber Estate. As former patients and friends of the old doctor, they had come from Hamburg. Emilie had been touched by their presence, by their affection for her uncle. They had had tea and talked. One hour stretched to two. They had held Morgan while they talked of their own home that had been destroyed in a bombing. They were living with a grown daughter in her crowded apartment. And they were looking for work.

"You know," Berta continued, "that morning Heinrich read the paper, well, it was the first time in months he had read the obituaries. You know, with the casualty lists taking up half the paper . . ." Her blue eyes sparkled. "You know, there are those who look at what is happening in Germany and say God has given up on us. Chastened us, yes, but abandoned never! Why, Heinrich and I see His hand more and more."

Emilie started to reply, but the stillness of the house was broken with the deep chime of the front doorbell.

She sat her cup down, immediately tense.

Berta patted her hand again. "I'll get it. I've been hoping for a proper chance to play maid. You know—and announce someone." She winked.

Berta reentered the library briskly. She scooped up the folded diapers.

"You have a guest, Frau Farber."

Emilie's eyebrows rose.

"Frau Heydrich is here to see you. You'll be fine. I'll bring another cup for tea."

"Yes, thank you, Berta. Show her in."

She was mistress of this grand house now, but she didn't feel an inch of it. She thought of Max's mother, so accustomed to the role of elegant hostess. Emilie could imagine her mortification—a guest was here, and the mistress was folding diapers! She stood with her hands clasped in front of her.

Elaina Heydrich was as nervous as Frau Farber, but she had had years of training in concealing emotion and anxiety. She entered the room and Emilie's heart dropped. The woman pulling off her gloves was tall, composed, and wrapped in furs. *This German woman could have been Max's wife.* Emilie was speechless and furious with herself.

Elaina crossed the room and suddenly smiled. "Frau Farber." She extended her hand.

It's a nice smile, Emilie decided.

"Frau Heydrich, welcome. Please sit down."

They sat across from each other.

"I apologize for not calling first," Elaina began as she arranged her furs with care. It looked so sophisticated to Emilie—it covered any shaking and gave Elaina something to do. "But to be perfectly honest, I . . . I decided to drive out here on quite an impulse. I can see I have surprised you."

"Well, yes . . . but . . . I'm sure I would have surprised you if you had been home yesterday."

Elaina smiled again. "That's true, you would have. It is strange, I suppose, that in all these years we have never met."

Was this a reference to Max or her brother? Berta entered unobtrusively with more tea and an extra cup. When she was gone, Emilie poured the tea. They looked at each other fully then, holding their teacups. One in silk and fur and jewels, the other in a white cotton blouse and dark wool skirt. Emilie decided Max's former girlfriend was a pretty woman—sad and a little frail looking—but classically Aryan. Perfect. She felt plain and looked to her cup.

Elaina could see in one swift perusal why Max would find this young woman attractive. *Very lovely, but grieving. Deeply grieving.* It stirred Elaina with an understanding compassion. She set her cup down carefully.

"I heard about Josef Morgan's passing, Frau Farber. I was out of the country at the time or I would have come. I was very sad about it. He was a very kind man."

Emilie's throat constricted. "Thank you." She had forgotten that this woman had known her uncle—really before she had. She couldn't continue. She couldn't say how she missed him. *Keep hoping, Emilie.*

She cleared her throat. She must get to the point. That would seem to be what this woman would want.

"I'm sure you must be wondering why I came to your home."

Elaina nodded. "I admit I'm intrigued."

Emilie looked away for a moment. *This is Reinhard's sister. How much did she know? What could she say? No, that was something else entirely. There is now; there is this important question.*

Emilie looked at her directly. "Frau Heydrich, I came to your house yesterday because I wanted to ask you if there might be anything you could do to help Max."

Elaina had had this suspicion. Yet for a moment Emilie's bluntness caught her unprepared. Now her composure was visibly shaken. She again set down her cup and rearranged her furs. Emilie could see she was agitated.

"Why do you think I could help him, Frau Farber?"

"I was ..." Emilie stopped. She set down her own cup. She leaned forward, her hands clasped together, her face appealing. "Elaina, I know you and Max were good friends and ... and I know that you helped him help the Jews."

Elaina's voice was crisp. "How do you know that?"

Emilie looked to her lap a moment. "I was with your brother in Prague when he found out."

There was a long moment of silence before Emilie spoke again.

"I thought perhaps you might have an idea or a ... a way we could help Max. I have some of his wealth, and you have influence and connections. Elaina, I haven't spoken to him since the day he was taken. I haven't been able to pass any word to him." She swallowed hard, her voice now hoarse. "He ... doesn't know about Josef, whom he loved. He doesn't know about his son. I don't know if Max is alive. I've just been living on hope." She couldn't hold back the tears.

Elaina froze. Finally she spoke with obvious care. "I know my brother swore Max Farber would never leave Tegel prison. I know he had him tortured to get information—"

"How do you know this?" Emilie asked hoarsely.

Elaina Heydrich had a heritage as blue-blooded as Max Farber. This American-German woman might have difficulty understanding family ties. She knew the depths of her brother's depravity, his hatred, his venom. Still she hated to say the words.

"I know because he boasted to me about it once when he had been drinking, shortly before he died. At a dinner party, oddly enough. I also heard high officials saying that no one would leave Tegel. The fuehrer has a particular anger against political prisoners."

Another long silence.

"Would you try to find out if Max is still alive?" Emilie asked. She stood up abruptly and walked to the fireplace, frowning. She had forgotten to be intimidated by the cool Elaina Heydrich. She turned, and Elaina was watching her. "That really isn't just it, is it? I want more. If I knew Max was alive ... In a way that's just as hard as thinking he's dead."

"You love him very much."

Now Emilie was surprised. "Yes, I love Max. We had such a short time together, but I love him very much."

Elaina stood. "I can try to find out if ... if he is alive, Frau Farber. I really can't promise anything more."

For just a moment Emilie was stunned. The sister looked and sounded very much like the brother. It chilled her, though she stood near the heat.

Then Elaina smiled faintly. "I wonder if there is something I could ask of you, Frau Farber, in return."

"Yes?"

A part of Elaina wanted to hurry to her car and drive away and forget this scene, to cry for what had happened to someone she loved, to cry for what she had given up. But this was a pain she must self-inflict.

"I'd like very much to see Max Farber's son."

31
Now an Altar

Through the small square window she could see the velvet-black sky. Already the jewels of the night were piercing the velvet, tiny scattered pinpoints of light and a translucent sickle of moon. Laying on her side, she felt a sweep of gratitude for this window. Life was now a series of small pleasures—like a room with a window that brought moonlight splashing across her bed. *The same moon ...* She twisted a length of her hair and felt again that same wonder that this moon shone on not just all of Poland and Germany, but all of Europe, and, in its revolving, all of the world! *This same moon ...* The length of hair was pulled taut by her fingers. *This same moon is shining on my father and brothers, if ... What a very large, very improbable if. I mustn't think about it. Not now, anyway,* she decided. Cloudless and still, it was a very cold night. It took all of her resolve and discipline to slip from the bed and the warmth of her mother's body. She sat on the edge waiting, as she did so many nights, to see if her mother would stir and waken and scold.

But Sophie Goldstein was deep in her precious dreams, and Maria stood. Immediately the cold grabbed at her, making her motions swift and jerky as she pulled on the blouse and wool skirt. It took all of her will not to gasp and pant. It was like this every night. *I should be stronger than this,* she told herself. Since they always slept in their wool stockings, she had only her shoes, belt, and sweater to gather up. This she did as she stole across the small room. She opened the door, paused to look at the sleeping shadow of her mother against the wall, then stepped into the hall. The draft again assaulted her. Now the smell of the ghetto. Her friends said they hardly noticed it anymore—this blend of human filth, sickness, disease, and decaying flesh. But Maria Goldstein noticed. It always twisted her inside, made her feel a little anxious.

She passed down the hall and through the sagging front door to the sidewalk. A shadow detached from the wall and fell into step beside her. She lowered her chin into her collar and didn't bother to look up or speak. They walked half a block before she turned, alone, into another building. She walked down the corridor into a small room. Here was a small clinic, and a light burned where a woman sat reading. She looked up and smiled and returned to her reading. Maria went to the basin and washed her face and dried it with the towel she had brought. She took the precious piece of mirror from the deep pocket of her skirt and set it on a shelf. From the other pocket came a fine tortoise-shell comb. Carefully, she combed through her dark, bobbed hair. This done, she touched a thin veneer of lipstick to her lips. Then she was finished. She gave a cheery wave to the nurse, then stepped back into the night. The shadow was again at her side.

"Can't see any difference," the voice teased.

Maria didn't turn or slow. "Then you have no eyes, Daniel."

They came to another building and hurried down the basement level steps. A sentry at the door leaned forward. "Shalom, Maria."

"Shalom, David."

The two entered a dark hallway. Voices could be heard from beyond a closed door, but Daniel restrained her with a hand on her arm.

"I do have eyes, Maria Goldstein." He pulled her to him and kissed her. "You are the prettiest girl in the ghetto," he continued.

"And you are the biggest flirt, Daniel. Now—"

But he kissed her again. Finally she pulled away. "We are late."

His arm didn't loosen. The usually playful Daniel was serious. He looked closely at her in the dimness. "You kiss me with your lips, not your heart, Maria. Why?"

She laughed. "That sounded very poetic, Daniel. Where did you read that?"

"I'm serious."

"And we are seriously late."

"Maria—"

"Daniel, this is not the time."

"When is the time? All day you are busy working in the school, or the kitchen, or with your mother, or watching children, or coming here! When is there time for us?"

"I am no busier than anyone else."

"That is not true. You fill every minute of every day, and half the night. Everyone knows they can ask Maria Goldstein to do something and she will help do it."

"There is nothing wrong with helping, Daniel, for goodness' sake. There is so much to do."

"The ghetto . . . the ghetto is everything to you."

Her voice hardened. "Survival and striking the Nazis are everything to me. There is not room for much else."

"For me?"

"For . . . us to be friends, to enjoy each other as we can, yes. But more? No. Look for another girl if you want more, Daniel."

His voice became as hardened as hers. "You are wrong, Maria. That is why there are schools and theater and concerts in the ghetto. There is more to life than mere survival."

"Not for me."

"I hate to interrupt this lover's quarrel, but we can hear you in here. And the meeting is underway."

Maria blushed and moved toward the open door; Daniel moved behind her with wooden feet.

"You look lovely tonight, Maria," the man in the doorway said smiling.

She gave him a saucy curtsey then entered the room. Maria Goldstein was ready for the meeting of the Jewish Fighting Organization.

• • •

Although Lieutenant Hugo von Kleinst was commandant of the Jewish ghetto, he was not in charge of police actions for the place. This was left to a superior officer, General Kruger. Von Kleinst's role was more administrative—he determined food quotas for the thousands and set up medical standards. Seeing how efficient and hard-working he was, they thrust upon him the additional responsibility of organizing the train schedule that brought empty cattle cars to the ghetto and took away full ones. Only by great effort had he been able to turn down a tour of the cattle-car destinations: Treblinka to the north, Auschwitz to the south. In memorandum and conference with his junior officers, he referred to this as the "export of Jewish passengers." At first they thought this quiet dignified man was being cynically funny. Much like other Nazi jargon, "resettlement" meant eventual death. Then they realized this man was squeamish on this aspect of his work. But the teasing went on behind his back. He was doing too good a job to criticize him for a little faint-heartedness. Von Kleinst abhorred this part of his work, yet he did it steadily and, after a time, mechanically. He was also responsible for granting entrance and exit passes to the ghetto, though after his first and only inspection he couldn't imagine why anyone would willingly enter that stinking place. Like this young man in front of him.

Von Kleinst motioned for him to sit. He leaned back in the chair and perused the application. Finally, he looked up.

"You are from Munich, Herr Picard."

Thomas nodded. "Yes. I've lived there all my life."

"I was in Munich before this assignment. I wish you had brought some Munich warmth with you."

Thomas smiled. "Actually it was very cold and cloudy the day I left."

"But in Munich the sun will come out and warm things up. Here . . . here even when the sun shines, it is cold."

Thomas had been praying for this man for two days, praying he would find favor with him. Now he could see this man was as melancholy as the weather he spoke of. But he was the picture of Nazi perfection that Thomas had seen so many times in Munich—a spotless, pressed uniform with shining black belt and mirror-shiny knee boots. This man had a patrician look about him with his silver hair and firm square jaw.

"I never had occasion to go into your music store, Herr Picard, but I passed it many times going to headquarters."

Thomas smiled. "It's a store sort of like the glockenspiel—been around for nearly forever. My grandfather began it sixty years ago."

"I'm not a musician myself, but merely a lover of it."

Thomas nodded. "Beautiful music has a way of soothing a troubled soul."

Hugo's eyes flashed briefly on him. "Yes . . . and now you have left Munich to come to this wasteland called Warsaw for what your application says, 'business opportunities.'" There was a touch of cynicism in the man's voice that Thomas detected but chose to ignore.

"I'm sorry. Is that not the correct phrase? I was certain your secretary said that was the—"

"Yes, yes. You have applied in the proper language. Business opportunities. Businessmen from Germany do it all the time. I call it exporting the wealth of conquered territories back into Germany. Others, a little crass I think, call it stripping the land. Either way, it is perfectly legal and sanctioned by the government."

Thomas hadn't expected this. It caught him off-guard. He had expected a Nazi-type eager to help him steal Polish wealth. Von Kleinst was bitter. Thomas relaxed in the chair, now freshly intrigued since he'd glimpsed this man's soul.

Von Kleinst appeared to have forgotten his presence. He was toying with his watch.

"You aren't sure you approve of this business opportunity, Lieutenant von Kleinst?" Thomas asked.

Now the Nazi was surprised. He had expected a fawning opportunist—not someone who would speak to him as an equal. It had been so long since anyone had talked to him like that. He studied the young man boldly. Some memory nagged at him.

"Well . . . yes, you are right, Herr Picard. I'm not sure I approve. But it doesn't matter because our government approves."

"As residents of a fair-weather city, please call me Thomas."

"You've come all the way from Munich to inspect the Polish pianos," he smiled tiredly.

"And violins."

"Violins . . ." Hugo tapped his knee thoughtfully.

"In Munich we hear rumors of great instruments that would profit the musicians of Germany being left behind. You and I know many in the army wouldn't know if they were using a Tassini or a Bechstein for firewood."

Again Hugo smiled.

"It piqued my interest. So I left my shop and decided to come and see for myself. Perhaps . . . pick something up for the store. Maybe, well, I confess it was sort of an impulsive adventure as well."

"But you want to enter the ghetto."

"I feel certain some of the best instruments have been hidden away by the Jews. They have been known to do that kind of thing."

"Yes." He picked up the application again.

"Though certainly I intend to snoop around outside the ghetto as well."

Hugo stood up and walked to the window. "Come here, please."

Thomas stood beside him at the window. He was looking over the wall into the ghetto. Thousands of Jews. A pall of dust hung over the enclosure. He could see bodies laying in the gutters. His stomach tightened. *Sophie and Maria were there ... at least they were eight months ago ...* He could see the railroad cars drawn up to a siding.

He could feel von Kleinst watching him and not the scene below. Thomas didn't look at him.

"What is the population?" Thomas asked in a hollow voice.

"We estimate between sixty and one hundred thousand."

"The trains? They bring more Jews in?"

"No. They take Jews out. They take them to the camps."

Eight months.

"I see."

A long silence.

"There is disease in that place, Herr Picard. You put yourself at some risk to enter it."

Thomas was still staring.

Amusement tinged the Lieutenant's voice. "You still want to make your hunt for pianos and violins? Perhaps just in Warsaw, now?"

Thomas turned then, steadying his voice with effort. "No, I'd like to go to the ghetto if you'll allow it, Lieutenant von Kleinst."

"Would you like an escort of SS to go with you?"

"No, thanks. When I find something, I'll call for them."

"We know there are resistance groups in the ghetto. They have weapons."

They studied each other a moment. Hugo returned to his desk.

"I'll give you a week pass. You'll need to leave by the curfew hour. Come back at the end of the week and tell me about your hunt."

The following day was bright and sunny, defying von Kleinst's words. Within a few yards, Thomas knew that his aerial view from the lieutenant's office had not given him a false impression. Here was a city within a city. But it was a poor decaying city, a crowded, suffering place. And in those first moments, Thomas Picard forgot about the Goldsteins. He forgot that he was a Christian in this city of Jews. He thought only of how he could bring comfort to a dying place. He stood in the middle of the street. Jews were passing on the streets casting furtive looks at him. But he stood there, his eyes closed. He was praying, tears streaming down his face. God had opened the gates, he couldn't leave. This was God's altar and here Thomas Picard would be poured out.

There were no words for what he was seeing. And he knew it would only get worse the farther in he went. The warm sun against his face, he stood there and felt the filling of peace. *I'll find the Goldsteins.* He turned and looked back at the entrance. Four SS had entered with him and were lounging and smoking at the gate, twirling their rubber truncheons, watching him. He turned and began walking.

Sophie Goldstein's narrow world of Blumenstrasse in Munich had widened. Now she only had a few thousand lives to watch, speculate about, and advise. It was a busybody's paradise. And it was the only thing that kept her from sinking into prolonged despair over losing her beloved Aaron, Abraham, and Issac. After the initial shock of this dreadful place—the loss of privacy, the privations, the brutality, the suffering, the death—Sophie had girded up her apron and gone to work. She was not alone: She had Maria, and she had a heart of service. . . . And there were so many practical matters to attend to—like finding a husband for her Maria. *Such a prize for someone,* she thought.

It had taken four full days before Thomas had a lead on the Goldsteins. He could see the conflict clearly etched in the faces on the streets—suspicion, distrust, yet wanting to accept what he could bring them. He was German; he was free. He could be a Nazi plant looking for Jewish resistance. He asked each person he talked to about the Goldsteins. He told them he would be at the gate at eight o'clock each morning if they would get a message to the Goldsteins and let them know. When that produced nothing, he walked the streets—every street—looking at each pale, haunted face. Hoping from some window he would be seen. *Perhaps Sophie hanging out a bit of wash.* When he watched the children in the streets, he forgot the Goldsteins.

He turned a corner. A young girl in a far-too-big black coat was crouched on the sidewalk. On her knees she was trying to feed something to another small child wrapped in a dirty coat. Thin bruised legs stuck out from the coat. Thomas leaned closer. She was feeding the girl moldy orange peel. The girl gnawed listlessly. The older girl looked up, squinting at Thomas.

"What do you want?" she rasped.

Thomas didn't know what to say. He squatted down. "My name is Thomas. I . . ."

He reached into his pocket and brought out the last roll of hard bread he had smuggled in. The girl looked a moment before she snatched it out of his hand. She took a ragged bite before she handed it to the smaller girl. Still she huddled protectively, wary, but interested in the tall man beside her.

He looked past her, now realizing the black bundle a few feet from them was another child—laying very still.

"My brother," the girl said in a listless voice.

Thomas spoke, but his voice sounded unnatural. "What is wrong with him?"

"Nothing now."

Thomas hung his head. *God, this is too hard. Take me away.* A shadow fell across him.

A deep, hostile voice jolted him. He thought it was the SS guards. "What are you doing to the child?"

"What?" Thomas asked as he stood.

Three men, ragged yet tough-looking, stood regarding him. Men like a rough-looking version of Wilhelm Mueller.

"I gave . . . her . . . the last of my bread."

"Why are you in the ghetto?"

Thomas didn't speak for a moment as he prayed.

The man shoved him. "Your SS escort is two blocks over. No one can help you now. We've been watching you since you entered four days ago. What do you want?"

"I'm trying to find someone."

"So you say. The German's send spies in here all the time. Many times they don't leave."

"I'm no spy. I'm looking for—"

They cut him off. One of them had jumped behind him and twisted his arm behind his back.

"In here," the leader ordered. They pulled him into a burned-out building.

"Loo—" Thomas began, but they pulled his arm tighter.

The two began to go through his pockets. They stood back to read his papers.

"Thomas Picard from Munich. A swine coming to loot us, eh?"

"Look, I'm telling you. I'm trying to find Frau Sophie Goldstein and her daughter, Maria."

He saw the swift look that passed between them.

"You know who I'm talking about," Thomas guessed.

The arm tightened and he gasped out in pain. "Please."

"We don't lead swine to Jews. That is why the children have not helped you on the streets. No matter how much you bribe them."

"I'm not trying to bribe anyone."

"Let's strip him and send him back out. Look at the shoes. They're my size."

They grabbed him roughly.

"Von Kleinst knows I'm in here," Thomas said steadily.

Their movements checked; their eyes narrowed.

"He signed my pass; he watched me enter from his office window. He knows I'm in here, and I'm sure he would personally take an interest in my treatment or disappearance."

One of them spat and swore. "Let me break his arm."

"I don't want to be the reason for reprisals in the ghetto," Thomas countered.

They shoved him roughly away.

"Look, I'm trying to find the Goldsteins. We were neighbors in Munich. I came to try to help them."

"How? How does a Gentile help us Jews?"

Thomas rubbed his arm and looked away. "I don't know yet." He sat down. "You know the Goldsteins. Go to Sophie. Tell her Thomas Picard is here. Her reaction will tell you if I am telling the truth or not."

"Why should we?"

Thomas looked at each of them slowly. He felt his heart wrench for what these young men had been forced to become. They could be no more than eighteen or twenty.

"Because you're decent fellows. The Nazis haven't killed that yet."

One of them laughed, and two of them left the building.

Maria Goldstein entered the room breathless. "Have you seen my mother?"

One of the woman nodded. "She's in there. She—"

But Maria was already moving toward the entrance. She had heard her mother's loud wailing.

"Mama, what—"

Sophie was across the room, and a man stood with his arms around her. He lifted his head.

It's Thomas Picard. Everything she had ever imagined she would say to him if she ever saw him again died on her lips.

"Mama?" was all she could say.

It was not loud but it broke through Sophie's weeping. She turned.

"Oh, Maria, look, look! He came!"

Maria staggered.

"What do you mean?" she asked slowly.

"Thomas! He came! Thomas!"

Sophie hurried across to her, tugging her arm, but her daughter didn't move an inch.

"I wrote him months and months ago. And look, look Maria, he came!"

"How did you get a letter out? You know the committee has to approve anything smuggled."

"Phooey on committee orders. I promised Eli an apple tart with my last apples if he would take it out and he did. And Maria, why are we talking about apple tarts? Thomas has come to Warsaw."

He came up to them then, his head slightly lowered.

"Hello, Maria, it's good to see you."

"Hello Thomas." Her voice was cool. "How's Gretchen?"

"Yes, yes, Thomas, I forgot to ask, forgive me."

"She's well. I left her in the care of a good friend, in Dachau?"

"Why Dachau?" Maria asked, and Sophie at last heard her daughter's tone.

"Maria!"

Maria ignored her mother. "Why is Gretchen in Dachau."

"We had to leave Munich suddenly."

Sophie linked her arm through Thomas'. "And of course, I must ask, is that good friend who cares for Gretchen a . . . wife perhaps?"

Thomas smiled and shook his head. *Blumenstrasse or Warsaw. It was good that some things never changed.*

"No, no. Just a friend. Perhaps you remember Jensen's Bakery. Frau Hilda Jensen is caring for Gret."

"Ah, that's wonderful, did you hear, Maria? Oh, Thomas . . ."

"Mama, I came looking for you to tell you I'm taking Ruth's shift this evening so don't wait up for me. I better go."

"But Maria!"

She gave her mother a swift kiss and left the room without a backward glance.

Sophie's mouth sagged open. Finally she sputtered, "To think! Well! I certainly thought Aaron and I had raised her better than that!"

Thomas smiled and placed his arm around her shoulders. "It's all right, Sophie. Maria and I just need to talk."

She thought she had cried a lifetime of tears when Aaron was taken away, then, at the suffering of the children of the ghetto. But Sophie Goldstein found she still had a wealth to shed at the sight of Thomas Picard. *He was,* she reflected later, *standing there so tall, like he always was, dependable and trustworthy and caring. Like he had been a thousand times on Blumenstrasse. Like a son to her.* Now her tears came from that wellspring of joy that hadn't dried up from her tide of sorrow.

They sat in a corner of the ghetto soup kitchen where Sophie worked. She and Maria shared one small room of a former office building. Sophie had accepted this as her home long ago, but suddenly, with someone from the past who had known what she had on Blumenstrasse, she was shy. She didn't want Thomas to see in this even more intimate light what life had become to them.

They sat in two chairs drawn up close to each other, drinking tea that Thomas had brought. Thomas leaned forward, elbows on his knees. *It's like stepping back into the comfortable past to be with Sophie Goldstein,* he thought. Sophie wept as they began their vast catching up, beginning with Maria Picard's final sacrifice.

"You know, Thomas, never, never did I believe that Maria had stopped loving me."

"I'm glad you know that, Frau Sophie, because she did love you— despite all that happened. With all we have to tell each other, I have to tell you quickly. I can bring a measure of good news with me—"

Her hand was holding his. "You are good news itself, Thomas."

"And you are healing to me, Frau Sophie. I have seen Isaac. I helped him leave Germany."

"My Isaac, safe?" She bent over weeping.

For two hours they talked. He told her of Gretchen and Hilda and Otto Beck. Of her letter that had come as an answer to prayer.

"And I sent it out so many months ago!" she exclaimed in wonder.

"It was ragged and worn by the time I got it. But I got it!"

She told him of their trip across Germany, their arrest at the Polish border, what their life had become in this place. "I believe my Aaron and Abraham are in this camp called Treblinka."

"I'll do everything I can to find out."

"I cannot tell you the half of what it is like, Thomas. I . . . the children . . ."

"I have spent four days looking for you. I saw the Germans shoot a man outside the ghetto for tossing a sack of bread inside. They shot him. I have seen the children. There are no words for this, Sophie. It is much more . . . than . . . I expected."

They were silent a long time.

"Thomas, I'm so sorry of the welcome that Maria gave you."

"Don't worry about that. Tell me about her. How is she? For a moment I hardly recognized her for her short hair."

"She had a fever when we got here. It was summer. And then there is the problem of, well, lice. We had to cut her hair." Sophie sighed deeply. "She works very hard. She's very popular with the young people."

"Some things never change," Thomas smiled.

Sophie nodded. "On the inside. Well, if Aaron were here he could get her to talk. I know she is afraid like we all are, feeling desperate. And . . . angry." Another deep sigh, then a smile. "She's hardly 'O Petted One' anymore."

Thomas looked at his watch. "Thirty minutes till curfew. I have to leave now. But I have three more days on my pass, then I'll go back to von Kleinst."

She clutched his hand with a sudden urgency. "Thomas, this is a dangerous place. There are shootings nearly everyday or roundups. The SS could pull you off the street, ignore you when you tell them you aren't a Jew. Not to mention the sickness that stalks us—"

He leaned forward to kiss her forehead. "Now that I've found you, you won't be able to get rid of me that easily."

Sophie had a son again. Thomas Picard had found his mother.

32
Wilhelm and Natalie

Though it was the middle of March, a night deep in the purple shadows and mists of a Polish forest allowed little comfort nor conceded any impetuous designs of spring. This night gripped as harshly as a night in January. The two men sat beneath the fringed branches of fir and pine, their bodies directed toward a fire. The older man sat back, appearing relaxed and comfortable, his arms crossed over a barrel chest, his thick legs extended and propped up on the fire's rock perimeter. His gray hair was thick and shaggy, his brows heavy, his face lined and chiseled. Glancing at him, the younger man knew it was this man's deep-brown eyes that saved his face from austerity. The eyes were inquiring and kind. The younger man wore similar, rough, peasant clothes. His face was framed in a brown beard, his cheeks and hands chapped from wind and cold. He looked, in garb and manner, a partisan, as much as black kneeboots, black uniform, and an armband denoted the SS. It was Wilhelm Mueller's newest identity.

A third partisan lay in a bedroll across from the fire, punctuating the night air with his snores. Neither man at the fire seemed to notice. A fourth man was positioned at the top of a ravine, huddled in the cold shadows—a sentry, an ancient, but effective rifle across his knees. With the rock terrain surrounding this camp, an approach must be made past this man who would kill anyone who didn't give the prearranged signal.

Yet a fifth partisan had ventured down the three miles and across the Vistula to Warsaw. He had been gone since just after sunset.

Wilhelm squatted forward and poured himself another cup of the tree-bark coffee. After six weeks he still winced at the first biting taste, but he had finally accepted it. It was warm. As he did so he felt the dizziness that came with any sudden forward movement. He cursed himself. He should know better after this long to move more slowly. Instinctively his hand went to the side of his head. The lump had finally decreased and was now only tender to the touch. His eyes traveled to the direction of the hill where the man he couldn't see stood watch. Willing to risk his life for Wilhelm now, when six weeks ago he had delivered the blow that had almost killed him.

"Saul's a good man, Wilhelm," the older man spoke up smiling while pulling a crusty pipe from his pocket. "He's very zealous for our cause."

Wilhelm was amused that this man seemed to read his thoughts. But his voice betrayed no amusement. "I'll remember Saul's zealousness with my next blinding headache," Wilhelm replied dryly.

Misha chuckled. "He would have clouted you harder if you hadn't been reciting a psalm. He didn't think a Nazi spy would be capable of that."

Wilhelm turned briefly to him. "I know that all of you saved my life ... even though it was a little painful in the process."

"It was Eli who convinced us to trust you. You have him to thank."

Wilhelm nodded. "I have."

Misha yawned deeply and shook his shaggy head. He stretched his hands to the fire, his voice pleasant. He didn't bother to look at Wilhelm. "So, you are in love with this girl that Eli has gone to Warsaw about?"

Wilhelm frowned. He knew Saul and Misha thought he was putting Eli at risk with this personal assignment.

"I figure Eli is a grown man and could have said no. I expect he'll accomplish more than just what I asked."

His voice was tinged in defensiveness, but Misha didn't reply in kind. His voice was still soothing. "I'm not suggesting the risk was not worth it, Wilhelm, not at all. Of all of us, Eli is the most skilled in the city. Love is a strong force that can't be denied. I understand that."

Wilhelm masked his irritation. "The fact is, Misha, I never said I was in love with this girl. She's like a sister to me. I've been trying to find her for years, that's all. I ... I felt I owed it to her grandfather. He was good to me."

Misha nodded. "You've thought about what you will do with what Eli tells you?"

"I've thought a little about it. I'm not sure what I'll do."

"The girl is a Jewish whore to a Nazi. I know you're smart enough to have thought about this—it brought you all the way to Warsaw."

Wilhelm swallowed his anger with effort. It had been the hardest thing of all to tell these four strangers of his very personal, very strange mission from Germany to Poland. He had seen the instant flaring of disgust in their eyes for Natalie Bergmann. But in those early days, after he had finally begun to recover from the blow to the head, he had been forced to tell them everything. It had saved him. These were men who didn't trust easily, who lived with a knife across their own throat as they wielded one at their enemies. They had taken in his incredible story. It had been Saul who demanded that he prove his Jewishness through circumcision and his knowledge of the Torah. Now, after all these weeks, Saul still had a smoldering suspicion toward him.

When Wilhelm slept, it was warily. He was living with a man who would cut his throat in his sleep without a thought. Saul had been indifferent to Wilhelm's joining the group, though he was a help with sentry and foraging he was also another mouth to feed. It had been Misha, and Eli mostly, who had accepted Wilhelm. And though he had been with them for six weeks, he knew this arrangement wouldn't last forever. He was a part of them without really being part of them.

Misha stood up, his voice still conversational. "Well, as long as you understand that what Eli learns tonight for you is very secondary to our purposes. And with you a part of us now ..."

"Yes, I understand."

Misha moved to the wood they had gathered. "I'm going to sleep for awhile. You should too, Wilhelm. Your head is still not completely healed."

He dumped some wood on the fire that sent up a spiral of smoke that made Wilhelm frown. He didn't have the forest ease they had acquired. Every snap of twig or rustle of leaf made him jump. *This fire,* he thought, *could be seen in Warsaw, perhaps all the way to Berlin. It casts up a column of smoke that the children coming out of Egypt could have followed.*

A thin, shrill bird call sounded. Wilhelm sat up straighter. The fifth partisan was coming in from his trip into the city.

•   •   •

The rain came down in torrents, in slanting curtains of silver—blowing, pounding, drenching. From her hotel suite window Natalie Bergmann tried to see the city, but everything was hidden. The world was wet and veiled.

"You would drown out there, little Moses," she said, smiling down at the kitten curled and purring in her arms.

It had been weeks since that shocking night when she had played the violin—the night he had shaken her with his question and she had fainted. He had taken her home and dealt with her with a detached gentleness when she came to. She would never forget that night, but he appeared to have forgotten it. Back at their hotel room he had made no indication that he had put this searching question to her. He was the same weary, preoccupied Hugo. They still slept together, ate together, carried on their simple conversations about books she read or the weather. On rare evenings she would see him smile at the antics of the kitten. Their eyes would meet for just a moment in tenderness, then the blinds would be drawn. He was the same, but she was different.

She no longer went to parties without Hugo, and even then only when he pressured her to go with him, which was rare. If he knew she was a Jewess, then there was the chance someone else would learn it too. Perhaps that was what he was afraid of. So she stayed away from the German nightlife. She took the kitten out each day when weather permitted. She occasionally went walking on the streets close to the hotel but no further. By Hugo's subtle design or her own making, Natalie Bergmann was a prisoner of Warsaw.

On clear days she could look east from her window and see the ragged perimeter of the Jewish ghetto. *That place ... is that where I really belong?* she often wondered.

•   •   •

If Misha was the brains of this small band of Jewish partisans, Eli was the muscle. His round, baby face, near-sighted eyes, and tousled curls belied his strength. Wilhelm had learned that very fast. He was

talkative and amiable—and as hardened as the others. He meant to out-
live these German brutes by every means possible or take as many in his
own death throes as possible. He came to the circle of fire, thrusting out
his hands as he knelt before it. His face was ruddy from the hike out of
Warsaw.

"So you waited up for me, eh?" He reached out and slapped Wilhelm's knee. "You must be in love with this girl."

Misha snorted from his blankets.

Although Wilhelm was tired of this speculation, he was grateful this
young Jewish partisan had not used the harsh epitaph Misha had. Wilhelm poked at the fire with a stick and didn't answer immediately.

"Well, if I am or not, will it matter to what you learned tonight?"

Misha snorted again and Eli chuckled. Wilhelm snapped the stick in
frustration. Eli pushed himself down on the hard-packed earth and
stretching toward the fire.

"I found her."

He gave Wilhelm the courtesy of not staring at his reaction. Eli's eyes
were fastened on the flames.

"Like I told you, I have three excellent contacts in the city. What I
didn't tell you is that one of them is in the Hotel Bristol. I went there first,
which was where I suspected your von Kleinst would live. I was right."

Wilhelm ignored the "your von Kleinst," his body straining forward,
as if by sheer will he could make the young partisan's words come
swifter. Eli was bringing Natalie closer. *If that was still a good thing* . . .

"They live at the Hotel Bristol," Eli repeated. "My contact has seen
the woman with the Nazi lieutenant. She has given her name as Natalie
Jensen. She has dark-brown hair and is very pretty."

He moved his foot against the stones, poking them. In the shadows
Wilhelm could see his frown. He was reluctant. Wilhelm didn't speak. He
wasn't sure what to say. *She really is here. A little over three miles away.
Living with a Nazi.* He had thought the shock of it had muted since
Hilda's words; perhaps Misha's bluntness had resurrected it. A minute of
thought stretched into five minutes of silence as the moon rose higher and
the fire snapped and crumbled.

Wilhelm drew a ragged breath. "All right, what else?"

Only now did Eli look at him steadily for the first time. "Von Kleinst
is the administrator of the Jewish ghetto, Wilhelm. That is what he was

brought from Munich for. He controls the starvation of our people. He is controlling the cattle cars that are taking Jews to their death."

Wilhelm felt as if he had been punched with the same force that Saul had delivered to the side of his skull. He had hoped von Kleinst was a minor Nazi official. He had never imagined this. *Natalie was mistress to an executioner.*

"I don't know what to say," he finally managed. His head hung low. *Natalie . . .*

"I'm sorry, Wilhelm. I know you've covered a lot of miles looking for her. It would be better if you forgot this girl. You have a place here with us."

● ● ●

This new life had given Abraham Goldstein a fresh appreciation for the night sky. It was as if he hadn't really noticed it back on Blumenstrasse. But now, it had come to represent continuity to him. This same starry heaven and luminescent moon hung over his family wherever they were. And this nighttime canopy gave Abraham Goldstein a feeling of peace, a calming to his anguished soul. It was a nocturnal tonic against the horrors of the day and the days to come. But he hardly noticed the sky as he hurried stealthily to the underground meeting.

He had been chosen for this dangerous assignment for several reasons. First, he had demonstrated his calm cool-headedness. He had shown his ingenuity by bluffing his Nazi captors soon after his arrival to Treblinka. The SS had stormed into the barracks looking for men skilled as roofers. The vast camp was still in the construction stages and needed many Jewish labors. The music store accountant had stood up and stoutly declared he had been a roofer in Munich before his internment.

"You better be good," the SS had barked.

It had been a lie even Sophie would have approved of. He was no longer expendable. He now had a permit to move more freely between the camp sections. The leaders of the underground had taken these assets and selected him for this most important task they had ever undertaken. If he failed, if he was caught, it would be instant death.

After a brief greeting, they handed Abraham his tool. They studied his reaction with eager faces. It appeared to be a camera, but for a Jewish prisoner it might as well have been a machine gun. Abraham turned it over slowly in his hands. It was a fine camera already loaded with film.

He didn't need to ask how it had been obtained. The victims of Europe had to deposit their valuables just inside the Treblinka gate. The warehouses were full of such treasures.

Abraham finally looked up, his face and voice betraying no emotion. "What am I to take pictures of?"

For an answer they doused the light and led him to the window. A pale hand pulled back the cloth. Even against the night sky the smoke from the crematoriums made a gray shadow that rose steadily and ominously. Every Jew of Treblinka knew the truth.

The shade dropped back in place. They didn't bother to light the lamp. Though a sentry was posted, their voices dropped to conspiratorial whispers.

"We got this assignment from Warsaw four weeks ago. And we are going to show them we can be counted on to pull it off."

"All right," Abraham said slowly.

"The roof of the crematorium is going to be damaged. We have the people in place to do it. That will mean you will have to be brought in for repair."

"I can't smuggle this in with my roofing tools. They look in it all the time, making certain that I haven't made a weapon. But," Abraham smiled one of his rare smiles, "I'm sure you have already thought of that."

"The crematorium doesn't have its own kitchen for the staff who work there. They bring the stuff in. Your camera will be in the false bottom of one of these kettles. We have already had it made and tested against leaking. It's ready to go. Once you're in, one of our people will slip you the camera. You put it in your jacket, take the pictures, get it back to the kitchen. They take it out. Your part is over."

"I am taking pictures of the people entering the gas chambers?" Abraham asked with a pounding heart.

They all nodded solemnly.

Abraham weighed the camera in his hand. Finally he looked up. "It will be an honor."

The day had come. Abraham appeared his usual unflustered self, but inside he was nervous with excitement. He cared little for his own safety—to live through this inferno was highly improbable, thousands were perishing daily in the chambers that worked without interruption. Even those like him who serviced the compounds were not without peril.

The Nazis regularly sent them to the pyres: The witnesses to this madness must be silenced. They had given him this task with only two days notice to quell his own nerves. In those two days Abraham had come to the realization that he wanted desperately to accomplish this mission.

If I am consumed by the fire, if I never see my family again, I can die knowing I did something to help my people. Something to silence the Nazi lies. I'm going to help tell the world the truth, he declared to himself.

The day dawned clear and crisp. Just after ten in the morning, he appeared at the gate to the crematorium compound. The guard examined the tools and tar. He glared at Abraham.

"You know where you are, swine?"

"Yes, Herr Commandant."

"I want you to stay at your job like a dog chained to a post. You stray for one minute and you won't come out of here alive, understand swine?" He fingered the sten gun in its holster.

"Yes, Herr Commandant."

The guard turned to meet a new transport. Just past the corner of the building Abraham was slipped the camera. He pushed it into his jacket with trembling fingers. He climbed the ladder to the roof. He sat the bucket down and proceeded to repair the building. He kept his eyes glued to the roof. Sweat made his thin shirt cling to him like a second skin. Though the stench from the nearby chimneys was great, he drew a deep, steadying breath. He thought of his younger brother Jacob, and it calmed him. He even smiled at the thought. *Jacob would be very surprised if he could see his mild-tempered, academic brother in such an adventurer's pose. Jacob . . . Papa.*

He looked back the way he had come. The guard was still in the distance. Abraham looked back to the roof and smeared the tar. Then he laid his brush down and looked north toward the crematorium. He had enlarged the middle buttonhole of his shirt to push the lens through, but his fingers seemed frozen. A crowd of naked women, perhaps a hundred, were being herded toward the chamber. Their cries of fright reached him. He snapped the picture. He turned slightly to the huge pile of corpses being burned.

After he was done with the repair, he went down the ladder and passed the camera quickly to outstretched hands. The guard eyed him at the gate.

"You look pale, swine. The work too hard?"

"No, Herr Commandant. The heat . . . but I'm all right."

But it took several hours for Abraham Goldstein to stop shaking.

• • •

The past few days had given Natalie Bergmann the hope that spring might be permitted to this wasteland. Now she needed only a light jacket when she carried Moses down for his daily time in the hotel garden. The garden was like the rest of the city—a memory of its former glory. The German landlords found no need to keep the garden; the Polish slaves had no time or energy. So the acre was merely an enclosure of manicured shrubs and roses in need of pruning and flower beds that had died long ago. The lawn was weed-choked and dead. One end of the garden had been turned into a trash dump. But Natalie had found her own little path through the ruins, past a carriage barn, away from the eyes of the hotel. She rarely saw anyone, occasionally a hotel employee dumping trash or a tradesman making a delivery. But that was rare. Most often she took the hour alone, the kitten exploring the gnarled trees and leaping at her from the bushes. Little Moses always came when she called him.

She sat on an old stone bench and watched her pet.

Somewhere to her left, from the corner of her eye, she saw a shadow, a movement. But she didn't bother to turn. Whoever or whatever it was would go away.

Wilhelm Mueller stood rooted, gripped as he had always known he would be at the first sight of her. They had tried to persuade him with arguments, then came the cursing. They told him it was suicidal to go to her. They told him she was not worth the great risk.

His voice had been quietly calm. "I've come this far. I'm not going to turn back now. I know all the risks. I know what she's done. But I know what I have to do. This won't bring any danger to you. If I don't come back, then you know I've failed and you will carry on."

"We have helped you, fool!" Saul spat. "You have eaten our food—"

"Everything I have eaten, I have helped you get," Wilhelm returned tightly.

"If you return, you will be given an assignment to test your loyalty," Saul said.

"I will return."

Eli had walked with him to the clearing.

"You think I'm a fool too," Wilhelm commented.

Eli smiled and patted his back. "Yes." He shrugged, "But we are all fools from time to time. Maybe these days more than most. God go with you, my friend."

"I'll be back tonight. Don't let Saul have my share of stew."

She was sitting with the sunlight falling upon her, and even at this distance he could see the look of sadness on her fine features. *Hilda had spoken only too sparingly. She had said lovely. This young woman was beautiful.* Wilhelm staggered. *This . . . this could not be the mistress of the Nazi.*

She tossed a stick at something, and Wilhelm saw a kitten pounce from behind a tree. The young woman smiled, and her face was transformed. It was the Natalie of Munich, the girl with the violin, the girl he had skated with.

A movement caught her eye and now she turned. A man stood thirty feet from her. And he was walking slowly toward her.

She hadn't forgotten him. His skates were still in the wooden chest in her hotel room. But she had never expected to see him again. He had vanished on that terrible night seven years ago. *But . . . this . . . this older man in such plain, worn clothes looked so much like him. He . . .*

He stopped six feet away and said her name.

"Hello, Natalie."

She stood up. She could feel the roaring blackness she had experienced that night with Hugo. She reached out to the tree trunk and steadied herself.

She paled and he spoke quickly.

"Please don't be frightened."

But she only stared at him, speechless.

"Do you know me, Natalie? I'm Wilhelm Mueller. We . . . remember when I came to your house in Nuremberg?"

In all his planning he had never really rehearsed a speech for what he would say if he ever finally found her. Suddenly he thought of Hilda and wished she were beside him. She would certainly have the words. The thought made him smile.

The smile brought back the memory of Nuremberg—the meals, the game of chess, the flashing smile. *Yes, this was Wilhelm Mueller, the young man I had known. There really is no escaping the past,* she thought. *I've always known that.* She sat down very slowly.

"Wilhelm Mueller," she said at last.

There was a flatness to her voice that he couldn't translate—except it seemed to fit the weary sadness in her eyes. Painful as it was to see, it stirred some kind of nameless hope in him.

"I really am sorry that I've startled you. If there had been some way to prepare you ..."

The kitten leaped into her lap and her hands enclosed it absently.

"I ... don't know what to say."

He nodded, smiling again. "I understand."

"This can't ... be an accident ... that you are ... here. I mean ..."

"Yes, I knew you came to this place every day."

"But how?"

"I'm with a group of partisans in the forest west of Warsaw. One of them has a contact here in the hotel."

Natalie had been stunned at Wilhelm's appearance, now she felt very afraid. He saw the look.

"You aren't being watched or anything like that. I just ... I had this man inquire around and find out. He was very discreet."

"You were looking for me?"

He nodded.

"How did you know ... to look here in the hotel?"

He wet his lips. "I had von Kleinst's name. I knew you were in Warsaw. Hilda told me."

She swallowed with difficulty then looked down to the kitten. Her voice was barely above a whisper.

"Leave me, Wilhelm Mueller. Please go away."

He had expected this reaction. He crouched in front of her, pulling at the dead grass. He was silent.

"It is dangerous here for you. Go back to your group in the forest." Still she didn't look up.

His voice was very calm and steady though he didn't feel either.

"I will go back, but not before I've said what I came here for. You're going to have to listen."

She stood up; her face was flaming. She clutched the kitten to her. He could see the tears in her eyes.

"Leave, Wilhelm, leave me!"

"No, not yet."

"I'll scream—someone from the hotel will come."

"No, you won't do that," he returned firmly. Their eyes locked before she looked away.

"Now listen to me. I have to leave this area for a few days. So I won't be back tomorrow. But I will be back in one week, same time ... and I want you here waiting ... for me. We'll talk again."

"We have nothing to talk about," she whispered.

"You're wrong. We do," he smiled. "You're growing up has made you stubborn."

Still she didn't meet his eyes. His voice gentled and he took a step forward.

"Look, I know this has been a great shock for you. I'm sorry I couldn't make it easier for you, but there it is. I think ... I think as far as I've come ... and all I've been through, you should let me speak."

"As far as you've come," she repeated dully. "Why have you come?"

Now he couldn't meet her gaze for a moment. *Deceptions, evasion, concealing truths* ... He looked back to her.

He was as nervous as a groom. "Well, I guess it's time for me to ... face the truth. In the States they call it 'fessing up.' I've come here to Warsaw ... to find you. For your grandfather ... whom I loved like a father, to save you from ..." He made an impatient gesture with his hand. He cleared his throat. "And because seven years ago I fell in love with you."

33
When There Are No Words

March 1943, Berlin

He didn't see the reaction on her face. He had turned and walked away. Spring had finally staked its claim in Germany. And though Emilie Farber sat where sunlight splashed across her, she felt a penetrating chill. Elaina Heydrich sat opposite her in an ornate, gold-patterned chair that Emilie thought exactly suited this slender, polished, decorous woman. But for all her elegance, her words to Emilie had been imbued with compassion and her own sorrow that she couldn't hide. They were vastly different women in looks, in temperament, in background. But they shared a love for the man in Tegel prison. Sitting there in Elaina's parlor, Emilie realized Max's old friend still loved him. It didn't threaten her now—that was over. She felt a sadness for this woman who seemed for all her wealth to have so very little. The unspoken knowledge that Elaina still loved Max gave Emilie some comfort. Elaina had lost Max as she, Emilie, had. But there was Morgan, living and growing and reminding Emilie daily that their love hadn't been a dream.

Elaina looked down at her jeweled hands clasped in her lap. Emilie could see her cool composure was shaken. Impulsively Emilie reached across and squeezed her hand.

The tears spilled over. Her voice came in undignified gasps. "I'm ... so ... sorry, Emilie."

Emilie managed to smile. It was good to hear her first name. Perhaps she had a friend here in Berlin at last, before she left Germany.

Emilie looked down at her own lap. Though she thought she had been prepared, upon hearing the words she found there was really no preparation for this. Tegel prison had been heavily damaged in another Allied bombing over the capital city's industrial sector. Two entire blocks of the old prison had collapsed. The Nazis were slow and apathetic in sorting through the destruction and chaos. There was no trace of Maximillian Farber. Presumed dead. Entombed as the prisoners had feared.

Elaina pulled a small envelope from the pocket of her dress. "When I saw ... your son a few weeks ago it reminded me of this. Max gave it to me years ago when we had a party where everyone had to identify each other from baby photos. He let me keep this."

Emilie pulled the sepia-tinted print from the envelope. A little boy sitting in a pony-drawn cart, smiling broadly. It was Max; it was Morgan.

"I ... I haven't been able to find any photographs of Max this young," Emilie said softly.

"There's another picture," Elaina pointed out.

A photograph of a boy of twelve in summer shorts and shirt, holding a fishing pole, proudly displaying a fish as he squinted at the camera. A man in whites and a straw hat, smiling, was standing with his arm around the boy. It was Josef.

Emilie leaned forward and they hugged. They cried together.

"What are you going to do now, Emilie? How can I help you?"

Emilie looked around the room and sighed. She looked once more at the treasured photographs. "You have done so much already, Elaina. I think Max would be pleased we're friends." "I think it's time I leave Germany. Perhaps you can help me with that."

• • •

Wilhelm had expected a challenging assignment from the partisans. He had not anticipated this. They had drilled him for two days on the roads, the surrounding terrain, the enemy movements, the local population from Warsaw to the concentration camp of Treblinka. He would appear as a Polish laborer.

"The Germans—"

"I'm German," Wilhelm pointed out with mock severity.

Misha had pulled at his beard and Eli had winked at him. Saul's face was set in a perpetual scowl.

"The Nazis are fanatical about road repairs and keeping things tidy," Misha said shaking his great head. "If they took such energy from killing Jews they might be winning this war instead of stalling in it."

"You want them to win?" Saul snapped irritably.

"We're getting off the point here," Wilhelm said as they bent over the crudely drawn map.

"Right. Now. You will slip into the line of road workers, Wilhelm."

"I won't have any tools."

"Ingenuity will get you some," Saul said.

They all ignored him.

"The package will already be out of the camp. The guard will be looking for you. I've already told you his description and the passwords."

Wilhelm stood up, scratching his head. "That's the worst part of this. Approaching a guard."

Misha nodded. "But there's no other way. It was supposed to go out when a food shipment came in but that fell through for some reason."

Eli took up the instructions. "Then you must slip back out of the line, back into the forest, back here." His eyes were riveted on Wilhelm. "You understand what you're carrying?"

Wilhelm nodded. He understood.

"If you're caught, you must do everything to destroy the film. If the Nazis find out there will be a massacre in Treblinka—worse than what they have already done. They will raze the place to get to the underground."

"I understand."

"If they torture you—" Saul began.

"I said I understand."

Eli's voice had been abrupt. "This assignment is too important for one man. I'm going with Wilhelm."

The others started an immediate protest, but one look from the young man silenced them.

Hiding out in the day, walking at night, Wilhelm was grateful for Eli's presence. He ran and hid and foraged with obvious skill. They passed within yards of an SS camp and remained hidden. The last night they camped within sight of the sprawling compound. They surveyed the scene on their stomachs from a nearby hill under the cover of sunset. Wilhelm would never forget the sight or smell. He rolled over on his back to face the starry night. Eli's shoulder wedged against his.

"No one will believe this," Wilhelm whispered. "I've seen it and I still can't."

Eli's voice was filled with a harshness that would have matched Saul's.

"They will have to believe the pictures."

"Eli, if something happens tomorrow—"

"I will go to the Hotel Bristol and tell the girl."

Wilhelm closed his eyes and began to pray.

He had shaved and Eli had trimmed his hair the first time he had gone to see Natalie, but now he was hardly thinking of his appearance. Now his face was shadowed with new beard, his eyes sunken, almost glazed. Natalie was nearly as shocked as she had been the first day. He was already at the bench when she slowly walked to him.

He looked up fleetingly.

"Thanks for coming," he said quietly.

He didn't move or offer her the seat.

"You are ill?" she asked at last.

"No, I'm just very tired. The last few days . . . have been long."

She wore an ice-blue dress, her hair was gathered with a bow. But he didn't notice her loveliness this time. He sat in silence, staring at the ground as if he had forgotten why he had come.

Natalie was alarmed. *He looked like . . .* Her hand went to her slender neck when she realized he looked like the young men she had seen entering the ghetto. *Hollow-eyed, ragged, gaunt, yet like a bow string pulled tightly. Fierce.* Finally he looked up at her.

"You've . . . thought about what I told you last week?"

His voice had a boyish quality. The old Wilhelm, hunted and desperate back in the Nuremberg days. Suddenly she saw him. *Will this man ever find peace, find safety?*

"I . . . I have thought of little else."

She was standing and he was sitting, and he finally noticed it. He stood up swiftly then swayed, groping out. Natalie hurried forward, taking his arm, steadying him.

"You are ill!"

He shook his head. "Just an old wound." He fingered the place on his head and closed his eyes. "You sit, I'm fine."

"No, Wilhelm, you need the bench."

His eyes opened. "Well, that's the second time you have said my name. We're making progress."

"You are keeping count of how many times I say your name?" she asked with unexpected lightness.

"I take it as hope," he returned with a slight smile, looking into her eyes.

She turned away.

"It is dangerous for you, coming into Warsaw, coming here. I wish you wouldn't," she said stiffly.

He sat down on the grass; she on the bench.

"We have a lot of things to talk about Natalie, but not much time to do it. Things are abbreviated for us; there isn't anything we can do about that. So we can't waste time with you saying things like you wish I wouldn't come. I'm coming until the Nazis take me or you come away with me."

Her eyes widened.

He leaned forward. "Yes, that's what it comes down to. It's what I told Hilda I would do. It's why I left Germany. I've been looking for you for years, Natalie. I want you to leave von Kleinst and come with me."

She stood up in agitation. "I can't go with you."

"Why?"

"I just can't. I'm leaving for Berlin in the morning." She couldn't say von Kleinst's name as easily as Wilhelm did. "I must."

He stood, his face flushed. His voice spared no patience.

"Again, why?"

"He . . . he has been called there for a sudden meeting with Himmler." She looked to the ground, avoiding his piercing gaze. "He wants me to go. We will come back."

"It would be a perfect time for you to leave him, a perfect time!"

She looked up, tears streaming down her face.

"Wilhelm, you have come . . ."

"Say it. I've come after you and you're telling me no thanks, take a leap."

"Please."

He gripped her shoulders. "You're making me say this, Natalie Bergmann. He isn't for you, maybe I'm not either. But this isn't you, this life, and you know it. I told you before I wasn't going to give up so easily, so you might as well understand that," he said harshly. He dropped his hands and took a step back. "It was one of the things your grandfather liked about me, my persistence."

"He loved you," she replied, avoiding his look.

Wilhelm looked toward the hotel. "I have to go now." He looked back at her. "Maybe you should trust his judgment."

They were a melancholy group sitting under the trees. The sun was high; there was no need for fire. The four sat at the top of the ravine looking toward Warsaw where Saul had just come from. They sat in stunned silence for several minutes. He had brought the news.

The Germans had found and executed the small Jewish underground of David Szmulewski. It made them feel their own mortality. They sat on the hill, ragged and hungry and hunted. How much longer could they all survive? This, on top of Eli's recent death, made them feel an overwhelming sense of loss.

Misha spoke finally. "Well, so this changes things. We've lost our contact to pass the film to. We just have to find another one."

Saul suddenly, savagely kicked at Wilhelm. Wilhelm was on his feet, his fist drawn back.

Misha was on his feet as well. "That's enough! That will not help." He shoved the two away. Saul swore. "He shouldn't have been allowed to go with Eli! He shouldn't have been allowed to join us in the first place!"

"Saul, you are not irreplaceable," Misha growled as he fingered the long knife in his belt. "Leave Wilhelm alone. It was not his fault. Now the thing that matters is the film. We have it, and Eli died to get it and Wilhelm put his own life on the line, and now we must get it to the right hands."

"Yes, let's just march down into the city and wave down one of those Red Cross trucks!" Saul snarled.

They sat for another five minutes in silence. Wilhelm leaned back in the sunshine as if he was dozing. But he wasn't. His mind was like a reel of spinning film, each frame stark and vivid and unforgettable ... Eli as they had run down the road with the sound of the German guns barking at their backs ... everything had gone so well until that final moment. In the woods Eli had slumped down without a last word. Wilhelm had dug into his jacket pocket for the package. Then he had stumbled to his feet and ran. Eli's eyes looking up, lifeless, to the trees.

Then Natalie in her pretty blue dress.

Wilhelm sat up suddenly, ignoring the spinning. He looked down at Warsaw before he turned to Misha. "I know how we can get the film out." He looked over at the simmering partisan. "Though of course Saul won't like it."

The man was so nervous the tea tray was rattling in his hands. He was pale and Natalie could see beads of sweat above his lip. He didn't want to meet eyes with her, yet when they did, they were pleading. He stood in the doorway to the hotel suite, dressed in the very plain uniform of the hotel staff. Natalie had seen him passing between the kitchen and dining room, but never above the first floor. He glanced back down the empty hall.

"I'm sorry but I didn't order tea," Natalie said kindly.

"Could I please bring the tray in," he asked as if he hadn't heard her.

She moved to let him pass. He hurried in, almost spilling the tray before he found the table. He turned around.

"The man in the garden said you might want tea."

Then he hurried from the room. Natalie looked at the mantel clock. Hugo should be back within the hour.

He looked the same, yet different. The same clothes and stubble of beard, the same restless energy, but not so weary. Resolved. They measured each other in silence.

"I'm sorry to take the risk to contact you that way, but it is important," he said curtly.

"What is wrong?"

"Are you still leaving for Berlin in the morning?"

She nodded slowly.

"Please sit down. Please."

He paced for a moment, thinking, looking toward the hotel. She watched him in wonder.

"I can't stay long." She hoped he understood without pressing her.

"Yes ... well ..." He stood before her, hands thrust in his pockets—a posture she remembered well from Nuremberg. She was finding in one week she had forgotten very little about this man.

"Natalie, I need you to do something for me. Actually, for ... our people."

She winced inwardly. He didn't seem to notice.

"I need you to take this to Berlin." He pulled a small cloth-covered package from his inner pocket. "People have risked their lives to get this." He looked away a moment and she could see the pain fill his eyes. "When I went last week ... away ... I went north to the camp at Treblinka." He licked his lips. He sighed. He looked at her deeply. "I saw ..." He turned away again, kicking at the dirt.

"The man who went with me was killed by the Nazis. I ... I survived. Again."

She paled.

"Natalie, these are pictures of what is going on in the camps—the slaughter. The Jews inside managed to get pictures. We need them smuggled to Berlin."

"But how?" she whispered.

"You with ... your escort. It's the safest way. When you get to Berlin, go to Tiergartenstrasse, number seven. There is a woman there, Frau Emilie Farber. She is an American and she has connections. Tell her what this is. If anyone can get it out, she can." He shrugged. "It's our best hope."

Time seemed suspended as he watched her wrestling with her thoughts. She could walk away as she had done years before. But this time she stretched out her hand toward him.

Berlin

She felt like a stranger in this house now. Too many rooms, too much silence, too many memories. It had been too long since the master of the house had roamed here. Everything was tidy and yet barren. His clothes hung in the closet, his silver comb and brush lay on the dresser, his desk quite neat, but his touch had long since departed. It was a hollow place. She didn't have Josef to hope for or tend to. She couldn't stay here. Morgan would have to learn of Germany from America.

Emilie had returned to Berlin. Someday the war would be over. She would return to Germany then and tie up all the loose ends of her life. Now it was better to leave. To start life with her son in Georgetown in America.

She sat on the stairs in the quiet house; Morgan was sleeping on his little cot in the library. She had sat here so many times. Josef had teased her many times.

"Are you going up or down?" he'd say.

"I couldn't decide so I'm taking the middle ground, Uncle Josef," was her reply.

"No middle ground now," she said aloud. And the tears came again. "I'm leaving Germany."

She hung her head. Nothing had happened quite like she planned.

Percy thrust his cold nose into her face whining. She threw her arms around him.

"Max always said you were a well-traveled dog. Well, we shall see how you do on the big boat. Now, you won't be chasing any rich lady's poodles, all right? Those really are dogs."

The doorbell pealed, which sent Percy into a wild fit of barking. Morgan began a companion squall above her. She raced to get him. Back down the stairs, she looked fleetingly in the foyer mirror. Perhaps it was Elaina with word on their visas.

Emilie was struck by her fragile beauty. It was not Elaina. This woman was young and very classic-looking in her tailored clothes. Her blue eyes looked at Emilie only briefly. She was watching Morgan, who reached a chubby hand to her. Finally she spoke in a low, hesitant voice.

"Frau Farber? Emilie Farber?"

"Yes."

She exhaled loudly and her eyes closed in relief. Then came a smile that nearly dazzled Emilie.

"I'm so glad!"

"I'm afraid I—"

Natalie reached out a slender hand. "No, you shouldn't recognize me. But we have a mutual . . . friend."

"Please step in."

Emilie hadn't gotten over her fear of Gestapo or SS surveillance. She closed the door firmly.

Morgan was still reaching for the visitor. "He is a very pretty baby. Oh, I suppose I should say handsome."

Emilie smiled. "It's all right. I think he's pretty too." She glanced around. The rooms were so dark. "I . . . well, I know it's very unconventional, but I was sitting here on the stairs. Please join me."

They sat together, Emilie, with Morgan in her arms, a little higher than Natalie. Percy kept guard at the door.

"I haven't had visitors here in so long, I never open up the rooms much. It's just Morgan and me, and we don't take much space."

Natalie was watching the baby with shy looks. She startled herself. "I always wanted a baby brother." She stretched out a finger, which Morgan locked on to.

Emilie laughed. "Careful. He's going to taste it."

They sat in comfortable silence for several minutes. Emilie could sense this young stranger rarely had these peaceful moments.

Natalie looked up and caught Emilie's gaze.

"I'm sorry. I should be telling you about myself. I'm Natalie Bergmann. Our friend is Wilhelm Mueller."

"Wilhelm! You have seen him?"

"Just a few days ago. In Warsaw, Poland."

"Poland!" Immediately her mind conjured up the horror stories she had heard of this occupied land. "Is he . . ."

"He was fine when I saw him. He is with a small band of Jewish partisans that operate outside of Warsaw."

Emilie was shaking her head in disbelief. "When I saw him . . . let's see, nearly four years ago, he was going to Munich looking for a girl." She laughed. "Will certainly gets around." She was surprised at the veiled look of pain that dropped over the pretty girl. She blinked and leaned forward, touching Natalie's shoulder.

"You're the girl?"

Natalie nodded.

Emilie stood, taking her hand. "Come along to the kitchen. We need tea."

They sat across from each other, Emilie still wide-eyed with surprise; Natalie pale as she struggled with the narrative. She told her only briefly about Wilhelm. Nothing about herself.

"He came to me four days ago in Warsaw. He had been to Treblinka. That is a concentration camp north of Warsaw. It is one of many camps where they send Jews."

"I've heard rumors of those places."

"The rumors are true," Natalie said steadily. "Wilhelm went there on the request of other underground groups. He got a package of film of what is going on . . . inside. The Jewish prisoners took these." She pulled the package from her purse and put it on the table between them. "The pictures are . . . They will tell the world."

Another long silence passed with only the sound of Morgan's fist-chewing.

"His contact to take the film, to pass it all the way out of Poland to London ... something happened. He thought of you. He said if anyone can get it out for us, Emilie Farber can."

Emilie stared at the tiny gray box. To take it would put the baby in her arms at risk. *If the Nazis found this on me ...*

"He wants me to smuggle again," she smiled wryly.

"Excuse me?"

Emilie shook her head, frowning. "He has great faith in my ability to trust me with this," she said slowly, as if to herself.

"It is very important to our people that the world know that—" She stopped, and her hands covered her mouth in shock.

"You are a Jew, Natalie?" Emilie asked gently.

Her voice was hoarse. "God cannot forgive me."

Emilie was startled again. Her eyebrows knit together a moment.

"God *can* forgive you. He loves you."

Natalie's head was bowed in silence.

"Ask me again, Frau Farber, ask me."

"What? You mean ... Are you a Jew, Natalie Bergmann?"

"I am a Jew."

"And God loves you very much."

34
Thomas and Maria

Maria, we have to talk."

There was no misunderstanding her mother's tone. Maria knew what was coming. She had expected it with the same certainty of waking up and looking down into the ghetto. Night hadn't changed the streets to Blumenstrasse, nor her mother from being persistent and blunt.

Still she offered an alibi. "Mama, I'll be late to the school."

Sophie's crossed arms and thunderous brows broached no excuses. She waved at the table she had just scrubbed, the table she had shared with Thomas less than twenty-four hours earlier. "Be late. Sit down here."

They sat across from each other. "Now."

"Mama—"

"How could you be so unspeakably rude to Thomas Picard yesterday?"

"Mama—"

"You were colder to him than my feet you say feel like ice in bed! Far ruder than Frau Hager on Blumenstrasse ever was!"

"Mama, I'm old enough to have my opinions," Maria said with matching tartness.

"Your opinions, ha! Like politics or the way Zelda wears her hair? No. I don't want your opinions, Maria. I'm asking you to tell me what the matter is. Talk to me, daughter of mine."

There was something plaintive in Sophie's voice that caught at Maria. In that moment she realized how much her mother must suffer in loneliness for her father. Half of her soul had been taken away. He had been the one whom she had talked so endlessly to. Now Maria understood this amputation. This was what it would be like to lose someone you loved so deeply.

"Why did you do that to him, Maria?" Sophie asked in a gentler tone.

But Maria couldn't speak. The sight of Thomas had stirred a strange conflict—a blending of comfort and hurt.

"I don't know if I can explain it to you, Mama. Seeing him . . . seeing him brings back a lot of hurt. I felt like he betrayed our family when we needed him most. He clung to his church that was hating us. I don't know, Mama. I don't understand what I'm feeling."

She stood up and walked to the grimy window that looked to the street. Three young boys were trying to play kickball with a wad of rags. *Racing and laughing, so thin and pale. What had Daniel said? "There is more to life than just survival?" Is there? Is there a chance for more? Dare I hope for more? For love? For a future beyond the bloodstained walls of this place?*

Sophie sat with restrained calmness. There in profile, with her poor clothes and cut hair, her daughter still stirred her pride. And stirred her hope that she would survive this terrible place with her faith—and the best of the Goldstein memories.

Maria stared at the boys as she spoke. "They remind me of Rudi and Jacob in a way . . . so eager. They don't care that in a few hours the Nazis may march in to take them away."

She turned to face her mother. Her voice was low, and she was trying very hard not to cry. "Mama, I see Thomas and he . . . he brings back all the past. Sometimes I wish there was no past so that . . . so that now wouldn't hurt so bad. I'm twenty-seven years old, and I still feel like a child sometimes."

She came and sat back down. They held hands.

"Maria, listen to me. I have to tell you these things because I know he won't. How can you say he betrayed us? He renounced the church. He's been running the store. He helped Isaac leave Germany."

"He has seen Isaac?" Maria gasped.

Sophie nodded. "Seen him and helped him leave Germany for safety. He moved our things into his house to prevent the Nazis from stealing more, so we could have them when we got back. And Maria, he came here, with all the dangers. He left Gretchen when he got my letter. If that doesn't prove his love for us, what can? He came!"

"Mama, I understand what you're saying and I want to ... forgive him. But I have to have a little time."

Sophie stood up. Aaron would have been proud and a little surprised at her restraint. She didn't voice her concern to her daughter. Time might be the thing here in the ghetto of Warsaw, Poland, that they had very little of.

• • •

The Hotel Bristol dining room was not as fine as it once had been, but it still retained a little elegance that satisfied the sensibilities of the many German officers who dined there. A chef had been brought from Berlin. To Hugo von Kleinst, who had grown up in the lap of luxury, it was a small oasis of finery in a city of rubble. With that perspective he had invited Thomas Picard to lunch. The SS lieutenant welcomed the opportunity to leave his stuffy office that overlooked the ghetto.

The dining room was crowded with men in uniform, all greeting von Kleinst with deference. Thomas couldn't miss the looks of curiosity they gave him. Seeing Picard's nervousness amused the SS man. He led him to a small linen-covered table.

"I hope you don't mind meeting here, Herr Picard, instead of in my office."

"No, of course not."

Thomas glanced over the menu—and thought of the starving children he had walked past only hours ago. He looked up and found von Kleinst's eyes upon him.

"You had a pleasant trip to Berlin?" Thomas asked.

"Pleasant enough, I suppose."

The flatness in his voice alerted Thomas again to some inner turmoil in this man. But his face was so polished Nazi, so perfectly controlled and, at times, hard.

They ordered and Hugo leaned back, eyeing the young man openly.

"And your trip into the Jewish quarter, Herr Picard?"

"I would say it wasn't equal to my expectations."

"Your search for musical instruments didn't meet with success?"

Thomas could sense he was being tested. He had been brought here for lunch when a message from the secretary would have sufficed. *His tone. The man was about to spring the trap.* He would spring it first. Better to lay the truth out.

"The fact is, Lieutenant von Kleinst, that I didn't come to Warsaw to look for instruments. I came to find two people."

"Two people. Why didn't you explain this when you first came?"

"These days we do not always ... encourage the truth, sir. I wanted to find these old friends very much."

"Quite a risk, quite a lot of travel for this search for old friends."

"Yes."

"Tell me about them."

Thomas hesitated. He was looking into the eyes of the executioner.

"A woman and her daughter. They were my neighbors in Munich."

"That would be Blumenstrasse, Pastor Picard?"

Thomas smiled and exhaled. "Yes."

"You knew I would look into your background."

"Yes."

"Then you can explain this search for you by a Gestapo chief named Otto Beck."

"I cannot, sir, honestly explain why my uncle searches for me."

Hugo leaned back. "You lied to me on your purposes here. You have likely smuggled things in and out of the ghetto. You are wanted in Germany. You are in an uncomfortable position, Herr Picard."

"I have taken small items of food into the ghetto. I have taken nothing out."

Von Kleinst was impressed with the young man's quiet courage. Their food came and Hugo talked of music as if the previous conversation hadn't taken place. Thomas tried to eat and pray and talk and listen.

Their lunch over, they lingered in the now-emptying dining room. Thomas could sense this man had no desire to hurry back to work.

"What are your plans now that you have found your two neighbors?"

"I've been around Warsaw long enough to see there are children on the streets. Polish children. There is a man, a priest trying to establish an orphanage outside the city. He is old and needs help. I'd like to stay and help him."

Von Kleinst toyed with his silverware, his voice bland. "I remind you, Herr Picard, smuggling Jewish children is a serious offense. The SS guards shoot without question."

"Yes, I have witnessed that," Thomas replied gravely.

Hugo's glass hesitated to his mouth. Now it was Picard's turn to give this man a penetrating stare.

"You want to continue to enter the ghetto?" he asked slowly.

"With your permission, yes."

"I'll grant you another week's pass, then you can report back to me. The same risks exist for you."

They walked out to the sidewalk. Hugo was pulling on his gloves.

"You must ... feel a great deal for these ... two ... friends."

"Yes, I do. They are like family to me."

"The ghetto is being emptied, Herr Picard," he said sharply. "You do understand that."

"Yes, Lieutenant, I understand."

They stood in the spring sunshine, only a few feet apart. Hugo von Kleinst peered at him critically. "Do you despise me, Herr Picard?"

Thomas was genuinely surprised. Von Kleinst would never forget the look on his face.

"Why no, Lieutenant, not at all. I'm praying for you."

Thomas had spoken truthfully when he said he had found his two friends. But von Kleinst hadn't forced him to admit the obvious—that they were Jews. Thomas considered this significant. He was also relieved and grateful the Nazi hadn't demanded more of his ghetto observations. Because of von Kleinst's trip to Berlin, Thomas now had spent almost a month of daily trips inside the walled city. He knew of the starvation rations as well as the Nazi masters who planned them from their impeccable desks. He watched the deportations on the crowded cattle cars, the sudden street roundups, and he saw what the twisted dream of Ayran supremacy really meant. The thought that he had stood with other men who supported this descent into evil threatened at times to bend and break him with guilt.

While daily life was truly a moment-by-moment survival, through Sophie he found the fuller life of the ghetto. He learned that von Kleinst had allowed the Jews to conduct plays, put on revues, and have concerts. There were five different symphonies in the ghetto using the instruments that had been left to them. As in any metropolitan city, there were evening lectures on scientific and literary themes. There were libraries. Von Kleinst had forbidden schools, yet they flourished in secret. All the religious observances were kept with spartan implements but zealous spirits. This activity surprised Thomas. It pleased and encouraged him and filled him with a new respect for these tormented people. It also saddened him. They were doomed, and there was so very little he could do. Now that he had found Sophie and Maria, how could he save them? The question plagued him at night in his hotel room, sending him to his knees.

"Have I come so far, Lord, just to see them die?" he prayed.

Sophie poured him a cup of weak tea. "Thomas, you look very pale and thin. There are shadows under your eyes. Isn't that hotel decent?"

He smiled. "I'm all right."

But Sophie saw something she hadn't seen on that first day.

"Thomas is struggling with all the sudden female attention he's been getting lately," a voice mocked. Maria entered the room.

Thomas looked up, smiling and shaking his head. Maria was teasing again. That was good.

Sophie frowned. "What female attention?"

"When we went to the play last night, half the girls there were all pushing around asking me who he was and flirting. It was quite shameless."

Thomas laughed. "Yes, shameless."

Sophie found this serious. "Now, Thomas, I must warn you, there are some girls in the neighborhood who are . . . well, have not been properly raised and in these conditions where we all live so closely, well, well . . ." Sophie was turning red.

Thomas and Maria were laughing.

Her hands went to her hips. "I'm only warning you."

He patted her shoulder. "I'm warned. But I'm not here for romance, so you don't need to worry."

"Well, I didn't say all the girls—"

She stopped and her blush deepened. Maria colored furiously; Thomas cleared his throat awkwardly.

"Anyway you forget I'm a Gentile among a brood of Jewish mamas," he smiled.

"That doesn't matter—" Sophie stopped abruptly as she glanced at her daughter. Maria's brows had lowered in heavy, menacing lines. Her face was still red. Her voice was crisp.

"It's time we leave, Thomas."

They walked side by side for several minutes in silence. It was the first time they had been alone since Thomas' sudden appearance in the ghetto. They walked, and both felt the old familiarity of the times they had walked together. Maria was pulled, at first unwillingly, into the memories. Thomas had been walking with her forever. Like she had walked with her father. She spoke suddenly.

"You know, I wish Papa was here with us, even though . . . things are so hard."

"I pray that he is well wherever he is," Thomas responded. He felt his words feeble.

"Thank you for what you did for Isaac," she said, not looking at him.

"I wish I could have done more."

She's talking to me, he thought delightedly. *It's as good as finding her alive. Now really alive.* They hadn't spoken of her coldness at their first meeting weeks ago. She still treated him with reserve, but she was slowly thawing. He could see her maturity and the girl of Blumenstrasse who, in small ways and precious ways, still survived.

"Tell me about this meeting we're going to."

"It's the Jewish Fighting Organization. We have about 600 members."

"You are one?"

She nodded. "Since the beginning. Before they sealed the ghetto I would go out in the city. Run errands for the underground." She laughed. "Put sugar in the Nazis' gas tanks. Little pranks. My Polish wasn't good enough like Wanda's. Now she was really brave."

"Who is Wanda?"

Maria's voice took on an edge. "Was. She was a Polish Jew. Younger than me. Blonde, very pretty. She would leave the ghetto on errands for the resistance. She was part of the group who blew up the train station and army installations. She went into the office of the Nazi who ran the ghetto before von Kleinst—"

"You know von Kleinst?"

"We know all about the Nazi leaders here. Our people keep tabs. Anyway, Wanda went into the office. She had gotten by the guards with a smile. Of course, with their filthy minds they thought she was his mistress. She went in, pulled out a pistol, and killed him. They retaliated the next day ... as we expected. They brought in a truck, and the Nazis machine-gunned the entire street. Sixty Jews, mostly children, were murdered that day."

"You actively participate in this group?"

"Yes. Whatever assignment they give me, I'll do. I'm not afraid, Thomas."

"Yes," he replied slowly, "I'm sure you're not." He stopped. "I ... understand, but ... Maria you have to be careful. I mean ... for your mother's sake."

They stood facing each other. She was no longer a little girl. He was no longer her big brother.

"Do you truly understand, Thomas? They are killing us."

He looked away.

"Thomas, I won't be taken just ... willingly. I can't."

He was looking at the sidewalk. "I'm trying to help you."

She swallowed with difficulty. She touched his sleeve.

"I don't think there is anything you can do, Thomas. And what you did for Isaac, for Mama. Please stop trying to do more. I know now."

Someone called her from the steps. The meeting was beginning.

They accepted him because Maria had prepared them. He told this gaunt-faced group of men and women as much as he could about the city, about the German preparations. He tried to explain von Kleinst and found that he couldn't.

"I think he is a man who is struggling with what he has to do. I ..."

"He's a murderin' Nazi and nothing else. If he had a conscience he couldn't do this. He'd leave if it bothered him," Daniel rasped.

A leader spoke up with a touch of diplomacy. "Herr Picard was only giving us his impression of the man, Dan. I think as long as we have a friend with Herr Picard, and he has a bit of a way with von Kleinst we should value that. Has he told you any specific plans about the ghetto?"

Thomas shook his head. "Only that the deportations continue."

"Then we continue to arm ourselves and make ready."

"What if von Kleinst asks you about the resistance here? He knows about us."

"I'll tell him I know very little." Thomas smiled. "Which is true. I'm trying to work out a way of getting medicine in. I think von Kleinst will look the other way."

"I don't know that we should trust you, German," a young fighter said angrily.

"Don't let jealousy color your judgment, Daniel," Levi said, and the group chuckled.

Maria turned her now-frequent red.

"You can trust me," Thomas said slowly. "I'm doing everything I can."

An older man stood to speak. "We all know what is coming. That is why we fight. And we understand that it will be a fight to our death. We wage war as flies against an elephant. And we die with honor."

"Mama, you have to try to talk some sense into him," Maria flung over her shoulder as she paced in front of them.

Sophie looked at her daughter then at Thomas. "Well?"

Thomas laughed. "I feel like I'm about to get in trouble."

"You're not too old for me to pull your ears," Sophie said tartly.

Maria shook her head in exasperation at this kind of talk.

"He's going to try to smuggle Jewish children out. He starts tonight! Mama do you know how dangerous that is?"

Sophie looked back to the tall young man, her son. "Maria is right. There are sentries all along the wall."

"Tonight there is a party for the commandant. There will be less sentries. The Muranow wall is least patrolled. I've watched it. I'll have fifteen minutes. That's a lot of precious children to safety."

"If you are caught they will be slaughtered on the spot," Maria countered savagely.

Sophie had never voiced the shared truth with her daughter. She had wanted to claim a future for her daughter. She had been optimistic.

She spoke slowly. "They will be slaughtered anyway. This is one way to try to save them."

Maria's eyes widened. *So Mama does understand. She does more than gossip and stretch the soup.*

"But if he is caught, Thomas will be killed with them," Maria said slowly.

Sophie took his hand in hers, her eyes on the lovely young girl. "I cannot stop him, Maria. Even as much as I love him."

And that night under a moonless sky, ten Jewish children slipped to freedom.

Maria was leaning against a wall. Daniel, in classic frown and suit of jealousy, stood beside her. She had been slowly walking back to her room thinking of the lilacs and daffodils in the Blumenstrasse garden when Daniel had accosted her. On a warm night such as this, she could smell the Blumenstrasse flowers' fragrance wafting through her bedroom window.

"You were the one who said there wasn't time for anything but survival."

She laughed. "Oh, Daniel, what are you talking about?"

"That German. Picard. He's with you all the time. He's a Gentile."

"So?"

"So he comes all the way from Germany. The two of you are in love."

"You are absurd, Daniel."

"I don't think so."

"It's your imagination. Thomas is just an old friend."

Daniel shook his head and moved away, his voice scornful. "You can't see the obvious, Maria. I see the way he watches you. Very possessive. And you look at him across the room as if he had hung out the moon for you."

"You are being even more absurd."

But she fell asleep with his words chasing her dreams.

The Warsaw ghetto robbed and ravaged. It was stalked by disease and despair and hunger—those attacks the eye could see and not ignore. But by its very nature, the ghetto could also bequeath. It had given Sophie Goldstein a resilience in herself, a steady calmness that Blumenstrasse could never have given her. The flame of the ghetto burned; the flame refined. Now in this moment, instead of former hysterics and hand-wringing, Sophie was in control and in command. It was Maria who wept uncontrollably, who was useless.

Thomas Picard lay stretched on the floor of the soup kitchen, chalk-white, bloodied, and unconscious. His second night of smuggling had ended with a ringing gunshot.

The four children had made it to safety under the cover of the black, stormy sky. The SS sentry had heard them and fired into the darkness. Thomas had staggered, and ghetto hands pulled him roughly through the tearing wire, through the mud to safety. The Jewish fighters were alerted for possible sudden retaliation. But the city was quiet. Just another shooting of a Jew trying to smuggle. The SS would stroll along and not make his report till morning.

The crowd in the kitchen finally thinned. It was nearly one in the morning. Now, of those who had helped Thomas inside, only two remained, along with Sophie, Maria, and the doctor and his wife. Sophie bit her lip, tears silently tracking down her face as the doctor dug into Thomas' shoulder with his crude instruments. Thomas moaned and cried out. She bathed his forehead and crooned to him.

"Just ... a ... little more and I'll have it," the doctor said as sweat dripped from his brow.

Sophie's voice was very controlled. "Thomas is a very good patient. I nursed him when he was seven, no, he was only five. It was Abraham who was seven. They both had scarlet fever. He was very strong. And when he was twelve he fell from an apple tree and broke his ankle. His mother, Maria, wasn't home so Aaron and I carried him to the doctor. He didn't whimper a single time. Do you remember that, Maria?"

But Maria was huddled in the corner.

"A little to ... the right here, see? It almost nicked a major artery. Lucky boy."

Sophie didn't like to look at the wound too closely. She snorted. "Luck, ha."

Their laughter eased the tension in the room. The two Jewish men stepped forward.

"He's awfully white."

"He'll pull through," the doctor said as he collected his instruments. "Anyway, it's the best I can do."

"Do you have anything for the pain when he wakes up?" one of the young men asked.

Now the doctor snorted. "I ran out of that months ago."

The doctor and his wife left. Sophie shooed the other men away with motherly pats.

"You come in the morning and help me move him to our room. Tonight he'll have to stay here."

The room was still and quiet but for the hiss of the single lamp and Thomas' ragged breathing. Sophie cleared away the bloodied rags, refilled the water, then tidied the room. Carefully she covered him with the thin wool blanket from her own bed. She smoothed the hair back on his damp forehead. She smiled. He was looking more like his father, Michael.

"Is he ... his breathing is so ..."

Sophie jumped, her hand clutching at her chest. She had forgotten Maria's presence in the dim room.

"He's going to be fine," she soothed.

"But ... he's so pale. He ..."

Sophie put her still-stout arm around the young woman. "He's pale; he's lost blood. But he'll be fine in a few days."

Maria turned into her mother's arms, weeping on her shoulder. Sophie's arms went around her. "There ... there. Now, Maria, stop or you'll make me cry. Thomas needs better than weepy nurses!"

"When they brought him I thought he was dead."

"No, no. Thomas Picard didn't come all the way from Munich to die in the Jewish ghetto! Ha!"

"Oh, Mama ..." She was shaking with sobs.

"Maria, Maria. Why you are crying like your heart is broken? He will be all right. We'll take care of him." She pulled her away to look at her. "What is it? You can tell me."

Long ago, so very long ago, Maria Goldstein had imagined she would find the man of her dreams and confess that love to her dear Papa. But now it was her mother, her mother who loved her as much as her Papa had. Of course. And of course she should be the first to know.

"I love Thomas, Mama. I love him."

Sophie couldn't answer as Aaron would have. She slipped back into her old Blumenstrasse ways effortlessly. Her voice was brisk and confident.

"It's about time," she said as she kissed her daughter's cheek.

It was another wedding in the ghetto. It had been a traditional ceremony, and now the friends and family celebrated with their meager gifts and loving hearts. For a few hours they could ignore the future, ignore the present. Tonight they celebrated love and life that the Nazis could not kill.

Maria and Thomas stood watching the dancers. Maria had danced with nearly every male except Thomas and was flushed from the effort. Still she swayed to the music, her hands behind her back. She was smiling.

"You know I could never do what they're going to do later," she said.

Thomas' glass stopped midway to his mouth. "Excuse me?"

"After this is all over, they'll go up to Mordecai's room. I just couldn't do that."

Thomas stared straight ahead and didn't speak.

"If I had just married the man I was passionately in love with and was, therefore, delightfully happy, how could I climb those narrow smelly stairs to that stifling little room with a window that looks on the alley? And they have only a thin wall to separate them from his parents. They'll look up at a water-stained ceiling, lay in a cranky, squeaky bed . . . and that's romantic?"

"That's all they have," Thomas offered awkwardly.

"That's all they have, but I couldn't do it. I will show you what I would do."

Before he could speak she had grabbed his hand and was pulling him from the room.

No one seemed to notice them leave. She led him out the building and down the twilight-shrouded street. Down another street, around a corner, up a flight of stairs.

"Maria, " he laughed, "where are you taking me?"

"To the stars, Thomas!"

They passed through a littered hallway and into an old abandoned room on the third floor.

"Looks like an empty room, right?" she asked.

He nodded. She opened a door to an old storeroom. Again empty. Only an old, rusty water heater in the corner. She pulled him to the corner. There was an opening, then a narrow flight of stairs. Up, up, then through a door. They were on the roof. But it was enclosed by a wall parapet and a stone overhang. It left the space of a small room.

Thomas leaned over the side. He could see the city, the streets below, and, because of the design, he couldn't be seen.

"I have the best view in Warsaw!" she boasted.

"How did you find this place?" he asked in astonishment.

"You're impressed," she laughed.

He nodded. "Very."

"One afternoon I followed a cat. I was tired of doing things, and I wanted to be alone. He came up here. I was so excited because no one else knew about this place. I could see out of the ghetto!" She pointed. "Look, you can see the Vistula and the forest. I suppose that way is Russia."

Thomas continued watching the city. Maria leaned against the cool brick wall and watched him. Finally he turned. She smiled.

"My groom and I would slip up here. I would have a bed prepared right there. I would have a bottle of wine. We wouldn't need a candle. We would have the stars! Right up here, above the world, alone!"

Thomas studied her a moment then turned back to the ledge. "Yes, it is very lovely up here." He could feel her eyes on his back. Finally he turned.

She stepped close to him. She reached out and touched the heavily bandaged shoulder.

"As I have told you a secret, and showed you a secret place that only a cat and I know about, I feel you are in my debt."

So. The Warsaw ghetto hasn't entirely killed the flame of "O Petted One," he thought.

He cleared his throat, his voice firm. "And as we have been friends for so many years, and know and respect each other, Maria, you know I am not like the boys who flutter around you like a moths to a flame. I seem to remember a time like this in our kitchen. You said you were through with conquests."

She smiled. "You remember that time?"

He nodded. "I remember it very well. I cannot ... I ... won't be teased."

She stepped closer and ran a slender finger over his lips.

"No, you are not like the others. I never imagined that, Thomas. Still in all fairness, I do think my confession warrants a ... simple kiss ... between friends." Her arms went around his neck.

"Maria ..."

"Yes, yours, Thomas ..."

Lieutenant von Kleinst had been put in charge of the arrangements because he had shown such a flair for management. So he chose the vast dining room of the city palace to hold this sudden meeting with the SS generals and Heinrich Himmler. His trip to Berlin had prepared him for this, but on this benevolent blue-sky spring afternoon he still felt nervous with anticipation and an unexplainable dread. The room looked impressive with the still-intact chandeliers, the gilded chairs, and the drinks on the side table. He had tried to strike a balance between the professional appearance of an important business meeting and the luxury that Nazi generals enjoyed and expected.

Himmler hadn't come alone. He had brought General Kruger, General von Sammern, and SS General Jurgen von Stroop with him. It was a heady concentration of power whose significance was not lost on anyone, small or large.

Himmler stood at the center of the table after von Kleinst delivered his report and had introduced the man. He repeated in his thin, didactic voice all the figures von Kleinst had meticulously and calmly stated.

"There are an estimated 60,000 Jews still living in the ghetto. There is a known armed Jewish resistance." Himmler brought the meeting to its purpose. "It is time, gentlemen, to liquidate the Jewish ghetto of this city. The transports to the camps take too long, expend to much fuel, and take up the energy of our men. It is time to finish this problem once and for all." He looked over the rims of his silver glasses and smiled. "I personally have chosen April 19 to begin the action. Our fuehrer's birthday is the twentieth, and I intend to give him a Jew-free Warsaw as a present. Yes, you look a little surprised. But that gives you two weeks to make the preparations. That should be sufficient. You will have General von Stroop in charge with the assistance of Generals Kruger and von Sammern. Lieutenant von Kleinst will assist with the obvious details." He consulted a paper.

"It will please you to know I have authorized the assistance of over 2,000 soldiers and officers of the SS. You will have three divisions of artillery. You will have two battalions of German police. You will have the assistance of the Polish police. Altogether, our forces will number nearly 10,000."

A hushed silence fell over the room. Hugo was angry with himself as he sat with a stoic, impassive face. *Why do I feel shocked, even . . . angry?*

Himmler was chuckling. "That should be enough to squash the Jewish vermin, don't you think?"

Polite nodding and smiles.

Himmler folded his notes. "I think this will make a nice present ... a burnt offering to our fuehrer."

• • •

They stood together under the canopy, their arms brushing against each other, their faces forward, smiling yet solemn. The old rabbi's voice was steady and, despite his weakness, rang in the clear night air. Maria imagined it somehow could be heard all over the ghetto through the skeleton houses, against the crumbling walls, sighing and rising, an offering to God.

"You that come in the name of the Lord are blessed. May He who is supreme in might, blessing, and glory bless this groom and his bride."

Her eyes left the wrinkled face of the rabbi. Sophie stood to her left. Their eyes met, and Sophie's tears spilled over as she smiled. Her hands were tightly clasped. *In this ... this inferno God has remembered my prayer. My daughter is marrying this night in April. My daughter is marrying Thomas! If only Aaron could see ...* Sophie closed her eyes.

The rabbi handed the cup of wine to Thomas. The couple turned at last to each other. He looked into her eyes as he drank, then passed the cup to her. He took the thin band of gold from his pocket and slid it on her finger. *Such a beautiful hand ...*

His voice was low. "By this ring you are consecrated to me as my wife in accordance with the law of Moses and the people of Israel. Before this assembly, before the God we both love, before my Lord, I take you Maria Goldstein with ... with great joy to love and cherish and serve you with my heart, my mind, my body all our days together."

He lifted her veil.

Her voice was steady and joyful. "Before this assembly, before the God we love, I take you, Thomas Picard, with great pride and joy to love and cherish and serve you with my heart, my mind, my body, all our days together." She lifted his hand and kissed the palm.

"You are my beloved, and I am yours."

They had slipped away from the gathering in the dining room. Except for the watchful eye of Sophie, no one saw them leave. She followed them to the hallway. Thomas stepped outside, giving Maria and her mother some privacy.

"You can have our room, Maria," Sophie began.

Maria kissed her cheek. "Mama, we've been over this. I've taken care of everything. Thomas is waiting."

"Yes."

They held each other. "You know ... you know how pleased I am, don't you, Maria?" Her voice sounded small and caught at Maria.

"Yes, Mama. You love Thomas."

"Like my own flesh. You could not have chosen better."

"Yes, I know."

"Papa ... he would ..."

"He will know, Mama. Someday we will all be together."

Sophie watched her skip away with a part of her own heart. Tonight would be the loneliest for her, the happiest for her daughter. As it should be.

"It couldn't be a prettier night," Thomas said as he leaned on the railing. He laughed. "The stars ... there are millions!" He shook his head. *God is so generous.*

He turned. His voice was shaky. "Well, we started out on Blumenstrasse. We make another beginning on a roof in Warsaw."

She had arranged the mattress, the bottle of wine, and some bread that was a gift. She stood back. So simple, yet so like she wanted it. Her bridal bouquet of daffodils sat in a chipped bottle of water.

She drew closer to him. "Another beginning on a roof in Warsaw."

"I never imagined ... never—even when you were the beauty of Blumenstrasse, and not when I came here. Yet I know I have loved you, Maria, in my heart for a very long time."

He kissed her, and she thought of those long-ago days when she had wondered what passion really was. Now she had found the perfect fitting of two halves—love and passion.

He kissed her eyes and cheeks and neck. She kissed his eyes and ears and chin. She took his hand and placed it across her heart. "And my heart speaks to you alone, Thomas. It always has and always will."

"Then He has led me here ... to find the treasure He gave me long ago."

He swept her up in his arms, not noticing the lingering pain in his shoulder. He carried her to her dreams under that perfect vault of velvet on a roof in Warsaw.

35
And He Shall Set the Captives Free . . .

T*he florid-faced, beady-eyed man seems to be vastly enjoying this process, drawing it out for as long as possible,* Emilie thought.

The officer eyed her application again. *Of course, it must be that American strain—that taint. That explained why she wanted to leave the Reich. He looked up briefly at the blond child in her lap. Such a handsome child. He would be perfect at the head of the Hitler Youth in a few years.* His mouth clamped downward in disapproval. He shook his head. *Disloyalty.*

"You will be permitted to take with you a certain amount of money, Frau Farber, the rest will remain frozen. Do you understand?"

She understood perfectly. The Nazis would strike at Max Farber one final time by stealing his wealth.

"This includes the country property, the house on Tiergartenstrasse, and all other assets."

She was surprised this man wasn't actually rubbing his hands in anticipation, as if he would be getting a cut. *He probably will,* she reflected.

"How much will I be permitted to leave Germany with?" she asked slowly.

He wrote a figure on paper and pushed it across the desk to her.

Enough for travel out of Germany, a steamer ticket, perhaps arriving on Ellis Island with enough to buy her and Morgan a sandwich.

She felt the color rise to her face. *This is blatant robbery, and the man knows it.* She looked up. He was smiling. Her color intensified.

"You are saying if I leave Germany, I leave my son's inheritance in the hands of the government."

"You are suggesting we are not good stewards, Frau Farber?"

He had the power to stamp "Refused" across her applications. To leave now would be to leave everything. She wouldn't want to come back.

"I'm simply saying that it would be very helpful to have a bit more to start my life in America with ... for my son," she said evenly.

His hands went out, palms up.

She leaned back and looked out the window. She felt more than stabbing sorrow. More than loss. *I'm turning over everything to the men who killed my husband, who killed Morgan's father. What would Max have wanted?*

She knew the man was watching her as she fought to stifle her tears. Like the things she would leave behind for them, if they mocked her sorrow, what did it really matter? *Max would want my happiness and safety. And he would want me to take the terrible burden of the film to safety. That could be the voice that would survive all of us. Yes, the film mattered most.*

"I'd like to take the next available train to Switzerland, please."

• • •

Elaina Heydrich was beginning to look at Berlin with the same jaundiced view as Emilie Farber. And perhaps, like Emilie Farber, it was time to leave. She could go to Switzerland and wait out what she considered the eventual toppling of the Nazi empire. Even the generals on furlough in the capital weren't above a little cocktail-party gossip—after the disaster in Russia the German army was faltering badly; the fuehrer and his cabinet were looking shaky. Goebbels' boasts on the radio were sounding very hollow. They were like old recordings being replayed to a duped public. Elaina Heydrich was smarter than that.

The phone cut sharply into her thoughts. The voice on the end of the line was curt and brief.

"Are you still interested in that property near Tegel, Frau Heydrich?"

"What? Yes, I ..."

The phone went dead. Elaina slowly lowered the phone, shocked. But there was no time to be shocked. She must be at the phone at the little cafe on Kurfurstendamm in thirty minutes. Then he would tell her without code about this property. Elaina felt some concern that the SS and Gestapo monitored her phone from time to time. *That old rivalry between her brother and Heinrich Himmler,* she thought bitterly. She snatched up her hat and purse. *Property near Tegel. News of Max.* She glanced at the phone. She couldn't contact Emilie until she had more information. *Max ...*

"Frau Heydrich?"

"Yes, yes, I'm here."

"You were interested in a certain prisoner at Tegel?"

"Yes, you know I am. You told me he was dead."

"I told you he was presumed dead. Your man has come back to life, shall we say?"

Elaina gripped the phone tighter. "What do you mean?"

"His block was one of the ones hit in the bombing. That part is true. There was a great deal of confusion and then the changing of the guard shifts. There were some victims and some survivors. It wasn't sorted out for over a week. Some of the survivors sustained injuries, others were moved to different blocks. There was no official record-changing ... you understand."

"He is alive."

"From my reliable information, yes. Injured but alive."

Elaina closed her eyes and struggled to keep her voice even. "I—"

"Are you interested in a deal?"

"Yes. Yes." She reclaimed her cool, business tone. "A thousand marks."

There was a pause. "The Farbers and the Heydrichs are very wealthy."

"One thousand marks," she repeated firmly. "How soon?"

"There is to be a movement tomorrow, an accounting of prisoners. Something could be attempted then."

Tomorrow night. Elaina closed her eyes again.

The oily voice spoke into her ear. "Even with all this confusion you know it is very dangerous for me. I will have to have help."

"There will be something for your help," Elaina said icily.

"Have a car down at the eastern gate at midnight. We will try to have your property."

• • •

Emilie sat waiting on the stairs with dry eyes. The doorbell rang and she hesitated only a moment. Percy began to bark, but she shook her head at him. She opened the door. Elaina Heydrich stepped inside.

"Hello, Elaina."

"Emilie."

Emilie was surprised at the aloofness. She thought they were past that. Well, it didn't matter now.

Percy sat with expectation between them, looking from one face to the other.

Emilie's voice was low. "I'm so grateful to you, Elaina, for taking him. I don't know why the authorities won't let me take him." She looked up at the woman a moment. "He . . . Percy was my first friend in Germany."

At the sound of his name, he laid down and placed his paw over her foot.

"I will take good care of him. He will have a good home."

Her voice faltered, and Emilie looked at her.

"Are you all right?"

She nodded wordlessly.

"We leave at six in the morning. Would you like to see Morgan?"

"I'm sorry," Elaina lied. "I have another appointment." She couldn't bear to see his son again.

"Oh. Well." She leaned down and snapped the leash on the dog's collar. She handed the leash to Elaina. Percy cocked his head.

"You will be a good boy, Sir Percy Blackney. You are old enough to . . . to not be foolish. You will mind, Elaina, all right? No chasing cats now. Just be a good boy for me."

Then she turned and hurried up the stairs.

• • •

A shrill wind had risen with the climbing moon as mottled-gray clouds slid against a vast sea of purple and ebony. The trees of the forest north of Tegel prison were bending and twisting as if pleading to the heavens. The air was moist and heavy. A storm was coming, and Berliners were grateful. It would help obscure their city as a target. To the man sitting in the dank hallway, it was a reminder of the storms when he had been a boy watching the trees in a mad dance from his window. He had been afraid of the storms then. But he wasn't really afraid tonight. He felt tired and listless from the events of the past week. It had disoriented and confused him. He could only remember that he was in Tegel prison. He didn't no where. Time and direction had vanished. This dark place had finally swallowed him.

He looked down at the bandage on his hand that made a gray smudge in the chilled darkness. He lifted it and winced. *I wonder if it will heal so I can play the piano,* he thought vaguely. Then he laughed at himself. The sound of it stopped him abruptly. *How long have I been sitting here?* He closed his eyes, but he couldn't remember much: the night of the bombing, the choking smoke, someone pulling on his hand when it hurt so badly. Someone had placed him against this wall. The storm was growing. He could hear the thunder rumbling and growling somewhere past his right shoulder. He must be on an outer wall.

He could see no pinpoint of light, hear no sound. *Where had the others gone, the men of block seven? What of Bonhoeffer?* He remembered the screams. Max sat rigidly still as the hair pricked on the back of his neck. Sweat broke out all over him, and he could feel his heart pounding in his ears. He began to tremble. *I'm alone in this dark place, forgotten. Is this a prelude to death?*

"What time I am afraid, I will trust in Thee," he said. Bonhoeffer had taught him that from the book of Psalms. No voice mocked him. And now the sound of his own voice didn't frighten him. If this was death, he was ready.

A sound to his right, growing, undefinable . . . still he didn't bother to turn. Silence. The scraping sound and the darkness at some distant point was giving way to a rectangle of less darkness. He squinted and leaned forward. *That sound . . . it was the wind! The storm! The rectangle was a door opening . . . opening to the outside.* He stared at it for a full minute. Finally he rolled to his knees and, holding to the wall, stood. He waited. *Still no movement. Nothing is behind me . . . no steps, no voices.* He staggered slowly toward the opening.

He stopped midway. The night air was rushing in on him. He felt it blowing the thin rags on him like a shroud. *Still no light . . .* Closer and closer, peering, listening past his own beating heart.

Then a form filled the space when he was six feet away. He stopped, frozen, feeling as if he might faint.

"Hurry up." The voice was very gruff.

Max leaned, then stepped through the door. The wind hit him and he swayed. He was squinting and breathing hard.

Then a hand reached out and grabbed his arm roughly. Only then did Max turn slightly. The dark shape in front of him was a car. *A car!*

Max turned to the man who pulled him, his voice not so very far from the dandy he had played so well many years ago, which had helped to bring him to this place.

"Well, then, I suppose you're not an angel after all."

He had spent hours and hours imagining what the first moment of freedom would be like. What he felt was incredible calmness. The darkness of the backseat seemed to enfold him in quietness and warmth. It was a sense of unreality, as those first abrasive moments of Tegel had been. He slumped back, feeling very thirsty and very weak. For the first few moments he wasn't the least bit interested in where this car was taking him or who was driving. It would be hours later, as this sudden dreamlikeness continued, before he would think of Bonhoeffer and the other men still entombed. Then he would feel the shattering guilt and sorrow—and salvation, again. Then he would try to think of everything Bonhoeffer had told him, everything he must treasure and not forget. Everything he had become.

Finally the car stopped, and the got out. The driver silently led him from the car, past a privet hedge, then through a door. An older woman took his arm unflinchingly and led him to a chair.

"You sit here and rest, Herr Farber. I've got broth here, and when you're finished we've drawn a nice warm bath for you."

He was vaguely aware that this man and woman were dressed and spoke like servants. But there was such a dreamlikeness to this that he felt no stirring of curiosity. When he drained the teacup, the man led him slowly up some stairs, through a bedroom, to a bath. The clothes peeled off painfully. He slipped into the warm, scented water and some vague memory was stirred, but he couldn't quite remember. Then the man led him to the bed and he was asleep before the man reached the bottom step. *This was a dream* ...

• • •

She felt emotionally ravaged, her nerves stretched taut over the past weeks. A hundred competing thoughts filled her mind as she packed her trunks and bags. If the Germans were going to loot Max Farber's estate she would take the things they wouldn't count as treasure, things that would bring something to his son. She stood in the library of the Tiergartenstrasse house surveying this room that was most stamped with the lingering presence of Max Farber. She selected a few of his favorite books and cried silently when she packed his old boyhood favorite, *The Scarlet Pimpernel*. She took all the pictures of Josef and Max. She carefully packed his telescope. *Perhaps Morgan will share his father's love of the stars,* she thought. She slipped the framed pictures of the Olympic games she had given Max before they married into her trunk. She stood in the middle of the room. It was so quiet, so painfully quiet, and a part of her rebelled at the stripping of this room. It should not have been this way. Her eyes fell on the ivory chess set. They had never played the game after they married. But those few years before there had been many games of heated challenge. Max had been so boastful and confident. She packed it as well. From his room she took his silver brush and stared at the fine, tangled blond threads. Finally from the mantel she took the one picture of them together—their wedding day. Josef had taken the picture with the Dresden fountain in the background. Both she had Max wore nervous smiles. *We began so unconventionally.* She carefully closed the trunk, then buckled and locked it. She sat back on her heels, chin on her knees. *Seven years in one trunk.* She was ready.

It had been no small matter to decide where to hide the precious film of Treblinka. The three of them, Emilie, Heinrich, and his wife, Berta, had pondered the problem for a very long time. They had gone through all the possibilities: trunk, smaller bags, hand bags, Morgan's small diaper bag.

Emilie shook her head. "No, I'm concerned about it being with Morgan. It's too great a risk to him. Not to mention what it would do to me if the SS started going through his bag."

"No we must not put little Morgan at risk," Berta agreed.

"Yet I want it close to me in the event the trunk is separated and lost from us," Emilie said slowly.

"Well, we know the SS are going to strip search each of us leaving Berlin and likely before we leave Germany, so we have to be prepared for that indignity," Berta said scornfully.

"Yes," Emilie muttered. She began to pace the library. *Is this too great a task Wilhelm Mueller set up? It's so important, but I feel like I'm about to crumble under the load of stress.*

Heinrich Dortmund was rubbing his chin thoughtfully, watching Frau Farber.

"We'll ask God to show us where to put the film."

And for the hundredth time, Emilie was grateful for this couple. They had chosen to leave Germany with her. They wanted to see her and her son safely out of Germany.

And so when the morning stars shone, Emilie looked one last time at the back garden, dewy and still, at each room in the house, then she locked the front door. The three were silent in the cab that took them to the station. Emilie wouldn't let herself think of Percy beginning his day in a strange house. Her hands gripped together, till the knuckles went white. She mustn't think of that now. The goal was to leave Germany and that was no small task.

There were no delays and at ten minutes past six the Berlin to Munich train slowly pulled from the platform. The young woman stood on the steps as the suburbs slid past in a blur. She didn't look back.

● ● ●

He awoke feeling stiff. The predictable gnawing of hunger was active in the pit of his shrunken stomach. His eyes focused dully on the sculptured ceiling of Elaina Heydrich's guest bedroom. He frowned. *First the dark hallway, the eerie, forgotten feeling, the opening, the night sky and wind.* He lifted his hand to examine it. He flexed his fingers. He lifted his left hand. Bandaged. He punched them together and winced with pain. His heart was racing now. He sat upright. *This was no dream.*

There were clothes at the end of the bed. He didn't bother to look at the room. Was this his old bedroom at Tiergartenstrasse? He was shaking so much it was difficult for him to button his shirt. He laughed out loud at himself. Max Farber was back.

He threw the door open and the man from the night before stood up stiffly from the chair.

Max lunged at him. "Where am I?" he laughed and shouted.

The man's eyes rose in shock. His voice was calm. "Please follow me, sir."

"Well, only if you're quick about it."

He led him down the stairs, Max gripping the railing as if he were drunk. At the closed, paneled doors the man knocked then slid them open.

The first thing he saw was Elaina Heydrich across the room. She was placing tulips in a vase. She dropped them as her hand clutched at her mouth.

"Elaina!"

She couldn't miss the gladness in his voice.

But a movement near her pulled his eyes away. A dog had risen to a sitting position. Its hair rose on his back in a stiff ridge. Max's smile dropped. He blinked rapidly against the light from the French windows. It was too much.

"You look . . ." Elaina said haltingly. "You . . . he doesn't know you, Max."

Then he remembered. His hands went to his face and his hair. He must look like an ape to the dog.

"Percy! You rogue!" he shouted.

The terrier let out a terrific yelp and hurtled forward, crashing into Max's arms. Max staggered, then laughed and looked at Elaina.

"Where is she? Is she here?" He swung around. "Emilie! Emilie!"

She knew then the old saying that some dreams die very hard and very slow was painfully true.

"Max . . ." she whispered.

He had fallen down to his knees in weakness. His voice was suddenly croaking as Percy lashed in his arms. "Elaina? Please, where is she?"

"She left Germany, Max."

His hands tightened around the dog. "Left? Elaina, this is Berlin?"

She nodded with the lump growing in her throat.

"And . . . and the war is over?"

"No."

"Hitler's still in power?"

She nodded again.

"Then . . . then I'm still . . . a criminal?"

Elaina looked up. "Please bring Herr Farber his breakfast. Max, I have a doctor coming at ten, a man we can trust who will help you and—"

"A doctor? Josef. Where is Josef?"

"I'm sorry . . ."

He reached out for her hand. He looked at it in his own. *So slender and pretty.*

"Elaina, what happened?"

"I found a way to get you out of Tegel. But we heard some weeks ago about the bombing at the prison. Max, Emilie believes you were killed. There was nothing left for her here in Germany."

It was happening too fast, much too fast.

"I . . ." he started shaking.

Her own tears spilled over. He could still stir her with one look from his eyes, with the sound of his voice.

"Max, she left only . . . this morning. We could try to get you to her before she crosses into Switzerland."

He squeezed her hand. "I've found out . . . with God all things are possible."

There was no time to attempt to get papers for Max. Not if he wanted to reach his wife before she left the Reich. And that was what Max Farber wanted now more than anything else. He had been fed, bathed, clothed, and barbered. The doctor had examined him carefully.

"Eat small meals slowly and frequently. Take these iron tablets. Take it easy," he had said.

"I have too much to do to take it easy, Doc," Max smiled. 'I've been taking it easy for quite a few months."

The doctor stood back. "You're grossly underweight and anemic, but I must say you look remarkable for all those months in prison, Herr Farber."

Max stood. "I know the risk for you to come here this morning. I'm indebted to you."

The medical man snapped the bag closed. "My only son was butchered outside of Stalingrad by the fools in the chancellery. I have no love for that gang." He paused at the door. "Good luck, Herr Farber."

"I have more than luck going with me now."

Elaina entered the room with some reluctance. Max stood at the windows, looking down on the street. He turned and smiled. He came forward, taking her hands in his.

"I have a lot to thank you for, Elaina, more than my words can say."

She looked away from his still-handsome face. "You told me we would always be friends once, Max, and so we have. I have only done what a friend would do. I only wish I had been able to do it sooner."

"I once thought . . . everyone I cared for had betrayed me. I was very wrong. You have been a faithful friend to me, Elaina. I'd better be going."

"I'm afraid for you all over again. Traveling across Germany . . . you know you'll be stopped."

"Please don't worry, Elaina. Whatever happens, happens. I've been made ready for it."

"You'll come back to Germany?"

He smiled. "If I can persuade my bride. Germany . . . Germany has wounded us both. But when the Nazis are gone, I'd like to do something toward helping the wounded. Besides you have this mutt you'll be very tired of. I wish I could take him."

Elaina thought of the son he didn't know he had. It was Emilie's surprise.

"You . . . you don't know the full treasure you have in your bride when you find her."

"Oh, I think I do," he smiled.

He had at least eight hours of driving on the autobahn in front of him. His first stop from Elaina's was the train terminal to find out all he could about the train Emilie had taken. It was expected to arrive in Munich at eight in the evening. "To Switzerland?" The man behind the grill had looked at him for an uncomfortably long time, and Max hoped the man didn't remember the scandal he had created three years ago.

"The train to Bern, Switzerland, departs at eleven o'clock. But there is always delays," he answered reluctantly, but when he looked up the tall young man was gone.

He was counting on train delays to catch up with her. He was counting on the loan Elaina had given him as bribes to any Nazi who chose to demand his papers. He was counting on his suddenly resurrected bluffing skills. Mostly Max Farber was counting on the God who had swung the prison doors wide.

36
Journey to Freedom

Munich Train Station

It had been an uneventful trip across the heartland of Germany. In business and pleasure he had traveled these roads many times. But never as an escaped convict, never as a man looking at the ordinary and seeing the amazing, never as a man so fervently praying. He felt pursued yet wrapped in divine protection. He felt afraid; he felt like laughing. To be so close to her but knowing she was slipping from him. He passed troop transits and SS men in open Mercedes with their fluttering flags on the hoods. He saw Nazis who would have shot him on the spot if they knew he had no papers—especially if they knew who he was.

It had long since been dark when he sped into Munich. He was tired, hungry, and weak. All of a sudden he felt like collapsing. But he must not. He hurried from the car and into the terminal. He froze at the entrance. There were only a few dozen civilian passengers, train officials and employees, and at least a hundred milling army personnel and SS. He had known there would be Gestapo among the crowd. *I'll stand out in this thin crowd,* he thought quickly.

Yet he drew a deep breath and approached the nearest ticket window. The moment had come.

He leaned forward and smiled. "Good evening."

The man nodded.

"The morning train from Berlin?"

"In hours ago."

"The train to Bern?"

"Leaves in an hour. Reserve passes only."

"Yes, I see. Thanks."

He left the window and went to the nearest pillar. He stood in the shadows, his face bent over a newspaper. His heart beat erratically. Yes, life in Tegel had taken its toll. His hands were shaking.

"Lord, I need You," he whispered. "No matter what happens, thank You."

He looked up and scanned the crowd inside the cavernous room. Emilie was not among the waiting crowd. *One hour. Did she make it here? Change her plans? She could be anywhere in Germany!* He closed his eyes as weakness washed over him.

He must decide what to do now. He opened his eyes. Something caught his eye and he saw the ticket man he had spoken to, speaking to another dark-suited man. They looked his way. The ticket man pointed. Max straightened and folded the paper. The man was cutting through the crowd toward him. He turned and the shout he expected came.

"You! Stop!"

Max was running for his life.

● ● ●

Emilie and the Dortmunds waited for their midnight train to Switzerland in their car. It had been a long day of delays, and Morgan had endured interrupted meals and naps with tolerant patience. But now his patience was gone. He lay stretched out on the front seat, his head in Emilie's lap, fast asleep. Emilie watched the tracks and fingered her son's curls absently. If there were no more delays, if their papers were accepted, she would leave Germany before this day was over.

Heinrich climbed in the backseat of the car. He handed his wife and Emilie paper cups of tea. He patted the sleeping boy.

"What did you find out?" Berta asked.

"They say it will leave on schedule in another fifty minutes, but I don't know now."

"Why?"

"Just as I was coming out here there was some kind of confusion. A man ran past and there was shouting—"

"The Gestapo are after some pour soul," Emilie sighed. "That will most likely delay the train." She rapped the steering wheel. "If they don't find him, they'll search the train again before it leaves. Another delay."

Berta patted her hand. "Now, let's not start worrying."

Emilie looked at the older woman. "I'm afraid . . . about the change. You know . . . I feel so responsible. Wilhelm gave it to me. And now you will have both the film and Morgan!"

They had been through this dilemma hours before, and Emilie still felt the tears that threatened. *To lose Morgan!*

Berta shook her head, lifting a baby bottle from the bag. "No Gestapo is going to deny a crying baby his bottle."

Emilie reached for it. "Yes, I suppose you're right. I just . . ."

She hefted the bottle. The metal cylinder that held the film was surrounded with cream. She hadn't wanted to put this danger so close to Morgan, but they had found no other safe place.

"Our papers are impeccable, Emilie. We've agreed they're more likely to detain a young woman than an older couple with a baby. If they question anything, it will be your papers when they see your name. It won't matter that you have the stamps that man in Berlin gave you. Some minor official can bungle everything. But I don't think that will happen. Everything will be fine," Berta soothed.

But with the Gestapo on a rampage, with citizens legally leaving the Reich . . . She looked out to the train station. Fifty minutes of danger, of waiting, of saying goodbye to this land of her joy and sorrow.

• • •

Max had started running with no distinct plan. After a few yards, he felt a rush blinding panic: *I'm the prey, and I'm far too weak and worn out to carry this hunt very far. I'll collapse soon. Without papers they can't identify me. Nameless, I'll be carried to the nearest prison or executed where I fall.* Still, for the first few minutes, he raced with the last of his fading energy evading the now-growing group of SS. The Munich station was huge. He felt that rather than dash into the night, he should remain close to this place. It was unreasonable, but it was what he felt impelled to do. Stay close to the trap. He dashed down the tile corridors, around corners, bumping into people and luggage carts. The pounding steps and shouts were close behind him. Around another corner, panting, he faced a staircase one going up and one going down. Instinct told him up, another voice, down. He leaped down the stairs. The marble splintered where a bullet shaved the corner.

Another long, dim hallway. He could hear them behind him, closer, closer. He couldn't turn around. One door that ... he fell against it and pushed it open. It led to a loading area out into the dark cover of night. He took a swift gulp of air. He whirled around. Two doors to his left. They were coming. Ten seconds and they would fire their weapons. He pushed against the door that led to possible freedom. It was stuck. Then he turned and opened the nearest door.

It was a large storeroom for the train terminal. He locked the door as he heard the nearing feet. *They think I took the obvious exit. They must* ... He slipped into the darkness, seeking a hiding place. He imagined they could hear his panting if they only stopped to listen. His fingers felt another doorknob. He turned it, entered, and locked it. Now he could see. He was in a basement room, hardly more than a closet. He brushed against crates and rough fabric. It was a place that smelled moldy. It brought back memories of Tegel. *There is some kind of light above me. Is this Tegel?* His body slid to the floor as the outer door was broken open.

• • •

"I think they will be calling in shortly, only another ten minutes," Heinrich Dortmund said softly. "We'd better be getting in line. Maybe things have quieted down now."

They had heard the gunshot, heard the screams. Yet the train remained with its slow curling steam as a steady reminder that it would move soon. This was the final challenge, the final hurdle, and all three were reluctant to leave the quiet safety of the car. Emilie looked down at Morgan sleeping so peacefully. Her hand went to his perfect cheek. She wanted to scoop him up in her arms. She looked up and Berta smiled at her.

"Yes, I suppose it is time to leave. I'll go first." She looked at the three of them. "I'll see you in Switzerland."

"We'll be behind you," Heinrich assured as he squeezed her shoulder. Emilie smiled and left the car. *The final journey begins.*

• • •

The SS man stood framed in the doorway as the other had rushed into the loading yard. His flashlight swept the storeroom. It seemed intact. A broom across the floor, he stepped forward, listening. Something brushed against his leg and his gun swung around. A cat ran past him. He looked a moment more into the shadows then closed the door.

Max woke from the faint chilled and disoriented. He lay rigid and panting. *Where am I?* Then he heard a high-pitched whistle, shrill and penetrating. He jerked forward in fear. He could hear voices and the rumbling of carts, the hiss of steam. He squinted in the darkness. A yellow rectangle across from him. A window, just like at Tegel. He closed his eyes. He would die here. He felt so spent.

The whistle sounded again. He leaned forward. He sat up. He stood on shaky legs. The small basement window gave him a view of the train platform. Panting, he drew nearer. *The Munich station! This was not Tegel!*

He could see legs and carts. *The train to Bern was leaving, and she is supposed to be on it!*

He saw the green-jacketed porters helping passengers on and handing up baggage. And then a pair of legs passed by him very close. The hem of a blue skirt.

Max Farber felt a sudden, incredible surge of peace. In these circumstances there was no explaining it. He felt an odd desire to laugh. He brushed at the grimy glass and leaned closer. People passed between him. It was difficult to see. The legs mounted the steps. Max raised on tiptoes. *I've seen those legs before. Yes. I can ... it has been over two years. It's Emilie. Emilie!*

They were pulling away the steps, the guards still posted as sentries. They stood unsmiling and severe. The cart had nearly knocked them over.

"Dummkopf! Watch where you're going!"

The train porter nodded and hefted the case to his shoulder.

"You're running a little late," the SS captain snapped.

The porter bent to his task. He laughed. "They say I was ten minutes behind my twin brother."

The train was slowly chugging to begin. The porter placed the case on the steps.

"Could you give me hand with that one?" he lisped and pointed.

The two guards looked at each other. They handed the case to him as he stood on the train steps.

The porter winked. "Vodka. Wouldn't want this to be left behind. The German ambassador's up in the first-class car. Thanks."

The train was pulling away. He held to the railing, smiling and giving them a wave. His voice was lost in the melody of departure.

"Heil Hitler and happy hunting!"

He opened the glass door to the last car. The noise was almost deafening. He pushed the boxes in and closed the door. He glanced down the companionway as the train picked up speed. *The lights flickering, the swaying* ... He sagged suddenly against the boxes and closed his eyes. *This sudden weakness is so strange. I'm not used to this*, he thought. And at that moment, Max Farber thought of Josef. *Josef.* He opened his eyes and looked out the small window. *I'm leaving Germany.*

"Are you all right?" a kind voice asked.

Again he jumped with surprise. *It's going to take some time getting my nerves steady again.* Only then in the dimness did he realize he was not alone in the train companionway. His eyes finally adjusted. A woman was regarding him.

"You looked like you were going to faint," she said with a slight smile.

Max ran a hand through his hair. "Well, I ... I'm not used to having to run, you know ..."

Then he heard the sound. *A gurgling.* He realized the woman was not alone. A man was beside the woman. Max straightened. The man was holding a child.

The train curved and Max swayed forward. There in the darkness he heard a baby's laugh. He peered closer.

"Our grandbaby," the woman said with a trace of nervousness that Max didn't notice.

Morgan stretched out a chubby hand toward Max.

"He's a bit odd in this way for a baby," the man said smiling, "he likes strangers."

The hand closed around Max's finger, pulling it toward his mouth as he laughed.

Max smiled. "What a beautiful child."

"We think so."

"You don't have a cabin?" Max asked.

"They were still getting it ready when we boarded," the woman said quickly.

"Ah, well, I better get to work," Max said. But the child wouldn't release his finger.

"Morgan, now, come on, let go," the man said laughing.

Max smiled. "His name is Morgan?"

The coupled exchanged a look and gave him a tentative nod.

"Fine German name. Well, hope you have a good trip. Goodbye."

He collected his broom and went down the aisle.

The Swiss-bound express was one of the few trains that entered or exited the Reich that hadn't been used by the German army at some time. Streamlined luxury remained in the plain but private berths and a small but efficient dining car. The train retained some of its former grandeur due to the very limited number of passengers it carried. Gone were the days of happy German families off to the Alps to ski. Now it carried foreign diplomats, neutral investors, SS high officials on rare holidays, and an assortment of spies. And those citizens with very rare and certainly very expensive special passes. Emilie Farber had secured a prized private berth on the fourth car for the ten-hour passage. The Dortmunds were booked in a similar berth on the sixth car.

The train sped into the darkness with a comforting swaying, like a rhythmic proclamation that with each click of the wheels the train was bearing one away from peril to peace. For Emilie, alone in her berth, it was a bittersweet time. She couldn't sleep even though exhaustion overwhelmed her. She hoped Morgan was sleeping now in the cradle-rocking of the train. *The film had made it safely past the Nazi hunters. If they knew what damaging evidence was passing through their hands . . .* She took a place on the edge of the narrow bed and stared out the window.

Max walked the length of the train, hunched, his head lowered, his eyes darting, his porter's cap pulled down low. He swept with his little broom and pan and looked for his wife. She wasn't among any of the few passengers in the nearly vacant seats. *Did I imagine her from the basement window in my eagerness? Or is she in one of the passenger cabins?* At the last car he felt an overwhelming fatigue. He had eaten nothing in hours. The swaying train was making him sleepy. He leaned in a corner near an exit platform. He would close his eyes for just a moment. *Emilie, so close. Please . . .*

Someone kicked the bottom of his feet. He was instantly awake. The guards had always wakened him this way—or worse.

"Wake up, you imbecile. What are you doing asleep? You should be fired!"

Max had slipped to the ground. He squinted up, groggily, "What?"

"Get up and work. I'm going to report you."

Max stood up. "Yes, yes all right, I'm sorry."

The porter looked at him coldly. "I haven't seen you before."

"I was called in at the last moment. Someone was sick. What do I do?"

"Some of the passengers want their breakfast in their cabins."

"Breakfast?" Max brushed past him to the small window. The landscape in the first pale brushes of dawns was still wrapped in shadow. *A beautiful dawn!* He ran an unsteady hand through his hair. He had slept too long.

"You're ill," the man said with growing suspicion.

"No, no, I'm fine. How long till we are in Switzerland?"

The man snorted. "You slept through the crossing."

"Bern?" Max asked.

"Three hours. Now, do you think you can push these carts and offer tea or coffee? Do you think you can do that or do you need a little more rest?"

Max bowed and smiled. "This I can do with pleasure."

His heart fell into an erratic beat, but he was going to ignore it.

"Oh, Lord, thank You," he whispered. He knocked on the first door. "Don't let her be afraid, let her know it's me."

The first cabin held an elderly gentlemen. *Coffee.*

Second cabin, no answer.

Third cabin, two elderly women. *Two teas.*

Fourth cabin, man and wife. *Tea and coffee.*

Fifth cabin.

"Oh, good morning!" Max greeted cheerfully.

Heinrich Dortmund stood with the door half open. "Ah, good morning."

"May I offer you tea or coffee, sir?"

"Two coffees, please."

Frau Dortmund was dressing the cherub-faced baby.

"And for the little gentlemen?" Max asked as he looked down the aisle. *She must be in the next car.*

"Oh, he has his bottle here. Morgan, can you wave?" Berta wagged his dimpled hand and he laughed.

"He'll have breakfast with his mother, thank you," Berta said. She gave a sudden look to her husband. *How could this cheerful porter be of any danger?*

"All right. Here you are. Well . . ." Max started to back up but the baby was leaning toward him.

He hesitated. He stepped inside and shook the baby's hand. He looked almost . . . familiar.

"I couldn't wait to see him. It's the first night we've been apart," a voice laughed behind him.

Max froze. He was blocking the way into the cabin. He could feel the Dortmunds' eyes on him, quizzical, waiting for him to retreat. The baby turned loose of his fingers and was reaching and gurgling for someone else.

"Excuse me," a voice behind him said politely.

Berta stretched forward toward him. "You look as you did last night. Are you—"

He looked at the blond-headed baby, his heart thudding in his ears. *It couldn't . . .* He turned very slowly, tears suddenly streaming down his face.

"Emilie!" he whispered.

He wrapped her in his arms and vowed he would never turn her loose. She cried though she had thought there were only tears of sorrow left. She kissed him and swore she would never stop.

Those first moments sped as quickly as the landscape passed by the window. Then the train slowed; the outline of a city was visible in the gathering strength of a new, clear morning.

Max Farber, holding his son, stepped onto the free soil of Switzerland.

37
Final Journey: Warsaw

Now that spring had finally come to Poland, the countryside not blemished and bruised around Warsaw held some attraction. The tides of war could ravage, but the fragile stem still struggled and blossomed from the rock. The sun was warm, the sky a canvas of porcelain-blue. The fields were brushed in green, the trees in shimmering leaf. The breezes were soft and gentle and carried the ageless, intangible stirring of hope.

The group of eleven men and four women crouched at a line of fir trees on the brow of the hill south of the capital. Wilhelm and Saul were stretched out on their stomachs sharing a pair of prized field glasses.

"That's thirty-seven," Wilhelm said after the dust had finally settled on the ribbon of road below them. He passed the glasses to Saul and glanced at his watch. "Thirty-seven truckloads of SS, and it's not even ten yet."

"With the six tanks yesterday and the ten this morning ..." Saul's voice trailed off. They looked at each other, their former animosity vanished under this test of survival. They knew what this military traffic meant. Yes, only one thing.

With this heavy concentration of Nazis, it was very difficult to resist the temptation to push further back into the relative safety of the Polish forest. They had already had to change their camp four times in the past two weeks. They had met and joined with another straggling, struggling group of partisans. Their group now numbered fifteen—a size that made Wilhelm uneasy. But Misha was still the leader—and Wilhelm took comfort in that. The leader had stated their purpose clearly and bluntly—they must help those who would try to escape from the obvious upcoming attack on the Jewish ghetto. And they would die in the effort. There was no illusion; the odds against survival were too great.

Wilhelm and Saul stood and walked back to the line of trees. All fifteen watched the road, now silent, a moment longer. Then Misha pushed away from the tree he'd been leaning against. He stomped into the brush with Wilhelm and Saul following.

Wilhelm noted the older man's hunched shoulders and the hands thrust into the pockets of the smock. His eyebrows were dark, heavy lines. Wilhelm knew this man felt the weight of the ghetto victims. *A courageous man with so little resources,* he thought.

"Well, let's see. We have nearly a hundred divisions of SS, Polish, and Lithuanian reinforcements, Polish police, the Werchmart, tanks, flame-throwers, and planes." He grunted. "Have the Russians entered the city, gentlemen?"

Wilhelm smiled wryly and shook his head. "Just the Jews with their broomsticks."

Misha nodded. "It will take them at least three or four days to set up their camps and get their plans finalized."

"And saturate themselves with vodka and schnapps to make them brave men against the women and children," Saul said sharply.

Misha stopped under a leafy canopy. He faced them. "Well, we know the way things are, and we know what to expect. That is something. We won't be surprised." He sighed and shook his shaggy head. "It will be a slaughter of course. And we must do what we can. At midnight we will divide into two camps and move in closer, nearer the breaches in the wall. We'll make contact inside. We'll set up escape routes. Then we'll send one group back into the forest to find a deeper camp for ... those who survive."

The two partisans nodded. Misha peered at Wilhelm.

"What of the girl?"

What of the girl? Wilhelm looked away.

"You have had no contact with her since she was reported back in the city," Misha stated bluntly.

"No."

"Well, what are you going to do about her?" he asked.

Wilhelm was surprised at the hard tenor of the man's voice. He would have expected this from Saul weeks ago. He realized this was the toll of anxiety on this man. And now the fuse was being laid for a terrible battle.

"I haven't decided exactly, Misha. I want to go back and talk with her—"

"With the Nazis in the city—thousands of them—you can't approach the hotel. It would be easier to just put a gun to your own head and pull the trigger."

"I can't leave her in there."

"Wilhelm, from what you have admitted, the girl doesn't want to leave her Nazi master," Misha argued bluntly.

Wilhelm's hands clenched. "She took the film, didn't she?"

Misha looked toward Warsaw. "We need you here with us. We need you in what is coming. If you go to the girl, you throw that away."

"I have to try one more time."

Misha shrugged and walked back to the group.

The Hotel Bristol had been her home for eight months. She felt some measure of ease here because she was left largely to herself. She could have her meals brought to the suite or wait till after the busy meal hours and eat in the nearly deserted dining room. She had her overgrown garden—that was dearer to her now. But suddenly, within the space of one short week, her home was invaded. Now, more than ever, she felt herself a prisoner. There were SS and German army officers everywhere— in the corridors, the parlors, the dining rooms. She could hear their voices and the sound of their boots from her window and through her door. Their trucks and cars rumbled past the hotel day and night. Watching from her window, soldiers crowded the sidewalks in a seemingly endless current. They lingered through the smell of their sweaty bodies, cigars, and liquor. Natalie Bergmann left her room only to take the kitten to the garden for an hour. She knew he enjoyed it so, stalking and playing. She could not deny him, even though it meant going past leering looks, murmurs, and raucous laughter.

She sat at her window seat for hours at a time with Moses curled in her lap. She was waiting. *Waiting for what?* she wondered. The interlude in Berlin had been brief and a slight relaxing of the tension between them, and Hugo was something of his old self. *Yet I'm different*, she noted. Wilhelm Mueller had come silently between them.

But now, back in Warsaw, Hugo retreated further into his distraction. She felt he had completely rejected her. He was pale and haggard, his eyes haunted. He was no longer the cool, confident administrator he had been months before. His words were now infrequent and sharp.

We can't continue this way much longer. I'm going to snap and crumble. And now all these Nazis. It could only mean . . . And her eyes were pulled toward the hazy district, the walled and doomed city.

• • •

The three days were in no way different or remarkable to the sixty thousand Jews of the ghetto. Another warm spring day. But vastly different and wonderfully remarkable to the man and woman who had made a temporary home on the roof of a ghetto dwelling. While the realistic life downstairs gave them danger, pain, and slow starvation, their love gave them a feast—a three-day banquet no one could steal from them. The sun rose, the moon climbed before them, and they stayed alone together. They found out what the years before hadn't been able to give them. In three days they learned of each other in every way. Three days of discovery and joy and drawing the cords that had begun on Blumenstrasse tighter.

She lay with her head on his smooth shoulder. His arms were around her.

"We don't have any more food," Thomas yawned, his hands in her hair.

"Well, we certainly don't have any if we go down," she laughed.

They lay in stillness as the sun warmed their skin. The sounds of the street filtered up to them, muted and, for the time, normal.

Her hand slid across his chest. "You know, I don't feel the least guilty about being here. I mean, everyone else is . . ." She laughed and he loved the sound of it. It was all Maria. "Well, we all need . . . pleasure for a change," she defended with a smile.

Thomas squinted into the clouds. "Half of this feels like a dream. And yet, knowing how generous He is, this is so real. God is so faithful to us, Maria."

"Yes, I know."

He began to pray aloud; Maria loved the sound of his steady voice. The voice she had heard before, for years. It was all Thomas.

"You see us here, Lord. You've blessed us so. We give our future to You. We trust You."

They were still and silent for several minutes.

She rolled to her side, resting on her elbow. They looked at each other and already they knew what the other was thinking. *What was the future for a Jewish prisoner and a Gentile?*

He smiled and laid a finger across her lips. "No matter what happens, Maria, remember He loves us." He traced her cheek and neck. "And you remember how much I love you."

For a moment her voice was small. "I don't want to go down, Thomas. Not ever."

"I understand. Don't be afraid, my love."

She kissed his shoulder and moved closer. "I think we have food enough, Thomas."

It was a combination effort of deportation and reconnaissance of the resistance. The Germans were no fools. They knew when they entered the ghetto that the Jews would mount some kind of response. The forces were therefore grim and nervous. The trucks pulled through the gates, and the soldiers poured from them. They began an immediate roundup of the unfortunate Jews who had been caught on the streets.

Sophie Goldstein had been a happy woman for the past three days despite missing the sight of her daughter and son. But she knew, wherever they had gone to spend their wedding nights, they were safe. They were happy. That was all she wanted. She had enjoyed the congratulations and blessings of the Jews around her who had thought beyond their own circumstances.

She left her room to go to the orphanage on Gensia Street to help there. It was good to be with children. She had been so absorbed in daydreaming about the beautiful children Thomas and Maria could have that she rounded the corner oblivious to the scene. It was too late. The screams reached her, jolted her. People running against her, knocking her down. Then a hard-faced young man loomed over her, pointing a gun at her.

She stood up, brushing herself off with dignity. She looked back over her shoulder only a moment. *This could take me to Aaron. Maria is safe.*

They pulled her forward.

"It's such a shame your work has destroyed the manners I'm sure your mothers took pains to teach you," she said haughtily. But the man didn't smile.

He held her, then kissed her forehead. She was weeping in his arms. *It had come too soon.*

"I have to go," he said softly.

Her arms tightened around him.

"I'll go directly to von Kleinst. I can reason with him."

"He won't let her go," Maria said hoarsely. She pulled herself out of his arms. "He won't let one Jew survive."

"Maria, I know how hard it is. I know you're afraid. But we aren't giving up. You promised me." He smoothed back her hair. "We've just begun."

She stood away from him. "If you leave the ghetto, you won't come back. They—"

He gripped her arms. "Maria, one way or another I'll be back. Just remember the things I told you. Stay on this street. Don't go any further out. I'll come back in tomorrow night at the latest. Please, please don't give up."

Thomas hadn't gone many blocks inside the ghetto before his heart was pounding in apprehension. It was early afternoon, but the broken streets were silent. Eerily silent. As he walked he could hear only the sound of his own steps. Nothing moved. They were waiting. They knew. He could feel the eyes of hundreds on his back. He was walking to freedom—while they were waiting to die.

But not entirely waiting. There were signs that the Jewish fighters had been busy while he and Maria had been on the roof of the world. Banners were hanging from the gaping windows, fluttering in the breeze, so gentle, but with the final salute to courage and defiance. Flags that bore the five-pointed star painted in blue. Slogans had been hastily painted on the walls. They called on the Polish population to stand with the Jews. Thomas paused. He looked to the nearest window. A man sat in the shadowy ledge. Thomas could see the thin tendril of smoke from his cigarette. He could see the rifle slung over his shoulder. *Waiting.*

Thomas turned and looked back down the silent street. *Maria ...*
Only by the strength of his will did he walk slowly forward. No matter
the obstacles, so looming, so large, he had felt he and Maria would be
together. That he could save both Sophie and her daughter. But now ...
As the man had said, the battle of a fly against an elephant.

He passed through the gate, barely noticing the looks of contempt
and disgust, the ill-concealed murmur of "Jew lover." He stopped as if he
had run into a wall. His feelings were confirmed. Tanks and trucks lined
the streets. There were thousands of soldiers. Camps, radio positions,
men hurrying everywhere in battle gear. He turned to the gate, but it
closed solidly. The match was about to strike the inferno.

• • •

By sunset Misha's group had divided and found concealed positions
within sight of the ghetto. They were very vulnerable hiding spots, and
every man and woman among them felt the tension. Misha stood in the
second-floor window of a gutted building. Four men below him were
working on a tunnel to the ghetto wall. He didn't bother to turn at the
sound of the steps behind him. Wilhelm entered.

The months of partisan living had left their mark on Wilhelm
Mueller. Hilda Jensen would have been horrified. The spartan forest diet
had left him anemic-looking and too thin. His eyes were darting; his
movements abrupt. He stood beside the leader. They watched the street
scene for several minutes.

"The butchers are in place," Misha said in a flat voice.

Wilhelm nodded. "They've got a heavy cordon around the perimeter
of the ghetto. The attack begins at dawn. They'll enter at the gate on
Nalewki and Gensia Street."

Misha nodded. "You can see them smiling and joking down there.
They are feeling pretty cocky."

"Is Saul back yet?"

Misha shook his head. Wilhelm could feel the radiating disapproval.

"Talking about me?"

Wilhelm turned. Saul had the stealth of a cat. Wilhelm swiftly took
in his blood-stained trousers. He tossed a uniform at Wilhelm and
slumped to the dirty floor with a rare smile.

"We found a little picnic out by the Vistula. Six army men lounging in the sun." He smiled broadly. "Let's just say they're really relaxing now and won't be entering the ghetto in the morning."

Misha swung around.

"Six sten guns," Saul continued flatly, "three belts of grenades, four pistols, one machine gun, brandy. A nice little haul for us, wouldn't you say? It's all downstairs."

Misha lumbered past him. He threw the words over his shoulders at Wilhelm, his tone resentful. "Good work, comrade."

Wilhelm picked up the uniform slowly.

Saul's voice was bland. "He doesn't understand you, Wilhelm. Neither do I. It doesn't matter though."

Saul stood up. "Try it on. You can get your girl with it."

• • •

They stood like two wary prize fighters. Each was shocked with the other's appearance. Von Kleinst looked like he hadn't slept in weeks. He wasn't like the smooth-faced officers on the street in their open touring cars that Thomas had passed. Caesars on conquest. Von Kleinst in another garb, in another pose, looked like a ghetto victim.

Thomas was likewise pale, his clothes rumpled and dirty. He looked edgy.

Von Kleinst didn't offer him a chair. His voice was testy. He didn't like the penetrating gaze of the young man.

"I am very busy. I was on my way out," he said testily.

"I've been waiting for five hours to see you, Herr Lieutenant."

Von Kleinst leaned his hands on the desk. "Where have you been? Your pass expired two days ago. Not to mention there was a certain shooting reported to me ten days ago. Know anything about that, Pastor Picard?"

"I've come to you, sir, about a woman who was taken off the street today. I know the transport hasn't left Warsaw yet."

"So?" he snapped.

"I'd like permission to remove her from the train. She's my mother-in-law."

Von Kleinst laughed hollowly. "Just like that. Take one Jewess off a train of thousands."

"It goes without saying that I'd like to take them all off, sir."

"You have a lot of nerve coming in here," Von Kleinst growled.

Thomas knew then that this man had changed since their luncheon meeting. But he couldn't give up. He stood silently and prayed.

"Why did you not come out of the ghetto on the appointed day?"

"I was getting married."

All color drained from the lieutenant's face. "Your ... bride is still in there, of course?"

"Yes," Thomas said softly, "of course."

Von Kleinst sat down heavily. His shoulders sagged and his head slumped forward.

"Leave me. I have work."

"Lieutenant von Kleinst, I understand."

He raised his head.

"Oh? Just what do you think you understand?" he asked wearily.

"That you are a decent man who has been forced to do indecent things—things that dishonor the name of the German army. You are being forced to participate in the slaughter of innocent people. You were trained to fight a legitimate enemy who threatens Germany. You are involved in this butchery, and it is killing you inside just as it is destroying them in body."

Von Kleinst shook his head. "There is nothing I can do. I am one man. Now leave, Picard, leave."

"My wife is in there."

Von Kleinst stood up, his voice shrill and sharp. "There is nothing I can do! Our leaders have decreed this. So be it! Get out! Go back to Munich, to your ... your music store. Leave!"

Thomas paled and his voice shook. He pointed at the lieutenant.

"The stench of what all of you have done reaches up to God, and you'll never get the smell of it away from you."

Von Kleinst was still screaming as Thomas slowly descended the steps.

● ● ●

The German command had assured Himmler he would be able to give the fuehrer the present he planned. It would take a mere two days of action, a third day of "mopping up." As the sun rose in the beauty and peace the Creator had intended, the German soldiers, some on foot, some in tanks, some wielding flamethrowers, advanced. They were greeted with a barrage of bullets, grenades, Molotov cocktails. After two hours of ceaseless attack, the Germans fell back in panic leaving their wounded and dead on the battlefield. The first day of the Warsaw uprising had begun. The first day was over. The Jewish fighters rushed into the streets, throwing their arms around each other, cheering and wishing each other further luck. The fly had bitten the elephant.

The city rocked with thunderous explosions all day. Smoke rose as a pall in the sky. At night the sky was brilliant with flame. Natalie no longer left her room. She hardly ate. She hadn't seen Hugo in nearly a week—since the battle had begun. She supposed he was sleeping at his office. She sat curled in her window seat and she thought. And she decided. She had packed a small bag that lay hidden under her bed. Knowing it was foolish, she had added the heavy skates last of all. She couldn't explain it, but she didn't want them to be thrown away by Hugo.

The door opened. Hugo stood in the doorway a moment, as if he was trying to recognize the room. Her eyes widened. She stood up. Finally he focused on her. He closed the door.

His eyes were bloodshot, his clothes disheveled. She had never seen him like this. *Has he been drinking?* she wondered.

"Hugo? How can I help you?" she asked.

"You can't."

He began stripping off his uniform. He went into the bathroom. Then the shower began to run. She sat down in the window seat, her mind keeping pace with her racing heart.

He appeared, shaven and cleanly dressed. He sat down across from her. They looked at each other for a very long time.

Her voice was clear. "Hugo, I have to leave."

He sat like stone.

"I should have left long ago. There is much to say, yet, there is nothing to say. It is too late. You were kind to me, and I'll always be grateful to you for that."

"Where will you go?"

"To my people."

He looked away. He stood. He left the room without looking back or saying another word.

Wilhelm had been given a description of von Kleinst. Standing in the evening shadow, he recognized him immediately. The man hesitated at the curb before he entered the black car. Wilhelm wondered if he felt he was being watched. Impossible. There were men everywhere. The car pulled away, and Wilhelm looked up to the lighted room of the third floor. He took a deep breath and said another swift prayer.

She opened the door with only abstract interest. It couldn't be the staff from the kitchen. She had vowed she wouldn't take another meal since the day before. With his old, brash confidence, Wilhelm hurried inside and closed the door. He slid the lock in place.

They hadn't seen each other in three weeks. She didn't know if he had gone away or been injured after he had entrusted her with the film. It didn't matter.

He regarded her with his hands on his hips. He didn't bother to ask why she looked as if she had been crying.

"Get your stuff together. One small bag, that's it."

She turned and went back to the window seat. Moses leaped into her arms.

"I can't, Wilhelm."

"You have to. Now hurry up."

"I am leaving here. But I can't go with you."

His brows furrowed. "What's that?"

"I'm leaving. I'll go."

"Where?"

But she wouldn't answer.

The truth dawned on him like the flashes that illuminated the night sky with their terrible testimony.

He went across the room in swift strides. "No. We are trying to get people out of there alive." He shook his head. "That's not your ... penance, Natalie. It doesn't work like that."

She started to speak but he shook his head.

"You're wasting precious time. Get your bag." His voice went tender. "You can even take that furry thing."

She shook her head.

"Look, Natalie. I'll carry you out across my shoulders if I have to. I promise you I will. And they'll see von Kleinst's woman being abducted and they'll shoot me."

"No," she said in a desperate voice.

He nodded and smiled. "Yes. And you won't let that happen because you love me. Hilda told me. Come on."

• • •

Thomas Picard watched in an agony that only a witness to tragedy can experience. It would have been impossible to return to Maria through the blaze of fighting—even if he could have passed through the heavy perimeter of SS men. And he also had the constant guard of the SS that von Kleinst had placed on him. He was a watched man. *Had von Klienst done this for his own safety, for spite, for some twisted sense of duty and honor?* Thomas couldn't decide and didn't try. He returned to the much-needed work of the orphanage just outside of Warsaw and waited and prayed. *Can Maria survive this holocaust?* he asked himself again and again.

• • •

Though the ghetto was catacombed with sewers, tunnels, and underground bunkers, after three weeks the Jewish fighters were running out of places of refuge. The Germans had flooded or burned and blasted block after block. The walled city was a city of ruins.

Mama is gone. Thomas is gone. And Daniel, Maria thought bitterly. Daniel had been shot helping her to a new bunker during the first week of the battle. She had pulled him, sobbing, into a doorway. He had smiled then died with his head in her lap. Now, ten days later she still wore the same blood-stained skirt. She had long since lost her precious comb and mirror. *What did it matter now?*

Yet something impelled her—perhaps it was the human instinct for survival that suffers a thousand sorrows but dies a slow death. It was the ageless battle between a swift death and the fierce passion to live. Then thinking of Sophie's hopes and dreams invested in her, Maria Goldstein decided she wanted to live. She had given up hope of seeing Thomas. She made the Molotov cocktails with swift hands, she helped move women and children to new hiding places, and she carried messages between resistance groups. Though she was weak from starvation, Maria was still the fleet-footed runner of Blumenstrasse. She would come upon huddled groups of Jews without weapons, fear and hope mixed in their look. They would give each other a timid smile then hurry on. She became attached to a group of four men and three women whom she hadn't known before the fighting had begun. They made their feeble attacks then retreated to their bunkers. Maria began to notice the silence as the third week dawned. There were fewer sounds of battle with each passing day. Her group had lost contact with the scattered others. At night, before snatching some sleep, she wondered if she alone would emerge from the debris, her hands raised before the victor's guns. *Can I do that?* she wondered.

She lay against a cold slab of rock in the near darkness of a small basement. The roof was partially caved in and the pale moonlight streamed in at her feet. She ached all over. She should try to sleep, but she didn't want to. She had seen too many terrible sights that she was certain her dreams would resurrect. *If I . . . If I do survive, will these horrors haunt me until I wish that I had also died?*

I'll think of Papa. Yes, that will help. She pictured them walking to the tobacconist. She visualized him praying over the Sabbath meal. And his words reached her from the comfort of her memory. There in the graveyard of the Warsaw ghetto, it was all Maria Goldstein had. She knew the others were awake as she was, but she didn't mind. Her voice was clear and steady.

> Turn Yourself to me, and have mercy on me, for I am desolate and afflicted. The troubles of my heart have enlarged; bring me out of my distresses! Look on my affliction and my pain, and forgive all my sins. Consider my enemies, for they are many; and they hate me with cruel hatred. Keep my soul, and deliver me; let me not be ashamed, for I put my trust in You.

• • •

In all his years, Wilhelm Mueller thought he had seen the far reaches of tragedy and misery and evil. Even as he was seeing this, he couldn't quite comprehend it was true. Yet the cries that reached him were very real. With the same stubborn purpose he had used to get Natalie Bergmann to safety, he now focused on the Jews under siege in the ghetto. *I must rescue as many of these helpless ones as possible,* he thought with determination.

This devotion pleased Misha. Mueller could be counted on to the fullest extent—even to a death that would be an honorable sacrifice.

Wilhelm and Natalie had escaped from the hotel and streets of Warsaw under great peril. Natalie was a woman to notice and, too late, Wilhelm realized he should have had her affect some sort of disguise. With a handful of SS in pursuit, they had escaped to the forest. He had quickly introduced her to the five partisans who had been left to secure a safe forest camp. Natalie's eyes had widened.

"You mean you want me to stay here? Alone?" she asked worriedly.

"Not alone." He motioned to the group. "With them. Getting the camp ready and safe."

"And you?"

"My place is back in Warsaw with the man I told you about. We have to try to help anyone escaping the ghetto. We'll stay there until there is no one to rescue."

"I'll go with you."

"No Natalie. It's too hard, too much, and you're not strong enough."

"Please don't ask me to stay here. I want to be with . . . them."

Wilhelm hesitated. *She wears fine clothes. She's accustomed to three daily meals. She's suffered no physical hardship like the women in the partisan group and the ghetto have. And I can't see her hurt. But I can see a determination in her posture that is equal to my own.*

"All right." He knew Misha would be angry. "But the cat stays here," he added firmly.

That had been almost four weeks earlier. Now they had been together almost a month. The fine clothes were soiled and blood-stained. Her face showed the marks of fatigue and fear, anxiety and hunger. They were rarely alone with each other. They had exchanged very few personal words beyond simple instructions. She held the light while he dressed wounds, she loaded the precious bullets, and she stood watch. She saw the horrors, heard the screams, smelled the smoke. She bit her lip and turned away and cried. She sobbed in the darkness when there was no comfort. She endured the other partisans' initial suspicions and aloofness. She was one of them—yet clearly not.

She waited for the sound of Wilhelm's voice, for his hurried step. She would see him search their hideout for her, then give her little more than a cursory glance. He addressed her with the same impersonal tone he used with the others. And when he sat hunched over the fire she knew he had retreated into himself, like all of them did, living in this unreal world of disbelief. As she watched him from the shadows, she felt forgotten.

And as the ghetto burned and the Nazis advanced, when her own life hung precariously in the conflict, Natalie Bergmann felt more alone and lonely than she ever had.

• • •

The smoke was still rising, thinner now. The silence of a graveyard settled over the streets. The Germans, heady with triumph at last, still toured the streets with smiling faces, but they kept their guns ready. Von Stroop surveyed the ruins sitting in his private car. His companion generals were in cars behind him. An occasional Jewish banner was sighted, bullet-ridden and limp in the pale sunshine. But there was no other movement. Von Stroop nodded in satisfaction and motioned his driver to turn. He had an important telegram to send to Berlin, its message quite simple: The Warsaw ghetto is no more.

• • •

It took nearly a week for the soldiers, police, and SS who had been brought to Warsaw to be reassigned. The city was still crowded with them, but the tension was relaxed on the streets. Thomas Picard walked to the gate he had passed through two months earlier. He could see down the broad avenue. There could be no living thing remaining there.

A young sentry watched him from his post. He sauntered up to him, his cigarette hanging limply in his mouth.

"Weren't thinking of going in there were you?"

Thomas glanced at him but didn't answer.

The man hitched up his belt. " 'Cause you aren't allowed. They don't want looting." He shrugged. "Can't imagine what would be left to loot."

"There isn't anything left," Thomas agreed slowly. *Lord, help me,* he whispered to himself.

A week later he left Warsaw for Germany.

• • •

It brought back her childhood fears of the darkness. She hesitated at the black, gaping hole. She had smelled it from yards away. Besides the blackness, the roar of water was both hollow-sounding and deafening. She felt herself break into a sweat and started shaking. *This is too hard, too much.* Emil's voice at her shoulder was both hurried and gentle. In that moment, Maria knew that human kindness still existed beyond basic survival.

"I know, Maria. It's hard and you're afraid. I was shaking like a leaf the first time. But I've been down there, and the first part is hard ... till your eyes adjust. There's a ledge, and Benjamin is there to help you."

"We must hurry, Maria," one of the women behind her urged.

"I can feel how cold it will be," she said hoarsely. "And we've heard the Germans have flooded the sewers and dropped gas too."

"Yes, yes, but they haven't found this one. It is the only way, Maria. We can't give up now."

Don't give up, Maria, Thomas had said so tenderly. For a moment she could imagine his warm lips on her skin. Emil placed his hand on her shoulder. She closed her eyes and pretended it was Thomas. *Thomas her beloved husband.* With her eyes still clamped shut, Maria lowered herself into the darkness.

They lived in the cold, filthy, stench-filled darkness for three days. They crawled miles. There was no longer fresh water or food. And they lived with the fear that when they reached the exit there might be grinning Germans waiting there.

Her knees and elbows were raw bloody flesh, her hands blue and stiff. Her body racked with pain, with spasms of coughing, with hunger and thirst that she thought would push her to insanity. And still they groveled forward. Still Emil led them, confident that there would be friends waiting at the end.

Finally they reached the prearranged point. Emil carefully lifted the manhole. He was temporarily blinded by the moonlight. As if in a fever, Maria heard the voices. She couldn't move her tongue to speak or to cry out. Then there was fresh water in her hands and a small piece of bread.

Emil spoke into her ear. "Just a little longer. They will come back tomorrow night. They are preparing for us."

But she knew there was danger. She closed her eyes and sank into a lethargy of pain and fear and sorrow. She lost all concept of time. Then voices again, so distant she could hardly understand the words. Except "hurry."

Hands were reaching for her, holding her. She winced at the sudden touch. She gasped at the sudden rush of air. Clean and cool. She felt faint. They were lifting her; she had no strength or will of her own.

Hands were pulling her up. She blinked rapidly. *A truck and people and voices.* She couldn't understand.

"Thomas?" she whispered. "Thomas?"

Then a face came close to her. "It's all right. Let me help you."

Still she couldn't see. "Thomas?" She began to cry.

"No ... I'm sorry. I'm Wilhelm and I'm going to help you."

Then a woman's voice, very soft. "Take my arm, lean on me. The truck is close."

Maria turned to look closer. The moonlight gleamed on the brunette hair. The woman smiled tenderly.

A black car pulled silently into the shadows. The driver was alone. He had heard there had been Jews spotted in this area. The forest partisans and the Polish underground were still active. Yet another duty, another part of the hunt. Seeing the old covered truck, he knew instinctively he had come upon a scene of danger and escape. When the stooped figures appeared stumbling from the sewer opening he knew these were Jews from the ghetto. Desperate they had been driven there. *Desperate.*

He leaned forward. There were women in the group. They were going to the waiting truck. He saw the gleaming brunette hair swing forward and the profile. He knew this Jewess. He gripped the steering wheel. *Natalie.* He could drive forward, his headlights cutting arcs into the darkness. He could step from the car and if they were unarmed he could arrest all of them. It would please von Stroop. It would bring him praise and reward. It would dispel the whispers of weakness he had overheard. They thought he couldn't stomach this action against the Jews.

But Hugo couldn't do it. He could feel their desperation to live as real as the waves of heat. *Had the things the people in Berlin said about these people been lies? Natalie* ...

The truck turned and sped from the city.

They found Lieutenant Hugo von Kleinst in his car the following morning with the revolver still entwined in his fingers.

May 1943
The Polish Forest

It was Wilhelm's turn at watch. It was sunrise. He sat with his back against a rock under a tree, the rifle across his legs. He was tired, but he knew even when he returned to camp he would have trouble sleeping. There was more time to think these days, though the challenge of survival had hardly lessened. There was still the feeding and safety of twenty-two people. *Like one large family,* he decided.

He had been thinking all night of the future. He now held the idea that the defeat of the Nazis was possible. It would begin with losing the war. *But if Germany is free of the grip of the Nazis, will life be as it once was or is that time forever gone? Can I return to Berlin or Nuremberg and take up some profession? Is that what I want? Will the new government be sympathetic to Jews? Can I live beside those who persecuted and tried to kill me? What of the future? I want to leave Poland. I want to quit this partisan life. But how?*

A step at his right brought him to his feet instantly, his hand swinging the rifle around. He was angry that his thoughts had distracted him. There were German and Polish spies in this forest.

Natalie came forward calmly as if she hadn't noticed Wilhelm's movements. They studied each other from a span of two yards. She still wore the skirt she had left the hotel in, now washed and worn. Her shirt was one he had given her, and she secretly treasured it. Her face was flushed from the climb, her hair tied back. She was paler and thinner. *She is . . .*

"Gosh, you're beautiful," he said impulsively, lapsing into American slang. He turned red and avoided her look.

She smiled slightly. "I brought you some coffee."

"You didn't have to do that. It's awfully early."

"I couldn't sleep."

He looked back into the valley.

"Why not?" he asked.

When a minute passed and she hadn't answered, he turned to her. She was looking at him.

Her voice was very low. "I can't sleep . . . for wondering if . . . you despise me for what I did. Wondering if you rescued me out of pity . . . or duty to my grandfather . . . or for love as you told me in the garden."

"I was shocked when Hilda told me," he admitted slowly, "but I could never despise you, Natalie. You're here because it was right that you should be." He paused. "And as I told you in the garden."

"These weeks you have hardly looked at me. You never touch me and rarely speak to me. Why, Wilhelm? It's made me afraid."

He looked at his feet a moment, younger-looking to her in his sudden shyness.

"I've been trying to keep us going. I've been thinking of our future, trying to figure it all out. And ... and I knew if I looked, if I spoke, if I touched, I wouldn't want to stop."

She stepped up to him. "I wouldn't want you to stop. Wilhelm, can you forgive me? I must hear it from you."

He studied her face without embarrassment then broke into a smile. He took her hand.

"Come on."

He led her to a clearing. She watched him, clearly puzzled as he dug into an outcropping of large stones. Then he removed a suitcase. He bent down, opened it, then came to her smiling broadly. He came with her violin outstretched to her in his arms.

"Someday you'll play for me, Natalie Bergmann," he promised with a smile.

Epilogue

Poland, 1945

The two inmates of Treblinka walked shakily toward the truck with the bright red cross. The older man was grateful that the American soldiers were gently helping people into the trucks. He knew he didn't have the strength himself.

"All right, sir. Just take hold and I'll help you," the soldier said.

The man smiled and nodded. He liked the sound of these confident Americans. He had been listening to them for the past several days. He liked their cheerful voices as much as the food they brought. He took his place on the bench and the soldier handed up the leather case.

"Yours?" the soldier asked kindly. "A violin?"

The old man nodded.

His friend spoke up. "Aaron played in the camp orchestra. He's a fine musician."

They sat together and the older man smiled down at the American.

"Thank you," he said slowly. "Thank you ... very much."

The man nodded and turned away quickly. The truck engine rumbled to life. So many months. He was leaving his son Abraham. His hands tightened on the violin case.

"You could say your music saved you, Aaron," the man beside him said with a tired smile.

But Aaron Goldstein was looking at the far horizon as he shook his head.

"My God saved me."

• • •

Aaron Goldstein died six months later of heart failure in a Red Cross hospital in Poland. He was fifty-seven years old. Sophie Goldstein perished in a gas chamber at Treblinka. She was fifty-two years old. Her oldest son, Abraham, age thirty-two, who had risked his life to take the photograph of the camp atrocities, died of typhus six weeks before the war ended. Isaac Goldstein made a successful escape from Germany and began a new life in Palestine. He studied and became a teacher in a kibbutz school.

• • •

In the spring of 1945, Himmler insisted that Pastor Dietrich Bonhoeffer had played a part in the assassination attempt on the fuehrer's life. In an act of revenge, Himmler ordered Bonhoeffer's execution. He was brought before the firing squad on a cold morning less than one month before the Allies liberated Berlin.

1946 Washington D.C.

The black-and-white checkered cab pulled to the curb with a slight wheeze and shudder. The couple in the backseat looked at each other and smiled. The driver reshifted his toothpick and pushed back his cloth cap. He glanced in the mirror again. *The brunette is certainly a looker,* he thought.

"So here ya are."

The young man stretched forward over the seat with the coins. "Thank you very much."

He opened the door and slid out. The young woman paused just a moment to turn to the cabby. "Yes, thank you."

The man's toothpick jumped and his eyes widened. *Such a heavy accent. Is it German?*

Leaning in, the young man saw the reaction and smiled. "We're Americans now," he said as he winked.

He took the woman's hand and led her up the broad steps. He stopped in the middle of the ascent and turned so they could look back over the mall. The cherry trees were in full, extravagant blossom. The sun glanced off the silver-blue sheen of the Potomac. He couldn't have chosen a better day to impress her with this sight.

"What do you think?" he asked.

She wore a tan suit and her dark hair was bobbed at the shoulders in the American way. It was glossy in the sun. Holding her hand, he had stopped to look at her several times during the day, as he had done for the past year, not trusting his eyes that she was really his. Any sight they would see this day paled beside her.

"I think . . . I think this country has a treasure here. Do they know it?" she asked.

He sighed. "I hope so."

He was back where he had stood ten years before. The memories of those years didn't cause him pain now. *I have a future, finally a future.* He thought of Hilda Jensen back at their hotel tending to his new baby daughter. *I'll bring my daughter here before she can walk!* he decided.

He turned to Natalie. "You know, when you said a treasure it made me remember something your grandfather said. He told me, 'Fortunate is the man who finds this treasure, my granddaughter!' He also said, 'If you are on God's side, you are on the winning side.' " Wilhelm shook his head in wonder. "Everything the old man said has happened. I guess he was a prophet."

And as she had done several times a day, as she had done for the past year, she threw her arms around his neck. "Oh, Wilhelm, do you know how much I love you?"

And he held her and laughed. Then he took her hand, still smiling.

"Come on, I want you to meet Mr. Lincoln."

Summer 1945
The Farber Estate

He was three years old and he sat on the broad front steps that led to the sweeping circular drive. He was absently picking at a scab over a sore on his chubby knee that sharp puppy teeth had inflicted. He shifted the sleeping puppy in his lap. The terrier opened one dark eye and licked the boy's arm. Morgan giggled.

A car was coming up the drive. Percy pulled himself out from under the bush near the steps and took up an impressive barking. The little boy stood, squinting into the sun. When he recognized the car, he started waving energetically with his entire small body.

The front door opened, and his mother emerged to stand behind him.

"Oh, Percy, leave off," she laughed.

She shielded her eyes against the sun, the other hand on the smooth roundness of her bulging stomach.

The car came to the steps and stopped. Morgan was hopping from one foot to the other; the puppy was squealing. Max Farber emerged from the car, smiling broadly, his arms outstretched to the little boy. He looked like he had the first time she had seen him—tanned and healthy and happy. *The same and yet different. Even better.*

Emilie met him in the middle of the steps. His arm went around her, her hand to his cheek.

"You're home," she smiled.

Warsaw, Poland, 1948

Thomas Picard had left something of his soul in Warsaw that spring three years earlier, when the ruins of the Jewish ghetto were still smoldering. His faith had suffered an invisible but real amputation. The chaos that post-war Germany faced was like a mirror to his own inner life. Those brief weeks in Poland had changed him, stripped him of everything he had thought had been firmly rooted. He had never returned to Blumenstrasse in Munich.

With Gretchen beside him, and the aid of his first church family, Thomas established an orphanage for refugee children near the grounds of the Dachau concentration camp. The past was firmly behind him—until he saw the notice of the ceremony being held in Warsaw honoring the Jewish ghetto uprising. Painful as he knew it would be, he felt impelled to go.

Now, standing by the memorial, he watched, stunned, as a woman singing walked toward him. *So familiar, so like . . .* His hopes, his long-held dreams . . . *People don't come back from the dead.*

Yet they both belonged to the God of miracles.

Gretchen ran into the woman's arms. Her friend was found at last.

Maria Goldstein Picard had been on her own pilgrimage that had led her to this night of a caressing wind and memories. Seeing him here, when she hadn't expected him at all, whispered to her of God's great love and protection for her. She cried for the joy.

She had escaped into the Polish forest that spring night three years earlier. For weeks she had been violently ill with typhus. The group had moved north, away from the Germans who were massing for confrontation with the Russians. On a cold summer night they had been separated, then captured by the Russians. Like thousands of others, though enemies of the Reich, they had been marched into the Russian interior as laborers. Between imprisonment and sickness, Maria had disappeared.

When prisoner exchanges were finally made, she was released. A long journey faced her. A slow journey back into the land that had tried to kill her. Her messages to Blumenstrasse had come back unopened. She had forgotten his mention of Dachau. Surely Thomas had died trying to reenter the ghetto—another body among the thousands. As far as she knew, she alone of her family had survived.

She remained in Poland, just another refugee, working in a hospital. She had quietly subdued all emotions. She tried to plan a future, to move forward, resume life, but her will had atrophied. In a way, the Nazis still wielded power through her painful memories. She was in her dormitory room when she read of the planned ceremony in Warsaw. She had tossed the paper aside. *I'll never willingly reenter that city,* she declared to herself. Yet the thought haunted her. *If I could return, bury something there, perhaps I can live again.*

• • •

Thomas walked closer. When he saw her he knew again how much God loved him.

Gretchen stood aside. *Thomas would be happy again. Really happy.*

Maria walked into his arms. She knew then how much God could be trusted.

As they left the ghetto later, the moon spun a golden path for them to the gate . . . and Maria remembered other moonlit nights.

Gretchen linked her arms through theirs, her voice sing-song. "Isn't this a fine night, Thomas? Look at the sky!" She waved toward the stars. "We see them! Thank you!"

The faith of a child . . .

Gretchen cocked her head to one side, her voice ruminative. "You know, the stars . . . the stars are like jewels in this evening sky."

Thomas looked at his wife, his bride, his miracle, still not quite believing she was here.

"Yes, Gret, jewels this evening."

> *"Trust in the Lord, with all your heart,*
> *And do not lean on your own understanding,*
> *In all your ways acknowledge Him,*
> *And He shall direct your paths."*

—Proverbs 3:5,6

Afterword

Jewel in the Evening Sky evolved in a surprising way. It started out as a book about the seduction of the Christian church and the struggle between Christian and Jews. But when Thomas finally found Sophie and Maria, I realized that the relationship between the Goldmans and Picards had added the beautiful testimony of the importance of family.

I hope you came to care about the people in this novel as much as I do. If you smiled and cried, if you put yourself in some of the situations, if you were stirred with gratitude to God, then I've accomplished my goals.

Most of the major events in this book are based on historical facts . . .

- There is a monument in Warsaw honoring the Jews of the ghetto uprising. It is made from stone originally ordered by Hitler for his victory monuments.

- A Jewish inmate of Treblinka smuggled a camera up on the roof he was repairing and took pictures of what was really happening in the concentration camps. These eloquent photographs still survive.

- Some prisoners in Tegel did escape during a blackout period of Allied bombing.

- The lecherous Reinhard Heydrich died from an assassin's bomb thrown at his car when he was on his way to work in Prague.

- Natalie's mistake of accepting communion by hand happened to a young Jewish woman who was trying to survive by masquerading as a Catholic.

- A handful of Jews managed to escape the massacre in the ghetto by crawling through the sewers of Warsaw.

- Some pastors did have the audacity to make comparisons between Jesus Christ and Adolf Hitler. All the speeches or quotes presented from the pulpits were taken directly from accurate documentation.

The Third Reich revealed the terrible consequences of a nation turning a blind eye to its leaders' moral character. It also accurately portrays what happens when a church is seduced away from Christ. When the church is no longer the salt and light God has called it to be, only darkness and decay can result.

If parallels between the Third Reich and our times can be drawn in fact or fiction, let us have the courage to learn from them.

In Him who is always faithful,
MaryAnn Minatra